‖‖ ‖‖ ‖‖‖‖‖‖‖ ‖ ‖ ‖ ‖‖‖ ‖‖‖‖‖‖‖‖‖‖‖ ‖‖ ‖‖

W9-AGV-638

MAY 0 5 2009

HAYNER PUBLIC LIBRARY DISTRICT
ALTON, ILLINOIS

OVERDUES .10 PER DAY MAXIMUM FINE
COST OF BOOKS. LOST OR DAMAGED
BOOKS ADDITIONAL $5.00 SERVICE CHARGE.

HAYNER PLD/DOWNTOWN

CHORAL SOCIETY

CHORAL SOCIETY

Prue Leith

Thomas Dunne Books
St. Martin's Press
New York

This is a work of fiction. All of the characters, organizations, and events portrayed in this novel are either products of the author's imagination or are used fictitiously.

THOMAS DUNNE BOOKS.
An imprint of St. Martin's Press.

CHORAL SOCIETY. Copyright © 2008 by Prue Leith. All rights reserved.
Printed in the United States of America. For information, address
St. Martin's Press, 175 Fifth Avenue, New York, N.Y. 10010.

www.thomasdunnebooks.com
www.stmartins.com

Library of Congress Cataloging-in-Publication Data

Leith, Prue.
    Choral society / Prue Leith.—1st U.S. ed.
        p. cm.
    ISBN-13: 978-0-312-56078-2
    ISBN-10: 0-312-56078-8
    1. Female friendship—Fiction. 2. Middle-aged women—Fiction.
I. Title.
    PR6062.E463 C47 2009
    823'.914—dc22

                                                            2008053056

First published in Great Britain by Quercus

First U.S. Edition: May 2009

10 9 8 7 6 5 4 3 2 1

F
LEI

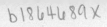

For Ernest

Acknowledgements

Thanks are due to Ann Cornwell, a member of the Medici choir, who kindly arraanged for me to attend a rehearsal, and to Jane Cluver and Sir Ernest Hall for checking the chapters on music and singing. Thanks also to Linda Lines for reading an early draft and for giving me the details of having her knees expertly fixed by the Harley Street knee-man John Lavelle, to whom thanks are also due for ensuring that my description of the procedure made medical sense.

Then thanks to Ian and Caroline Cormack for checking my Cornish geography and the passages about sailing.

And to Francisca Sankson, my long suffering PA, for keeping control of far too many drafts, for expert copy-editing, but mostly for patience and for liking the book.

Thanks too to three Janes: Jane Dystel, my American agent who stayed keen in spite of my taking four years to deliver the book; Jane Turnbull my British agent who sold *Choral Society* and has been a great enthusiast; and Jane Wood, my exacting but always encouraging editor at Quercus.

Chapter One

The women behind the counter were filling orders and shouting to customers over the lunchtime din.

'Two chicken pesto?'

'Hold the mayo?'

'To go, or eat in?'

'Want mustard with that?'

'Any beverage?'

'Still or sparkling?'

'You paying separately?'

Only in this city, thought Lucy. Their speed and skill were marvellous. At her end of the counter, three women, Korean maybe, were rolling dough into long rectangles, slamming baking trays into ovens and pulling out cooked loaves which they flipped onto boards. One hand held the bread flat with a padded glove while the other, with a few quick saws, split them horizontally. Down the line, more women, those doing the shouting and serving, used latex-gloved hands to turn the still steaming bread into sandwiches. From the refrigerated wells in the counter they deftly extracted prepped ingredients (cheeses, grilled veg, rocket, tomatoes, salamis, chicken, ham, beef, you name it) to cover the bread in a thick even layer.

Their hands flashed and their arms weaved across each other's as they reached for ingredients, drizzled sauces, flicked spices, scooped salsas, spread pastes, sprinkled bacon bits or pine-nuts.

On with the crusty top, a firm but careful push to consolidate the mass into a sandwich, then into the paper wrapper and over the counter to the customer.

The smell of hot bread and coffee, the crowded, noisy, none-too-pristine sandwich shop, the Manhattan lunch-hour ritual, produced in Lucy a wash of pleasure. I love this city, she thought. This is real food, cheap, fresh, and available on almost every block.

But her pleasure was almost immediately followed by a familiar backwash of grief. That's widowhood, thought Lucy, it permeates everything, gets into your life like fog through the cracks. For over thirty years she'd telephoned her husband from all over the world and he'd shared her pleasure (or disappointment or fury) from an Islington armchair and, later, from a Cotswold bed.

David had hated 'abroad', but he enjoyed her delight in travel, food, friends. He liked her to do what she liked to do, and he wanted blow-by-blow bulletins. If she didn't telephone him at seven p.m. every day, he'd fret.

Lucy looked at her watch. It would be just seven p.m. in London now. David had been dead for nearly six months, but some inner clock still told her, wherever she was, when it was time for that phone-call. Thirty odd years of pre-supper drinks or drinks-time telephone calls could not, it seemed, be expunged.

Yet it should be liberating, she thought, that I can now go anywhere I like without worrying about anyone, without checking in, without reporting back. I could disappear for days, maybe weeks, and no one would object – or indeed notice. That's good, isn't it? It's freedom, independence, self-sufficiency . . .

Or will be one day. Meanwhile, she thought wryly, there's no comfort like food. She turned her attention to her sandwich.

The layer of mozzarella and avocado on the base crust was receiving a libation of olive oil and a scattering of black pepper. It set her mouth watering. Why, she asked herself, am I eternally hungry?

Her mind then made a well-trodden journey. That sandwich was probably seven hundred calories on its own. She should be in the salad line, not the sandwich one. Indeed, she should be skipping lunch altogether since this evening, and every evening this week, she'd be eating in a new, fashionable restaurant and telling herself it was her bounden duty, as food critic for London's *HOT Restaurant* magazine, to sample every dish she possibly could. She'd have to lose a stone when she got back to London.

Lucy had these interior conversations with herself all the time, especially about what she wasn't going to eat or drink. Monday I'll go on a diet; I'll skip lunch today; tonight I won't drink at all. But she knew she wouldn't keep these promises, any more than she'd keep the ones about taking up swimming or joining a gym.

Her sandwich in a bag, Lucy started up Fifth Avenue, intending to walk all the way to 58th Street, but somehow her arm stuck itself out at the sight of a yellow cab and five minutes later she was at her hotel. Before she went in, she picked up a double espresso at the deli opposite. In the lobby of the hotel, she installed herself in a corner by the window, and ate her sandwich and drank her coffee, alternately reading the *New York Times* and watching the world go by. It was very pleasant, and the sandwich was everything it should be, except, as always in the US, it was super-sized. But of course she ate the lot. It would have been wicked to waste it after all.

She liked the Winchester and always stayed there if she could. The hotel had certainly seen better times – there was no room service, the shower-head needed fixing and the curtains did not quite meet. But her room was large and airy with high ceilings and a big firm bed.

And the staff all knew her. They'd been there for ever: the cheerful doorman, the woman pulling and inserting plugs on the ancient switchboard, the trio of old men who took turns manning the hundred-year-old lift, swinging the lever to stop the car precisely at floor level with one hand, clattering the metal gate open with the other. And she liked the chute into which, at any level, you could drop your mail and it would fall through the floors to the mail-box in the lobby. Lucy never wrote letters or postcards –

email had done away with that – but it pleased her that the mail-chute still worked.

In spite of the double espresso, the combination of full stomach, jetlag, and the sight of her bed, made a siesta irresistable. I'll just have half an hour shut-eye, she thought.

She woke three hours later, refreshed and eager to get to her desk, which she was glad to see was a decent one. What modern hotel would provide a proper desk that did not have to double as a dressing-table? She wished she could write about the faded grandeur of the Winchester and its like – very few left now – or Cosi's honest sandwiches. But the *HOT Restaurant* brief did not include unfashionable hotels or old-style sandwich chains. Lucy felt a small shadow of despair, a fleeting awareness of being out of her time.

Once she could sit in this room, or one very like it, and write a well-researched article about the influence of MFK Fisher on modern food writers, or the vestiges of 18th-century kitchen English (like skillet or scallion) still current in American speech. But today's editors wanted punchy pieces about scandals and food scares, or gossip about trendy people and fashionable food.

She shook her head, irritated with herself for brooding, and pressed the key. The screen flickered and steadied. She read:

Lucy Barnes. New York Restaurants for *HOT Restaurant*, May issue. 1200 words

One of the appealing aspects of New York is its unabashed love affair with itself, its pride and confidence in its brashness, its bigness, its New Yorkness. Whether in the famous art deco skyscrapers, the 80s' bling of the Trump Tower or today's elegant new MoMA, New York architecture has always been uplifting, sometimes breathtaking.

So I confidently expected the new Time Warner Centre with its 'vertical retail' to be a breathtaking success, gleaming with money well spent, echoing to the tap-tap of well-heeled women on marble floors. It is not. It is positively depressing: for all the expensive expanses of atrium and lobbies, the comfortable sofas, enigmatic art installations and whole floor of restaurants, I cannot fathom why anyone goes there. The ground floor is uninspired, the shops unexciting and the restaurant floor gloomy. It is also extremely expensive.

Even with an exchange rate of two dollars to the pound, Barbarella is as over-priced as it is over-hyped. A narrow windowless room with a few closely packed tables and a preposterous bar of giant dimensions. A glass of water costs $10 and the cheapest wine . . .

Boring, thought Lucy, but it will have to do. She worked on, tapping the keys fast, eyes on the screen. She finished the piece, and checked her word count. Years of journalism had given her the ability to produce the right number of words as if by instinct. She was only forty words over, but she edited fast, losing those that were unnecessary. Editing down was a job she liked, knowing that her copy would be the better for it. She was running a final spell check when a window popped up:

'You have mail. Two new messages.'

One was from Sandra, her editor on the daily *Globe*, the other from her daughter, Grace.

She opened this one first:

Mum, what are you doing in New York? Don't you ever stop working? When will you be back? Archie and I wanted to come down this weekend. It's half term and we've got tickets for Stratford.

Lucy raised an eyebrow, and mentally added 'and you could baby-sit the children while we are at the theatre, do our laundry and cook Sunday lunch.'

She tapped her reply: *Back Friday morning. See you for supper then. XX Mum*

Still, she was glad they were coming. It would be good to see her daughter and even her ultra-conservative son-in-law Archie. But mostly she looked forward to having the grandchildren around, adding noise and activity to a near-empty house now more used to silence. And having people to cook for.

Lucy read her daughter's email again and found she slightly resented the demanding tone. She loved Grace of course, but she could be taxing. Since David's death, Grace had taken to dishing out advice with a subtext about retiring gracefully. Get a decent haircut; buy better clothes; spend time with your grandchildren; join a choir.

Lucy opened the email from Sandra and was surprised at its length. Her boss's editing skills had honed her writing to terse essentials. Her communications seldom exceeded 50 words.

Dear Lucy,

You aren't going to like this and there is no way I can wrap it up, but I'm afraid we will not be renewing your contract next month.

This is not personal. You are a great cookery writer and you've done wonderful copy for the Globe *over the last twelve years. But you will know that we are keen to attract a younger readership and the research done by Focus has identified that the younger reader, though very into food, is more interested in the 'celebrity/dining-out/what's hot' scene than in real cooking. If they do cook, they want to do it quickly, with fashionable ingredients ready prepared — hardly your sort of thing, you will agree. (Your famous piece on osso bucco, 900 words if I remember right, is a memorable piece of writing, but when confronted with it as part of the research, the target audience failed to get it at all.)*

I'm sorry I didn't manage to catch you before you left for NYC. But the decision was only made the day you left. I'd have liked to have at least bought you one more good lunch.

Of course we will publish the two pieces we have in the pipeline, but April 8th will be the last.

I'm so sorry Lucy. If you can bear it, let's have lunch anyway.

Sandra

P.S. You should know I have engaged Orlando Black as our new food columnist. The page is to have a complete revamp, plus colour.

Lucy read the email without moving a muscle. Part of her mind told her it could not be true, that they wouldn't, they couldn't. The *Globe* was one of the few daily papers that had not gone down market, that still published serious stuff. And Sandra *loved* her writing. In a memory flash of a second, Lucy remembered a whole hour's conversation, held not a month ago, when they'd been plotting a series of pieces on sweet yeasted doughs: gugelhopf; savarin; brioche; rum baba, pannetone. She'd have followed Carême from the kitchens of Talleyrand to the Russian court, and the migration of pastry cooks from Florence to Paris in the wake of Catherine de Medici. It was to be a little bit of history and some perfect, infallible recipes with all the butter, cream, rum and brandy that such lavish times demanded. An antidote to today's diet-mania. Sandra had even agreed to illustrate the piece with Carême's own drawings.

Sandra could not be sacking her. Her reputation as a writer rested significantly on the *Globe* job. If she lost her column she'd no longer be in the top tier of journalists – she'd be a mere freelance with a monthly column in *HOT Restaurant*, a minor magazine read principally by chefs.

When she got to the P.S., disbelief gave way to rage. Her mouth and eyes opened wide and she felt the sudden heat of pumping blood. She jumped up from the chair, crying out, 'Orlando Black! Orlando bloody Black! It's ridiculous!'

Orlando Black! He was a minnow. A silly, pretty, telly-made know-nothing, whose gastronomic celebrity was founded on his making a passable Spanish omelette on some reality show. They could not do it. How *could* they do it?

Orlando Black was a fake. Even his name was made up. And could he write? Unlikely in the extreme. Certainly he could not speak the Queen's English. 'Wow, brilliant' was about the limit of his verbal expression.

Lucy rubbed her hands over her face and again thought this could not be happening. Weaned on Elizabeth David and André Simon, she was in an honourable line of serious authors from both sides of the Atlantic: Jane Grigson, James Beard, Julia Child, Matthew Fort.

To replace her with a non-writer was bad enough, but Orlando Black was not even a restaurant chef. If they'd sacked her for Jamie Oliver or Gordon Ramsay maybe she'd have understood. Celebrity is a powerful seller of newspapers, and at least they could cook. But to replace her with an androgynous show-host of vacuous intellect and zero talent . . .

Lucy stood at the window, seeing nothing. She still had her hands on her hot cheeks, but now her fingers were wet with tears. Her mind ranted on: was her knowledge, and yes, scholarship, to count for nothing? She belonged to that top echelon of food writers who read widely, who knew the social importance of food, who could cook themselves. Who published good, well-researched and well-tested cookery books that people read and *used*.

She started to weep in earnest, and went to the bathroom to bury her face in the bath towel. She carried it to the bedroom and sat on the edge of the bed, rocking and sobbing in uneven gulps.

Lucy realised she was crying as much for her dead husband as for the loss of her job. She wanted David. She needed him, damn it, needed to shout down the phone. She wanted his steadying voice, his balance, his ability to make her laugh when she was crying.

Oh, how *could* the *Globe* replace her with a pipsqueak who rose to fame because he dyed his hair orange, wore ridiculous chef's pants in green checks and pranced about saying 'Cool'?

She stared at the carpet, tears running down her cheeks.

Ten minutes later she straightened up and said aloud, 'Bloody hell, this is ridiculous.' She rubbed her face with the towel, flung it in the general direction of the bathroom and strode back to her desk. She emailed her copy to *HOT Restaurant*, pulled on her coat and stamped out of the hotel.

She took a taxi downtown to Rivington Street and was greeted by a blast of good smells and convivial noise at 'inoteca. Good, she thought, comforting Italian food is what I need. I'll have ribollita, that wonderful Tuscan soup with bread in it, followed by pasta. Or maybe risotto. Anyhow, something made of solid carbohydrate.

Chapter Two

Rebecca stared at the jumble of clothes on her bed, her fingers raking her hair. Why am I stressing about what to wear, she thought, it's not as if the place is going to be stuffed full of gorgeous men.

She pulled on the turquoise T-shirt for the second time, now over her sea-green panelled skirt, which, long and flowing, hugged her hips but flared below her knee. It made her feel jaunty, yet elegant.

She rummaged in her belt drawer and extracted the string-and-shell affair she'd borrowed last week from her daughter's bedroom. She felt a twinge of guilt. Angelica minded if her mother took things from her drawers. Of course she does, thought Rebecca, no young woman wants her mother rummaging through her things – think what she might find! But what Angelica did not understand is that *this* mother would never be shocked: not by purple condoms or tart's underwear, rude love letters or sex toys from Ann Summers. She supposed a packet of cocaine would disturb her, or a briefcase full of stolen money or casino chips, or half a jack of whisky under the pillow. But there was no chance of finding any of these things in Angelica's room. Angelica was the most sensible of daughters, with no apparent hint of rebellion in her soul. So presumably she just didn't want her mother in her room, period.

Rebecca acknowledged this fact and did not resent it, but she did not understand it. She never minded who borrowed things from her. She loved to lend her friends her clothes, her jewellery, or anything. She liked nothing better than Angelica borrowing from her, which she did less than she used to. It was funny, but when Angelica returned stuff to her, Rebecca always felt a little shaft of rejection. She would have liked her daughter to keep whatever it was, or at least to want to keep it. She always offered, and Angelica always refused.

When Angelica was little Rebecca would let her play with her jewels (the good stuff as well as the beads and junk), use her expensive make-up as face paint, ruin her Emma Hope shoes by traipsing round the garden in them. She'd never minded other people driving her car, sleeping in her bed, borrowing their flat if they were away. It drove Bill, her ex, mad. He used to say she'd lend a perfect stranger her toothbrush.

Rebecca slid the belt through her fingers. It was a mix of turquoise and orange macramé with two-inch discs of mother-of-pearl. I must put it back before she comes home for the summer, she thought, knowing the chances were she'd forget. She fastened it low over her hips and turned to the mirror, an expectant smile on her face.

But the smile faded. It would not do: she looked ready for lunch under a beach umbrella, not a singing group down the seamy end of Notting Hill. She took the belt off and dropped it on the bed, followed by the skirt and top.

She considered her lilac tunic, made of slightly knobbly alpaca. It was months since she'd bought it but she hadn't worn it yet. She felt the fabric, cool and heavy to the touch. It would hang well and look great with jeans. But she didn't feel like jeans.

Don't dither, she told herself, and put on the navy trouser suit with the pink shirt. Nothing wrong with good classic clothes, and you don't get more classic than YSL. Turning this way and that in front of the mirror, she smiled gamely.

Oh God, she thought, shrugging off the jacket, I look like a secretary. Dull, dull, dull.

She went back to the black dress she'd started with, muttering, That's it, no more faffing about. Get *on* with it. Just go.

Rebecca scooped up the pile of clothes and took them back to the walk-in cupboard. She dumped them on top of the laundry bin, promising herself she'd sort them out when she got back. She could have left them on the bed of course, but she had a rule, never confessed to anyone but firmly held since adolescence: at least leave the bedroom looking good. You never know.

One more look in the mirror, and this time Rebecca's smile was real. The thin jersey dress had little cap sleeves and a scoop neck which showed off her tan – fake, but who was to know? – and the combination of black and the cut of the skirt turned her from a size twelve into a ten.

Hurriedly, she reached for her handbag, the navy Prada bucket, but it was quite wrong with the black.

By the time she'd transferred everything to the cream Gucci with all the pockets and buckles, and found the black and cream wooden beads from Carole Bamford, Rebecca was definitely, definitely late.

She hurried along the street, striding as wide as her narrow skirt allowed, feeling good now. She was pleased that she could still put that swing into her gait that made her look more forty than fifty (OK fifty-four), at least from behind. Rebecca was proud of her legs, especially when they were tanned, which somehow disguised any hint of cellulite. And she knew she had a great bum. I should hope so too, she thought: all that puffing and heaving at Pilates must do something.

This end of Westbourne Grove always struck Rebecca as another country, or countries. The bookshops were Arabic, the butchers halal, the newsagents Pakistani; the restaurants were Thai, Indian, Chinese, Lebanese, Greek. You didn't hear English spoken for the first couple of blocks, not until you got halfway down, to the organic food shops. From there on to the Portobello Road, almost everyone in the designer shoe shops, fancy beauty therapists and chic cafés was white and loaded. Most were female: yummy mummies in their natural habitat.

God, she thought, with a stab of longing, I wish I was rich.

Rebecca lived at the Paddington end of Westbourne Grove, but the Notting Hill end was where she knew she belonged. Getting her legs waxed in Elemental cost her £80 but the reverential attention they paid her calves and knees as she floated off with the whale music made it worth the money. Sometimes she felt guilty, knowing she could pay £17 at her end of the Grove, where Bella did a perfectly good job in her basement room under the mobile phone shop. But the cramped cubicles, peeling ceilings and the therapist's nylon tabard were too upsetting. There, she felt her toes curl in protest as she put her shoes back on, fearful of touching the horrible lino.

But tonight she was not spending money on what Bill called fripperies. No one could disapprove of educative evening classes. According to the Sing Your Heart Out website, she was going to 'experience the endorphin rush of deep breathing combined with the emotional satisfaction of singing with others in harmony'. Well, good, she thought, I like singing a lot, but what I want is to meet new people, preferably male. Unlikely, I know, but I have to make the effort.

As she swung down Ledbury Road she tried not to be distracted by the designer clothes so artfully displayed in the shop windows. She kept her mind on the task in hand: to find a new man. She'd been on the hunt now for quite a few years. She wanted a permanent chap. Of course she would never admit it to anyone: she was terrific at pretending the single life was just fine and dandy, allowing her to play the field, have fun, stay young. But lovers were getting harder to find, and she wasn't made for celibacy – too withering and lonely. It hadn't been so bad when Angelica was at primary school and took a lot of her time, but the last ten years since Angelica had gone to boarding school had been hard.

Her married friends were no help; they'd written her off as far as men went. If they asked her to dinner these days they never invited a man for Rebecca, but stuck her next to Gran or between a couple of gay blokes or at best, twinned her with some old boy whose wife was in hospital.

They probably thought she was beyond desire, too old to even think about love, or sex. Or maybe they thought she couldn't sustain a relationship? OK, she had to admit her record so far wasn't great, but she'd been really unlucky. Her first marriage, to Kieran, had been a mistake from the start. They'd both been too young, and at least they'd sensibly given up on it as soon as they realised the relationship was going nowhere, and before they had children. Lots of people make a disastrous first marriage. She didn't think it really counted.

And she'd stuck with Bill for thirteen long years, hadn't she? Even though he drank like a fish?

And then, she thought, a little lick of anger echoing a long-ago fire, I'd have made the thing with André work if he'd had the guts to leave his wife. She'd wasted six years of her life waiting for him to do the deed, but of course he never did. Men are such hopeless wimps.

And then the divine Israeli, Joseph, had turned out to be a world-class con-man. Any woman would have fallen for him. They'd married within three weeks of meeting and Rebecca had gloried in the recklessness of it, the romance of a whirlwind courtship and flying off to Tel Aviv where he'd showered her with gold necklaces and lovely clothes, and returned with armloads of presents for Angelica. He'd been wonderful with Angelica. She'd really believed he would be the perfect father. Now her jaw tightened at the memory of her bank account emptied and the trail of debts she'd had to honour.

None of those disasters were my fault, she told herself. Some women are just unlucky with men and I'm one of them. But, hey, that doesn't mean I'll always be unlucky. Somewhere, sometime I might meet the perfect man. Maybe tonight, who knows?

Chapter Three

Joanna sometimes took visiting colleagues from the States down the Portobello on a Saturday. They found its mixture of real antiques, tat and rip-off merchants quaint. But otherwise she seldom ventured this far north, and certainly not at night. And never, until now, alone.

So she was suspicious, and a little scared, of the young black men in hoodies and puffa jackets slouching in the hall doorway. She hesitated on the bottom step, forcing herself to smile at them and say good evening. One lad, who looked more fearsome than the rest with a black bandana round his head and wraparound dark glasses, replied, 'Good evenin' to you, lady' and opened the door for her. Relieved, and a little ashamed of herself, she smiled her thanks and walked in.

Joanna was early. Anxious about the singing session, she'd determined to check the lie of the land in advance. She hated not being on top of things.

The internal door to the main hall was open, and she went in. The room (tall Gothic windows, wooden stage at one end, plastic stacking chairs, neon lighting hanging a long way down from the high arched ceiling) had the sad look of community halls the world over.

She lifted one of the grey chairs off the stack and staked her claim with her suit jacket over the back and her briefcase under. Then, thinking that the jacket was too expensive to lose, she put it on again. Irritated with herself, she thought, do you really think your fellow singers are going to nick your jacket? But she kept it on.

It was not like her to be so nervous, but she knew without a shadow of doubt that she was about to make a fool of herself. She would be the one unable to make a sound, any sound, come out of her mouth.

Joanna was not used to failure and in an effort to bolster her confidence she ran through a quick list of her upside: head girl at school, a First at Oxford, still a club-standard tennis player for all that her legs, now screened from view under white trousers, were fifty something. Pretty stylish on the ski-slopes, she was also a good public speaker who could acquit herself creditably on television. For pity's sake, she lectured the timid non-singer inside her, I've managed hundreds of people, bought and sold businesses, made large amounts of money – still do. I'm a grown up, confident woman: I've even been given a gong by the Queen, for God's sake. I should be able to handle my downside. So, I can't sing. Big deal. Lots of people can't sing. But the difference is, I'm dealing with it.

But that cringing twelve-year-old was still there. The girl who, fresh from junior school and with all the self-confidence she'd imbibed with the constant praise of teachers and proud parents, had wanted to be in the senior school choir. As soon as she'd seen them processing into church in their red tunics and white surplices she'd wanted to be one of them.

It wasn't just the choir-boy costumes. The choristers wore special school blazers that set them apart as better than the other students. And they had a common room with a piano and a radiogram in it, and they had a permanent 'town pass' because they were trusted to walk to the cathedral without a detour to the shops.

No doubt about it, the choir was the key to status, privilege and a red velvet collar on your standard-issue grey flannel jacket. The school orchestra won prizes and several ex-students were successful musicians, but it was the choir that was the pride of the school – events in the cathedral were always packed out and they had even made recordings which were on sale in the high street music store.

The head of music (and choir master), Mr Randall, was a legend in the Melbourne music world and everyone was in awe of him. But when Joanna and a bunch of other hopefuls from the new year's intake at the Peter and Paul Academy of Melbourne appeared for their choir audition, she'd never spoken to him, nor he to her.

Now he did so. Squinting myopically at his notebook, he had barked,

'Joanna Carey, you first.'

'Yes, sir.'

'Speak up, girl. If you cannot project your voice so I can hear you talk, how do you think you are going to be able to sing?'

'Sorry, sir,' Joanna had mumbled.

Mr Randall rolled his eyes to heaven in a gesture that even the child Joanna recognised as theatrical, *God give me patience*. 'Joanna, what have I just said?' he asked.

'You said to speak up, I think, sir.'

'You think? You think?'

She felt the hot blush rising up her neck and cheeks as Mr Randall ordered her to stand next to him at the piano. Then he addressed the rest of the class.

'Right, we will start with Joanna. The rest of you can sit down and listen.'

As the class settled on the floor, Joanna felt herself, tall and awkward, being abandoned to her fate. Now the only one standing, she felt peeled of the protection of her peers, exposed to the terrifying Mr Randall. Oh, why had she ever thought of being in the choir?

Mr Randall now ignored her as he instructed the rest of them.

'What you are listening for are two things: is she in tune? And if she is, then do you like the sound she makes? Being in tune is good, but there are plenty of singers who hit the note but sound unpleasant, if not atrocious, and they will not be in my choir.'

He made her stand up straight, feet slightly apart, head up, hands by her sides. And then he hit Middle C a couple of times and told her, 'I will play a note, and you will sing it, loud and clear. OK?'

She nodded, really frightened now.

He played Middle C again, and sang Aaaaa, long and strong. 'Right, your turn.'

Joanna took a deep breath, her chin up, determined to do her best, and sang the note. She managed a steady sound and held it for as long, she hoped, as Mr Randall had done. Then she dared look at Mr Randall's face, hoping for encouragement. But he just frowned, and struck D. Joanna followed the piano, singing the notes with increasing confidence. He then played a short phrase, the first three notes of 'Three Blind Mice', and she sang that too.

The group sat silent, conscious of their own ordeal to come.

Eventually, Mr Randall turned to the class. 'So, was she in tune or not?'

Waiting for a steer from the master, no one dared venture an opinion. Impatient, he snapped, 'You have ears, haven't you? Well, was she in tune or not?'

Finally a gangly lad with glasses said, 'I think she was flat on the high notes, sir.'

'Well said, young man. Too right she was. Flat as a pancake. And did you like the sound she made? Was it pleasing to your ear?'

Again, he got no answer.

'Heavens above, has the cat got all your tongues? It's a simple question. Did you like it? Did you like the sound? Do you like notes sung flat?'

Heads reluctantly shook, and Joanna burst into tears, her face aflame.

Mr Randall turned to her.

'Oh, for goodness sake, girl, what are you crying for? Yes, we have established you cannot sing and you won't be in the choir, but it's not the end of the world. You can presumably play hockey, or join the cookery club or something. So off you go now.'

And that had been that. No jacket with a red collar, no making that wonderful, all encompassing, magical sound with a band of friends. No belonging to the choir. At first she had tried to tell herself she didn't want to be in the choir anyway with such a horrible teacher, but she knew that the music students would go through fire for him. If you were in the choir, you became one of his protected pets and he was nice to you; no one ever wanted to leave the choir.

Now, forty years later, here she was in this little community hall, determined to overcome the legacy of Mr Randall.

She pretended an interest in the pile of exercise mats and plastic steps for aerobics classes in one corner. Joanna used to enjoy step classes at her gym and was good at the routines. She liked the competitive nature of them. But now, at fifty-five, her knees were getting a bit dodgy and aerobics made them worse. So she swam a lot and used the gym machines with care.

She wandered over to the upright piano, rather battered but a Steinway, and looked through the music sheets lying on top of it: Singing for Beginners; Songs from the Musicals; Schubert; Mozart.

A pile of sheet music for 'Cry Me a River' gave her the nasty thought that they might be expected to read music. She could not do that either. Maybe I should just quit now, she thought, I don't have to do this. I could just grab my briefcase and go. Walk away.

But suddenly there were footsteps and voices in the hall and four or five people came in and it was too late to leave. One man (tall, black, forty-five-ish, maybe Jamaican) was wheeling a bicycle.

'Hi lady, you here for the singing?' he said. He balanced the bike with one hand, and stretched the other towards Joanna with a big beamy smile. 'I'm Nelson. I teach this class.' He waved to include the others. ''Fraid I can't introduce nobody to nobody. But when everyone's here we'll go round the room and get the formalities done. Meanwhile, welcome.'

By the time Nelson had propped his bike against the wall, and cheerfully explained that he'd had his last two bikes stolen from the street outside, another ten or so people had drifted in and they got down to business.

'We'll start,' Nelson said, 'with something simple to break the ice.'

It was a vaguely familiar gospel tune that Joanna realised anyone would get in five seconds, and she knew she could sing it if she was alone.

But with the others there, it was the same old story. Her throat tightened almost at once and as the familiar ache overlaid the wheezy near-silence of her efforts, she felt a wash of frustration and disappointment.

Everyone else, of course, sang beautifully. With Nelson's encouragement they were belting their hearts out, and sounding mellow and rich.

Joanna mimed along and watched the others. Some of them, especially the younger ones, were smiling at each other across the room as they sang, their faces softened and lit by the pleasure of it.

It was preposterous at her age, she thought, but she could feel the prick of tears behind her eyes. Oh, why can't I do that? What's the matter with me? *Why* can't I sing?

She was standing next to Nelson, who would have to turn fully to verify that she was not singing. This was a relief to her. She did not want to be shown up, now she just wanted to get the class over with and go home.

Chapter Four

Rebecca had walked fast but the class had obviously started. She could hear singing through the open windows of the community hall. For a second she considered ducking out, but the singing sounded really good, some sort of gospel hymn she guessed. Besides, she could hear male voices in there. She listened intently, trying to count them. Half a dozen at least, she thought. Worth a little look.

Her mind made up, Rebecca swung into the room with drummed-up confidence. She dropped her bag beside a row of others against the wall, hoping it wouldn't get nicked.

About twenty people were standing in a loose circle, feet apart, backs straight, heads up, concentrating. Some of them were clutching their midriffs, testing the depth of their breathing as they sang.

Some looked up and returned her smile while still singing, others just kept going without acknowledging her.

About a third were men, most of them a lot younger than her. The big black dude with a lot of hair was obviously Nelson, the teacher. He held his right arm bent, with his elbow sticking straight out from his shoulder and his hand flat. He lifted his arm up and down as the sound rose and fell.

Still singing, he smiled at Rebecca, and with his free hand waved her to stand between him and a little bearded guy, who seemed reluctant to give up his place next to teacher.

A distinctly classy woman (drop-dead suit, Issey Miyake probably, must have cost a fortune) on the other side of Nelson had to shift up to make room for her. She smiled her thanks, and looked round at the circle of singers.

How do they know the words? she wondered: this is lesson one, and they don't have any song-sheets. But Nelson gave her another big toothy smile and she found herself following him in a repeating round of the same few phrases:

> *Wadin' in the water*
> *Wadin' in the water*
> *Wadin' in the water*
> *God's a gonna trouble the*
> *water*

They prolonged the last mellow notes, commanded by Nelson's hand, then stopped cleanly as his arm flicked up in a decisive halt. They smiled at each other, pleased and surprised. Nice chap, thought Rebecca, dead friendly.

'So,' Nelson said, 'we establish everyone can sing. So we won't have no crap 'bout how you's tone deaf or nuttin'. Everyone in the whole wide worl' can sing. B'lieve me. They just need showin' how.'

He stepped back to the piano and banged the lowest note at the bass end repeatedly with one finger. 'You hear that?' he said. Then tinkled the high end with the other hand. 'An' that? Do they sound the same to you?' He glared round the circle. 'There's a difference OK? Anyone can't hear the difference?' He hit low and high again. Low and high. His glare moved round his class, holding everyone's gaze for a second, aggressive but smiling. 'Anyone still want to tell me they tone deaf?'

They grinned sheepishly at each other, mumbling 'No' or shaking their heads.

'Good,' said Nelson, 'now we knows y'all can sing, we go round the room, introduce oursel'.'

It was the usual mixed bag, thought Rebecca: four couples, one of them proudly lesbian, and five or six singles under forty. Among the over-fifties, she counted three single women besides herself: Joanna, the posh suit on the other side of Nelson, who turned out to be a businesswoman, a big black woman with a great voice, and an overweight food writer in a shapeless trouser suit and terrible haircut called Lucy, who could certainly sing. But of single men over forty there was, of course, a dearth: just the bearded ecologist who introduced himself as a bird-freak, and one old guy, very tall and completely bald, who declared himself a medical scientist.

When it came to Rebecca, she described herself as a partner in an interior design business. Not exactly true, she thought. What I should have said is I'm the dogsbody in my ex-husband's company, for which he pays me peanuts.

After the introductions, they followed Nelson in stretching, breathing, humming and making unmusical animal sounds. And then they were back to 'Wadin' in the Water', then 'Motherless Child' and finally 'Swing Low, Sweet Chariot', sung sweetly and gently, hardly recognisable as the maudlin rugby anthem bawled by oafs on the terraces.

Within an hour they were into three-part harmony, and Rebecca was singing with real pleasure, smiling at the others, happy and relaxed. Even her man-hunt had been temporarily forgotten.

Chapter Five

Lucy knew she'd been bullied into joining the choir by the combined forces of her daughter, son-in-law and grandchildren.

They'd won the battle one Sunday a few weeks ago. It had started with Grace in her kitchen.

'Mum,' Grace had said, 'you can't go on mouldering in the country for ever, eating junk and watching daytime telly.'

Lucy had tried to ignore her daughter's aggrieved tone. 'Why not?' she'd asked, sliding the Tesco pizza out of its box. 'And this won't be junk for long anyway. I'm fixing it.' She cut off the wrapping and slid the pizza onto a baking tray. 'And my mouldering, as you charmingly put it, doesn't make any difference to you, does it?'

'Yes, it—'

'Darling, you should be pleased. You were always pleading for "real sausages, like we have at school"; "proper ice cream from Wall's", "white bread from the shop, like normal people . . ."'

'For God's sake, Mother, that was twenty years ago!' Grace had flicked the tea towel off the rail and dried the saucers with a lot more energy than necessary. 'And of course you staying at home day after day makes a difference to us. The children don't see you enough for a start.' She'd faced Lucy and her voice had softened. 'And we worry about you. Besides, Dad wouldn't want you moping, would he?'

Irritation had licked at Lucy. She knew Grace was motivated by genuine concern, but it felt like interference. Grace never gave up and, true to form, she persisted,

'You don't go walking with that group any more, and you've given up the choir. Why not just give that singing group off Ladbroke Grove a go? I think it sounds perfect, and you could stay the night with us, and the children could see something of their gran.'

Lucy had shaken her head, feeling obstinate, even truculent. No, she thought. No, why should I?

Grace, however, had not finished.

'You've even stopped cooking, Mum. Tesco's pizza for God's sake! You used to be the kind of cook who bakes her own beans!'

Suddenly Lucy had felt more defeated than defiant. All this family emotion was so *tiring*. It was bad enough feeling wretched herself; considering the feelings of her children seemed beyond her.

What Grace had said was true, of course. At first she had tried to keep up the habits of her marriage. She'd gone to church. Gone walking with the Cotswold Wardens with whom she and David had hiked for years. But the empty pew beside her had been horrible, and the walkers' sympathy had made David's absence worse, not better.

And she could not have borne going back to her old choral group to sing the music she and David had learned together, rehearsed together, performed together. Even a snatch of Fauré's *Requiem* on the radio was enough to make her cry. Singing it would be impossible.

As for cooking, what was the point? Cooking was about love and caring and togetherness. Cooking for one was a waste of time.

She'd watched Grace stacking the mugs on the shelf, her back speaking heroic patience with an obstinate mother. She hasn't a clue what I feel, Lucy had thought. She thinks I should just pull myself together.

'Mum, for God's sake, just give the choir a go. It's perfect. Not quite *St Matthew Passion* I know, but you like gospel, don't you? You used to sing it to us all the time.'

Lucy had closed her eyes for a second before responding.

'Grace, could we give it a rest, do you think? I'm trying to cook lunch, and you are being horribly persistent.'

Lucy had known her voice sounded dead and unfeeling. Her daughter's heavy sigh and resigned shake of the head as she resumed unloading the dishwasher had not surprised her. Grace's clear belief in her own rightness, funny as a child, now grated. Two weeks before, she'd insisted Lucy go to the doctor, who told her she was depressed. Depression is caused by a chemical imbalance he'd said. Not your fault. Just take the tablets.

Lucy had refused the tablets and rejected the diagnosis. She was unhappy, sure, but she had good reason to be. If your husband died and you were not unhappy, what kind of marriage would that have been? Certainly not one to spend half your life on. And wasn't losing your job, one which gave you everything a good job should – challenge, opportunity, satisfaction, interest, status, interesting colleagues, money – a reason to be down in the mouth?

She had then made an effort to stop swatting mental flies, and concentrated on adding slices of sun-dried tomatoes, chunks of mozzarella and a few squashy olives to the pizzas. She poured a thin dribble of Italian olive oil over them and slid the tray into the oven.

'Lunch in ten minutes' she'd said briskly. Then, relenting, she'd touched Grace's arm and said, 'Don't worry about me, darling. I'm not desperate. Just rather poor company at the moment.'

Grace had gone in search of the children and Lucy had laid the table, thinking about their conversation. Maybe what she resented wasn't Grace's bossiness but the fact that she was not allowed, or at least not expected, to grieve. You had to do things. You had to 'move on'. Horrible phrase. Resume everything you did before, accept all the invitations of kind friends. Lucy thought there was merit in the ancient tradition of wearing black and mourning, when people accepted that you didn't feel up to much, certainly not up to singing.

But Grace was right about the cooking. Why had she collapsed into convenience food, stopped doing what she'd loved doing all

her life? Before David's death a ready-made pizza, even with home improvements, was unheard of. Even after he died and she still had her column, she managed a real interest in the food she was writing about. But it was an academic interest, a conjured-up enthusiasm from remembered or imagined meals, markets, ingredients. It did not extend to her own shopping and cooking.

Now the fridge was full of shameful things – shameful for a respected food-writer anyway. Ready-made meals from the farm-shop, bottled mayonnaise, chiller-cabinet soups, roast chicken from the rotisserie, salads in puffed-up bags, Marks and Spencer's panna cotta.

These things were for when the family came down. When she was on her own, which was most of the time, Lucy ate fingers of cheddar and a fresh pear, or maybe a banana. Or yoghurt straight from the pot. Occasionally she made a tomato and cheese sandwich, or poached eggs on toast. Sometimes she just ate chocolate.

That same afternoon, when they'd been watching Johnny and Clare petting the donkey in the paddock, Archie had a go at her too. He'd put his arm round her shoulders (rather tentatively as though he knew the gesture was required but could not feel any real affection for his mother-in-law to go with it) and said, 'Lucy, you know Grace is right. Why not join a London choir? Just for fun?'

'I am not after fun. And it wouldn't be fun.'

'Really, Lucy, it's not just about the choir. You could combine it with a night or two with us, and you could meet a friend for lunch, go to a gallery or something. Make something positive about not having to work. And Johnny and Clare would love it.'

Lucy had not replied that she would rather be at home with her cat than any of this. She had protested that she still had to work: she'd lost her newspaper job but there was her column in *HOT Restaurant* and she had a cookbook well over her publisher's deadline. Archie had let it drop.

But when, over tea, her grandchildren, obviously put up to it by Grace, had added their pleas for her presence, Clare wheedling,

Johnny tugging her hand and saying, 'Go on, Gran. Give in', she'd crumbled. She could not let the children suspect that she was uneager to spend time with them. Indeed, she was ashamed of her reluctance and worried by it. She used to so love their company, rather more than their parents' in fact, but somehow they did not delight her as before.

A week later Lucy was in the train, on her way to London. She pulled her eyes away from the Cotswold landscape sliding past the window and returned her thoughts to the matter in hand. She booted up her laptop and found her file: 'Draft One. Peasant Soups'. To her irritation the font size had somehow gone back to the factory setting that twenty-year-old techies working in Microsoft might be able to see but she couldn't, even with her glasses on. Why were computers so maddeningly disobedient? For the umpteenth time she reset the default to font size fourteen.

Lucy worked steadily for an hour. When she got to the recipe for ribollita she paused, wondering if her preference for Italian sour-dough bread was born of snobbishness or because its toughness stopped it falling completely apart in the soup. And did it have to be cavalo nero, or could you use spinach or chard? Suddenly a wave of acute boredom engulfed her. Who gives a toss, she thought. I don't, that's for sure. She closed her laptop and rubbed her eyes, boredom transmuting into anxiety.

This singing thing isn't going to work, she thought. I don't want to pay fifty pounds every week to come up to London on this inevitably late train, stay in Johnny's bedroom with nowhere to put my things and the bathroom down the corridor, and, worst of all, a Thomas the Tank Engine duvet. I detest duvets. And all so I can sing in a group that Grace thinks will do me good. I don't want anything that will do me good.

She gazed out at sloping valleys, sun on stone, picture-book sheep with laughable lambs gambolling about, a spring scene to lift the heart. But Lucy's heart remained unlifted.

Her mind picked at her crossness with her daughter. Why had Grace turned out so controlling? She, Lucy, had never been strict with her. Neither had David. In fact, when Grace was little, she'd longed for her husband to be a bit more Victorian and a little less indulgent.

Now Grace claimed her instincts for order were a reaction to her over-lax childhood. She thinks David and I should have made her go to church and tidy her bedroom. And that we should have said no to pierced ears, loud music and boys. It's true we hardly ever said no. Except maybe to junk food.

Lucy sighed, and closed her eyes. It must be Archie's influence, she thought, he is such a middle-aged thirty-five-year-old. *Daily Telegraph*, pinstripes and umbrella, well-shined shoes. Even ironed cotton shirts at the weekend.

With an effort, Lucy wrenched her mind out of complaint mode. She must stop this constant brooding. She sat up and smiled at the woman opposite, who reacted with a nervous half-smile and a swift return to her book.

Be positive, Lucy told herself. She resolved to enjoy singing gospel and blues.

And she did. The teacher, Nelson, was a pro. He used that 'patterning' gesture with his hand held flat to signal higher or lower, while keeping eye contact with everyone in turn, and somehow he managed to lift the group above the only-just-in-tune into the spot-on tuneful. It was good to feel her lungs fill and her diaphragm working. The sound, round and true, seemed to fill her head. She had forgotten how liberating singing could be.

The little hall off Ladbroke Grove had great acoustics, and there were some excellent singers – a big black woman with a huge rich-as-velvet voice, and two tenors who had clearly sung a lot before. One chicly-dressed woman, with obvious money and style (she'd arrived late in a black jersey dress and strappy leather sandals) had a quiet but very pure alto. There was really only one dud, a rather uptight woman next to her, whose voice didn't seem to work at all.

After the class, she forced herself to stay a few minutes and make polite conversation with her fellow singers, then excused herself, explaining she was due back at her daughter's for supper. She walked slowly, enjoying the replay of melodies in her head, reluctant to break her pleasant mood. Even a little reluctant to face her grandchildren. She'd have liked to go on singing.

Chapter Six

For Joanna the whole evening had been a disaster. They'd sung nothing but gospel songs you can learn without words or music. Even she could tell that Nelson was a good teacher, and by the end the group was singing complicated three-part harmonies worthy of Harlem, and most of them were swaying and moving in a wholly un English way. Joanna had made sporadic efforts to join in, but the pain was intense and the sound almost non-existent, so she quickly returned to miming.

At one point, still conducting and grinning at the group, Nelson had leaned close, his ear near her mouth. The game was up . . .

She'd endured the agony, longing for release. But then, at the end, when everyone else was flushed with success and talking about next week, Nelson came over and took her arm.

'Come with me, lady,' he said.

She'd followed him to the piano, out of hearing of the group.

'This group's no good for you,' he went on, 'not by itself. You gotta fin' yo' singing voice, and right now you don' know how or where. Right?' He looked seriously into her face, forcing her to meet his eyes. They were big, slightly bulging and intense.

Joanna nodded. 'Right,' she said, almost crossly, 'but it's no good you saying everyone can sing.' Her voice didn't sound right in her own ears. Why was she getting so emotional about this? 'I can't do it. I just can't.'

Nelson did not challenge this. 'What happens when you try?'

'You listened to me. No sound comes. Even if you asked me to sing 'Three Blind Mice', I could not force any voice through my throat. It just closes, tight and hard. And it hurts.'

He did not say anything for a moment, just looked straight at her.

Then he said, 'I bet you sing fine on your own – in the bath. In the car?'

He was right. If there was no one around, she could karaoke away with the best of them, sing Cole Porter while watering her posh little garden, or belt out 'Toreador' while boiling pasta. She shook her head and said, 'OK, I sometimes sing a bit on my own, but I don't suppose it's in tune.'

'That don' matter. Point is, you can sing without hurting, which means yo' trouble is in yo' head.' He looked hard at her, forcing her to look at him. 'I can make you sing, lady, I promise.'

She shook her head, and said, 'No, forget it.'

But Nelson cheerfully insisted. He took Joanna's telephone number and said he'd put together two or three people from the group, and they could come an hour early, and together they would get her singing. He opened his arms wide, all smiles, and said, 'And then the Albert Hall!' and roared with laughter.

Joanna suddenly realised how ungrateful and feeble she must seem. Indeed what a wimp she was being.

'I'm so sorry, Nelson. You're a really nice guy. You don't need to do this, do you? All you signed up for, presumably, was to give a singing class, not nanny me through my problems.'

'No sweat,' he said.

Joanna went home surprisingly cheered, and found herself singing 'Wadin' in the Water' as she drove up Kensington Park Road. There was no strain and no pain, just the pleasure of singing.

Chapter Seven

Lucy's serene mood after the singing class gradually evaporated as she walked up the hill. She began to worry that she was late. Grace did not approve of the children staying up. She pulled her jacket close and, head down, quickened her pace.

Suddenly she was startled by a too-close bike skidding to a stop beside her. She jumped round.

It was Nelson, the teacher. 'I'm so sorry. I didn't mean to frighten . . . So sorry. I couldn't remember your name to call you.'

Lucy, smiling with relief, said, 'No, no, it's fine. I'm Lucy.'

'Oh, yes of course, Lucy. I wanted to ask you a favour.'

'Go ahead,' said Lucy, wondering what on earth a forcibly retired food columnist and glum widow could do for a confident, charming, talented (and fashionably black) blues teacher? Whose accent, she noticed, veered from broad Jamaican to the Queen's English. Was that for show? Self parody?

They were standing outside a pub, and it was hard to hear above the noise of music and drink-raised voices. Nelson said, 'Let's walk. Where are you going?'

She told him Pembridge Square. As they set off up the hill Nelson asked, 'Did you notice that the woman between you and me didn't sing at all? Just pretended?'

'Yes, I did. She looked so miserable. Joanna wasn't it? The business-woman?'

Nelson grinned. 'That's right. That's her.'

Lucy could not think where this conversation was going.

'She's got a problem,' Nelson went on. 'She can't sing with other people. Her throat constricts from anxiety, and then no sound will come. It's quite common. I thought we could help her.'

Lucy looked into Nelson's face and could see his concern was genuine.

'We? I can see you could . . .'

'She needs a couple of singers who'll have semi-private sessions with her. It's the big group that paralyses her. She can sing on her own, she says. I thought I'd ask Rebecca as well. The blonde lady with the alto.'

Hmm . . . thought Lucy, the middle-aged trio together. But of course she agreed. How could she not? And besides, the woman's predicament intrigued her. She'd heard plenty of people who sang flat, or sharp, or were too shy to try, but never someone who tried, but couldn't make the sound come out.

The family had waited for her, and of course the table was properly set, with real linen napkins and candles. Grace had roasted a chicken with lemon and tarragon, and the children were bathed and looking angelic in their pyjamas. Lucy, hugging her granddaughter, noticed that her wide mouth, so like David's, was now sporting serrated new front teeth.

There was a bottle of robust red wine, and ten-year-old Johnny went round and poured it like a waiter, with one hand behind his back and a napkin on his arm. It was sweet and funny. He'd learnt waiter behaviour for a play at school, he said.

'It's cool you having my room, Gran,' he said.

'It's good of you to let me. But why is it cool?'

'I like sleeping on the sofa.'

Clare said, 'That's because you put the telly on in the middle of the night.'

'I do not!'

Grace interjected, 'I'm sure you don't, Johnny, and Clare, don't try to get your brother into trouble. Eat up, both of you.'

The children obediently returned to their food, glowering at each other under their brows in a half-hearted way.

Lucy, as always, was impressed with her daughter's control of the children. When Grace had been little she could only, it seemed, govern with her consent. But Grace was the boss here, and her children knew it.

Once in bed Lucy found herself, as she still did most nights, talking to David. Not aloud of course, just in her head. She knew some widows actually wrote to their dead husbands, or kept a sort of mourning diary. She just carried on mental conversations, observations and accusations.

Darling, it's been over six months now. The worst of my life. But tonight I forgot about you for a good three hours. And I felt a stirring of real affection for my grandchildren, making faces at each other below Grace's radar. Now I'm under the horrible duvet, but feeling mellow and not sad. Progress, don't you think?

Chapter Eight

When Joanna got home after her disastrous singing class she was in such a good mood that she did something she had not done since Christmas. She rang her parents in Australia.

She needed to be feeling brave to do this, to face the inevitable accusation from her mother, uttered or unsaid, of having been the beneficiary of a pampered childhood and privileged education and given them nothing back. There was some truth in the charge. She had fled to Europe as a twenty-two-year-old, and never returned.

Her parents had visited her once but, almost from the moment of their arrival, she had been desperate for them to leave. Her dad had been as generous and affectionate as ever, but she was still in her thirties and not grown up enough to be relaxed about his Crocodile Dundee clothes, coarse manners and expansive loudness. In front of her smart City friends with their pink-striped shirts, button down collars and mobile telephones (they were new then and the size of bricks, but they were the mark of the new elite) he embarrassed her quite as much as her mother did. More in fact. Her mother, as ever, nagged both her and her father mercilessly but at least she liked London, and didn't tell people they were talking cobblers, or insist on drinking Foster's in smart restaurants.

It was nine in the morning in Melbourne, so Joanna reckoned she should get her mother. She would not be downstairs yet, since she always dressed slowly and late, stuck in some interior vision of herself as a sort of Scarlett O'Hara, surrounded by servants and adorers who do everything for her, but marooned in a ranch miles from the excitement of the city.

Her mother was almost eighty now, but she had been Miss Australia and had been headed, she reminded everyone frequently, for a glittering career on the stage. Instead, she had made the mistake of marrying Joanna's father, who seemed a good bet at the time since he was the richest property developer in Melbourne.

But when he'd made his pile, he'd sold up and bought a 30,000-acre cattle ranch in the middle of nowhere and imprisoned his beautiful bride in it. At least, that was the version her daughter had been fed throughout her childhood. It wasn't until she could do the arithmetic that Joanna worked out that her mama had been forty something when they moved to the ranch, long past any spin-off glory from her nineteen-year-old flowering as Miss Australia. Poor woman, thought Joanna, I should have had more sympathy for her delusions and her unhappiness, but she irritated me then, and irritates the hell out of me now.

She dialled the number and almost immediately heard her mother's voice.

'Hullo, is that you, John?'

'No, Mother, it's me.'

'Who? Who is this?' Her voice held a touch of disdain.

'Me. Your daughter. Joanna.' Joanna spoke loudly and clearly. Her mother was slightly deaf.

'You don't have to shout you know. I'm not deaf.'

And I don't have to ring you up, thought Joanna. But she said, 'OK, Mum. How are you? How's Dad?'

'I thought you were John. I'm waiting for a call from John.'

'Who's John?'

'My hairdresser. He's good enough to come all the way out to this godforsaken place to do my hair because my back is too bad to jolt over these awful roads.'

'God, Mum, that must cost a fortune!' The ranch was fifty miles from the nearest town, and there was a nine-mile drive along the gum-lined drive once you were on the property.

'Your father can afford it. It's the least he can do. And John stays for lunch, so at least I get some civilised company for once.'

Joanna sighed. How could her mother have been married for sixty years, and still be complaining? Why didn't they divorce years ago?

They discussed her mother's bad back, her thinning hair, her isolation (as always), the weather (drought, sheep dying, farm labourers quitting) – which seemed to give her more satisfaction than concern.

Joanna waited to see if her mother would ask her one single question. But no. It was always the same. These conversations were only ever about her mother. Joanna still minded, and always noticed. In a way there was a kind of grim satisfaction in each time noting that her mother never showed any interest in her, any concern or affection. Yet when she'd been little her mother had been proud of her. Like a performing monkey or a designer accessory, thought Joanna.

When she had run out of complaints, Joanna asked, 'Is Dad still there? I'd like to catch him before he goes out on the ranch.'

'I've no idea.'

But she did put the call through, and Joanna heard, with guilt and love combined, her father's broad Aussie accent.

'Darling girl,' he boomed, his voice at eighty-five as strong as ever. 'Great to hear you. Tell all. How's the best head-hunter in the western world doing then?'

Joanna laughed, 'Oh Dad, you know I'm not a head-hunter any more. I sold the search business years ago and I now work for Innovest, the venture capital guys.'

'So you did, so you did. I'm getting senile. Well, how is the best venture capitalist in the western world doing then?

She told him about her new life, working for Innovest and doctoring companies in trouble, and she felt like she used to when she came home from school with a good report. He was so pleased and proud of her. Then they talked about the ranch, how he was herding sheep by helicopter now. And yes, of course he had learnt to fly it. He had been flying single-engine flat-wing planes for years, so it wasn't difficult. He loved the chopper, said it was so manoeuvrable you could be a sort of aerial sheep dog. But he still rode out every day on old George, his chestnut gelding — but for pleasure (and to get away from Mama, thought Joanna), not to inspect the sheep or cattle. And come shearing time, he still liked to do his bit.

'I can't keep it up all day any more,' he said, 'but I can still have a fleece off a sheep faster than the lads, and without a single nick.'

When father and daughter had done boasting to each other, Joanna reluctantly replaced the phone. Why am I not mature enough to put up with her carping? If Dad can, why can't I?

Chapter Nine

'But darling, you've left home, haven't you? Surely you don't mind if I put some stuff in here?'

Rebecca watched her daughter yank her clothes cupboard open, lift half a dozen hangers off the rail, each heavy with two or three dresses or coats or jackets, then turn to face her before she answered. 'No, Mum, I haven't left home. I'm at university. I still need a home!'

Rebecca waved her hand to encompass her daughter's bedroom.

'How many times have you slept in this bed in the last two years? Half a dozen?'

Angelica dumped the clothes on the bed and looked at her mother with a mixture of dismay and affection. She rolled her eyes with exaggerated patience and said, very slowly, as to a recalcitrant four-year-old,

'Mum, I am a student. I have to be in Edinburgh most of the year. Last year I was travelling on my gap year, remember? I was "growing up", "broadening my mind", "learning to earn my way", "loosening the apron strings". All your phrases by the way.'

'And now you are grown up and free of my apron strings you have quite rightly left home.'

Suddenly Angelica laughed. 'Mum, when did you ever wear an apron! I've been tidying up after you since I learnt to tie my shoe laces. Which Dad taught me, by the way!'

Rebecca didn't know how to react. The conversation had taken a turn she did not like. She felt the accusation, and she minded. It was true she was untidy, true she wasn't domesticated, but it was unkind of Angelica to point it out, and particularly cruel to bring Bill into it. And anyway, Angelica was dodging the question.

'What have my domestic talents, or lack of them, or your father's abundance of them, got to do with my clothes in this room?'

'Oh, Mum . . .'

Angelica came across and put her arms round her. Rebecca was tempted to turn away but she left it a second too late: as Angelica hugged her, a wash of comfort replaced her anger.

She loved the smell of her daughter: it had not changed since she was little, warm and clean. She suddenly had a vision of Angelica, aged five, telling her and Bill that just because they disagreed with each other, they didn't have to shout. She *smells* sensible, thought Rebecca, breathing in. It would be good to have a little cry against Angelica's neck.

Angelica spoke into her mother's hair. 'Mum, I have to have this room. I'm not completely independent. I still need some place to call home, and you don't seriously want to chuck me out, do you?' She stood back a little, looking into Rebecca's face. 'Oh, Mum, you look like a child whose balloon has burst.'

In an instant Rebecca melted. She could never feel put out with Angelica for long.

'Oh, darling, it's fine. You are quite right, I've been a rotten mother—'

'Oh yeah?' Angelica interrupted. 'Well, I guess if a rotten mother means someone who can't make a bed or bake a cake, then yes, you are a rotten mother.' She gave Rebecca a little shake. 'But I think you're brilliant. Fun to be with, indulgent, tolerant, interested in me – very important! – and with great clothes I can nick. Pity your trousers are now too short.'

Angelica returned to the question of her room and convinced Rebecca, as a mother does a child, with a mix of explanation, threat and reward.

'Problem is, I've got a ton of stuff that I'm not allowed to leave in my room at uni. I suppose I could ask Dad if he can store stuff for me and put me up in the vacs, but Mum, I'd much rather be here with you. Look, why don't we have a go at your wardrobe and make some room? I like sorting stuff.'

Rebecca heard the threat, and knew she'd been manipulated, but the prospect of her daughter helping her do what she was so hopeless at, and of having time with her, vanquished Rebecca.

'OK, sweetheart, you win,' she said, scooping up an armful of coats and dresses and heading back to her own bedroom. 'But let's have a little lunch first. I've got some really nice cheese and a packet of prosciutto from Carluccio's and some great bread from Planet Organic and half a bottle of bubbly. It will give me the courage to chuck stuff out.'

Rebecca rather wished Joanna and Lucy were not in the pub with her and Nelson. The presence of two other women in their fifties put her in an 'oldie' bracket she did not think she belonged to. Guilty by association.

It wasn't that she didn't like these women – she did – but you had to be honest. Both Lucy and Joanna looked *much* older than her and she knew that if it had been just her and Nelson, people would take them for the same age. His age.

They were in the upstairs room of the pub, which was heaving with bodies, both black and white, and pounding with reggae. No one took any notice of Nelson with the three of them, which surprised Rebecca a little. They made such an unusual table: one young black guy in his natural habitat and three white, middle-class old matrons right out of their comfort zone. It was impressive that Nelson was prepared to bring them there and risk being ridiculed by his mates. But he was cool about it and when a couple of Rastafarians came past he introduced them.

'Malcolm, meet these good ladies. They all learnin' to sing gospel. Ladies, this is Malcolm who owns a nightclub, and his brother Mark who is a villain.'

Mark said, 'Yeah, man,' and punched Nelson's arm, grinning, pleased at the compliment.

'And this here's Lucy, voice like an angel. And Joanna, shit-hot business lady, and this chick here's Rebecca.'

Rebecca knew he was joking, but hey, it was still nice to be referred to as a chick. Mark and Malcolm moved on to the bar, and the women went back to discussing Joanna's problem, which was still a problem, but maybe a diminishing one. Tonight they'd had their third private lesson before the group session, and Joanna had sung 'Motherless Child' by herself with no help from anyone and then started blubbing. It was sweet really, thought Rebecca, she's the hard-boiled business type who never cries: she'd been so embarrassed, laughing and mopping her eyes and saying sorry, sorry.

Nelson had put his great bear paws round Joanna then and the green-eyed monster had given Rebecca a little stab.

But then when the main group arrived and they had all sung 'Motherless Child' again, Joanna couldn't do it, and Rebecca had thought she'd burst into tears again, this time with frustration. But she didn't. She just mimed away, her face long as a wet November.

Thinking over this, Rebecca concluded that that was why Nelson had suggested a drink. He was a softie really and didn't want his students crying into their pillows.

Now he put one of his big warm hands on Joanna's wrist and said, 'Joanna, babe. I tol' you it was gonna be like this. One step at a time. Soon you'll be singin' like Tina Turner.'

The wine (they'd downed a bottle and a half of red between them) had made Joanna look less of a schoolmarm. Her face was flushed and her eyes shiny, but whether because she was glad or sad it was hard to tell. She hadn't said much but now she blurted out, 'Nelson, I really am so grateful.' She included Lucy and Rebecca in her frowning, earnest gaze. 'And you two. You've been really wonderful to me. So kind. You mustn't feel you have to continue—'

'Nonsense,' interrupted Lucy. 'We like it, and it's a good warm-up for the classes.'

Rebecca was sorry for Joanna but couldn't understand why she was so wound up about the singing. Not being able to sing was hardly the end of the world. She chipped in, 'Don't worry, Joanna. It's good fun. Besides, we want to see if it works, don't we? Like being part of an experiment.'

And there was another reason of course. Nelson. She knew that a black preacher who taught gospel singing to white middle-class residents of Notting Hill wouldn't exactly *do*, but he was definitely, definitely a turn-on.

She turned to him. 'Nelson,' she asked, 'have you ever done this before – trained someone out of tight-throat syndrome or whatever it is?'

She wasn't really interested in Joanna's singing problems, but she knew the way to a man's heart was to ask him questions so he could talk about himself. Nelson was no different, and answered with a grin.

'Yes, a few times, once for a professional singer who could not sing if his wife was in the audience. I ended up teaching the whole family. The wife now sings in one of the choirs her husband performs with.'

He talked about his work with school children and community groups, with private clients and professionals.

He's magnetic when he's talking about teaching, thought Rebecca. He forgets to do the Jamaican street slang bit and sounds educated, confident and relaxed. She looked at the others. They were as fascinated as she. Three ageing groupies, transfixed by a very tasty guy.

Then Lucy, who stayed with her daughter and son-in-law on singing nights, said she must go. Rebecca knew Lady Luck was really on her side when Joanna decided to leave too. Quickly, before Nelson could organise a general exodus, she whispered to him, 'I'm for finishing the bottle, what about you?'

'Sure thing, babe.'

He helped Joanna into her jacket – Armani, Rebecca noticed – and they said their goodbyes.

The two of them sat down again and Rebecca returned to her task of wooing him with flattery and questions. She reminded herself that this was just for fun, for flirting's sake, not to be entered into seriously. Nelson hadn't any money, and she simply could not afford a real relationship with someone who could not improve her lifestyle.

She was surprised to learn that Nelson had never married, and he didn't have children. She'd thought there would be a wife and a flock of kids. Another surprise: he was forty-eight! Only six years younger than she. He looked more like thirty-five.

They ended up in his flat, which Rebecca was sorry to see was in a council block in Westbourne Park. She'd never been inside a council block, and rather expected it to be all graffiti and piss in the corridors and young men in hoodies loitering with intent. But it was a low rise, solid, brick building, perfectly nice, and Nelson's flat (once they'd negotiated the impressive array of front door locks) was a pleasant surprise. It had white walls and wooden floors, with a pale kilim rug under a glass coffee table. There were large, rather good, modern pictures, a cream leather sofa, an upright piano, and bookshelves crammed with orange Penguins. It was neat, spacious and classy.

Rebecca tried to disguise her surprise, but Nelson spotted it.

'I don't do badly with the teaching. And I run singing sessions for big companies and organisations on their away days – sort of corporate bonding sessions. Team building, they call it. Pays well.'

He came and stood behind her at the bookcase, where Rebecca was pretending an interest in *The Great Gatsby*, *Ulysses*, *Middlemarch*. There were lots more like that – books she had heard of but never read. She'd better deflect him from any discussion of them.

'Nelson, how come you talk afro-slang in company and proper English now?'

He laughed. 'I don't know. It's true though, you aren't the first to notice it. I just fall into the Yo Man stuff when I'm with my pub mates, or playing the part of the black blues teacher. Maybe it's for the street cred with the kids I teach so they'll give me "respec". They're great on being given "respec" though it seldom occurs to them to earn it. But it's not really me. Both my parents spoke good English – they were civil servants.'

He is intriguing, thought Rebecca, no doubt of that. She watched him roll a couple of joints, feeling good that he accepted her as someone who would not disapprove. They sat on the sofa, smoking and listening to Haydn.

He asked her about her marriage. Rebecca, at first flippant and jokey, found herself becoming serious as she told Nelson about Bill's problems with drink, how she'd hoped in vain that the birth of a longed-for child would sober him up, how their shared devotion to their daughter had seemed a competition in parenthood rather than a mutual delight.

'And the truth is,' she said, 'I encouraged him to drink. I guess I was what they call a "facilitator" – the person who gave him permission to do what he shouldn't.'

'Sure. But it's tough being a policeman.'

'And Bill was so much more fun with a few glasses in him. He wasn't a destructive drunk at all, and never violent. But he didn't do much work either, and after a bit a good business looked like it was going down the tubes.'

'And did it? Is he still drinking?'

'Oh no! Divorce was the best thing that could have happened to Bill, though he's never exactly thanked me for it. He met this thoroughly dreary advisor from the bank, who took him in hand, sent him to AA and married him.'

'And?'

'And now they have two boys, the business is booming, and it's all happy happy happy.'

'You don't sound happy.'

Rebecca flipped her hair back and smiled into his face. 'Oh, I am. Bill is a good chap, but off the booze he isn't a ball of fire. So no complaints, I'm fine. I've got a nice life. And a wonderful daughter.'

It had crossed Rebecca's mind that she might be wise to keep quiet about having a grown-up daughter. But she could have had Angelica at twenty, which would make her only forty. And she couldn't resist boasting about her darling girl.

So she told him about Angelica, the adorable, sensible twenty-one-year-old who had sailed above the divorce of her parents and being the single child of a single mother, to become a quiet achiever who was doing well at university. When Nelson said, 'I'd like to meet her,' Rebecca was pleased. She wondered if he was just being polite. But yes, she thought, they would like each other.

When Nelson came back from the kitchen with a bottle of water and two glasses, he put them down on the coffee table and leaned over and kissed her. It was a gentle kiss, eyes open. Nice, but not electrifying. He seemed to be watching her. Then he pulled away, a little solemn, and she stared back at him. Rebecca did not quite know how to play this one. She had never been with a black guy, and was ashamed that her mind kept sidetracking to Aids and worrying about condoms.

He said, 'We *are* going to bed, right?' He didn't wait for an answer but kissed her on the nose. 'Just for the pleasure of it, not to get serious, right?'

She liked him more and more. He was upfront and straight. And surprising.

'Agreed,' she said, cool as a teenager.

Chapter Ten

Joanna was debating whether or not to take her jacket off. It was warm in the boardroom but she knew she looked the business in her Savile Row pinstripes. She generally wore trousers, partly because they looked good on her long skinny legs, partly because they disguised her slightly swollen knees but mostly because they so effectively made the woman-wearing-the-trousers point. It was part of her psychological armour for the job.

She decided to keep the jacket on. Her shirt, though classic and expensive, was soft silk crêpe with a ribbon at the neck and would not give her the right air of authority: she knew it was easier to play the part if dressed for it.

She struggled to pay attention while the routine stuff went on (minutes of the last meeting; chief executive's report; last month's results). She was worrying about her paper and calculating who would back her and who would not. When she'd joined the Greenfarms board back in the spring all the existing members were hostile. They'd tried to hide it, but she was the necessary evil, the 'company doctor'appointed by the firm's chief backer to dish out the medicine no one wanted to swallow. Six months of board meetings and discussion had not improved relations much. Most of them still resented her and she didn't blame them – but she had a job to do.

Several of the board were family members which made it a tough call. Hardly a level playing field, although Stewart, the chairman, could go either way.

Joanna admired Stewart. He'd got bags of experience and was a heavyweight captain of industry with a reputation in the City for delivering shareholder value. He'd made one fortune in carpets and another in property, and now sat on half a dozen boards, most of which he chaired. And he had fun investing his fortune in go-ahead enterprises – including this one, his daughter Caroline's organic food business.

Joanna watched him as he came through the door, his papers in a pigskin leather folder embossed with his initials. He could have been made by Hollywood, she thought – elegantly greying, sophisticated, confident, rich, charming. He'd got that presence and toughness which women find sexy and men admire. If this were not his daughter's business, he'd certainly back her conclusions. But as it stood, he might just go on indulging Caroline.

Which, if you knew Caroline, was understandable. She was really something. She had a fine-boned face, big green eyes and a wide full mouth, deep red even without lipstick, which she never wore. Her red hair bounced about her narrow shoulders and down her back in great unbrushed ropes. As she strode into the room, she looked, Joanna thought, like a pre-Raphaelite angel. But angelic she was not. When opposed she was intolerant, foul-mouthed and completely unreasonable. But you had to hand it to her: Greenfarms was her baby and she had grown it from nothing.

Caroline had started the business ten years ago in her own kitchen, making organic soups for a market stall, and went on to build a profitable company with a ten million pound turnover. She was still as idealistic as ever. Her products were all certified organic by the Soil Association, packaging was sustainably sourced and bio-degradable, the factory was powered by a heat pump and the heat generated by the refrigeration, and excess energy went into the national grid. And she still rode her bike everywhere and her house and office ran on methane gas from the farm and on solar energy. It meant she had to put up with great ugly solar panels on the roof and in the garden. Which Joanna could never do. But Caroline's principles were absolute.

Which means, mused Joanna, we are going to have a major fight – one that I could easily lose.

As the directors settled themselves round the table, Joanna continued her mental tour of the board: Amin, the finance director, was a small neat Indian, nervously twirling his pencil in his fingers. He was new, and she had no idea which way he'd go. At least he was not family.

Mark, the production director, was Caroline's elder brother and perfectly hopeless. He was jealous as a snake of his sister and resented working for her. With luck he would go for Option A just to spite her. But then again, he might realise Option B would be safer for him. He would never survive the shake-up if she, Joanna, got her way.

The sales director was a relation too, but a more distant one. He was Caroline's cousin, Alasdair, and he was good. He'd doubled turnover in the last two years, mainly by getting three of the big four supermarkets to list Greenfarms' chilled ready-meals, and two of them to take their organic fruit and veg. He'll go with me, I'm sure, thought Joanna.

She was not so sure of Phyllis, the company secretary, though she liked her and was pretty sure the liking was returned. Phyllis was a careful and lawyerish company secretary. The trouble was, she'd been Caroline's friend for years and they were very close. Personal loyalty might conquer common sense.

Joanna returned her attention to what was going on and realised they were about to get to Item Five. Something lurched in her chest. How silly, she told herself, it's not as if this is the first time I've had to do this at a company board. But her heart continued to thump. She forced her hands to lie still in her lap as Stewart put another tick on his Agenda and looked across at her.

'Right,' he said, 'now, to the meat of today's business. Joanna, will you introduce your paper?'

Joanna smiled at him, nodded, and looked round the table. Most of the board caught her eye briefly and then looked down as they shuffled their papers, finding the first page of her report.

Only Stewart and Caroline met her gaze steadily. Stewart's expression was professionally neutral and polite. Caroline's was anything but: her jaw was set and she was leaning forward, hungry for a fight.

Joanna spoke quietly and mainly to the two of them, her eyes resting on one for a few seconds, then on the other, occasionally sweeping the circle of the others and talking directly to anyone who lifted their eyes to hers. She had learnt years ago that the quickest way to alienate someone was to exclude them from eye contact.

'I am afraid radical change is inevitable,' she said. 'This business has to change or it will not be here in a year. You've all read the report, so I won't go through it blow by blow, but I would direct you to page eight, which covers the options in front of us.' She opened her copy at the right page, flagged with a yellow sticker, and waited until everyone had followed suit. 'Perhaps we could spend a little time understanding those before moving on to the report's recommendations?'

Stewart and some of the others nodded. Caroline sat unmoving, her face stony.

'OK then. Option A. This route assumes that we retain the big retailers as our main customers. But if we are to do that we have to take twenty-one per cent out of our costs for the coming year, and probably a bit more the following year. This is achievable, but only if we do all of several things.'

She counted down her list on her fingers.

'One: we must invest in new automatic packing machinery for the raw produce range. Two: we must face up to the redundancies made possible by this automation. Three: we must abandon small customers for whom delivery is uneconomical. Four: we must import more produce from countries where labour is cheap. And

Five: above all we must move from our small UK suppliers to bigger cheaper ones.'

She paused, every eye upon her, then said, 'Later, we will almost certainly need to take out some head office jobs.'

Mark's head went down and Joanna addressed his bald patch. 'And possibly outsource the ready-meal production.'

Mark's head jerked up again. Joanna looked at him and said, 'But I have not done the figures on those yet. I'll need Mark's help, and there was not time before today. So I have, for the moment, left the factory costs as they stand. But there could, and should, be further savings there.'

For a moment it looked as though Mark was going to protest, but he said nothing.

She went on. 'You will see from the table at the top of the page that the bulk of savings will come from better buying. Our current growers are, I think we all agree, loyal and committed, but they just cannot compete with the big boys in the Eastern counties, or the produce from abroad. The supermarket contracts—'

Caroline, her chin forward and eyes narrowed, could not stand it any longer and interrupted.

'So, we just chuck farmers who have stuck with us through thick and thin onto the scrapheap—'

Stewart cut her short. 'Caro, if you could wait until we've heard what Joanna has to say? We can then discuss it. Go on Joanna.'

Caroline flung herself back in to the chair with a muttered 'fine'. She crossed her arms and stared at Joanna, who remained cool. She had been here many times before and knew that founders of small enterprises were often unbusinesslike. Full of passion, vision and mission, often great inventors or innovators, they were generally lousy at people management and even worse at making that difficult transition from a niche business to a big one. Which was why Innovest had sent her in to sort them out.

Keeping her voice even and polite, she said, 'If you turn to the next page, you will see that the average supermarket selling price of organic produce has been going down for four years. This has been driven by hard bargaining from the supermarkets, who buy increasingly from eastern Europe and the third world, but also by more efficient UK producers with large farms going into organics. The public's increasing enthusiasm for ethical sourcing, their dislike of air miles and growing awareness of the need to support British farmers has meant that, for example, large poultry farms in East Anglia are converting to organic production.'

Caroline, her face flushed, interjected. 'Poultry farms! You call them farms! They are bloody great factories! They may give the poor things organic feed, but it's monoculture on a terrifying scale. Acres of birds—'

Again Stewart stopped her. 'Caro, we must allow Joanna to finish. She is explaining the two options. We will debate their pros and cons in a minute.'

Stewart was the only person able to handle Caroline. His expression was tolerant and his voice low but there was no doubt of his authority. Joanna wondered if Stewart was once as passionate and difficult as his daughter. Probably.

Caroline, pouting childishly, muttered, 'Well, it's stupid. We all know where she's going with this. She wants to destroy the business.'

Joanna ignored this and turned from Option A to Option B. She explained that Option B would mean withdrawing from the big supermarket contracts and returning to Greenfarms' roots: buying from traditional organic suppliers; radically reducing their own ready-meal range; delivering vegetable boxes to domestic addresses; selling locally at farmers' markets and to small stores and health food shops. And, crucially, selling through the internet.

She stood up to reach her computer, already hooked up to the AV system, and pressed it into life. She took them through the research, indicating with the laser wand which figure in a column or which line of a graph she wanted them to focus on. She covered the growth of local food markets and festivals, the explosion of 'alternative' lifestyle choices, the rise in spend on quality food products and the increase in healthy-eating publications.

She turned off the computer.

'So . . . there is no doubt that there is an increasing market for ethically sourced organic food. But if we are to profit by it, and fill the hole left in our business by the loss of the supermarkets, we will need to build up direct sales via the internet very fast. Which, of course, will need considerable investment in the website and in marketing.'

She directed them back to her paper, saying briskly, 'The financials are summarised on page ten.'

By the time they had been through them, Caroline was looking less truculent, and Joanna realised with dismay that she might have done too good a job on Option B. Almost all the board would be more comfortable with this option. Only Alasdair was shaking his head.

God, thought Joanna, it is truly astonishing how cowardly boards of directors can be, like a lot of ostriches with their heads in the sand. Surely it must be clear to them that Option B isn't really an option at all? It's there because the board needs to have an alternative to the obvious so they can tell themselves they – not I – are making the decision. I'm like a photographer giving the picture editor the one good pic he wants used and only supplying duds to compare it with.

She looked round the table, hoping to see some sense there. They must know it, she thought. They've read my paper. She had known the answer to the problems at Greenfarms ever since Innovest first asked her to look into the company. Indeed, they had invested the money on her advice with the intention of making just the changes she was now proposing. Joanna looked at Caroline and felt a wash of sympathy for her. Poor girl, she thought, the truth is staring her in the face, but she will not see it.

'Is anyone unclear about anything?' she continued.

Head-shaking all round. Stewart said, 'Right, Caro, you wanted to say something?'

Caroline pushed the fingers of one hand into her hair and looked at her father. 'Well, everyone knows where I stand. I'd sooner die than turn Greenfarms, which provides almost all the jobs in this village and a whole lot more in the factory, into Option A.' She raked her hair back from her face and continued. 'Companies should not be there just to make City investors rich.' Her glance, full of fire, flicked towards Joanna. 'They are there as part of the community, and they should bloody well be of benefit to that community.' She turned towards Mark and Alasdair. 'Christ, guys, what benefit would it be to local farmers and the people who live in this area if vegetables are grown in East Anglia? Sure, it will mean starvation wages for some poor seasonal workers from eastern Europe or illegal immigrants from somewhere else. But that doesn't help Joe who grades our potatoes here, does it?'

Caroline closed her eyes for a moment, obviously struggling to remain calm. 'Of course I'm for Option B! That is how we started. I'm sick of dancing to the supermarkets' tune. They are bloodsucking bastards who get you dependent on them and then screw you. They talk a lot about supporting small farmers, but it's all crap.'

She was into her stride now, her face slightly flushed, her whole body tense with the strength of her conviction, her eyes wide and impassioned.

'Our products fly out of Planet Organic and the Health Food shops. We can build up our wholesale sales on their expansion. We are not a tin-pot business, we win awards all over the place, we make the fastest-growing brand of baby food in the country—'

'Only because it's sold in the multiples,' interrupted Alasdair.

Caroline jumped up, and for a moment Joanna wondered if she was going to assault her sales director. But she just glared at him.

'We've got an amazing company here,' she went one. 'It is not just that we are good at food, we do things other companies don't. We do the right thing by our suppliers, by the environment, in animal husbandry, for our local area. Do we really want to go from being loved for all these things to being hated as the bastards who sacked all the locals? If we decide to do that, I'm out of here.'

Joanna could feel them falling under her spell. Indeed she was in danger of doing so herself. Caroline was so passionate and sincere it was hard not to be seduced by her. By the end of it, they were all looking at her, except Alasdair who leant back in his chair and studied his fingers.

Stewart's eyes stayed on his daughter, who sat down slowly, still glaring around her.

God, he worships that girl, Joanna thought. This could go seriously wrong.

Stewart turned his gaze to his nephew. 'Alasdair? A or B?'

'I'm for A, I'm afraid. I'm sorry Caro, I know how hard this is for you, but personally I want to be part of a company that's going places. Which we are. We've done well to get onto the supermarket shelves. We just need to stay there. If other companies can get their costs and prices down, so can we.' He looked across at Mark, who said,

'Yeah, easier said than done, mate, You . . .'

'Mark,' said Stewart, 'let's be businesslike about this. Are you for Option A or B?'

'B. I agree with Caro.' Mark looked defiantly at Alasdair who sighed and shook his head but did not rejoin the argument.

'And Phyllis?' asked Stewart.

'I'm with Caro too,' said Phyllis. 'She's built her business up before. I am sure she'll do it again.'

'Amin?'

'Caroline, I am very sorry. I must look at this as an accountant. Our best option is to stay with the big retailers and get suppliers' costs down. Option A.'

Stewart had been making notes. 'Right,' he said, 'that looks like three for A (Joanna, Alasdair and Amin) and three for B (Mark, Phyllis and Caroline). I don't like boardroom votes. I would far rather discuss the matter until we have a natural consensus. But in this instance, I don't think anyone is going to change their position, and as chairman I have a casting vote.'

Joanna held her breath and looked at Caroline twisting her pencil in her fingers, round and round.

But Stewart seemed in no hurry. He tapped his gold fountain pen gently on the writing pad, eyes down, face serious.

Suddenly the pencil in Caroline's hand snapped with a sharp crack. Everyone jumped, then smiled briefly, acknowledging the tension in the air.

'C'mon, Dad,' said Caroline, 'I can't bear it.'

Stewart looked to each of them in turn as he spoke.

'I agree with Caro that swimming in the big seas with sharks is dangerous. But I don't underestimate the effort it will take to crack the internet route either. Hygiene regulation and cost will mean we cannot send ready meals by mail. We will have to expand the bigger ticket items – meat and smoked produce. But on balance, if we think we can do it, we probably can. We need to examine the figures more carefully, but if they stack up, then I'm with the CEO.'

Joanna felt as though he'd thumped her in the solar plexus. She could not believe it. She kept perfectly still, her face carefully impassive as she watched Caroline jump to her feet then sit down again as suddenly.

'Sorry, Joanna,' Stewart continued. 'I know you are convinced of the merits of Option A, but I'm afraid I am not. I favour a planned retreat from the supermarkets, an expansion of the bigger margin lines and the preservation of the brand's reputation. '

Caroline said, 'Thanks, Dad,' and closed her eyes in relief. Her lower lip trembled but she bit it, holding it still between her teeth.

Stewart glanced at his watch and started to gather his papers into a neat pile, tapping them briskly on the table to line the edges up. He smiled. 'Right, I'm afraid we've run a little late. Forgive me.' He looked round the circle of faces. 'Has anyone any other business?'

Joanna took a deep breath, looked him in the eye.

'I'm sorry to do this, Chairman,' she said. 'It seems pedantic, but I'm afraid I have to object. It has just occurred to me that Phyllis is not, strictly speaking, a board member. Her vote is therefore invalid, which brings us back to a three–three situ—'

Caroline interrupted with a bark. 'What rot, of course she's a board member! Aren't you Phyllis?'

Phyllis, her hand over her mouth, shook her head. 'No, Joanna's right. I'm so sorry. I didn't realise that was a formal vote. We've never had to actually vote on anything before. Stewart has always treated me as one of you for discussion, and I thought he was asking my opinion, so I gave it. If I had realised it was a vote, I'd have reminded you that I am only "in attendance" at the board, not a member of it.'

Stewart, for once, looked nonplussed, but before he could rally his thoughts, Joanna fired her last volley. She had known all along she would have to do this if they rejected her recommendation, but she had hoped to get them to vote for the medicine and not have to force it down their throats. She braced herself.

'I've one more thing, Chairman. Before we confirm the decision, or reverse it, the board needs to know that Innovest favours Option A. If the board decides on that, then they are prepared to continue to back the company and provide the funds for restructuring. However, if we go for B, they are not. Venture capitalists, as you know, are interested in companies able to grow at a pace that will provide the highest returns for their investors.'

She knew Stewart would have got it before she had completed the first sentence, but he waited for her to finish.

'So they'd turn off the tap if we don't follow your recommendation?' he said.

'Yes.'

'And in that event, what about their equity?'

Joanna had been hoping to avoid this question. Even though she was used to it, she did not enjoy destruction.

'Innovest would liquidate their investment in Greenfarms. Of course if you could find an alternative buyer for the shares . . .'

'It would be a miracle,' snapped Stewart. 'And if Innovest cashes in its chips, we go bust.' He looked, not at Joanna, but at Caroline, her mouth open in disbelief, her face ashen. 'Well, that's clearly understood,' he went on. 'If we don't agree with you, you not only turn off the investment tap, you pull the plug and hang us out to dry. We lose the business.'

He looked round the table, and came back to Caroline. 'And Caro, you lose your farm and house too. It's part of the business. And you all lose your jobs. Not much of a choice is it?'

Chapter Eleven

The Porchester Baths had been taken over by some private company. They had added a gym and made a half-hearted attempt at a spa, but the place still had a whiff of public facility about it. Rebecca had asked the girl at the desk why they put so much chlorine in the water.

'Trust me,' she'd replied, 'you don't want to know.'

Rebecca had shuddered. 'You're right, I'm sorry I asked.'

She'd have liked to walk out and enrol at the Langton Club further down the Grove, but she could not afford the fees: not with paying so much for Pilates and a personal trainer.

Now, as she rolled over to do backstroke for the next length, she felt a little glow of pride at her flab-free belly and firm upper arms. Since she'd met Nelson she'd been trying hard, and the months of swimming and working out had paid off. The things I do to look good in a bikini, she thought. Pity there's no one to see. And then she went into a little fantasy about Nelson walking in and watching her.

Nelson had occupied rather too much of Rebecca's mind over the long summer. The memory of his muscular arms conducting his singers, sleeves pushed up to his elbows, his deep voice with the exaggerated afro-accent, his spooning a taste of jambalaya into her mouth, his wet back visible through the glass in his shower – these images kept invading her thoughts, unbidden.

She'd resolved to stick with the singing – and stick with Nelson.

Of course she was side-tracking from her sensible mission to find a husband, but she reckoned a little fun on the way couldn't do her any harm.

The truth was she had been lonelier than she thought she would be when Angelica went off to university. She was grateful to Joanna and Lucy. They'd all become friendly over their semi private sessions with Nelson, and she and Joanna had been to Lucy's big stone house in the country and walked the Cotswold Way. It had been surprisingly enjoyable and they'd got mildly tiddly in the pub, swapping confidences about men. Or, rather, she'd told them about her chequered past and about Nelson, and Lucy had talked of David and had cried a bit. Only Joanna was reticent, saying that she was happy to be single.

In London Rebecca missed her daughter's presence and her bevy of clever, interesting school friends. Angelica was a mystery to her mother, like a changeling. How could she have a daughter who was so sensible, so even-tempered? But Rebecca was as proud as punch of Angelica's achievements: her straight As at A level, her History scholarship to Edinburgh, the way Angelica was so together, not all over the place like she'd been at her age. Still was now, come to think of it.

Rebecca liked to think that she and Angelica were more like sisters than mother and daughter: they did things together, movies and musicals, went shopping, had lunch. Though Angelica could be *too* grown up. Last month when Angelica was home for a weekend and Rebecca was reading the pop music reviews, she had proposed they go to a Prophets concert at Wembley,

'Mum, you cannot want to see that lot. They're rubbish!'

'No they aren't! And anyway, I like the atmosphere, the excitement, being part of it. You should come, darling. Loosen up a bit.'

'You mean scream your head off with a bunch of teenagers. No thanks.' Angelica put her hand on her mother's arm. 'Come on, Mum, grow up. I'll take you to a proper concert. Mozart and Brahms. Or Bach. You like classical music, don't you?'

'Of course I do. You know how many CDs I've got. Stacks.'
Rebecca had dropped the magazine and changed the subject. She
didn't want Angelica pointing out that she seldom listened to those
CDs, but sometimes left them lying around to impress her friends,
or put one on just before her guests arrived.

But now she even missed her daughter's reproving eye on her.
Without Angelica's gentle tick-offs about mess and clutter, Rebecca
knew she was getting messier. Sluttish even. She winced at the
word sluttish. She wasn't a slut. But her possessions did seem to
fill the house in a way they hadn't when Angelica was at home all
the time.

Rebecca recognised, of course, that there were advantages to
Angelica's being away. She could be out almost every night without
feeling guilty, and she could have her friends in without competing
for space with her daughter and *her* friends. And Nelson could
spend the night without Angelica knowing. Rebecca had not told
Angelica about Nelson.

She needed a bigger flat, that was the bottom line. Somewhere
she could bring people to without them having to step over cases
of wine in the hall, or negotiate their way to the sofa via the cross
trainer and the exercise bike in the living room.

She'd just have to tackle Bill again. She should ask him for an
extra £20K a year. That should do it. After all he was a lot richer
now than when they'd made the divorce settlement. True, her
payments went up with inflation, but the increase was also *limited*
to inflation, and his income wasn't. He didn't have to put up with
a measly few per cent annual increase, did he?

OK, thought Rebecca, so I'm a little late, but it's hardly the end
of the world? She saw Bill get up from behind his fancy Italian
desk, which she happened to know cost fifteen grand after discounts,
and swing round the end of it, looking like thunder. He yanked
open the glass door of Inside Job just as she pushed hard on it. She
stumbled inside, stilettos skidding on the marble.

Bill, of course, did not apologise, nor put out a steadying arm. 'Becca,' he hissed, 'this is hopeless. We've got to talk.' Then he grabbed her arm and hustled her back out of the shop and along the pavement.

Rebecca saw the lie of the land and gave him her best smile. 'What's up darling? You look . . .'

'I can't keep bawling out my own wife . . .'

'Ex-wife,' she reminded him.

'. . . in front of the staff. You cannot just roll in when you feel like it . . .'

He went on in the same vein, while Rebecca did her trick of listening but not listening. She'd heard all this before, and it was better not to let it penetrate, or she'd get upset.

Once in Starbucks, he stopped ranting and almost pushed her into a sofa. 'What do you want?'

'Darling, how lovely,' she said, pretending this was a nice cosy little outing. 'A decaf cappuccino. And a chocolate chip muffin.'

She didn't really want the muffin, but it drove Bill mad that she could eat like a horse and stay slim while he only had to look at food to get another chin.

While Bill queued for the coffees, Rebecca ran her mind over the issue – her job, her relationship with Bill, her money. He did have a point, she thought, she was a rotten employee, but then he paid her almost nothing. And she hated the job. She was a glorified receptionist: her main duty was to tell the walk-in shoppers, politely of course, that this shop was not for them. And to make appointments for Bill to go schmooze the real punters in their smart houses or loft conversions. She might occasionally get to deliver sample books and swatches and sit down with rich women on their immaculate silk sofas and help them choose something else – a different silk this time perhaps, or hand-printed fabric from Italy. But if it was anything more than a chair to be upholstered, she had strict instructions to refer the matter to the boss. Then in Bill would sweep and sell them a whole new look:

maybe a thirties-style white leather suite plus brand new Eames chair and footstool, retro lighting, a new floor (last year this shop alone must have devastated a few forests, but the wood craze was fading and now they were back to pale stone and paler carpets), hardwood doors that reached from floor to ceiling, a dining room table made of translucent marble lit from underneath, a professional kitchen to make a real chef weep but which no one would ever cook in. No bones about it, he was good at selling. By the time he'd finished with her, our customer could have bought a new house for the money.

Rebecca did so long to be rich. She knew she'd be good at it. She'd not want to just walk into Harrods or Fortnum's and buy stuff. She'd still shop carefully because her shopping was a serious business and she gave it due attention. She knew she had terrific taste – never boring but never vulgar – even in clothes, where sometimes the line between designer frivolity and street market tat was hard to find. She had smiled at Lucy's accusation, made only half in jest, that she spent a fortune to look cheap. Dead wrong. She spent very little to look a million dollars.

Lucy's idea of a bargain, thought Rebecca, is something from an Oxfam shop, or Nike trainers from a market stall, whereas she would never ever buy street-market rip-offs. They were rubbish and they looked it, but good fakes were identical to the real thing. Once she'd even taken her imitation Cartier watch, bought in a shop in Bangkok, into Cartier's in Paris to get a link taken out of the strap and they did it without a word, and for free.

It's not just clothes, she thought. She knew where to get everything Bill sold, all the furniture, soft furnishings, lighting. Sometimes he sent her to do the bargaining. That was part of the fun, getting a great deal. But even for bargains you needed money.

And her ex-husband was her only source of money.

When Bill came back with the coffee, Rebecca was ready for him. Before he could say a word, she leant forward, smiling into his face, contrite.

'Look, darling, I'm really sorry. I was late at the gym. But Mandy was holding the fort. It's not as if the place was deserted.'

'The point is, Becca, I don't have to employ you, you know. I could get some girl for half the money who'd be twice as good. I only hired you because you can't live on the money I give you, though God knows it should be ample . . .'

'Oh Bill, let's not go down that route . . .' But he was in full flood and not about to be deflected.

'I pay you a fortune in maintenance. Naturally, you don't think it's enough, but if you applied for more you'd get laughed out of court, and you know it.'

This was an over-familiar script, and Rebecca's answer was as well-rehearsed as his.

'Darling, of course I can't live on the money you give me, even with the salary. Which is a pittance by the way. I was going to put in for a raise. It's ridiculous. My rent is five hundred a week.'

'Yes, and your clothes bill just about matches it, and so does your holiday bill, to say nothing of the lunching and the taxis. Rebecca, one way and another you and Angelica cost me a hundred grand a year, which is more than Jane, our two boys and I cost together.'

Rebecca did not want to follow this path, which she knew from experience would lead to unfair comparisons of her tenure as his wife (thirteen years during which she decorated his arm, helped him drink a lot of Bollinger, made him laugh and gave him a beautiful daughter) and Jane's (fifteen years spent breeding sons, ironing shirts, cooking meals, and boring the pants off him). So she interrupted, aiming for peace.

'Look, Bill, I'm sorry I was late. I'll try harder – God knows I need the extra money.' She looked into his eyes, her face open and friendly. 'But darling, you could afford to stump up a bit more, surely? Inside Job made more than my annual salary just on the profit of those Chinese marriage chests you brought in for Lady Child, and what did that cost you? A couple of phone-calls. You

65

didn't even have to lay out any cash since her fifty per cent deposit more than covered what that poor Chinese dealer got.'

Of course in the end her lateness was forgiven and Bill promised to review her allowance. Then she told him how she was saving money by going to cheap singing classes down the seamy end of Notting Hill instead of to smart restaurants up the posh end, and made him laugh with gossip about her new singing companions – the uptight Joanna who struggled to get a note past her lips and the criminally fashion-averse Lucy. Rebecca felt a bit bad poking fun at them. She'd had few women friends in her life and she really liked them both. I shouldn't mock them, she thought.

She told him of her plans for secondary shopping, since the expense of primary shopping bothered him so.

'One day I aim to do a complete makeover on Lucy,' she explained, 'choosing the clothes while she spends the money. Joanna thinks Lucy's seriously depressed, and what any depressed woman needs is retail therapy.'

'I'd send her to a doctor rather than on a shopping spree.'

'No, I don't think so. She's just unhappy about losing first her husband and then her job in swift succession. Anyone would be.'

Bill raised an eyebrow at her, and Rebecca laughed. 'OK, depends on the husband and the job. And I don't want to lose my job, darling, really I don't.' She leant over and kissed Bill lightly on the cheek, and was gratified to see him smiling. It seldom took much effort to get Bill into a good mood. She went on.

'Lucy's a really nice woman and not bad looking. She could lose a stone, sure, but it's more important that she gives up dressing in Oxfam. Definitely time for a trip to Harvey Nicks.'

When they got back to the shop, friends now, Bill went off to see a client, and Rebecca felt free to flick through the décor mags and dream. Most of the pictures were conservative and lifeless. Good taste, but dull. And ridiculously expensive; she could achieve that look, or better, at half the price. She wished she had clients of her own. It would be wonderful to do what Bill did, and completely transform boring interiors into something stylish and original so that people stood stock still and open-mouthed on entering a room.

But she knew Bill would never let her loose on a house, or even a room. He had an unshakeable image of her as frivolous and unreliable, based on a few tiddly nights, lost car keys or missed trains. Which she considered mighty unfair since those incidents were spread over a thirteen-year marriage. She looked up at the Justin Mortimer portrait of Bill on the wall (a present from her for his fortieth) and said aloud, 'I am neither frivolous nor unreliable. And your boozing was a worse problem than my spending, damn it. And I raised Angelica pretty much on my own, didn't I? And made a damn good job of it too.'

Rebecca looked intently at the picture. Bill had been slimmer then, in spite of the drink, but he had not aged that much in the last twenty years. He was greyer of course, but still with thick wavy hair that gave him a slightly Bohemian look. He's not a bad old stick, she thought. He had pretty well promised to come across with a bit more money. And he never denies Angelica anything.

Sometimes Rebecca thought she should have stuck with Bill. But how was she to know AA would get him off the drink and that he would get, not just rich again, but a whole heap richer? She'd thought he was a sinking ship.

And the awful thing was that she would never have stayed faithful to him, rich or not. I'm fond of him, she thought, but sex matters to me, and sooner or later I'd have come across someone as irresistible as Nelson, and we'd have been back in familiar territory, with me behaving badly and him on the booze.

Chapter Twelve

As she stepped onto the platform at Paddington station, Lucy was curiously excited, almost nervous, and she could not think why. She was only going to have tea with Joanna and yet it seemed like some kind of test. Joanna was so elegant and self assured, so *independent*.

While she, Lucy, seemed to have *lost* confidence over the last months. She'd never been smart or fashionable of course, but she was bloody good at what she did. Why feel anxious?

Lucy looked at her watch: twenty-five past three. It wouldn't take her more than fifteen minutes to walk to the Palace Tea Rooms in Westbourne Grove. If she set off now she'd be half an hour early and could read the paper till Joanna arrived.

And yet she did not want to. Fashionable restaurants had never intimidated her in the past – indeed their owners, chefs and head waiters were more likely to be nervous of her, Lucy Barnes, the scary restaurant critic. But here she was, reluctant to arrive early in case some slip of a girl told her that she could not have a table.

She decided to delay setting off and put the time to good use on the station. She'd do boring things like buy a railcard, get a couple of ballpoint pens at Paperchase, the kind she liked with free-flowing ink but which leaked in your handbag if you took them on aeroplanes, a fact she routinely forgot. And she'd buy Grace some little present as a thank-you for the months of weekly Bed and Breakfast.

She had to queue for ages for her reservation, but was surprised to see when she looked at her watch that it was only quarter to four and she still had time to kill.

She bought the pens and sifted through the racks at Accessorize but it was all cheap tat which she knew Grace wouldn't like, so she ventured deeper to the shops at the back of the station.

At Tie Rack she nearly bought a pretty purple pashmina, and at Monsoon she was marginally attracted by a beaded bracelet. Eventually, irritated with herself for being so indecisive, she abandoned the search for a present for Grace and joined the queue at Costa Coffee.

As she sipped her coke slowly, staring idly round the station, she noticed the station clock was wildly wrong: three quarters of an hour fast. How irresponsible, she thought, station clocks, of all clocks, should tell the right time.

Then the woman at the next table said to her little boy, 'Cmon, Tom. Did you hear? That's the four-forty. Platform Nine.'

Four-forty? The woman must be mad. Lucy looked at her watch, and saw that it still said quarter to four. She started to tell the woman her mistake, but the child had darted ahead and the woman hurried after him.

And then Lucy looked again at the station clock on Platform One. It said half past four.

Realisation crashed in. Her watch had stopped. She'd been on the station for a good forty-five minutes. Of course she had. How else could she have trawled all those shops, bought the pens, got her railcard, had a coke?

Lucy grabbed her bag and ran out of the station to the taxi rank. There was an enormous queue. Oh God, she thought, panic mounting, Joanna will have left. What is the matter with me? Why didn't I realise my watch had stopped?

She fished for her mobile phone, buried deep in her handbag. It was turned off, something that irritated her daughter enormously. She must remember to keep it on.

She pressed the on button and sure enough, she had a couple of messages.

'Lucy. It's four-fifteen. Just wondering where you are. I was expecting you at four. I'm at the Palace Tea Rooms. See you soon.'

And then a second message.

'Lucy, hope nothing horrible has happened. Perhaps I misunderstood. Anyway, I'm off to the singing class. Hope you'll be there. Call me.'

She left a message on Joanna's voice mail.

'Oh Jo,' she said, 'you won't believe this, but my watch stopped, and I've been on Paddington Station waiting for it to be time to meet you. I can't explain it. How could I not notice?' She ended abruptly, knowing that if she said another word, she'd cry.

Lucy hurried along Bishops Bridge Road, mortified at her stupidity. And then she suddenly stopped. With appalling clarity she knew that her worst fears were realised. It's happening, she thought. I knew it would. I am going mad, just like my mother.

The young woman shook the painted wooden pieces out of a drawstring bag onto the table between them. There were red, green and yellow ones of different shapes.

'As you can see,' she said, 'these pieces are different from each other. I'd like you to sort them into three piles, so that like goes with like.'

Lucy quickly pushed the round, triangular and square discs into different piles.

'Good,' said the woman. 'Is there another way to sort them, like with like?'

Lucy slid them into groups by colour: green, red, yellow.

So far so good. But Lucy knew the assessment would not all go so smoothly.

She'd been coming to the Memory Clinic once a year for several years now. David had said her fears were unfounded nonsense: everyone forgot things sometimes, and as you got older you naturally forgot a bit more – it did not mean you had dementia.

But Lucy's mother, and her mother's mother, had both gone doolally in their early sixties. Both had lived to be well over eighty, needing constant care during the last twenty years of their lives. If it was to happen to her she wanted to know soon enough to make her own arrangements. She wasn't sure what those arrangements would be, but she wanted to be in control, not like her mother, denying to her death that there was anything wrong with her. Her mother had gone on driving her car and getting lost until Lucy took it away from her. That was just awful: her mum was beside herself with fury, convinced Lucy was stealing the car. And when Lucy had put her in a care-home, her mother became paranoid, sure Lucy was shutting her away for devious reasons of her own, convinced the staff were trying to poison her.

David had been reassuring and relaxed about it. 'Why worry, darling?' he'd asked. 'If it happens, it happens. I'll look after you. Why keep going to the clinic year after year to be told you are fine?'

She hadn't said she could not bear the thought of him having to answer the same question five times in five minutes, of having to coax her into cleaning her teeth or changing her shirt, of having to lock her in if he went out in case she wandered off. Instead she'd laughed,

'I go so I'll be first in the queue when they find a cure. Or so I know when to do myself in.'

He hadn't believed the suicide bit of course. And indeed she hadn't really meant it. As long as they were together, even if one of them was ill or mad, life might still be worth living. Of *course* one would look after the other.

Only she would prefer it to be her that did the caring. The prospect of David's inevitable irritation with her senility, his consequent loss of respect for her, his doing things out of duty rather than love, had been horrible.

But David was dead. And now, since the incident on the station, Lucy was again anxious. Until then, the fear had come and gone, interspersed by long periods of relaxed confidence. But right now she felt she faced only three options: ruining Grace's life by burdening her, living out her days with other mad old women in a nursing home, or seeing herself off with an overdose. Who would not choose the latter?

As the tests progressed, Lucy was convinced she was doing badly, even on tests she'd performed well before, like joining dots in number or letter order, or spotting anomalies in drawings, or doing Kim's game: remembering a selection of animals, tools, gem stones, etc.

She was hopeless at numbers; always had been. She could feel herself losing concentration as she tried to do mental arithmetic or remember strings of digits. The process did not test your innate ability, but only indicated deterioration or improvement since the last time, so this did not worry her. But the effort tired her and her performance depressed her. By the time she saw the consultant, a rite that took place when they'd had time to compare her scores with her last session, she was feeling frayed and close to tears. God, she thought, I must not cry. I've blubbed more in the past year than in my whole life.

Dr Wilson always looked exhausted, but his eyes were steady and kind.

Lucy, not waiting for the formality of smiles and greeting, plunged in. 'Not good news, is it?'

Would she feel devastated or relieved at knowing the worst, her fears confirmed? She swallowed.

There was a tiny pause as he considered her, and then, 'Why do you say that? There's no cause for concern at all.'

Lucy could feel the sting of tears behind her eyes and kept them open. Blinking would expel the tears, and then she'd not be able to stop.

'There's some deterioration in concentration, that's all,' Dr

Wilson went on. 'Which is very common with bereavement. How long is it since your husband died?'

'Almost a year.'

It was no use. She fumbled for a tissue, could not find one. She pulled off her glasses and used the backs of her fingers to stop the flow.

He pushed a box of tissues towards her. She grabbed at it gratefully, forcing a smile. 'You're prepared for hysterical women, I see.' She blew her nose, her head down.

'You are not hysterical. You are suffering from grief. It's normal. It will affect your moods, your concentration, your confidence.' She could feel him watching her. 'But it will lessen in time.'

'Will it?' She raised her head. 'I hate being so hopeless.'

Then she told him about the incident on Paddington Station, and he listened attentively. He told her that sometimes people in a tired or anxious state focused on one factor, excluding all others, as she had on her watch, so the brain could not make a proper judgment.

'Were you anxious about the meeting with your friend? Was it something that seemed very important?'

'Well, oddly, yes, I think it was. I was excited and a bit nervous. She's a fairly new friend, and very smart and competent — a businesswoman — and I didn't want to look like a Bohemian writer or country cousin, I suppose. And the Palace Tearoom is stuffed with Notting Hill young women in designer gear with investment banker husbands making zillions. So yes, for some reason I did feel a bit anxious.'

'Yes, that might explain it. Your confidence is obviously not very high at the moment, but I'm fairly sure your problem that day was more to do with grief than anything.'

'Really? Why would grief affect my ability to absorb information?'

'I'm not sure why, I'm not a psychiatrist. But I do know it does.' He smiled at her. 'Sadly, we see a lot of widows in this clinic and our statistics show that concentration, and the ability to process information, is affected by grief. And grief, because it causes anxiety, affects memory function too. The situation almost always improves by the next assessment.'

I believe him, thought Lucy, he's not patronising with that irritating reassurance: trying to con you into believing what you both know is not true. Dr Wilson continued.

'If that sort of incident, the loss of time at the station, happens repeatedly, and is still happening in a year's time, then, I agree, we need to take it seriously.'

'But maybe my lack of concentration is caused by growing dementia, not grief?'

'That is not my judgment.' His formal, but gentle manner pleased Lucy. 'You are not showing the pattern I would expect with early dementia or Alzheimer's.'

Lucy nodded, a wash of gratitude making it difficult to speak. She thought, I'd like to ask him if this rollercoaster of blubbing, feeling fine, feeling dead, feeling indifferent will lessen too. Or ask him if my gaining weight is caused by grief, and the pounds will fall off as time passes. But he will tell me he is not a psychiatrist.

The thought that he would not pacify her with psycho-babble, would not stray out of his area of expertise, comforted her. She felt both cheered and strengthened. Of course I'll stop blubbing eventually. Everyone does. And I'll lose weight when I stop stuffing my face.

The thing to remember, she thought as she walked to her car, is that this happens to *everyone*. Loved ones die, brain cells drop off, waists thicken. Either you die young, or you get old first and then you die.

Chapter Thirteen

Three weeks after the board meeting at Greenfarms, Joanna had again gone north, this time for a follow-up meeting with Caroline and Stewart. It had been tough going and she was glad that her return train was half empty. She found a first class seat at a table for two, confident she would have it to herself. She stretched her legs out under the table, easing her stiff knees. She had been gardening at the weekend, kneeling on the stone terrace while she weeded and planted and her knees were protesting. Sometimes, when she got up in the night, she had to make an effort not to hobble to the bathroom like an old woman. That was another boring thing about getting older – going to the loo in the night.

She opened her laptop and went to Slides. She had a PowerPoint presentation to complete for this evening when she was due to persuade a group of high-net-worth oil traders to put their spare cash with Innovest.

But she did not look at the screen. Her mind returned to the meeting. Caroline had been openly hostile and had implemented none of the new strategy. She'd not attached the costs, actioned the redundancies or changed any suppliers, and Joanna had had to insist. She disliked being the hard-hearted banker, cold and determined. The truth was she wanted Caroline and Stewart to like her, especially Stewart. But of course they hated her. She stared out of the window as the train left Wakefield station and made an effort to think of something else.

But immediately the thought of her friend Lucy deepened her frown. The poor woman had been in such a state after that mad thing on Paddington station, where she'd resolutely refused to accept the evidence of her own eyes and ears or draw the logical conclusion that her watch had stopped. Poor Lucy! It had taken the combined hugs, clucking and soothing of both Rebecca and herself, not to say a large glass of Chardonnay, to get her to join the class.

Mind you, thought Joanna, I don't blame her for falling apart. If that had been me I'd have checked myself into the madhouse.

Joanna could not imagine not being on top of what she was doing. She always knew exactly what time it was and could probably operate without a watch at all. But maybe, she thought, that was because her life was chopped into meetings all day every day, or just about, and Lucy's – since she'd lost her job – had no structure to it at all.

Lucy had seemed fine when they'd first met in the spring but over the summer her widowhood seemed to weigh on her more. Last week she had not turned up at the singing class and she wouldn't answer her telephone, though she did respond to text or email. Joanna thought she knew what Lucy was up to: you can write a cheerful little text: *All well. Sorry so out of touch. No offence meant – just trying to meet a deadline. Lots love. XX* and that way no one would hear the misery in her voice.

Joanna was trying to help Lucy without it showing. She and Rebecca had been to stay with her a couple of times and she'd suggested that Rebecca drag Lucy round some designer shops and beauty therapists, which, if only Lucy would agree to go, might do her good. Rebecca was such fun and Lucy could do with a bit of self-indulgence. She needs lightening up even more than I do, thought Joanna.

She returned to her laptop and tried to concentrate. But it was no good, her mind would keep coming back to Lucy or Greenfarms. The very word Greenfarms made the unease and vague feeling of guilt return to squeeze her gut. Yet she had behaved with exemplary professionalism. Her research was thorough, her argument good, and she had never once let the matter get personal. But she kept seeing Stewart and Caroline's faces as she'd explained that if Caroline did not implement the agreed strategy Innovest would refuse further funding, the company would be liquidated and Caroline would lose her job, her company and her house. Caroline's face was pale and blank, Stewart's stony with suppressed anger and derision.

Of course if it ever came to that, Stewart would bale his daughter out, of course he would. If he really believed in the organic local route, why didn't he back her himself anyway? He'd got mega-millions.

Joanna's troubled thoughts continued to churn until they pulled into Doncaster, when she made an effort to concentrate on her presentation.

She ran through her slides, making small changes, until someone dumped a briefcase on the table behind her open laptop and a grey worsted jacket brushed her shoulder as its owner stretched up to cram a raincoat into the rack above her head. Irritation flared: why could he not sit somewhere else? The train was hardly full. She looked up in annoyance and was met by the smiling face of Stewart.

'Whew, that was a bit close,' he said. 'My driver had to race the train from Wakefield.' He eased himself into the seat, and then immediately stood up again. 'I've got a better idea,' he said. 'Lunch.'

What was he doing here? He'd not said anything about catching the London train. He sometimes did, it's true, if he had business in London, but then they'd be chauffeured to the station together.

'What . . . ?'

'Come on Jo, we need to talk. But let's do it over lunch.'

Joanna shook her head, about to say she had to work, but he said, 'I need a drink, don't you? That was a bit of a sticky meeting.' He lifted the armrest on Joanna's seat and stood back, giving her no choice but to consent or seem ungracious.

As she hesitated, he leant over and closed her lap-top without bothering to close it down, and slipped it into his briefcase. She watched in indignation and surprise as he then stuffed the briefcase under his raincoat on the overhead rack and said, 'I'll go first, shall I, and hack a path through the masses.'

'Hey!' she said, but then faltered: he was already halfway down the aisle, oblivious of any offence. She followed, torn between indignation at his taking her consent for granted and his closing her laptop without a by-your-leave, and concern that his briefcase, and more importantly her computer with tonight's presentation on it, might get stolen.

She considered sitting down again and refusing to follow him, but dismissed that as childish. She had to hurry to catch up with him which annoyed her too. Walking behind him (like a good squaw, she thought) she noticed that the heels of his shoes were as polished as the leather, the creases in his trousers were perfect and his jacket was, as always, elegant and expensive. Probably makes the life of his valet hell, she thought – and those of his driver, secretary, and the rest. The trouble with the super-rich is they are too used to having their own way.

Once they sat down, his good humour slowly dispersed both her indignation and her angst. He might be a touch too masterful, she thought, but here he was, smiling, full of goodwill, apparently unaffected by the tensions of the meeting. Could she have *imagined* the derision on his face?

He ordered smoked salmon salad, and Joanna followed suit. Then he asked the waiter for a bottle of champagne.

'Not for me, Stewart,' she said quickly, 'I've got work to do. I'd fall asleep.'

'OK,' he nodded, and changed the order to half a bottle.

How can he be so equable and relaxed? wondered Joanna. Not two hours ago he was tight-lipped with anger.

The waiter arrived with the fizz and two glasses, assuming they were to share it. On Stewart's urging, Joanna gave in and accepted a glass. She reasoned that she might need it if they were to talk Greenfarms and supermarkets.

She took the plunge and said, 'OK, shoot, what's on your mind? You do know that Innovest won't reverse their decision?'

'I agree, but let's not talk about that yet. Let's give ourselves a lunch-break first.'

He smiled at Joanna and she found herself smiling back, relieved. We are, she thought, like two conspirators playing truant. They ate in silence for a minute or two, then he said, 'You know, I know next to nothing about the real Joanna. What do you do when you aren't working?'

'What everyone does,' she said, a little defensively. 'I go out with friends. Dinner. The theatre. Watch television. Fix my house. I like gardening . . .'

'Do you?' He leant forward. 'What kind of garden?'

She found herself telling him about her classy little Chelsea garden, with its round lawn in the middle and triangular beds at the corners, bordered with box. How the planting was all white and grey, and formal. How the beds that surrounded the paved grey terrace were sunk so that the white Kent roses held their flowers at ground level and looked like a carpet.

'That's interesting,' he said. 'Does it work?'

'It does, yes. You prune them flat on top, like a hedge, a good foot below the level of the paving, and when they bloom, they are pretty well level with it.'

He pressed for more information and she went through her flowerbeds.

'Well, I've got white hydrangeas in the shade, those ones with huge mop-heads; clematis, climbing roses and jasmine – all white varieties – up the trellised arbour at the back. And white tulips in the spring followed by big white peonies; lilies and phlox in summer . . . Do you really want to know all this?'

'Yes, I do. Go on.'

Joanna laughed. She was enjoying herself. 'OK, you asked for it. There's lots of grey-leafed stuff that likes the sun – white lavenders, cistus and santolinas nearer the house—'

'But,' he interrupted, 'santolinas don't have white flowers, do they? Don't they have bright yellow buttons?'

So, he's a gardener too, thought Joanna. 'They do but I never allow them to flower.'

'You're a control freak, that's what. I can just imagine it. Not a weed allowed; every box hedge clipped; the tulips standing to attention, not daring to sway with the wind; out with anything that dares pop up the wrong colour.'

He said it kindly, it was a joke, but Joanna did not like it. It was too close to the truth. He seemed to sense this, and put a hand on hers, just for a second.

'You remind me of Elaine. You never met her, did you?'

Joanna was not sure who Elaine was, so she just shook her head. He said, 'My wife. She died two years ago.'

Joanna started to murmur the usual platitudes of condolence, but he shook his head, silencing her.

'She was a wonderful gardener. Had our garden organised to within an inch of its life. Paths deep in gravel, lawns edged, beds weeded, flowers deadheaded. It's got rather wilder and woollier under my direction though. My excuse is that Caroline explodes if I use insecticide or pesticides – she was always lecturing her mother, who took not a blind bit of notice. Elaine was brilliant at both ignoring her daughter and loving her to distraction. A remarkable woman.'

Joanna did not know if she should encourage him to talk about Elaine or not. Lucy had told her that the bereaved needed to be allowed to talk about the dead, and that they resented the fact that no one let them. But Joanna wanted him to stick to gardening. His gardening or hers, but not Elaine's.

Maybe he sensed this, for he ran his fingers up and down the stem of his empty champagne glass and said, 'I prefer the garden as it is now, though. Rather disloyal I suppose, but it's good to have some part of one's life that's *not* organised, that can surprise you. Under Elaine's regime I never knew that poppy heads made great seed pods, that rugosa roses had wonderful hips, that grasses looked so beautiful in the frost. She'd have had the lot off as soon as they'd bloomed.'

Joanna was surprised, and rather elated. She had always admired Stewart and in the last six months of knowing him personally, she'd got to like him a lot. But she'd not had him down as a gardener.

She'd only had one glass of champagne but a pleasant sense of relaxation had crept over her. She gazed at the passing countryside. The autumn sun was on the fields, highlighting an orderly pattern of combed brown plough and pale stubble, with occasional squares of green pasture dotted with sheep.

Stewart ordered another half bottle of champagne and Joanna did not object. She waved her hand at the view. 'Lovely, isn't it?'

'Indeed, the smiling English countryside, nothing better.'

This led the conversation to English churches and then to medieval villages in Tuscany crowning vineyards and olive groves, and to the Alps in May with wild flowers thick underfoot. 'I've got a chalet in St Moritz,' he said, 'but I seldom ski. Elaine got me hooked on walking in the mountains. So I go more in the summer. Caroline and Mark and Alasdair all ski, and sometimes I join them for Christmas or New Year.' Joanna told him that for the last few years she had taken herself off on walking holidays rather than sitting on a cruise deck or a beach drinking margaritas served by a uniformed flunky. She did not tell him that now her hiking days could be over on account of her knees.

She tried questioning him in turn, but he brushed enquiry aside, insisting on talking about her. It was a very long time since anyone was interested enough to question her about anything other than business and Joanna was flattered. She told him about the singing group.

He put his glass down and grinned at her.

'Joanna Carey, you and I have much more in common than I realised. I sing too.'

He told her that he and his wife had been in the Wakefield Choral

Society for years and had performed together at festivals and even at the Albert Hall. Joanna felt a twinge of jealousy. It must be good to have someone to share an interest with. And he sounded fond of Elaine and so balanced. It must have been a good marriage.

'We've not really got singing in common,' she said, almost crossly. 'I go to my singing group because I cannot sing a note.'

His eyebrows went up in surprise. 'Tell me about it.'

So she found herself talking about the terrifying school choir master, her ability to sing alone but not with others, and how she longed to do it properly. She told him of the slow progress she was making with Nelson and the group, and that Rebecca and Lucy had become her friends. Stewart listened with interest and sympathy.

Then, to her own surprise, she said, 'I think I was too scared to retire. I was sure all my friends were business colleagues and that I'd end up a lonely old woman reading gardening catalogues. But now with Lucy and Rebecca, maybe it won't be like that.'

'Of course it won't,' he said, 'you're interesting, talented, good-looking and (forgive me) rich. You'd never end up lonely.'

Joanna was suddenly embarrassed at the turn the conversation was taking and asked him if business still interested him as much as it did.

'No, it doesn't. I'm too old for the City jungle. As I get older I find myself agreeing more and more with Caroline's sentiments. I like the thought that business should be a force for good.'

Joanna did not want to go there. She was enjoying the little cocoon of warm intimacy and she knew talk of Caroline would lead them into conflict. So she nodded but said nothing.

Stewart wanted to know what had brought her into Innovest. 'I'd have thought,' he said, 'with your record, you'd have started another business. You could do whatever you want! Veuve Clicquot Businesswoman of the Year, Queen's Award for Industry, Order of the British Empire, London Entrepreneur of the Year, half a dozen honorary degrees . . .'

'Stop, for God's sake! Heavens, you've certainly done your home-work!'

'Not difficult these days. I Googled you. Do you think I'd have let Innovest put someone on the board that I didn't approve of?'

Canny old charmer, thought Joanna. She refrained from pointing out that he'd have had no choice: the piper calls the tune, and with seventy-five per cent of the Greenfarms equity, Innovest was definitely the piper.

She told him she'd sold her head-hunting agency because she'd wanted to retire and spend at least some of the money she'd made doing the things a long career in business had left her no time for. But then she'd found retirement less exciting than work so was drawn back into business.

'Technically, I work as a freelance consultant,' she said, 'but Innovest have so many fingers in so many pies, I do all sorts of jobs for them. And I sit on their board of course.'

'And you enjoy it?'

She was about to say what she always said, that she loved it, that business gave her a buzz, that it was great working with young imaginative entrepreneurs, etc. But instead she found herself saying, 'Not all the time. I did not enjoy the board meeting last month.'

He looked at her for a moment, an evaluating, measuring look.

'No, that must have been hard. But you handled it well. Kept your cool. I was impressed.' He smiled and added, 'Can't say I did as well. I do tend to lose it when I can't get my way.'

Joanna realised they could not put off a discussion about Greenfarms any longer.

'I'm sorry, Stewart,' she said, 'it's a horrible situation. But you must have thought about it. It cannot have been a surprise.'

Before he could reply the waiter appeared with the bill, saying they were about to arrive at King's Cross and he needed to cash up.

Stewart paid, and then said, 'We'll have to go somewhere to talk. Can you bear the first class lounge on the station?'

Joanna shook her head. 'I'm due at a meeting, for which, thanks to your company and your champagne, I have not done my prep. Besides, don't you have an appointment or anything?'

'Jo, I came so I could talk to you.'

'What! Don't you have any business in London?'

'Only you. How about after your meeting?'

The train slid to a stop, and people started pulling down bags and bumping through the corridor. Joanna stood up.

'We'd better collect our stuff before someone steals it or they call the bomb-squad.' She started down the train back to her original seat.

Stewart followed in silence. But when they were out on the platform, he said, 'Jo, we've got to meet. When?'

'I can't do today. After the meeting I'm going to now, I'm due to see a client for a drink. '

'Where are you meeting him?'

'American Bar in the Saxon. But Stewart, I don't know how long I'll be with him. He's flown in from the States to check his investments and decide on new ones and it may take hours.'

This seemed to satisfy him and he said nothing more until they reached Joanna's taxi, waiting with a yellow board reading INNOVEST in the window.

Stewart opened the door and Joanna climbed in.

'I'm sorry, Stewart. We should have talked on the train.'

'I'm glad we didn't,' he replied. 'Or rather I'm glad we talked of more important things.' He smiled into her eyes, familiar and friendly. 'I'll be in the Saxon Grill from seven-thirty. You need only walk down the stairs, and you'll be there.'

He slapped the roof of the taxi as he might a horse, a sort of dismissal and a goodbye, and walked briskly away, not waiting for an answer.

What makes him think that I'll be there? thought Joanna. That I'll have dinner with him? How dare he assume I have nothing to do after my meeting?

But the truth was she was not at all indignant. She was, against all the rules of feminism, impressed, and she would *love* to have dinner with him.

But as her taxi crawled through the traffic, she made a calculated, strategic decision. She needed to keep her relationship with Stewart on the right footing. She had to win on the Greenfarms issue and she must not let him get the better of her on a personal level. She took out her BlackBerry and texted him. *Sorry Stewart. Can't do tonight. Call me.*

Chapter Fourteen

Through the grey thicket of sleep the high buzz of the front door bell threaded its way to Lucy. She realised it had been ringing for some time. She turned over, pulling the duvet over her head.

She wanted more sleep, but some residual obligation to proper behaviour intruded. I should get up, she thought, but who's to know? Grace has abandoned her campaign to reform me and has taken the children to Majorca.

Grace had called ten days ago, and it had not been a good conversation.

'But *why* won't you come to London?'

'Because there's no singing class this week because it's school half-term and I'm perfectly happy at home.'

There was an exaggerated pause and Lucy could see her daughter shutting her eyes and taking a patient breath.

'But Mother, we won't see you at all if you won't come up this week. You know we're going to Majorca on Monday. The children should see their grandmother.'

Lucy was tempted to retort that grandmotherly contact was not the children's *right*, or her duty. Instead she said, 'You could bring them to me. They love it here. We could go blackberrying. And it's perfect autumn weather for once.'

'Oh Mother! You know I haven't the time. I'm much too busy. But you're retired . . .'

'Grace,' Lucy retorted, 'I am *not* retired. Six months ago I lost

one important job. Not the same thing. I'm still writing, as you
well know.'

'But not full time, Mother. You've never been able to write more
than four hours a day. So why can't you write one morning, come
up one afternoon, stay with us, and return next day in time to do
another four hours?'

Lucy was angry now, but she tried not to bark.

'Darling, don't you think that since you hold that being a full-
time mother is the most important work in the world, giving the
children some country air would be—'

'Mother, don't moralise. I can't bring them down, and if you
won't come up, we'll just have to see you when we get back.'

Lucy had put the receiver down, furious, but feeling ticked off
all the same.

She'd heard nothing from Grace since then, and had felt
increasingly guilty for being so unobliging. But not guilty enough,
she told herself sourly, to text her daughter or ring her up.

The ringing at the door stopped. Lucy was just drifting back to
gentle oblivion when a new noise, the old-fashioned uneven clang
of a real brass bell, sounded strangely through the house. Her caller
had found the iron bell-pull set in the stone to the right of the
door. It was attached by a chain to an ancient interior bell. It took
Lucy a second to place the noise. No one used that bell any more.
She was surprised it worked.

Whoever it was did not give up easily. Lucy clambered out of
bed and looked down from her bedroom window. A Parcel Force
van stood there with its driver's door open. She leant her forehead
against the window pane and listened to the door bells, both
electric and antique, ring at once. They stopped together, and Lucy
closed her eyes in relief – but she did not move.

When she opened them, the driver, a fat packet under his arm,
was walking briskly back to his van. She knew what was in the
packet – the book she'd ordered on Polish soups and stews. She
needed the book to cross-check some recipes, and to steal (well,

be inspired by) some others. She wanted a few more hefty Eastern European dishes, full of garlicky potatoes or chickpeas, with big chunks of cabbage, spicy sausage or veal that could be slow-cooked for hours at the weekend for freezing or reheating in the week.

Lucy knew she should open the window and call out to him. She needed the book and he'd tried so hard to do his job and deliver it. Yet she could not. She could not face having to talk, to apologise, smile, go downstairs, open up, apologise again for her state of undress, sign things. Smile, smile, smile. She just didn't feel like smiling.

She watched him toss the parcel across to the passenger seat, pull himself into the cab, slam the door, drive away. And then she went back to bed. There was relief in curling up under the covers, her hands around her knees.

At lunchtime she did get up, and made some toast and tea. She did not dress, however. What was the point? No one would see her.

She resolved to spend the afternoon at her desk. She would work, she'd be cheerful, she'd pull herself together and just get on with it. It was a year since David died and surely, surely, she should be OK by now?

But the hours were not productive. She had no energy, and little interest. After two cold calls (double-glazing and Sky television) she unplugged the telephone. When her mobile rang, she cancelled the call without answering it. She looked at the screen. Seven messages. She rang one-two-one and listened to the last of them. It was from Joanna.

'Listen Lucy, I'm worried about you now. I've been calling all day. If you don't ring back I'm coming down. Or maybe I'll send in the cops. So pick up the phone, you idiot, and ring me.'

Lucy frowned. She couldn't have Joanna in the house. It was a mess and there was no food. And anyway, she was trying to work. She'd have to stop her, but she could not face a conversation and texted her instead.

Darling Jo, sweet of you. Sorry about silence. Trying to finish book on bloody soup. See you next week for singing. Don't worry. Luv

Lucy sent the text and forced herself to listen to the rest of the messages. She deleted them as soon as she'd got their gist, sometimes as soon as she recognised the voice, without waiting for the message. Three of them were from Joanna, the first a friendly enquiry, but becoming more worried. (Why had she not come to the last singing class? How about going to a concert to make up for no singing over half-term? Was she OK?)

Oh, God, thought Lucy, Joanna is marvellous, a truly good friend. But such a control freak. You'd think having all those companies to run would be enough for her. If only I could convince her – and Grace – that there is nothing wrong with me, except that I don't feel sociable. I am just not up to shopping with Rebecca and listening to her banging on about Nelson. Or entertaining my grandchildren or going to a concert. And I can't seem to get enough sleep.

She managed to finish the chapter on cheese soups with a Danish Samsoe soup and a Derbyshire Stilton one, but she wasn't pleased with it. She decided to leave it and go back to correcting and editing earlier chapters.

When she'd corrected the whole tomato soup chapter, with hardly a typo or a word wrong, she realised she'd already edited it. She'd only done it yesterday, but she had no memory of it.

Usually she liked correcting and editing. She always did the first read-through on screen and then printed off her pages to correct them again by hand. But today she could not concentrate. She abandoned the typescript and added it to the pile of unopened mail, then made a foray to the kitchen for a lump of cheese which she ate in her fingers at her desk, shaking the crumbly bits from her papers, disgusted with herself.

She opened her laptop and returned to her chapter for a glossy book, *Great Victorians*. She had agreed to write an essay on the Reform Club chef, Alexis Soyer – partly because she needed the money, but mainly because the man fascinated her – but she deleted almost as many words as she wrote, and the chapter did not advance.

Lucy read what she'd written. It was concise and well constructed. But lifeless. How could she have removed the fire from the captivating Soyer? He should be a gift to a writer. He'd founded soup kitchens in the Irish famine; he'd revolutionised hospital catering behind the front line in the Crimea; he'd masterminded a catering extravaganza to cream off the visitors to the Great Exhibition; he'd invented countless kitchen appliances and gadgets. All that before you even touched his day job, or his eccentric dress, or his young wife, soon to die.

She closed the laptop and put her head down on top of it. The truth was, even Soyer failed to interest her. I have to pull myself together, she thought. *Tomorrow*.

She wasn't sure how long she stayed like that. Maybe she slept briefly, but when a stiff back roused her, she again wandered through to the kitchen to open the fridge and peer into it. She extracted a pot of yogurt and a bottle of Sauvignon Blanc. She put a teaspoon and a corkscrew into one dressing gown pocket and a glass into the other, and, clutching yogurt and wine to her with one arm, she managed to scoop up the cat with her free hand. She would watch the news with Magnificat on her lap and a glass in her hand. The thought lifted one thin layer of grey from her spirits and she said aloud to the cat, 'Right Mags, time for rest and recreation. I am going to drag myself out of the wretched pit.'

And indeed she quite enjoyed the catalogue of a government minister's indiscretions and the good news story of villagers seeing off a supermarket development. But then, the ever-cheerful Orlando Black appeared in the middle of a row of well-known cooks, clearly the chairman of a celebrity cook's quiz show.

Lucy's first thought was that she'd been going to chair this show, and that the irrepressible Black was filling yet another pair of her shoes. But then she remembered she'd refused the job because she'd thought the format vulgar – for every question the participants got wrong, they'd lose points which they could buy back by eating something disgusting: sheep's eyes, live flying ants, etc.

The show was quite as dire as she'd imagined it would be. The contestants displayed abysmal ignorance of ingredients, culinary history and culture, even of classical recipes, and then shrieked and gagged over deep-fried grasshopper or mopane worms.

She flicked off the TV and stared at the blank screen for a few seconds. Then she put her head back on the chair and started, once more, to cry. Her face wet with tears, she wailed, '*Oh David, David, when will the misery start to lift?*' She held Magnificat tight and buried her face in his fur. But he struggled free, jumped down and, with an irritated twitch of his tail, took himself off.

Even the bloody cat rejects me, she thought, and smiled despite herself.

Chapter Fifteen

A week after the train ride with Stewart, Joanna agreed to meet him for dinner.

He'd booked at the Saxon. She was early and, since she'd come straight from a drink with her colleagues at Innovest, she headed for the Ladies and spent some time re-doing her make-up, with a touch more on her eyes than she wore during the day.

Her charcoal jacket, fine for business, was now too formal, so she decided to carry it and wear her pink and purple pashmina (she always carried a pashmina in the back pocket of her briefcase against over-zealous air-conditioning). She draped it over her shoulder and was pleased that it went well with the soft mauve blouse.

She turned her head this way and that, closely inspecting the skin round her eyes and jaw. Sometimes she looked positively wrinkled, but tonight she looked good, not bad for fifty-five. And then she admonished herself: what was she trying to do – seduce her chairman? It was ridiculous. She was a confirmed spinster and happy that way. But she did feel pretty upbeat. Maybe having that frozen daiquiri in the pub was unwise.

The truth was she felt a fluttering in the gut she'd not felt in years – not since her disastrous affair with the glamorous Tom. That had come to grief when the prospect of marriage and children had him dodging for cover like a rabbit with a dog on his tail.

She looked steadily into the mirror and asked herself if there had been, on Stewart's part, any more than professional interest in her on the train last week. Yes, she concluded, there had been. It was probably nothing, but he was the kind of man who could not help but charm women. She had better be on her guard.

And then she convinced herself that she had imagined his interest. She'd been flattered by his attention and elated by the champagne, that was all. After all, why should Stewart be interested in her? Most men his age (sixty-two? Three?) go for forty-year-olds. He was just softening her up so he could get round her on the Greenfarms question. That must be it . . .

It was a relief to see Stewart sitting in the corner – at the best table – when she arrived. Filippo greeted her with his usual skill.

'Ah, Miss Carey, how good to see you. So tonight you are to be the guest! But I have still given you your favourite table, you will see.'

Joanna, weaving her way through the tables in Filippo's wake, thought how impossible it was not to be flattered when a maître d' pretended that you were important. Of course she knew the good ones did it to everyone, remembering faces they seldom saw, and pretending to remember those they didn't, but still, it did make one swish through the restaurant like a star.

Stewart rose with old-fashioned courtesy as she approached, his face alight with welcome.

'Oh, thank God. I thought you might blow me out.'

Joanna smiled and slid into the banquette seat diagonally opposite him. 'I'm not late am I?'

'No, I was early, anxious to ensure they'd got my booking.'

'And were you suitably gratified to find you had the best table? I'm impressed.'

'I did it by dropping your name to Filippo.'

Joanna didn't think this was true, but the flattery got to her, and once again she told herself to beware: this was all about Greenfarms, not her. It was a deliberate charm offensive, and she was not going to fall for it.

Dinner was delicious, and after a couple of glasses of very good Gigondas, she began to relax. After all, she thought, I know and trust Stewart, and if he has something to say I should listen.

Stewart admitted that her rigid analysis of the Greenfarms business could not be faulted by conventional business wisdom. But then Greenfarms was not a conventional business. And didn't she recognise that there are some companies that do well in an unorthodox way?

'Caroline built Greenfarms on conviction,' he said. 'On a passionate belief that you can combine high-minded principles with making a profit and providing employment. I was sceptical at first, but I was wrong. She did extraordinarily well.'

Joanna made a determined effort to pull her mind into business mode instead of thinking how attractive Stewart was when serious. His eyelids sloped down over earnest brown eyes, his slightly shaggy eyebrows softening his all-over polish. 'Stewart,' she said, 'I would not be on your board if that were true. You know better than anyone how deep in trouble Greenfarms is.'

'Agreed,' he replied, 'it is now. And it's largely my fault. I thought the supermarket route was a wonderful opportunity. I saw it as a City man would, but Caroline was always against it. She felt we were somehow compromising the brand – and she was right.'

'But . . .'

'Joanna, forget for a minute that you represent Innovest. Just imagine that this was your business, and you wanted it to survive. You care more about its soundness than its growth. You don't need to become mega-rich, you don't want to float on the stock market, you don't want to sell out to a global conglomerate. You just want to provide good food to people who want to buy it, and to do well enough to keep growing steadily, so you can do more of what you do – spread the mission, if you like.'

For a moment Joanna was spellbound by the intensity of his tone. He could be Caroline, proselytising for the organic movement.

'OK. But I'd still advise Innovest to sell up. A slow-growing life-style mini-business is not what they invested in. They want, and always have wanted, good returns to satisfy investors who are hugely demanding.'

'I know that. I am not asking you to prevent them selling. I want to buy them out. Have a family business again.'

'And you want me to persuade them to give up their shares for a peppercorn?'

Stewart smiled. 'Well, maybe two peppercorns. They'll be more interested in cutting their losses, getting out before we go into loss, won't they? They will know that there won't be another buyer out there wanting to take on a struggling company, losing supermarket contracts. Other venture capitalists will know very well that if Innovest couldn't make Greenfarms fly, they won't be able to either.'

Joanna was back on the business ball now.

'Stewart, you're telling me that you're a buyer, and you're asking me to tell my employers that there are no buyers. And that therefore they should just give their shares to you.'

'No,' he countered. 'I'm asking you to be the honest broker. Do a deal that will avoid us having to call in expensive advisors, negotiate for aeons, and end up with both sides feeling they have been robbed. That's what I'm asking.'

Joanna agreed to think about it. 'But Stewart,' she said, 'are you sure about this? Are you really convinced by Caroline's plan for recovery? And if she wasn't your daughter, would you hire her as the best person to lead that recovery?'

She thought he might be offended. He was so besotted with Caroline. But he gave a snorting laugh. 'Hell, no,' he said. 'Of course not. But when was business a perfect world? And if you stayed on the board, between us we could probably manage her.'

'Me stay on? After Innovest has pulled out?'

'Why not? You are the best board member we've got. And you'd enjoy it.' He put a hand over hers and she was struck by how cool it felt and how his long, manicured fingers had just a few hairs on the back of them, between the knuckles. Oh Lord, I'm slipping again, she thought.

She frowned and withdrew her hand. 'Stewart, I'll look at her plan again. And I'll think about it, take some advice . . . and come back to you.'

When he'd paid the bill and they'd been bowed out of the restaurant, Stewart put her into a taxi with old world courtesy and paid the driver in advance.

She wound down the window to thank him.

He put both hands on the window sill and leant into the cab.

'Joanna, you're too good for that City rat-race. You should give up Innovest and have some fun. With us.'

Chapter Sixteen

It was late November, and Rebecca had decided the time was right to put her Lucy makeover plans into action. Joanna had told her she was worried about Lucy. Bring on the cavalry; Rebecca to the rescue, she thought. She opened her mobile, wondered if Lucy would answer it. She did.

'Lu-Lu,' Rebecca told her, 'I've got a great idea.'

'Don't call me Lu-Lu.' Lucy's protests were routine: she always objected to her Lu-Lu, but Rebecca never took any notice.

'What great idea?' Lucy sounded suspicious.

'Let's go shopping. For clothes. For you.'

'Rebecca, you've tried this before. But why? I hate shopping.'

'That's because you don't do it properly.' Rebecca could not understand anyone not liking shopping. 'It's supposed to be fun, not a death sentence! We'll have lunch in the middle. Get tiddly and buy stuff you wouldn't buy sober. And which you'll not regret, I promise.'

Rebecca could hear Lucy's heavy sigh.

'But Rebecca, I don't *need* new clothes. I've too many . . .'

'You do. Trust me, you really *really* need new clothes. And you need a clear-out. That'll be fun too. We'll give them all back to Oxfam where they came from.'

Oops, thought Rebecca, maybe I've gone too far, she'll take offence. But she didn't. 'Not all of them came from Oxfam,' Lucy said. 'There are other charity shops, you know.'

She's great, thought Rebecca, I love her.

'What has brought on this sudden desire for retail spending?' Lucy wanted to know.

'I'm having withdrawal symptoms. I can't shop because I'm broke. You, on the other hand, can afford it. Also, I'll make a great personal shopper.'

'And I bet Joanna has been telling you I need rescuing or some rot. Has she put you up to this?'

Rebecca thought. Why lie? 'Sure,' she said, 'she's worried about you. She thinks you've been down. But I've been itching to use my makeover talents on you ever since we met.'

'You have, have you?'

'Sure. You're the perfect victim, clueless when it comes to fashion, but great raw material. You're good looking under that awful haircut, and if you would just swing your hips a bit, people might notice what a great bum you've got. The before and after pics will be terrific.'

'That bad, is it?' Lucy sounded quite unruffled.

'Worse.'

To Rebecca's surprise Lucy agreed, and they settled on Friday.

On Wednesday Lucy tried to back out. She rang Rebecca on her mobile, sounding hesitant.

'Rebecca, look, I can't do Friday. You don't mind if I cry off do you?'

'Yes, I do. No crying off allowed.'

'I'm so sorry, but I really can't come.'

'Why not?' Rebecca was not going to let her off the hook. Apart from anything else, she thought, Joanna would kill her.

There was a pause and then Lucy said, without much conviction, 'I've got to finish some work . . . I . . .'

'Lu-Lu, that's not true.'

'Don't call me Lu-Lu.' Long pause. 'OK, Rebecca, it's not true. Or rather it is, but that's not the reason. The truth is that I don't want to go shopping. I can't face the Christmas jingle bells and

Rudolf. Can't face lunching either. Or having my hair done, or getting my face covered in mud or essential oils or whatever nonsense they dream up.'

'Darling, if you don't come up to town on Friday both Joanna and I are coming down to you, and that will be much worse, don't you think?'

This was bluff – Rebecca had only just thought of it and had no idea if Joanna would agree. But she knew that a month ago, when Lucy had been really down, Joanna had done exactly that – landed on her doorstep, stayed the night and frog-marched Lucy to London for the next choir practice.

'You'll feel obliged to tidy the house,' she went on, 'and make lunch, and entertain us. Much more effort than getting on the train and then letting me take over.'

In the end Lucy caved in, and agreed to meet Rebecca at Costa Coffee on Paddington Station.

Rebecca lay in bed, periodically telling herself to get up, but mostly thinking about her friendship with Lucy and Joanna. Didn't true friendship mean telling each other everything, like schoolgirls? Or maybe as you got older you got more easily embarrassed? I never tell either of them how badly I need men, for example. How much I still need sex. Does any woman of our age discuss this I wonder? Or only with their shrinks? Do they confess to fantasising and wet dreams and masturbation? Indeed, do they even *do* these things? Perhaps I'm a freak or something, but I do prefer it with real men, rather than making it up on my own.

She thought that maybe Lucy might be still too damped down by grief and widowhood to need a man, but Joanna, surely, must long for someone to make love to her. If she did, she hid it well.

They both, she thought, disapproved of her affair with Nelson. She guessed they'd grown fond of him and suspected she was messing him around, wasn't *serious*. Well, it was true Nelson wasn't for keeps, and they'd only stay together while the sex was good.

But Joanna and Lucy probably considered sex at their age undignified. As if sex at any age was dignified!

This led her to wondering what Angelica got up to. She wanted her daughter to have a lot of fun, and satisfactory sex. And a real love life. But Angelica, though she sometimes mentioned a boyfriend, never gave her mother any details. But maybe daughters just don't tell their mothers. She certainly did not discuss her love life with Angelica.

Rebecca flung back the duvet and stretched. She must get up. Today she was taking Lucy shopping, and she loved shopping. She even liked shopping for groceries, but her favourite place was Harvey Nichol's Designer Room, which was her idea of heaven.

When she was about fourteen her foster father had complained that she never did her homework.

'Well, what do you expect? I'm fourteen! All I think about is sex and shopping.' It was true, and she thought it was true of nearly all her friends, but it wasn't supposed to be admitted.

I'm not that different now, thought Rebecca. Shopping is still a thrill, and so is sex, but I no longer get them both together. Sadly. Nelson just would not understand the point of shopping. He saw shops as the enemy, trying to relieve him of his hard-earned cash, he didn't see that it was like dancing, or eating, or drinking, which have a value quite apart from their main, practical function.

Nothing could compare with the kind of shopping she had once done in Harvey Nick's, or in Bond Street, with Faisal. That period of her life, just before she married Bill, had combined the high point of both her sex and shopping life, and Rebecca often thought of it. Nelson was a great lover, but Faisal had been something else.

Faisal was Jordanian, rich, Oxford-educated and urbane. But no new-man European ideas had penetrated: he was all unreconstructed male. He liked women to be beautiful and he liked to both spoil and command them. He would never have done for a husband, but he was a five-star lover.

He had sat in the Designer Room's upholstered armchair,

champagne (courtesy of the house) in one hand, while the 'Personal Fashion Consultant', an exquisite Frenchwoman wearing a YSL dress of fine silk jersey, produced the clothes. She showed them first to him – she knew who was paying her wages all right – and then, if he approved, Rebecca would put them on in the 'Personal Shopping Suite', then step out and give him a twirl.

She had loved it. Faisal's close inspection was such a turn on: his eyes were on her like a trainer's on a racehorse, except that his gaze was lazy rather than intent, and she felt the challenge of keeping it there, making him want her. She knew he could so easily lose interest and turn that gaze to the demure curves of the Frenchwoman.

Soon it had become a sort of secret sex game. Somehow he knew that the process excited her, and he played along. Instead of immediately spinning about to show off the dress, she would stand before him, like a schoolgirl awaiting instructions. He'd keep her there, expectant, while he slowly looked her up and down, down and up. Then, without a word, he'd describe a circle with his fingers, and she would slowly turn in a circle. That the elegant Frenchwoman had to stand by, a servant in attendance, pretending nothing was going on but routine shopping, somehow excited Rebecca more.

They would try all sorts of clothes. A smart little suit with a short full skirt had him sending mademoiselle off for knee-high boots. When Rebecca had pulled them on he had put out his hand to take her foot. She'd stood there on one leg while he held her heel in one hand, and caressed the soft suede of the boot with the other. As his hand went from ankle to knee Rebecca longed for it to slip over the top, meet the cool flesh of her thigh, go higher . . .

An evening dress with a low scooped neck allowed him to discuss the design with the saleswoman. He took no notice of Rebecca other than to trigger electric messages of lust with one well-manicured finger tracing the neckline over her breasts, or stroking her hip while apparently inspecting the cut of the skirt.

When she tried on tight lycra jeans, she'd stood close to him with her legs a bit apart, back slightly arched, bum out. Under pretence of turning her to inspect the stitching, he had put one hand lightly on her bottom, one on the front of her thigh and trailed his fingers over the cloth as she turned, legs melting.

Once, leaving the store loaded with carrier bags of designer loot, they'd been alone in the lift. He'd put down his bags and leant close to her. She raised her face and closed her eyes, confident he would kiss her. But instead he'd whispered in her ear,

'You'll have to wait, won't you, my horny little bitch.'

She remembered how the blood rushed to her face, half shame, half desire.

And once into his big stretch limo, he'd told the chauffer to go into Hyde Park and drive around it, down Park Lane, then round again until he ordered otherwise.

He had pushed the button to raise the dark glass screen behind the driver. As it rose Rebecca had met the driver's eye, just for a second, and he'd looked at her – expressionless but knowing.

Without ceremony Faisal had pulled her onto the plush carpet and pushed her head down. Rebecca knew she was to play the whore, to thank him for the clothes as he wished to be thanked.

That the driver knew what was going on heightened her desire. She wanted to break Faisal's studied indifference. She did too, though she noticed he had control enough to flip the intercom switch to off before letting go.

Another time, after a Bond Street spree, he'd given her tea in Fortnum's, and all the time they were eating elegant little sandwiches and tiny éclairs, he'd had his hand under her skirt on the banquette. He had not removed it when the waitress poured the tea, nor when the manager brought the bill and talked to him of the store's revamp. When she'd tried to cross her legs at the approach of a waiter, he'd leant close to her and whispered, 'Open your legs, little whore.' And she had.

Hot and aching, she had been unable to concentrate on the conversation, and the torment had continued when they got back to his Eaton Square apartment. He'd had her model the new leather trousers and fur jacket he'd bought, with nothing underneath except a gold slave collar from Asprey's. And then he'd stripped her of the clothes, slowly, until she was frantic.

'You're gagging for it, aren't you?' he'd said. It was true.

He'd finally fucked her, well and truly, on the long upholstered footstool. It was not long enough to support her head and legs and it lifted her body like an offering. It was half real, half fantasy. Even the gold collar digging into her neck as her head fell back excited her. Rebecca was all the things modern women are supposed to object to. She was his object of desire, his plaything, his chattel. And she loved it.

But the thing was, Rebecca thought, she was never powerless. Even with Faisal over her, in her, holding her down, the footstool juddering and shifting with the violence of every thrust, he was dancing to her tune, acting out her fantasy, giving her what she craved.

She would do anything to recapture some of that. Nelson was lovely, but he wasn't in the same league.

Rebecca looked up to see Lucy approaching across the station concourse wearing a too-tight tweed suit, well-polished black pumps and carrying a basket. She was smiling, apparently unaware of the blaring Christmas Carols.

Oh, I do love her, thought Rebecca. She's a fashion disaster, but she's really tried, abandoning her pleated skirts and awful trouser suits. And she's had her hair done.

They went first to Rigby & Peller, the posh people's undies shop in Knightsbridge. Lucy protested that there was nothing wrong with Marks and Spencer, but Rebecca was firm.

'Sorry Lucy. When did you last buy a bra? Be honest.'

Lucy admitted it had been a long time ago, five years maybe, and reluctantly entered the shop, muttering, 'A *doorman* for a lingerie shop! Good God!'

Rebecca loved Rigby & Peller. It was quaint and cramped yet so chic. Today it was crowded with two distinct types of customer: stick-thin young women with botox lips (and silicone breasts I bet, thought Rebecca), who were perched on a narrow upholstered bench, and well-padded Knightsbridge matrons in sober but expensive clothes. They overflowed the minimal seating.

All were waiting for appointments, but no one waited for long. Every minute or so, one of the corsetieres appeared through the door to summon a customer into the inner sanctum of fitting rooms.

When two of the matrons had been ushered off, Lucy and Rebecca took their seats and watched the shop at work. A young assistant up a ladder was searching through the stacks of bra boxes, other assistants were at the till, busy with Christmas gift wrap, charging, bowing goodbyes and thank-yous, or running upstairs in search of stock.

'That woman just paid eighty pounds for a bra!' Lucy whispered. 'I can't afford that!'

'Yes, you can,' Rebecca replied. 'If you are going to spend six hundred, maybe a thousand, on a suit, you need a great shape under it. Just as you need a decent pair of shoes and a good handbag to set it off.'

'But I'm not planning on the shoes and handbag either!'

'Ah, but I am.'

Quite soon it was Lucy's turn. The fitter introduced herself as Sofia. Her smile was professional yet reassuring, like a good nanny's. 'And what can I do for madam today?'

Rebecca got in quickly. Given half a chance, she thought, Lucy will bolt.

'We are on a mission to get the perfect, tailored suit, and Lucy needs a good bra and some latex knickers to show her bum off a bit—'

'No I don't!' Lucy interrupted. 'Just the bra. That will be fine.' Rebecca did not argue. Plenty of time.

Sofia was authoritative. She slipped off Lucy's blouse and looked with concentration at her clean but certainly not new bra, at her pale breasts bulging gently from the sides of it, at her pushed-together cleavage, the skin wrinkled at the join.

She stood behind Lucy looking over her shoulder into the mirror.

'Mmm,' she said, 'lovely bosom. But your bra is the wrong size and the wrong shape — it doesn't do you justice. See here . . .' she pulled a bra strap to one side exposing a deep red groove '. . . the bra back is giving you no support so the straps are doing all the work and cutting into you. Not very comfortable, is it?'

'No,' replied Lucy, 'but all bras are uncomfortable. It's the nature of the beast, isn't it?'

Sofia smiled. 'You'll see.'

She cupped Lucy's breasts in her hands to lift and separate them, and all eyes concentrated on the mirror.

'What we want is enough lift to give you some cleavage, but not too much, which would wrinkle the skin.' She lifted Lucy's breasts higher and the skin above her bosom puckered, instantly adding years.

Sofia's shrewd eyes assessed Lucy's body like a Cruft's judge awarding dog-show prizes. Then she disappeared briefly but was soon back with an armful of bras.

She picked one and instructed Lucy in the art of putting it on: she had to bend over so her breasts fell into the cups. Then Sofia fastened the back. Then, diving a hand into each bra cup in turn, she adjusted Lucy's boobs unceremoniously.

'You have to lift each breast, and let it settle back into the cup. And then you use your forefingers to get maximum separation.' As she spoke she stuck her two forefingers deeply down the central panel of the bra and smoothed first one, then the other breast from the middle to the side.

They all studied Lucy's transformation. The smooth cream satin fitted, wrinkle free, over each breast. The neckline was scooped slightly, so that her breasts, smooth and creamy as a young woman's and now separated, swelled gently above the lacy edge of the bra.

Lucy had lost her air of mixed embarrassment and irritation at this whole performance, and was pleased. She did not say so of course, but Rebecca could tell from the way she turned her body this way and that to see herself in the mirror.

Lucy could not decide between the various bras, and Rebecca talked her into two: one black and lacy, the other flesh-coloured and plain which would be invisible under anything.

Lucy was so delighted that she needed no persuading to buy a pair of support pants with a panel in the front to flatten the tum, clever elastication to lift and shape the bum, and legs to reduce her thighs.

Rebecca made her wear the plain bra and the pants since their next stop was Harvey Nick's for the suit. She insisted Lucy consign her old underwear to the bin. 'We can't have you keeping your new things for best and never wearing them,' she said.

Rebecca had arranged for a personal shopper to help with the suit.

'Can you believe it?' she said. 'There's a six-week waiting list for personal shoppers? But I blagged our way up the list by telling them that "my client" needs a whole wardrobe before she starts filming again in a week.'

'You did not!'

'Yes I did. And don't fuss. Just don't blow our cover.'

Lucy looked distinctly unhappy at this, but Rebecca just laughed and said, 'Don't be grumpy. The saleswoman would far rather be serving a film actress than anyone else so we are actually doing her a favour.'

The personal shopper, badged Georgina, was young and friendly. She had already selected half a dozen suits in Lucy's size.

Lucy stripped down to her new underwear and Rebecca guessed she was relieved that she didn't have to stand before the young saleswoman in ancient M&S. But she was uncooperative, standing in front of the elegant cheval mirror without enthusiasm.

And she's right, thought Rebecca, the suits were nice enough, but they sure didn't make the heart beat faster. So she went with Georgina to look through the racks of Max Mara, Nicole Farhi, Jil Sander, Chanel — classic designers more interested in fabric and cut than in fripperies.

As soon as Rebecca saw it, she knew they'd hit the jackpot. It was a purply-blue Donna Karan in the finest wool. The jacket had built-in ties at the waist, in the same deep purple satin as the wide revers of the collar. Below the waist was a short flared peplum. The skirt was long and narrow with a matching flare at the lower calf, revealing a flash of satin underskirt.

It was perfect: frivolous and severe at the same time. Comfortable yet formal. You could go to a wedding or a funeral in it, a formal dinner or lunch with a girlfriend.

Georgina held the skirt over Lucy's head and let it slither down her body. Lucy shrugged into the jacket, and Georgina looped the ties together.

The rounded neckline was wide and low, showing the curves of Lucy's breasts, but none of her bra. Lucy clutched at the lapels, trying to make them meet.

'Wait a sec,' said Georgina, as she produced a silver pendant on a narrow ribbon and hung it round Lucy's neck. The purple stone lay on the gentle swell of Lucy's bosom.

'Wow,' said Rebecca, 'you look beautiful, Lucy.'

'But I'll never wear it. It's too glamorous.' But it was obvious that she wanted to be told otherwise, and Georgina and Rebecca obliged.

Georgina produced a plain cream T-shirt (£130 Rebecca noticed, but happily Lucy didn't) and Lucy put it on and tried the jacket again. The cream silk V at the neck had changed the look from evening to day.

Rebecca was delighted at the effect on Lucy. She looked in turns thrilled, almost smug, and disbelieving. She opened the jacket to inspect the glowing lining, tied the soft belt loosely, turned to admire the way the skirt undercut her bottom, extended her leg to see the flash of kick-pleat. Slowly her anxious uncertainty was replaced by a childish excitement.

And when the suit was laid out on the desk for folding, Rebecca noticed that she could not resist putting a hand out to stroke the fine wool, feel it slip smoothly over the silk lining. She's experiencing what I know so well, thought Rebecca – the lust for possession.

Suddenly Lucy said to Georgina, 'I'll take the necklace and the T-shirt too.'

Ha! thought Rebecca. Result!

Chapter Seventeen

Joanna set out for the meeting feeling guilty and gloomy. She walked along the sunny Wakefield streets, taking no pleasure in the crisp winter air. She had been dutifully telephoning her parents in Australia every few weeks, but the enjoyment of talking to her father was almost always cancelled by her mother's downbeat take on everything.

During their conversation last night her mother had complained.

'I hate these phone calls. You always want to speak to your dad. I can tell you are longing to get rid of me.'

'That's not true, Ma. I want to speak to you both. And if you want to talk to me more, why don't you ever ring *me*?'

That stopped the argument but Joanna was left facing the fact that the last thing she really wanted was more talk with her mother.

And it wasn't just her mother. She was mulling over the uncomfortable fact that for the first time in her professional life she'd let her emotions get in the way of business.

The truth was she had compromised because she was becoming increasingly attracted to Stewart. She half feared she was in love with him. The only comfort was that he did not know that – neither the attraction, nor that she'd given in because of it. He – typical man – believed he'd convinced her with the power of his argument that Caroline could be an effective CEO. Joanna was perfectly sure she could not, but she harboured a small hope that, against all the evidence, Stewart would prove to be right.

It was true, of course, that Caroline had commitment and energy and passion and all that. But she was a lousy manager – disorganised, upsetting her managers, refusing to listen.

Joanna could not believe she'd been so weak. She should have insisted that Caroline be replaced by a good CEO as the price for her stumping up for a third of the shares. If this had been any other negotiation, she knew she would have got her way or she would have walked.

The one ray of comfort was that she'd got Stewart to agree to buy her out after six months if she was still unhappy with Caroline. But of course if it came to that, it would be she, Joanna, that was shown the door, not Caroline. She'd have her money out, true, but the business would still be a dog. And it would mean she'd not see Stewart again.

What a perfect fool I am, she thought, as she pushed open the pub door. But then she saw Stewart and her heart lifted. As she walked towards father and daughter sitting at the far end of the room, her head came up and she told herself she'd do her damnedest to make this work.

The meeting had to be held in the pub: they couldn't meet at head office for fear of starting a rumour mill. And the rest of the board had not yet been told of the proposed rescue-package – that Joanna was to buy into the business, that Stewart and Caroline would buy back the rest of the shares, and that Joanna would go half-time with Innovest so that she could spend two days a week helping Caroline restructure Greenfarms. Innovest had agreed to sell for very little, taking an overall loss on the venture, but they'd been happy to get out. And Stewart and Joanna would have to provide a lot more finance for the needed investment, mostly the on-line side.

Stewart came back from the bar and put the drinks down on the table. As he lowered himself to the banquette between the two women, his arms went wide to pull them to him. Joanna felt an immediate warm charge and wondered if he felt it too.

He looked, she thought, like a cat with the cream. He adores his daughter and he likes me and here we both are, tightly in his web: emotionally, financially, and professionally. And, right now, physically.

'God, Joanna,' he exclaimed, 'am I glad to have *you* with us, rather than the soulless Innovest!' He swept a happy, triumphant smile over them both.

Joanna looked at Caroline. She was smiling at her father, but it was a careful smile, hiding anxiety.

They toasted their new beginnings and then settled down to discuss Joanna's plan. There was a lot to do, and she produced a spreadsheet with the tasks, a six-month timetable of when they would be done, by whom and at what cost. Under the heading Internet Sales were web redesign, pilot trials, evaluation, roll-out. Under Marketing and Public Relations: maximising farm sales, expanding farmers' markets, targeting health-food chains, publicity campaign. Under Employment: staff consultation, factory reduction, head-office retrenchment, outsourcing. And so on. With the detail, there were two double sheets of it.

Of course there was not much chance of an easy ride from Caroline. She was no fool, and as soon as she spotted the heading 'staff consultation' she said, 'That's mealy-mouthed code for putting the poor buggers out of work, isn't it?'

Caroline's outbursts always had the effect of making Joanna super-cool and unemotional. She replied, 'It means we need to make at least half of the factory staff redundant, yes.'

In the end Caroline behaved much better than Joanna had expected. She was, Joanna supposed, so relieved at the prospect of getting her business out of the big retailers' clutches she swallowed her objections to everything: the redundancies, mothballing half the factory until they could replace the supermarket sales, hiring a professional web-sales company.

But then they got to the trickiest item.

'The next thing is awkward,' Joanna said. 'But it has to be tackled. We do not have a strong enough executive board. It was probably

fine for a small family company five years ago, but it's not now.
The programme of change we've just agreed will need strong
leadership to push it through.'

Joanna caught a flash of the familiar Caroline hostility. When she
spoke her voice was bitter.

'I presume it's the family members you are gunning for. Which
of us has failed the test then?'

As always, Joanna ignored the tone and answered the question,
saying evenly, 'I am principally concerned about your brother. Mark
is just not up to the job of operations director. Do you not agree?'

Caroline's head came forward, chin rising. 'He's been with us
from the start and he's as loyal—'

But Stewart cut in. 'I agree with Joanna. Mark is not capable of
doing the job as it will be. He lacks the necessary energy and drive.
It would be different if you were more—'

Caroline jerked her head from Joanna to him. 'So it's me now
is it, Dad? What's the problem with me? I hardly lack energy.'

Stewart smiled at her. 'Indeed you don't. I was going to say you
hate the boring bits of business, so your doing any of Mark's job
would be a waste of your talents, and, though Mark can do them,
he'll never do them anything like fast enough.'

Caroline, mollified, relaxed slightly and Stewart went on. 'Mark
needs a change. He's been too cosy here, working for his sister,
living under her shadow. He needs to get out from under. I'll talk
to him. It will be all right.'

Joanna was constantly amazed by Stewart. He might have a blind
spot when it came to Caroline but he faced everything else so
straightforwardly. Sacking his own son would not be easy, but
because he thought it right he did not duck it for a second.

All through the meeting Stewart was businesslike and brisk,
pushing them through the agenda, and Joanna managed to forget
how much she was attracted to him. But when they moved to the
routine stuff, agreeing a new lease, ratifying the audit committee
decisions etc, desire came flooding back.

I want Caroline to go away, she thought. I want Stewart to talk to me, to me alone, his eyes on mine. And I want him to talk about anything at all as long as it's not Greenfarms.

She had not felt like this – longing for a man's call, thinking about him all the time, hanging on his every word, his tone of voice, his every gesture, for years – not since her thirties when she was in love with Tom.

She'd met Tom when he'd registered with Joanna Carey Executive Search and she'd placed him in his first chief executive job, with the new and growing broadcaster, City TV. He was forty-five, small, dark, dynamic, and a huge egotist. When he'd landed the job he'd telephoned her, not to thank her, but to tell her how brilliantly he'd handled the interview, and how, if he needed to hire any executives for his new company, he'd expect a whopping discount on her fees.

She now thought that what had so spellbound her was his being unafraid of her. All her life men had found her intimidating: too clever, too confident, too successful, too rich. But Tom, with a background perfectly suited to his new job, half of it in television, half of it as a hedge fund manager, was every bit as successful, and a lot richer, than her. Far from resenting her accomplishments, he gloried in them, crowing to their friends about her achievements as though he were responsible for them. He boasted about her doings almost as much as he boasted of his own – which he did without shame and with boyish zeal.

At first intrigued, then admiring, she'd found Tom addictive. And had ended up deeply in love with him.

It had been a four-year affair: four years of parties, expensive holidays, great clothes. Tom had made her see the difference between good sensible clothes and truly beautiful things, made from exquisite cloth by great designers; the sort of clothes that made her look the part even when she was secretly nervous.

Their love affair had fallen apart as suddenly as it had begun. For some months, the endless round of London life had failed to satisfy Joanna and she'd attributed her lack of pleasure in it to overwork and tiredness. But she'd not have said she was unhappy, or out of love with Tom.

One evening, after a day on a friend's boat in the South of France, she'd abruptly decided to tackle her fears.

'Darling,' she'd said, 'I need to know where we are going. I love you to bits, but is this it, do you think?'

He'd been trying to light a cigarette on the harbour front at St Tropez and he'd gone on flicking the lighter, head down and hands shielding the flame from the wind. He'd said, the cigarette between his lips,

'What do you mean, is this it?'

'I suppose I mean, are we going to progress at all?'

'Progress?' He was still clicking his lighter without success.

Tom could be irritatingly stupid sometimes. She spelled it out for him.

'Yes. Get married and have children.'

He'd looked up at her then and said, 'Good Lord, no! Why? You don't want to, do you?'

It was as though he were asking, 'You don't really want an ice cream do you?' Or, 'you don't really want to go to that restaurant, do you?' He was simply unaware of the importance of her question, as unaware as he had been of her growing anxiety about children, about their future, about his commitment to her.

He had just never noticed how she felt when their friends showed off their new babies, when she peered into a stranger's pram or gazed into shop windows of infant clothes.

'Yes, I do,' she said. 'I'm nearly forty and if I am to have children I have to have them now. So – she'd tried to smile as she said it – am I to have them with you, or someone else?'

He'd realised how serious she was then, and had taken her by the shoulders and told her he loved her, and sat her down with a large glass of red and reminded her of what a great life they had, how good they were together, how faithful to her he had been,

'But,' he'd said, 'I can't do marriage. I just can't: a house in the country, children, schools, in-laws, the whole bit. They'd completely ruin our lives.'

She'd never found that someone else to have babies with, and if Tom hadn't almost immediately replaced her with a younger model, she'd have gone back to him, she knew, and on his terms. The truly painful thing had been that within eighteen months he was the proud father of twins, with a double page spread in *Hello* magazine trumpeting his new-found happiness in fatherhood.

And now, thought Joanna, there was Stewart. Or rather, she hoped there would be.

The truth was that over the last few weeks of negotiations, discussions with Innovest and planning for the future, Joanna had been falling in love with her chairman.

Apart from their business acumen and the ability to handle Joanna's success, Stewart had little in common with long-gone Tom. He never voluntarily talked about himself, and he would never, ever boast about anything, not even about his beloved Caroline. He was also infinitely more civilised. In the years since her affair with Tom, Joanna had discovered the pleasures of art, music, theatre, even of playing tennis. Her life now was much richer and more interesting than the glitzy socialising Tom had provided. And Stewart, she knew, would understand and share her love of concerts and opera or of trailing round museums.

But was he remotely in love with her? She had no idea if he felt what she felt. Maybe he was just flirting with her . . . Sometimes it seemed as though they were tipping into something close and deep, but then she would decide that this was wishful thinking. That they were more than colleagues was certain, but she could not tell if he desired her.

They normally lunched together when she was in Wakefield or he was in London, and he made a point of discussing personal stuff before business. It was one of the most attractive things about him – the way he was interested in her life: her garden, her friends, what she did with her time. And, if she pressed him, he talked to her honestly about his marriage, his children, even admitting his unfair preference for Caroline over Mark, and the unexpected hole in his life when Elaine died.

'To be honest,' he'd said, 'I didn't think I'd miss her as I did. I suppose I took her for granted. We seldom had a cross word, and we rubbed along together just fine. But there was no longer any excitement in it, though we both loved the Wakefield choir. I seldom thought of her, never telephoned her during the day, didn't look forward to holidays, though we went to great places together. And yet I missed her terribly.'

'And now?'

'No, I've got used to her absence. And, in truth, it had become a rather dull marriage by the end.'

'But is there ever excitement in a long marriage?' Joanna had asked. 'I've never been married, but I imagine you'd have said pretty well everything you have got to say to each other after thirty years, wouldn't you?'

'Maybe, but if so, it's sad. Anyway, I feel badly now. Because Elaine was a bit deaf and refused to wear a hearing aid – vanity I suppose – having a conversation could be a strain, and I'm a lazy bugger and I didn't make the effort.' He'd sat back, shaking his head. 'So latterly we didn't discuss anything really.'

Joanna had been struck by the generosity of this remark: it was *his* fault for not trying, not Elaine's for refusing the hearing aid. It was typical of him. He seldom had anything unkind to say of anyone and his ability to see the good in people was very appealing.

'The thing is,' he'd continued, 'what I remember now is not our later years, though of course there were still some good things: dinner on the table, someone who cared. I think more of the way we used to talk when we were young, when we discussed every detail of each other's lives, and were genuinely interested. Her work in a primary school, mine as a travelling salesman.'

'A travelling salesman! What did you sell?'

'Batchelor's Surprise Peas.'

'What on earth . . . ?'

'Don't you remember them? No, you were probably in Australia then. They were freeze-dried peas, tiny little things, electric green, and they plumped up with boiling water. They were huge sellers for a few years until frozen peas saw them off.'

'And you sold them. Who to?'

'Mainly village grocers. I used to bump all over the Highlands of Scotland in a Morris Minor van demonstrating the marvels of my peas to independent grocers and village stores.' He'd chuckled at the memory. 'I learnt a lot about the grocery business, that's for sure.'

'Like what?'

'Like what a hard job it was. And that I should definitely do something else with my life. If you were the village grocer in the Highlands of Scotland in the seventies, you had to get into the store hours before it opened to shake the weevils out of the walnuts, and scrub the ox tongue you'd fished out of the brine tub, and put fresh sawdust on the floor.' His face was alight with his tale, and Joanna felt her enthusiasm being kindled by his. He went on. 'They were great characters, those grocers. Heart of the village. Making sure Mrs McFee got her pilchards in tomato sauce or her corned beef, stocking both fine and coarse oatmeal so that porridge could be made to suit the laird in the Manse or Mrs Douglas down the road. Giving thieving school kids a clip round the ear . . .'

Joanna loved the talk, but increasingly found herself looking at Stewart's eyes, or mouth, often his hands, as he spoke.

Up until last Wednesday, she could tell herself that she was just having fun, enjoying the attention, and maybe a bit of flirting and fantasy; that any attraction wasn't serious and she could walk away anytime, no problem.

But last week, after they had concluded the deal with Innovest and were walking down Cheapside looking for a cab, Stewart had put his arm round her neck, pulling her to him, like students and children do.

'Jo, let's go across the river and have a drink. To celebrate your getting us out of Innovest's clutches, and, more important, your throwing in your lot with us. Anyway, I don't feel like a two-hour train journey back to an empty house. What about you?'

Her heart had given a triumphant little lurch. Maybe tonight's the night, she thought, giddy as a teenager.

They'd sat side by side on a sofa with a view of the river. The winter light quickly faded to dusk, and they watched the water darken as the embankment lights went on. Golden oldies were playing in the bar, and they got mildly drunk on Bellinis and hummed along. They discovered that they both knew all the words of 'Smoke Gets in Your Eyes', and of 'Raindrops Keep Falling on My Head'. They ended up eating tapas and talking, like they had on the train, for hours.

Lightheaded with drink, warm in their winter coats but with cold cheeks and misty breath, they had ambled along the Jubilee Path on the south side of the river, talking about everything and nothing. They'd crossed Westminster Bridge, admiring London like tourists. They stopped in the middle, silenced by the spectacle.

The riverfront was mesmerising. The tide was in and the water glittered darkly below the floodlit buildings and sparkly bridges, with St Paul's so serene and confident among her brasher neighbours, the millennium wheel a joyous thing, the familiar parliament buildings still magical.

And then they walked on, along the Embankment towards the City again, her arm through his, both of them softly singing 'Smoke Gets in Your Eyes'. Joanna's throat did not tighten and she didn't miss a note. Stewart teased her.

'I thought you couldn't sing. Was all that about your throat closing a fiction then? You sing like a dream.'

'I'm better than I was, thanks to Nelson's lessons. But my throat can still clamp up if I'm not relaxed,' she said. 'I'm relaxed with you. You feel close and on my side.'

'I'm glad,' he said, looking at her solemnly. They were outside the Howard Hotel now. She knew he had a permanent suite here, but he'd never invited her to it. Now Joanna waited for him to usher her in.

But he guided her instead to the row of waiting taxis.

'Joanna, you are a dangerous woman. Dangerous to me, that is.'

There was an intensity in his voice, and when he kissed her on the cheek, he held her hard, just for a second, and then almost pushed her away. As he opened the cab door for her, his voice flattened and he said, almost formally, 'But you will be wonderful for Greenfarms. I know it.' His face broke into a grin. 'And with luck it will make you even richer.'

Joanna forced a smile, disappointment enveloping her. How could he follow that merry drink, the long deep conversation, that walk through the glories of London with a peck on the cheek and a quip?

Joanna had not seen Stewart since that evening, and now, sitting in the pub, she was finding concentration on Greenfarms business almost impossible.

They wrapped up the meeting just as the citizens of Wakefield began drifting into the pub, and Stewart offered to drop her at the station. But she needed the loo first, and followed Caroline down the swirly red and blue carpet to the distant Ladies, her mind playing with the thought that Stewart might follow her onto the train as he did before, but this time in romantic rather than business pursuit.

When she came out of the cubicle, Caroline was washing her hands. Joanna smiled at her in the mirror, but though Caroline looked up and their eyes met, she did not return the smile. Joanna bent to swish her hands, dried them on a paper towel and followed Caroline to the door.

Suddenly Caroline spun round, her back to the door, barring Joanna's exit. Joanna stopped in surprise. Caroline's eyes, narrowed and hard, held hers.

'Just don't mess with my father, Joanna,' she said. 'You may be good news for the business. We will see. But you are not good news for the family, and Dad does not need another woman in his life.'

Joanna was too astonished to utter, and anyway Caroline turned away, opened the door and walked out. As she went, she said, 'Just so you know.'

Chapter Eighteen

Lucy waited for Joanna and Rebecca at Bentley's corner table. Joanna had offered to treat them to a pre-Christmas lunch, and Lucy was feeling rather good. She was used to a deal of fawning and fussing by head waiters — she was a restaurant critic after all — but the maître d' had told her she looked like a movie star, and on the way to their table she'd met a former colleague from the *Globe* who greeted her with, 'Lucy, what have you done? You look fantastic!'

The fact that she hadn't been able to remember the woman's name, did not, for once, worry her.

Now she looked at her reflection in the mirror opposite. Her face, carefully made up, was framed by stylishly cut straight hair, shiny as a shampoo commercial. Until Rebecca had got at her she had seldom worn make-up at all, and when she had, it was what Rebecca called her Women's Institute look — pale pink mouth, and a tentative smudge of lilac on her lids. Now her skin was subtly smoothed with some expensive foundation, the shape of her wide cheekbones accentuated by blusher, her eyes satisfactorily dark and smudgy and her lipstick several shades browner than she'd ever have chosen unaided. At last, she thought, at the age of fifty-nine, I look as one might expect a successful globe-trotting journalist to look. And, damn it, I'm still that, even without the *Globe* column.

Her famous Donna Karan suit was buttoned up in winter mode, and the purple pendant was barely visible. The softness of the fine wool skirt and the slipperiness of its lining still pleased her. David wouldn't recognise me, she thought, I really feel fine, confident and in control – for once not sorry for myself or panicking about losing my mind. And a clear sunny day in December is such a treat. Cause for celebration. She signalled a waiter and ordered a bottle of champagne.

The others arrived together, and Lucy found herself smiling at the sight of them. Rebecca's backless high heels click-clacked across the hard floor and her skinny dress looked, Lucy thought, like a petticoat. She must be freezing. Joanna was elegant as ever in a brown trouser suit with a big pink cloth bow on her lapel. God, thought Lucy, I'll be a fashion writer next. When have I ever noticed clothes before?

Lucy endured her friends' exclamations and congratulations on her new look with embarrassed pleasure.

'I told you I'd make you beautiful!' said Rebecca. 'Aren't you thrilled?'

Lucy laughed while Joanna protested, 'Rebecca, how about a bit of modesty here? Maybe Lucy was beautiful already! Anyway, you look great, Lucy. Congratulations, both of you.'

The waiter appeared with the champagne and three flutes.

'Oh, I'm sorry,' Lucy said, her hand out to prevent him pouring it. 'I just ordered the house champagne, not the Bollinger.'

'There is no mistake, madam. The champagne is with the compliments of Mr Corrigan. And these.' He indicated a platter of oysters being respectfully laid in the middle of the table by a second waiter.

Lucy could not help being pleased and flattered, especially as Rebecca and Joanna were so impressed.

'Wow, Lucy,' said Rebecca. 'Does this happen wherever you go?'

Lucy shook her head, smiling. 'No. When I review a place I book in another name and am seldom recognised by the staff. But if the owner sees me, I might get fêted a bit. Bribery, I guess. But since I'm no longer on the *Globe*, and only doing reviews for *HOT Restaurant*

I'll get less of it in the future. The ridiculous Orlando Black will get the treatment.'

'Well, I could get used to this,' said Joanna. 'This is such a treat. Isn't it odd that however old you get, there are some things that still feel very "grown-up" and special. I feel as if I'm playing the part of a lady who lunches. But we *are* ladies who lunch.'

'Well, today anyway,' said Lucy. 'I've eaten in countless smart places but almost always for work. Very seldom like this, just with friends, and no note-book recording every mouthful.'

The oysters, Lucy noticed, had been carefully thought out. There were nine of them, three of each variety. Three were topped with a green salsa, three with a red one, and three plain. The women all ate one of each variety, throwing their heads well back and inserting the oyster shells deeply into wide open mouths.

There was much oohing and aahing about the coriander and lemon dressing, and the kick of the chilli in the tomato and red pepper salsa. They followed the oysters with lobster tagliatelle and then Chef Corrigan's retro-chic rhubarb and custard, and drank the champagne with rueful remarks about middle-age spread. But for once Lucy did not feel guilty – she had lost six pounds and a single blow-out on really good food wouldn't hurt.

Then, over coffee, Joanna said, 'Listen, you two, I've got some news and a proposition.' Caught by her serious tone, Lucy and Rebecca looked up, expectant.

'Go on then, out with it,' said Lucy.

'Well,' said Joanna – colouring slightly, Lucy noticed – 'I think I'm in love, or something pretty near it.'

'Jo! How wonderful!' Rebecca exclaimed. 'It's Stewart from that greenie company, isn't it? I knew it!'

'How did you know that? I've never said a word!'

'Yeah, but every time you talk about the business, it's Stewart, Stewart, Stewart.'

Lucy leant across and put her hand on Joanna's arm. 'I hope he's in love with you too?'

'Well, no, I'm not sure that he is. Sometimes I think . . .'

'Has he said so?' demanded Rebecca. 'You don't want him messing you around, Jo-Jo.'

'I don't think he'll do that. I know he likes me. And he thinks I'm the business when it comes to managing companies so I guess he respects me too. And we talk for hours and hours about everything under the sun. And he's affectionate . . .'

'C'mon Jo, are you sleeping together?' Rebecca demanded.

'Becca,' Lucy remonstrated, 'give the woman a chance.'

Joanna shook her head and Rebecca said at once, 'Well, does he kiss you? Do you . . . ?'

'No, we aren't, and he hasn't. Not yet. But I have a feeling he's holding back. Sometimes I am sure he's attracted to me – I know it – but then nothing happens.'

Lucy said, 'Isn't he a recent widower? Maybe he's still grieving.'

Joanna thought about this for a moment. 'Could be, though his wife's been dead quite a while now. Or it could be his daughter. Perhaps he's scared of complications.'

She told them about the scene in the Ladies with Caroline.

'What a bitch!' said Rebecca. 'Why shouldn't her father . . .'

'No, no, Becca!' Lucy interrupted, 'Caroline is just jealous and frightened. She's lost her mother and she's scared stiff she'll lose her father too.'

Joanna suddenly sat back and said, 'I can't believe I told you all this. I wish I hadn't because maybe nothing will come of it. Anyway, enough of Stewart. What's up with you two, besides shopping? Rebecca, how is our singing teacher? Is it getting serious?'

Rebecca said, 'No, no chance. The passionate twice-a-night-bit never lasts longer than six months, does it? But . . .'

Lucy laughed. 'Rebecca, I don't know about Joanna, but I've not done enough personal research to know. So we'll believe you.'

'It's true,' Rebecca went on. 'I heard some guy on the radio explaining why, but I've forgotten the explanation. Anyway, after six months it gets to be more good friends than lovers, or goes off the boil altogether. We're still bubbling along after, let's see, April to Jan . . . Good God, that's nine months!' She looked at them in astonishment. 'That's a long time if you aren't serious, isn't it?'

'And you aren't serious?'

'No, of course not. Nelson is hardly husband material is he? But he's a lovely guy and I have to say he's blissful in bed.'

Joanna signalled for the bill, writing in the air with a raised hand to a passing waiter. She hated the inevitable wait to settle up at the end of the meal.

There was a slight argument about the bill, both Rebecca and Lucy wanting to pay, but Joanna insisted it was her treat, and anyway her company would pick up the tab.

'You canny thing. You can't put us down to expenses can you?' said Rebecca.

Joanna passed her the chocolates and said, 'Probably, yes. Remember I said I had some news and a proposition. Stewart is the news. Now comes the proposition, a business one.'

Joanna reached down and removed a folder from of her briefcase. She pulled out two full page photographs and handed one to Lucy and one to Rebecca.

Lucy looked at hers. The photograph was of a wide two-storey house perched on the edge of a cliff, the distant sea dotted with sailing boats. The picture had been taken from the side so that some of the terraced garden in front of the house could be seen. It had palm trees to the side, and a mass of flowering rhododendrons and azaleas to the front. On a terrace on the cliff side was a long slate table and iron chairs.

Puzzled, Lucy and Rebecca swapped pictures. The second photograph was of the same house, but taken from the sea. It showed a shingle beach, a small quay and boathouse, and a precipitous set of stone steps zigzagging up the cliff with the enormous house, low and many-windowed, at the top. The sky was picture-postcard blue behind the palms, the froth of rhododendrons riotously pink.

'Good God, Joanna, you haven't bought this, have you? Where is it? The Caribbean?'

Joanna laughed. 'No and no. It's in Cornwall.'

'Cornwall? What's with Cornwall?' Rebecca asked.

'I've been asked by Innovest – you know, my company – to look after this place,' replied Joanna. 'It's called Pencarrick and it's a sort of holiday resort with summer school attached. They teach all kinds of stuff – cookery, sailing, painting, jewellery-making and so on. I went there last week and it's really something.'

Lucy was confused. 'But I thought Innovest were investors, or business backers or something?'

'The owner wants to borrow a shedload of money to turn it into a much posher hotel, and to add a spa, etc,' said Joanna. 'The rest of the Innovest board are not too keen, but I've rather fallen for the place, and fancy spending some of the summer there. So I persuaded my colleagues to let me do a feasibility study about future expansion, property values and generally assess the business potential. Even if we invest, we won't be doing any alterations until after the season anyway, so it's a good opportunity to check the owner's business nous and see what's what.'

'Doesn't sound like a money-spinner to me,' said Lucy. 'It must be very seasonal, and I doubt if they can charge much for a kids' sailing course.'

'No, I agree,' said Joanna, 'but money has been pouring into Cornwall lately. The idea is that with Cornwall's good weather, and airports becoming an increasing nightmare, the rich might like an exclusive, five-star resort where they can learn things or just get pampered. It's only four and a half hours from London by motorway or train, so there might be an all-year-round market for luxury short breaks. But the idea is that I investigate.'

'Could be fun.' Lucy put a chocolate truffle into her mouth and let it melt before swallowing slowly. 'Where in Cornwall?'

'On the south coast, miles from the caravanners and teenage ravers. There are wonderful walks along the cliff-tops—

'OK,' Rebecca interrupted, 'the commercial sounds terrific. But where do we come in? You said you had a proposition?'

Joanna stirred the froth on her cappuccino and said, 'I thought Lucy could teach a few short cooking or cookery-writing courses, which would give us an idea of what the market is, and Becca, you could advise me on the décor. The survey didn't find any structural problems but the interior is shabby and the current designers haven't a clue.'

'Brilliant! I'd bite your hand off!' exclaimed Rebecca, eyes alight with excitement. 'Bill never lets me do a whole job. But I swear I'm better than him!'

Joanna laughed. 'Don't get too carried away. All we'll do this summer is plan the décor, run the place much as before with guest tutors, see what works and what doesn't, and make recommendations.' She turned to Lucy. 'What do you say, Lucy?'

Lucy was suddenly sure this was all an elaborate subterfuge. Joanna was inventing the plan, or somehow bending it, into a Save Lucy project.

'Joanna, are you including us to stop me getting depressed?'

Joanna, Lucy was relieved to see, looked completely nonplussed. Oh God, she thought, now I'm being paranoid.

'No, OK, I'm sorry, Jo,' she went on, 'but I seem to go up and down like a bloody yo-yo. I was feeling great on account of this posh suit Rebecca made me buy, but I'm so neurotic . . .'

'Forget it, darling,' said Rebecca, her hand on Lucy's. 'Joanna is a control freak but she isn't going to stage a summer in Cornwall just to get you on an even keel. Are you, Joanna?'

'Lucy,' replied Joanna, 'your husband died, what, maybe a year ago? You are allowed to be as neurotic as you like. But you've still got to come to Cornwall. I need you.'

The women met again that evening for the singing class. Lucy had very nearly cancelled. Was being chronically sleepy in the afternoon a product of stress or of old age? Or too much champagne at lunch?

But a pot of tea, made for her by Grace, had restored her

somewhat, and the thought of the argument she'd get from her daughter if she chucked the class had her changing out of her smart suit and into comfortable trousers and top.

The group's singing was improving. The choir had expanded and been joined by some good singers. Over the last year they had progressed from blues and simple gospel hymns to Schubert and Handel. There was talk of them singing Handel's *Messiah* at Christmas, and tonight they had another go at the Hallelujah chorus. Lucy knew she'd sung it better, many times, with David, but it still had the power to exalt. It is singer-proof, she thought. The most untrained school choir would enjoy doing it, and even if they did it badly, something sublime would get through.

They sang carefully at first, all eyes on Nelson, but as the tempo increased and hallelujah piled on hallelujah, Nelson loosened the reins a bit, and the singers began to lose themselves in the sound. It was the first time they'd sung the chorus right through and Lucy realised that Nelson, for once, was letting them just enjoy it unchecked.

After the last note there was a tiny moment of complete silence, everyone still lost in the glory of the music, reluctant to return to earth.

Lucy looked at her fellow singers. They all shared that open, fulfilled look that singing brings, their eyes alight and their bodies relaxed. Only Joanna had her eyes closed. She stood with her fingers resting lightly on her throat, her face suffused with a deep content.

Lucy watched as Joanna opened her eyes and met those of Nelson. He nodded slightly, gravely, a tiny gesture of approval and congratulation. Joanna's face slowly broke into a smile, and then a grin. Lucy, standing next to her, put an arm around her and gave her a quick squeeze.

Nelson punched the air with an exultant fist. 'Wow, that was good, guys, really good! And you see,' he said, turning to Joanna again, 'you found yo' singin' voice, Jo! I told you we'd do it, didn't I? All you needed was time and a little help from yo' friends!'

Chapter Nineteen

In February, on her fifty-sixth birthday (though she did not tell him that) Joanna invited Stewart to dinner. For months they had met in restaurants or pubs, and of course in the Greenfarms or Innovest offices, but he had never been to her house.

It was a Friday and she took most of the afternoon off. As she plumped cushions, tidied magazines, arranged flowers and cooked the dinner, she became more excited and more nervous.

She dressed in a cream wool skirt, clingy and long, a cream silk shirt, short stone cardigan, flat shoes. No jewellery – just careful make-up so she'd look good without seeming to try too hard.

Stewart arrived with a present, a pretty sea-green bracelet made of flat glass beads linked with silver wires.

'Oh Stewart, it's so pretty. Really lovely. Much more delicate and feminine than the things I usually wear! Thank you.'

She wriggled her hand into the bracelet and held her wrist against the cream of her skirt, admiring it.

'It suits you,' he said, taking her wrist and turning her hand over to look at it. 'You should indulge your frivolous side sometimes.'

She noticed how cool his hand was on her wrist. 'Where did you get it?'

'Some gifty shop in St Moritz. We were staying at the chalet.'

Joanna didn't question him further. 'We' would have been he and Caroline, and she did not want to hear that they'd bought a job-lot of presents, or that he'd bought the bracelet for his daughter and she'd rejected it. He would not, she was sure, have deliberately set out to buy her a bracelet, but she was thrilled with it anyway.

Joanna showed him round the house and turned on the garden lights so they could look at it through the windows, without venturing into the cold. To her eyes it looked rather bedraggled and wintry, but he was full of praise.

When she led him into the dining room, he looked at the carefully laid table, surprised.

'Just me? I'd somehow imagined a dinner party?'

Oh God, thought Joanna, he's feeling cornered. Did I mean to corner him? Do I mean to?

'No. Oh dear, I'm sorry, were you expecting interesting glitterati? I'm afraid it's just me.'

'Good.' He sat down, smiling. 'Dinner for two is just fine.'

Joanna had played safe with the food: really fine smoked salmon to start, a couple of lamb shanks bought ready cooked from the deli, a green salad made exclusively of romaine with a lot of avocado in it, and cheese. It was good, Joanna knew, but she was still, in spite of two glasses of wine, a little nervous.

I'm talking too much she thought, but Stewart's capacity for silence and his steady gaze on her were unnerving.

He was spreading goat's cheese on a biscuit when he suddenly dropped his knife and biscuit on the plate and stood up.

'Stop talking, Joanna.' He came round and pulled her to her feet. He said, very quietly and deliberately, 'There's no help for it, Jo, I have to make love to you. Now.'

She let him take her hands and for a second closed her eyes. Oh, God, it was happening. She had longed for this moment for months. He led her into the bedroom and turned to face her. Neither of them spoke as he pushed her cardigan slowly off her shoulders. It fell to the floor behind her. When he reached for the top button of her shirt she saw that his hands were trembling and she had to help him. He pushed the shirt off her shoulders as he had the cardigan.

Her eyes on his, she reached behind her back to undo her bra.

He held her gaze as she slipped her arms from the straps. And then he dropped his eyes and whispered, 'Oh, Joanna'.

Her heart was thumping as he pulled her quickly into his chest, one strong arm around her back, one hand under her breast, his warm breath on her neck. She wanted to stay like this for ever.

She stayed still, feeling the rise of raw lust invade her. She could feel the texture of his jacket against her bare breasts – she thought she could feel the exact herringbone pattern of it. She could smell the sharp lemony scent of his aftershave, hear every gradation of his rapid breathing.

She could no more help herself than a puppet. Her head went back and his mouth came down on hers. 'Oh, Stewart,' she said, 'Please, please.'

For a second Joanna looked at the empty bed beside her and thought it had not happened. A grey wave of loss engulfed her. Was last night a fantasy; a figment of her longing?

And then the bathroom door clicked and Stewart walked in, a towel around his waist.

She sat up, almost sick with relief. She wrapped her arms around her knees. 'Oh Stewart, I thought for a minute that it didn't happen. That I'd imagined last night!'

He came and sat on the side of the bed and took her face in his hands. She could feel a foolish grin spreading across it.

'Silly girl,' he said, as though she were a child. 'Let's fix the memory a little more firmly then.' He pushed her knees flat and pulled the sheet off her. Then he yanked her by the ankles to lie her flat and stood looking down at her.

Joanna immediately worried that he would notice her knees. They looked all right bent, but when straight she really hated them, especially the right one which was worse than the left. She brought them up a little to iron out the creases. But Stewart was not interested in her knees.

'You've got the body of a young woman,' he said, his voice deep with desire. He leaned over to run his hands over her breasts, feel her ribcage and belly as if she were an animal he intended to buy. As he slid his hand between her thighs, he added, 'With the responses of a very grown-up one.'

It was true. As soon as he'd flipped back the sheet, even before he'd touched her, a warm flood of longing had run through Joanna. And now that his voice was enveloping her, transfixing her, all concern about her age, her legs, evaporated. She could not prevent her body squirming slightly under his gaze and her breath quickening.

His skin was damp from the shower and smelled of soap, and his fresh-shaved cheeks were smooth and delicious. He made love to her slowly and so deeply that he had her crying out. And then, as she was drifting into sleep, she felt his kiss on her neck.

'I want more, darling, we have to do it again,' he whispered. Joanna wanted only to lie still, to sleep and drift, but he would not listen and caressed her again and again to a pitch of pleasure, each time more agonising than the last.

When he finally let her rest, and held her as she lay on his shoulder, she felt completely drained, floating on a sea of exhaustion. He told her she was the lover he always wanted, the more desirable because she was not a girl. Joanna did not really believe him, but it did not matter. She'd never felt such deep content.

They slept for an hour then. When they woke again, she said, 'I've never had such a good birthday in my life.'

'What? Is it your birthday?'

'Was. Yesterday. And you gave me this.' She showed him her arm, the bracelet on her wrist.

He kissed her wrist and palm below the bracelet and said, 'Very inadequate birthday present. We'll go to Bond Street and improve on it.'

She shook her head. 'No. I love it.'

'You're one hell of a woman, Joanna. Under that pin stripe

business persona is a very sexy beast.' He sat up and ruffled her hair as one might a child's. 'How old is the birthday girl?'

'Much too old and wise to tell you that.'

'Ah, well,' he said. 'Wise you may be. Old you are not. But more important: can you fry eggs? Because I like mine sunnyside up and on toast. I'm going for the Sunday papers.'

Joanna wore happiness like a coat. It was such a cliché, and she never thought it could happen to her again, but she felt giddy with longing. When she saw the name Stewart on her mobile phone display, her guts would turn to water, and she would have to close her eyes while she listened to his voice.

And he was so surprising. One evening he was hanging his trousers neatly in the trouser-press when something heavy fell from the pocket.

'Oh yes,' he said, bending to pick up a small leather box. He tossed it onto the bed in front of her.

'I bought you this today.'

It was a Patek Philippe watch.

It was beautiful. So classic and pared-down. Elegant and special, but no flash or bling about it.

'But . . . why?' she said, puzzled. It's not my birthday . . .'

'I know. But I saw it and thought you'd like it, so . . .'

'But . . .'

'You do like it? You can change it.'

Joanna swapped her workday watch for the flat-faced square one, buckling the gold bracelet with care. She could not help thinking that this watch must have cost a fortune. She was a little ashamed of her pleasure in the thought. Being bought an expensive present was a buzz she'd seldom felt.

She looked up to thank Stewart, but he was already in the bathroom, electric toothbrush whirring. She stretched out her arm turning her wrist to admire the thin roman numerals, her mind going back to the time he brought her the bracelet from St Moritz and they'd gone to bed together for the first time.

This Darby and Joan romance should be embarrassing, she thought, but I don't care.

Her whole life was suddenly exciting and pleasurable. She was now convinced that Greenfarms would come good. And working only part-time for Innovest meant that she could meet Stewart for lunch or dinner more or less when she liked, that she could sneak up to meet him in the Wakefield Hotel when he couldn't come to London. None of his family knew of their affair, and they both preferred it that way. Caroline would be jealous as a snake and she had enough to do restructuring the business without wasting time hating Joanna.

And Joanna was enjoying playing house – fixing intimate dinners for two, candlelight included. And having someone to talk to about her plans for the garden, and showing off her efforts after a morning of clipping or planting, were new pleasures. You forgot, being single and working all the time, how good it could be to share things, and how satisfying domestic nesting was.

She could not believe it. Being with Stewart was exciting, yes, but also comforting and relaxed in a way she'd no experience of. Being the centre of someone else's life was new to her. Even her serious affair with Tom, with both of them working flat out apart or playing flat out together, had been somehow part-time. And her parents' marriage had been less than loving, her mother demanding, her father trying to understand.

As a child she'd desperately wanted more of her father, but he was out on the farm all day and gave what time he had at home to her mother.

Once, she'd thrown herself off a ladder in the stable yard, just so he'd have to pick her up and kiss her better. To this day she could remember the bliss of that moment: his concern; the warm smell, horse sweat and leather, of his hands on her face; his enveloping arms; his kissing her eyes. Her tears had been genuine since she'd twisted her ankle and bruised her arm, but it was worth it.

Stewart's love was like that – all encompassing. She felt loved and safe, and more relaxed. And yet more energised too.

She was also excited about the Pencarrick project in Cornwall. She'd been doing some work on the business plan and the summer bookings were not bad. It had, she thought, real potential.

So life at the moment was all upside. Even another scene with Caroline failed to dent her happiness. Her mobile rang as she was walking from the warehouse to the factory. *Caroline* on the display screen.

'Hello, Caroline. What's up?'

She thought Caroline was going to raise some issue about the redundancies they were trying to effect. She was being impossible about them, refusing to bite the bullet and endlessly finding reasons why some nice old chap was vital to the business.

'I want to see you. How long will you be here?' Her voice was tight.

'I'm catching the four-seventeen.'

'I'll be in your office in five minutes.' She hung up before Joanna could tell her she was not in her office, but in the delivery bay outside the warehouse. She headed back to the office, walking briskly through the chill spring wind, hugging her jacket around her and thinking bleakly that this had got to be about Stewart. Why else would Caroline's tone be so peremptory?'

Caroline was there ahead of her. She followed the young woman's bouncing step and swinging red hair into the building. Caroline did not stop in Joanna's office but swung through it to the boardroom. She shut the door behind her and leant against it as if to imprison Joanna, just like she had in the Wakefield pub loo.

Joanna took a deep breath but said nothing. The greatest weapon in any dispute is silence, she reminded herself. If you can keep your mouth mostly shut, your opponent will generally talk themselves into a compromise. Or lose it completely, which also gives you a kind of victory.

'What are you doing with my father?' Caroline said, her voice high and hard.

'Professionally or privately?' Joanna countered, deliberately cool in spite of a thumping heart.

'Privately of course. And anyway the question was rhetorical. I know very well what you're up to. You're screwing him, aren't you? What I want to know is why?'

'Caroline,' Joanna said, as gently as she could, 'I'm not going to discuss Stewart with you. If you want to ask your father anything, of course you can.'

Caroline lost it then. 'Don't fucking lecture me about what I can or cannot say to my father! You come here as Innovest's bloody vulture, picking the guts out of the business, destroying what the rest of us have slaved for years over, but that's not enough for you, is it?'

She was red-faced and near to tears, but she kept going. 'You have to go and shag my dad too. Maybe if you were a straightforward gold-digger after Dad's money and wanting to take my mother's place, it wouldn't be so bad, but it's all a power game with you lot, isn't it? How much money you can make, how much of a company you can grab, how many men you can shag, how many poor sods you can put out of work.'

There was plenty more in the same vein. At first Joanna found the tirade unfair and wounding, but as Caroline began to stumble and tears started to leak down her cheeks, Joanna felt sorry for her. She was so thin-skinned. She had lost her mother, she was still in danger of losing her business and she believed she was losing her father to her, too. She wasn't of course, or not entirely, but Caroline would not see that.

Poor girl, thought Joanna, she's neurotic as hell, but I feel for her. Only, I cannot play her game.

So Joanna just stood there, silent, until Caroline finally ran out of steam and slammed out of the room. Then she picked up the telephone and rang Stewart's direct line.

'Darling, Caroline has obviously found out about us – it seems your housekeeper has been less than discreet . . .'

'Oh God – where is she?'

'She's jumped into her car, so I expect she's going home like a wounded animal. Maybe you'd better follow her?'

Joanna did not know what Stewart had said to his daughter, but the next time the women passed each other, although Caroline did not respond to Joanna's greeting, she did not lay into her either.

Joanna had continued her strategy of cool professionalism, but she wasn't easy about it. She almost admired Caroline's rawness and outspoken passion. She, Joanna, could never open herself up like that: allow anyone to see that she cared that much. Being self-possessed and in control had been her strategy for all occasions. She'd never known any other way to play it.

But just recently, she mused, she'd been more vulnerable, less buttoned up. Was that weakness, or a good thing? Bursting into tears over her inability to sing had been humiliating at the time but had brought warmth and understanding from Rebecca and Lucy, and falling in love with Stewart had opened up a whole new way of behaving, one she had a lot less control over, but which certainly made life more valuable, more meaningful.

She stood at her office window, looking across at Caroline's house and the forest of solar panels marring a pretty view. Poor girl, she thought, my refusing to engage in a row must have been maddening for her. But the last thing she wants to hear is that I truly love her father – that would be much more of a threat to her than the story she's invented of my lust for power over all things.

The following Thursday, after several days of intense work and intense love in Wakefield, Joanna met Lucy and Rebecca at the community hall. Rehearsals for the *Messiah* had started in earnest and they were all enjoying it. Joanna had had no return of her throat problem and she wondered if a satisfying love life could help one's singing?

In the pub, after the rehearsal, Joanna told them about Stewart.

'You sly thing,' said Rebecca, admiration and envy sharing her face, 'you never said. When did he succumb? We need all the gossip, Jo-Jo. No holding back!'

Joanna had been a little ashamed about her previous confidences when she'd told Lucy and Rebecca about falling for Stewart. It was so juvenile to let on about one's secret desires, and she'd worried about how foolish she'd feel if nothing came of it. So it was both a relief and a pleasure to be able to tell them now about Stewart's sudden declaration of desire.

Joanna and Lucy teased her for stalking him for so long and she protested that she hadn't really been after him, and then had to admit that, yes, of course she had.

'But the problem was I wasn't sure he felt what I felt. It took him longer than me to give in and realise what was happening.'

'Of course,' said Rebecca. 'What's new? Men are slow.'

Lucy declared how delighted she was for Joanna, but worried about the damage that Caroline could inflict and fearful that Joanna would get hurt. She questioned her about Stewart's motives. Joanna laughed and protested.

'Lucy, for God's sake! Any minute you'll be asking me if his intentions are honourable!'

'And are they?'

'Yes,' she said, and she knew it was true. 'He has not said he loves me. But he does. And I love him.'

Three weeks later Joanna was again back in Wakefield. Stewart had asked her to help Caroline with the redundancies. It was over two months since she and Stewart had bought out Innovest, and relations with Caroline had not improved. Neither woman made any reference to Caroline's attack about Stewart. Joanna was briskly polite, Caroline unresponsive and unsmiling. And she was still disorganised and unfocused and had barely implemented any of the agreed plan to slim the workforce.

Joanna asked Caroline to go through the staff roll with her, help her understand who did what, what their talents were, who should go and who should stay. As the discussion continued, Joanna became increasingly frustrated as Caroline found a reason why every member of staff should stay and no reasons why anyone should go. In the end Joanna said, 'Caroline, we need some help here.'

She picked up the telephone and asked Alasdair to join them.

Caroline burst out, 'But Alasdair has nothing to do with production. He won't know any of the factory staff!'

'No, I agree, but only you and your brother really know the production side and Mark is hardly going to be the coolest judge since he's on notice himself. And you are reluctant to lose a single soul. So someone has to help. Alasdair has a cool head and a pretty good idea of how the factory runs, even if he doesn't know the individuals' strengths and weaknesses.'

Alasdair got the picture immediately. 'Let's leave the personalities out of this and draw up our ideal staffing picture, assuming we are going to achieve only five per cent more output next year than this. What would that give us?'

Within thirty minutes they had a list of jobs with a salary against each executive, and an estimated wage, based on likely hours, for each worker.

'Right,' said Joanna, 'now, Caroline, I'm sure there are some managers you'll want to keep more than others, and even some workers who work harder, or are pleasanter to be around, than others. If you do not help us pick the best, then we'll just have to do it with a pin.'

Caroline shook her head, the bouncing of her red hair exaggerating the gesture. 'But surely we have to obey the last in, first out rule, don't we? So that long service and loyalty counts for something?'

Alasdair said, 'Caro, before you get all stoked up, let's take the jobs one by one, and decide who you think would do them best. This is just a paper exercise. We need to start somewhere, and we need to make some assumptions. OK?'

Caroline looked from one to the other. 'But surely we cannot just pitch out the ones we don't like?'

Joanna did not react to Caroline's high-wire tone.

'If the job hasn't changed and we are happy with the job-holder, then obviously there's no problem. But if we know someone is no good, or is a square peg in a round hole, we may prefer to give that job to someone else. And of course that makes it easier for him or her to bring a case of unfair dismissal. We need to be careful as well as fair.'

'But what is fair about putting someone on the dole?'

'Caroline,' said Joanna, her voice firm but patient, 'we have to do this. For some people it will be hard. But you understand as well as any of us that if we don't trim costs to fit our new, smaller business, then everyone will end up out of work.'

'And,' added Alasdair, 'we will be as fair as we can. The losers will get their redundancy payments.'

'But you can't argue redundancy when their job is still there but you are giving it to someone you like better,' snapped Caroline.

'Agreed,' replied Joanna, 'which is why we need to see everyone personally. We need to see what sort of help the losers need – maybe they'd like early retirement, maybe they'll want retraining for another skill. There are options out there and we need to explain them to everyone. You and I should see them together, Caroline. It is important that they realise that you care as much as you do, but are nonetheless behind the plan.'

Caroline was gradually drawn into the discussion, and after nearly two hours, they had, on paper at least, halved the factory staff and got the best people in the jobs.

The next morning they called a lunchtime meeting of the workforce. They assembled in the factory on the empty side where most of the supermarket products were made. Stewart welcomed them and then handed over to Joanna, whom he introduced as one of the new owners of the business. Joanna stood on a couple of stacked pallets and addressed the room without a microphone and without a note.

'Good afternoon' she said. 'I will get straight to the point, which of course you have already guessed. We would not be standing in this inactive factory if there was work to fill it, and money to pay for that work. But the company had a simple choice: we could go on supplying the supermarkets and go slowly broke or we could go back to our roots and sell direct to our customers.'

She talked for fifteen minutes explaining in straightforward terms the situation they were in: the board's legal obligations; the need for cost reductions; the process ahead of them; the board's belief in a new future for Greenfarms. She ended by abruptly turning to Caroline and saying,

'That is all I have to say, but I know that Ms Muirhead wants to say something too.'

Caroline, startled and horrified, shook her head. But Joanna went close up to her and whispered, 'Just say what you feel. Tell them. Just tell them.'

Caroline stepped on to the pallet and looked around. She opened her mouth but, at first, no sound emerged. Then she cleared her throat, lifted her chin, and spoke.

'If I had known this day would come, I would never have started Greenfarms.' She looked down at her shoes, fighting tears, then jerked her shoulders back and looked to the back of the room.

'No, that is not true. If that were true I would never have got to know any of you. I would not have learnt from Joe (her eyes scoured the room, looking for Joe, found him and lifted her hand in greeting) what a hard and miserable job potato picking is. I would not have discovered from the Smythe family just how cold it is to pack spinach and cabbage in the winter.

'I would not have discovered what wonderful cooks Damien and Sally are. After a day in the fields in winter we all know how good Greenfarms soup can be.

'I would not have been able to open a profitable farm shop if Dana had not come into our lives and worked every hour God gives to make it pay.

'We would not have had the excitement of our first factory, with geothermal heating and solar generated electricity.

'The truth is, even if we had to close Greenfarms today, I would be grateful for what we – all of us – have done here. We've trodden lightly, not damaged the soil, not polluted water or air, not poisoned anyone. We've done our bit for the community, and for the planet. We are the good guys.'

She paused and again lifted her head, 'And we will do it again. We will grow direct sales, and supply more schools with proper meat and veg.' She looked across at her father, who nodded slowly. 'The only bugger, and it is a real bugger, is that it will take time before we again employ everyone who wants to work for us. In the meantime, we will, I promise, do the very best we can for you.'

There was absolute silence, every eye upon her. Joanna saw that, far from being glad the ordeal was over, Caroline was almost reluctant to leave them, like a singer having to break the spell after a great song. Finally, she seemed to come out of her trance. She took a breath, said, 'Thank you,' and stepped off the pallet.

Someone started to clap, others took it up, and soon everyone was clapping. They had, in their understanding of Caroline's passion and their affection for the company, momentarily forgotten that tomorrow they might not have a job.

Stewart walked back to the office between his daughter and Joanna. His arm round Caroline, he turned to Joanna.

'She's quite something, is she not?'

Joanna nodded. 'She is. I've never seen anything like it.'

'Well, it's hard for me to admit this,' Caroline said, 'but, Joanna, you were very good in there.'

'I was good? Good Lord, Caroline, you were absolutely brilliant.'

'But you knew I had to speak to them. I didn't. Why didn't you warn me?'

'Because you would not have spoken as you did. You'd have rehearsed something and it would not have come from the heart.

It was a risk, but I was pretty sure the real Caroline would come through.'

Stewart and Caroline paused at the office steps, and Caroline faced Joanna.

'The real Caroline?'

'Yes,' said Joanna, her hand lightly touching Caroline's arm, 'the transparent, driven, idealistic, just great Caroline.'

Chapter Twenty

The 'Rebecca suit' and purple and silver pendant were getting another outing. Rebecca had invited her to dinner.

It was the first time since David's death that Lucy was going out, alone, to a formal social event. Of course she often went to restaurants on her own, or to meet people she was writing about, and occasionally to friends for supper, but setting out, without a mate, to go to a dinner party where she would meet strangers, was new. She hoped she'd got it right and was not going to find everyone in jeans and T-shirts.

It was ridiculous at her age to feel apprehensive. She found herself wishing Joanna was going to be there, but Joanna was in Wakefield. I'd better get used to it, she thought, walking alone into a roomful of strangers is the single woman's price for any social life at all. I should be grateful. Not many people invite lone women – it upsets their table plan.

On the way back from the hairdresser Lucy had stopped at Baker and Spice and bought a box of tiny ginger biscuits covered in chocolate. They smelt delicious and she was glad the salesgirl had sealed them in a fancy little carrier bag. If she'd been able to get at them she'd have eaten at least a couple in the taxi. But she arrived at Rebecca's flat with her present intact.

'Oh, yum,' said Rebecca, tipping them out into a dish. 'We'll have them with coffee.'

Rebecca's daughter Angelica was there, and Lucy was struck by her physical resemblance to her mother. She was dressed in black trousers with a black cowl-neck top and flat patent shoes like ballet pumps. Her blonde hair was tied at the back of her neck in a demure velvet scrunchie, but she wore no jewellery, not even a watch. She was pretty and feminine, with creamy skin, and Lucy wondered for a moment whether Rebecca was proud of her daughter's appearance or irked by such a constant reminder of how she herself had once looked. Probably both.

While her mother darted about, looking distracted, Angelica sat quietly on the sofa, talking to, or rather listening to, two men.

They must be the father and son pair, thought Lucy. Rebecca had told her and Joanna that she had designs on the son, who was something big in computer software, for Angelica. And this little dinner party was to set them up. Lucy, watching Rebecca abandon her attempt at arranging flowers – presumably a gift from one of the guests – in favour of sitting herself on the arm of the older man's chair to join the conversation, wondered if perhaps Rebecca had designs on the father for herself. She had not invited Nelson, Lucy noticed.

Lucy accepted a glass of champagne from the remaining male guest, who introduced himself as Bill, Rebecca's ex-husband. He had a friendly, open face, a little fleshy, and Lucy liked him at once.

After a few minutes of pleasantries, he said, 'Maybe I'd better fix those roses. Rebecca has obviously forgotten them. Will you excuse me?' He picked up the flowers and their wrappings, scissors and vase and disappeared into the kitchen.

Lucy, thinking she might help, followed him, and looked round in horror. The kitchen was a complete tip, the sink full of dirty pots and pans and every surface covered with food in various stages of preparation.

'Ah!' joked Bill. 'This brings back rather forcibly what marriage to Rebecca was like!'

Lucy laughed and quickly cleared a space, and between them they cut short the rose stems and put them into a different, squat vase. Bill carried them through to the drawing room, while Lucy calculated how she could best get some order into this chaos. She had just found an apron (under a carrier bag of groceries) and put it on when Rebecca came in.

'Lucy Barnes, will you get out of here!'

'But Becca, you could do with a hand, couldn't you? It will only take a minute for me to clear—'

'Lucy, you are so bossy! Go away! I know what I'm doing, really. So go and be a guest please. I'm fine.'

'OK, OK, I'm going. But yell if you want help.'

The guests had all arrived by eight-fifteen, but by nine-thirty there was still no sign of any dinner. Rebecca had made several forays into the kitchen, though Lucy had not dared follow her. She noticed that Rebecca was becoming increasingly flushed, whether from the strains of hostessing or from the champagne, she did not know.

Angelica was quietly serving more drinks, and Lucy went up to her.

'Angelica, do you think I should help your mum? I did offer, but . . .'

Angelica looked worried. 'Poor Mum, she's hopeless at this sort of thing, but she's just bitten my head off for interfering, so I'm waiting for her to demand help, which she will any minute.'

'Will she? It's nine-thirty!'

Angelica gave a rueful smile. 'Well, she'd better, because we're running out of champagne.'

Lucy had noticed that an attempt to lay the table had foundered. This is crazy, she thought. We will all be dead drunk if Rebecca does not produce some food soon.

She strode back to the kitchen and put her head round the door.

'Becca, can I at least lay the table?'

Rebecca turned from rootling in the fridge, and as she did, a large glass dish slipped from its perilous position on top of something else and crashed to the floor, splattering floor and fridge with what Lucy now recognised as trifle. The glass dish was in pieces.

'Jesus, Lucy, if you would just not interfere . . .'

Angelica had heard the crash, and came in. She looked from Lucy to Rebecca and then quietly fetched kitchen roll and dust pan.

'I'll do it,' said Lucy taking the cleaning things from her. 'You do the table.'

'Thanks, Lucy.' Angelica turned to her mother: 'Don't worry Mum, no one needs pudding.'

Rebecca rounded on her daughter. 'Angelica, you may think I am a waste of space but I am just about capable of clearing up this mess! You can't ask a guest to—'

'It's fine,' said Lucy, 'I offered.'

Rebecca made a grab for the dust pan but Lucy held it aloft.

'Mum,' said Angelica, 'everyone is starving. Let's just get them fed, shall we?'

'God Almighty!' exploded Rebecca, 'could you *not* use that nursemaid voice on me? The patient, long suffering voice of reason! It drives me mad.'

Angelica, miraculously, did not fight back.

'Fine, I'll go and lay the table.'

But Rebecca, who was, Lucy realised, quite drunk, was not going to leave it at that. She caught her daughter by her arm.

'Just do as we agreed, Angelica, and pour the drinks.'

'Mother,' said Angelica, her voice finally betraying suppressed anger, 'the champagne is finished. Everyone has had too many drinks, especially you.'

'So now I'm a drunk like your father, am I?'

'Dad has not touched a drop for years as you very well know. And no, Mother, you are not a drunk. But you're a useless cook. Why don't you do what you do best and go and chat up those men out there?'

Oh God, thought Lucy, this is heading for a full scale family row. She left the dust pan and brush on the floor and steered Angelica towards the door. 'Go and lay the table,' she said.

Angelica hesitated, her face pink and her bottom lip not quite steady, then she nodded and turned to leave the kitchen. At that moment Bill came in.

'What's going on girls? Any chance of dinner anytime soon?'

'Oh, fuck off, Bill,' snapped Rebecca.

Bill blinked in surprise but did not react. He looked at his flushed ex wife, his stony-faced daughter, Lucy bending to clear up the mess on the floor, and said to Rebecca,

'How about I take everyone out to dinner?'

Rebecca would not agree to this, but Bill did persuade her to rejoin the others with him, leaving Angelica to lay the table and Lucy to rescue the supper.

Lucy really enjoyed it, in spite of the mess, lack of space and need for urgency. She was doing what she was good at and she spun round the kitchen like a dervish, stacking stuff to make room, and working deftly and skilfully to get the show on the road.

First, where was the main course? She eventually found the dish, stone raw, in the cold oven. Rebecca had prepared two fat salmon fillets on a bed of sliced onion and potato. The fillets were sandwiched together with some sort of stuffing, and covered in foil. Rebecca had put them in the oven but failed to turn it on.

Angelica reappeared as Lucy was dismantling the fish.

'Wow, Lucy, what are you doing?'

'Well, I think speed is what we need, don't you? So I'm heating the soup, and we can eat that while I grill the fish. Your mama had forgotten to turn on the oven.'

'But what are you doing to it?'

'I'm afraid I am ditching her original idea. To heat the oven and bake this recipe would take at least an hour and anyway it's a bad idea. The salmon would be overcooked long before the potatoes were anything like ready.'

'But we had sea bass on potatoes like that at Geales the other day, and it was delicious. That's why Mum wanted to do it.'

'But they would have pre-cooked the spuds in a bit of fish stock.'

'Ah.'

Lucy turned the grill to maximum, separated the fillets, rinsed off the stuffing, and cut them across into smallish portions. She turned the pieces in a mix of honey and soy sauce.

'Could you find a bit of oil or butter or something and grease a sheet of foil to go on the grill tray?' she said.

'Why can't the fish go straight on the grill?'

'Because grills are hell to wash up, and the fish will stick to it.'

She smiled at Angelica. What an amazing girl, she thought. Any other daughter would have slammed out of the house after an exchange like that with her mother.

Lucy discovered the soup on the cooker and looked round for a spoon to taste it with. She couldn't see a clean one so dipped her finger into it and sucked it. You're not on telly now, she thought, there will be no calls from viewers on the need for hygiene. And anyway, heating the soup will kill the bugs.

The soup was OK. Spinach and pea, she guessed. But it lacked flavour. She looked around for something to gee it up with. She found some Marigold vegetable bouillon, a lemon, and best of all, a box of coconut cream.

'Why would a non-cook like your mother have coconut cream?' asked Lucy, 'or is it yours?'

'No, it's Mum's, but it's for making piña coladas.'

Angelica watched her doctoring the soup. 'I wish I could cook,' she said.

'I'll teach you if you like.'

'Would you? Really? I'd love that.'

'Well, I will. Why not?'

Lucy liked Angelica and felt for her. It could not be easy with a mother like Rebecca.

'What are we going to do to replace the potatoes?' asked Lucy. 'We need something that cooks fast. Pasta, or rice maybe?'

Angelica stared into a cupboard. 'How about couscous?'

'Even better, takes no time at all.' They couldn't find a steamer so Lucy poured half a packet of couscous into a serving dish and guessed how much boiling water to add. Then they chopped some of the spring onions and rocket intended by Rebecca for the salad. 'We'll reheat the couscous in the microwave and add this lot, and a handful of these peanuts, at the last minute. How about you finish making the salad and I'll have a go at the pud?'

'But that's a goner if you remember! It's in the bin.'

'There might be something we can do,' said Lucy, opening the fridge – cautiously to avoid a further cascade on to the floor. There was half a pint of thick cream in it and Lucy found a large pot of plain yogurt. She mixed them together, spooned them into coffee cups and topped them with maple syrup.

'I'd have preferred muscovado sugar. It liquefies into a wonderfully treacly syrup, but never mind, maple syrup is good. We could have used honey, like the Greeks do, but we've got honey on the salmon.' She put one of her Baker and Spice biscuits into each saucer.

'The soup's hot, my little commis chef,' said Lucy, giving Angelica a pat on the back. 'I'll stick the fish under the grill while you go ring the dinner gong.'

'That's amazing, Lucy,' said Angelica. 'That whole Ready-Steady-Cook performance took ten minutes. You're a genius.'

Lucy laughed. 'And the washing up will take for ever.'

Chapter Twenty-One

Both Lucy and Joanna had been dead reluctant about coming salsa dancing, Joanna with some nonsense about wanting to go back to Wakefield, and Lucy – more honest – just saying she wouldn't enjoy it. But the whole point was that the three of them should have a night out together, and they *would* enjoy it.

For a moment Rebecca feared the brute of a bouncer would not let them in, and of course neither Joanna nor Lucy was any help, telling her to forget it and that maybe salsa dancing wasn't such a bright idea after all. But Rebecca indignantly claimed they were guests of the owner, Clemente, and surely the man could recognise Clemente's mother when he saw her? Just as well he couldn't.

And were Lucy and Joanna grateful? Or impressed that she'd blagged their way in? Were they, hell. They were full of moral tut-tutting and anxiety about being too old for this sort of thing.

Anyway, here they were in the New Salsa Dive, which Rebecca thought was great. Expensive, but worth it. Most salsa clubs were small, hot and seedy, but this one was amazing. It used to be the basement of a vast postal sorting office.

A deafening blast of amplified music hit them as they entered, and Lucy looked at Rebecca with panic in her eyes. Joanna was as cool as ever, though Rebecca suspected she didn't want to be there either. Her smart red skirt, pencil-thin to her calves and her teetering heels would be impossible to dance in anyway.

The huge interior of the club was one giant fake: a film-set

Havana plaza, complete with decayed baroque colonnades round the sides. One whole side housed the bar. The restaurant was visible above, with filigree iron balconies and tall French windows. A wide pavement surrounded the dance floor, with café tables and giant cane armchairs, and along one side three real nineteen-fifties American cars with leather upholstery were parked at the kerb. And what looked like the crumbling paving and irregular cobbles of a run-down Cuban square was all trompe l'oeil – it was a dead-flat dance-floor.

The place was heaving. Professional dancers, really cute young guys, were there to partner unattached women, just as luscious young hostesses pulled in the single guys. Couples were shimmying around the floor, groin to groin.

Lucy put her mouth to Rebecca's ear and shouted, 'I can't do this, Becca,' but Rebecca shouted back, 'Don't be a wuss! It will be great,' and took her hand and dragged her along, Joanna following. They edged past the line of cars, two of which were occupied by couples groping each other in the back seat. As they drew level with the big Buick with no one in it, Rebecca opened the back door on impulse and climbed in. The others followed, and they all sat in the back seat, laughing.

Rebecca leaned over the others and pulled the door shut. It clunked heavily, instantly halving the volume of sound. She said, 'I guess these cars are so you can pretend you are in the back seat of mom's Studebaker on Prom night. But they are good for talking too.'

'God, how does anyone talk in that din?' asked Joanna.

'They don't. No one talks to anyone,' replied Rebecca. 'They are all here for the dancing.'

'But,' said Lucy, 'I'd want to know if I liked someone before I danced with him, wouldn't you?'

They really are out of the ark, these two, thought Rebecca. 'Hell no,' she said, 'I want to know if he can dance. And that takes six seconds.'

Joanna asked what happened if he couldn't. 'I dump him of course. Just walk away.'

'I couldn't do that,' said Lucy, 'it's so rude.'

Rebecca decided not to take offence at this, and they sat in their sound-proofed igloo looking out at the dancers. Joanna looked aloof, Lucy anxious.

'They aren't all young,' Joanna remarked. 'Some are in their forties I suppose, but none as old as us. Rebecca, are you sure about this? Who's going to want to dance with us? '

No one if you look so bloody miserable about it, Rebecca thought but did not say. Lucy answered Joanna's question,

'No one,' she said, then shifted round to look directly at Rebecca. 'I'm sorry to be so feeble, Becca, but I didn't care for being a wallflower at sixteen and I don't want to repeat the experience now.' She looked at Joanna. 'Jo, I'm for cutting our losses and leaving if you are.'

Rebecca was getting seriously fed up with this. It was like wading uphill through treacle. You'd think she'd invited them to a sex orgy in a brothel, they were so determinedly negative. 'God, you're a pair of wet blankets,' she said. 'At least give it a go – how can you knock it if you haven't tried it?'

She saw Joanna and Lucy look at each other, undecided whether to walk out or to trust her. 'C'mon,' Rebecca insisted, 'let's get you some Dutch courage.'

They climbed out of the car and Rebecca pushed through to the bar, Lucy and Joanna reluctantly in her wake. Rebecca ordered three mojitos.

It's a good thing the music makes talking impossible, thought Rebecca, because Lucy and Joanna were so tight-lipped they would not be talking anyway. Lucy looked cross and unhappy and Joanna's expression had gone from cool to icy. Fuck the pair of them.

Within minutes a middle-aged man with broad shoulders and tiny feet took the near-empty glass out of her hand, put it on the bar, and led her onto the dance floor.

He was seriously good. God, what a relief, thought Rebecca, this is what I need.

They stamped and twirled and moved together like cogs of the same machine. Rebecca could feel her short skirt lifting and falling as she jiggled her bum and flashed her feet. She knew her legs looked good in her dancing shoes (she always wore her chunky Jimmy Choo sandals to dance in: they were not too high, with wide strong straps, and they had style).

Rebecca gave it her all. She was showing off, she knew, but why not? She liked being looked at. I'm sure that po-faced pair are full of disapproval, she thought, but what are we here for?

The man was a fantastic dancer. Rebecca was good, but he was better and he lifted her game. Some of the surrounding dancers fell back to give them space and were now watching. Rebecca found the audience a real turn-on. The beat got faster and faster, but the dancing had taken over now and she didn't have to concentrate. She could feel the sweat running down her spine and she was panting, but she felt she could keep going for ever.

When the music changed, they stopped and gave each other an involuntary high five and a kiss of congratulation.

As they headed for the bar, they met Joanna and Lucy at the edge of the dance floor. Both were grinning and they patted Rebecca on the back as though she'd won something. Good, she thought, at least they've stopped sulking.

Neither of them had been on the floor. Rebecca was aware of the very Latin-American convention in salsa clubs that women didn't ask men to dance. So under the pretence of going to the loo, she got weaving and found partners for Lucy and Jo. All the pros were dancing, or hiding, and she had to bully a couple of regular punters she knew into asking them to dance.

But within minutes Lucy had been dumped by her partner, and a few minutes later, Joanna was back too. She shouted above the noise that her dodgy knee was giving her trouble, but it didn't matter because she couldn't follow her partner anyway.

The three women went upstairs to the restaurant and ordered rice and black beans with fried sweet potato and mince. It was, as Rebecca knew it would be, awful. Normally, she'd never eat here. The dancing was great but who wants nineteen-fifties' Cuban food? But she had to do something with Jo and Lucy.

They were half way through the meal when Lucy suddenly said, 'Oh God, there's Orlando Black. Keep your heads down, he mustn't see us.'

'Why on earth not?' asked Rebecca. 'Do you know him Lucy? I'd love to meet him.'

Lucy muttered something about Orlando writing the column she used to do on the *Globe*. She hardly knew him; she'd seen him on the box, that was all.

He had the look of someone who knew he was turning heads. He had a half smile on his lips and a slightly detached gaze as he weaved his way between the tables. The look seemed to include everyone while never quite focusing on anyone in particular.

He walked past their table and Rebecca called out, 'Orlando!' He turned, looked confused, and then saw Lucy, who was apparently searching for something under the table. He stooped and picked up a napkin.

'It's Lucy Barnes, isn't it? Is this what you're looking for?' Lucy, obliged to straighten up, took the napkin, and smiled a forced thank you.

Rebecca filled the gap. 'I'm Rebecca,' she said quickly, 'and this is Joanna. Would you like to join us?'

He smiled into her eyes, a huge professional smile as if she'd offered him something wonderful. 'I'd love to, but I'm meeting someone. I'd better go find him.' He shrugged, apologetic. Then he turned to Lucy. 'But Lucy, I'm so glad we've met. I need to talk to you. Shall we do lunch? I'll call you.' And he was gone.

'Wow, is he gorgeous or is he gorgeous?' said Rebecca. 'He's—'

'How could you do that, Rebecca?' interrupted Lucy, her face flushed with anger. 'I told you I didn't want to meet him, told you

I didn't want him to see us. And you bloody call him over!'

Rebecca was amazed at this onslaught. 'Of course I did. He's cute. And famous. And I wanted to meet him. What's the matter with that?'

Joanna joined in. 'Becca, the point is Lucy had made it clear she didn't want to see him. Don't you think you owe her some loyalty?'

This is mad, thought Rebecca. 'Loyalty? What is this? A lacrosse game? How can Lucy remotely mind if I say hello to someone she knows?' She looked at Lucy. 'And anyway, what's the problem, Lucy? He could not have been nicer. And you've got a lunch date with a drop-dead gorgeous telly-star out of it. I'd say you owe me one, sister!'

Rebecca genuinely did not get it. She watched as Lucy shook her head and said, 'Forget it' in an uptight way, and saw Joanna close her eyes and sigh. Obviously, they thought her beyond redemption.

They drank their coffee in silence. Rebecca was about to suggest that her misery-guts friends go home and leave her to have some fun, when Orlando reappeared with another guy in tow.

'Ladies, can we join you after all? We couldn't find a table and then I remembered Rebecca's offer. It is Rebecca isn't it?'

Rebecca was pleased he'd remembered her name. He introduced Juan, his producer on *Know Your Onions*, the telly quiz show that he presented. Juan was tall, skinny and Spanish-looking. Late thirties, maybe.

Rebecca decided things were looking up. They now had two good-looking guys, both young and friendly.

On the women's advice, the men skipped the dinner menu and ordered pizza. They tried to buy drinks all round, but Joanna said three mojitos was more than enough for her and Lucy asked for mineral water. Rebecca had a Cuba libre with an extra shot.

Juan ate half his slice of pizza and dropped the rest of it, at the same time pushing his plate away.

'Not good,' he said. He turned to Rebecca. 'Would you like to dance?'

He had a theatricality and an 'Old Europe' affectation about him, which was both a spoof and, Rebecca thought, real. He held out his hand and she followed him down to the dance floor, her palm resting on the back of his raised hand, like a couple about to take the floor in *Come Dancing*.

He was nothing like as good a dancer as the little fellow she had partnered earlier. But he was a lot sexier to smooch with. As soon as the music slowed up, he had his hand opened wide across her bare back, pulling her to him. He was taller than her, so when she looked up she could smell the aftershave on his neck. Guerlain she thought. He dropped his head to nuzzle her ear, and she bent her neck a bit to make it easier for him. She smiled at the thought of how shocked Joanna and Lucy would be. They seemed to think you had to know a guy for weeks, and maybe even love him, before you felt the tug of lust. She was sorry for them really. They missed so much.

Rebecca was not made like them. She knew already that Juan and she would spend the night together. Maybe not all the night, but enough to satisfy them both. And why not? Angelica was back in Edinburgh so she did not run the risk of shocking her so-shockable daughter, and what was she meant to do? Live a life of celibacy? She just gave thanks that the lighting in this place was so minimal. Otherwise Juan would certainly have rumbled her age and been after younger meat.

They danced for maybe half an hour, by which time they were kissing a lot, and, especially when doing the rumba, she was encouraging the hardening lump in his trousers by some judicious bump and grind, and by occasionally letting her fingers accidentally trail across his groin when turning. She loved the feeling of power that came from a guy really wanting you, when he could not deny his horniness and you could orchestrate matters to keep him on a high wire.

When they both knew it was time, they just left. Rebecca did feel a genuine pang of guilt at abandoning Joanna and Lucy, but told herself, hell, they are grown women, and anyway they had probably left already. They'd been keen to quit all evening anyway, hadn't they?

Next morning Rebecca woke up early – and anxious. She hadn't had a hangover like this for a very long time. She blundered into the bathroom and looked forlornly in the mirror. Crumpled with sleep and her face still smudgy with last night's make-up, she looked a hundred. Thank God Juan had left. He'd gone, she thought, about three. Nice guy. But she knew she would not see him again. And she did not really want to either.

She made a mug of tea and sat at the kitchen table to drink it. Why did she feel so wretched? It wasn't just the hangover. About once a month she drank a bit too much, occasionally a lot too much, but nothing criminal. She just liked to party, that was all.

Actually, she thought, I know what is making me feel so awful. It's guilt, that's what. Guilt at abandoning her two friends in the club, guilt at being unfaithful to Nelson for no good reason, and guilt at her behaviour last week at dinner: she'd lost it with her daughter, been really rude to Bill, and landed her friend with cooking the dinner.

She had to do something about all of them, she decided. But what she needed right now was a decent breakfast. It would settle her stomach and give her the courage to put all this right. Suddenly cheered by a decision, Rebecca showered, pulled on trousers and a sweater, plus her mac – it was still April and showery – and set off for Carluccio's. She ordered scrambled eggs and pancetta, the bread tin with fig jam, and a latte.

Halfway through the eggs, she rang Lucy.

'Lucy,' she said, 'I'm really, really sorry. Will either of you ever forgive me?'

'Oh, hi Rebecca. Forgive you? What for?' Then she laughed, 'You mean that horrible club? Neither of us will ever, ever forgive you for that!'

At Lucy's tone Rebecca felt herself relax with relief. 'No, I'm utterly unrepentant about the club. Everyone should experience a salsa club once in their life. But I do feel guilty about abandoning you.'

'Abandoning us? We abandoned you! We left you wrapped around that Juan fellow. Didn't think you were going to peel apart for a while, so we scarpered while we could.'

'God, that's a relief. I woke up feeling so horrible. And not just about last night, Lucy. I also owe you a huge apology for my dinner party. It was supposed to be a treat for you, not a busman's holiday. I'm really, really sorry.'

'Becca, forget it. I enjoyed doing the food, and that daughter of yours is an absolute star. You should be proud of her.'

'I am,' said Rebecca, her anxiety returning, 'but I behaved appallingly to her too. And to Bill.'

'Well,' said Lucy, 'you were a bit rough with them, that's for sure.' She paused, then said, 'Did Angelica tell you I'm going to teach her to cook?'

'You're not! Are you really?'

'Yes. She wants to learn, and says everyone in her flat at uni lives off crisps and pizza, and buying decent ready-meals in Waitrose costs a fortune. So we thought she should get a couple of friends together and I'd teach them the basics.'

Rebecca put the phone down with mixed feelings. She was delighted Lucy was so full of praise for Angelica. And it was really kind to give her lessons. But she felt left out. Angelica had not told her of this plan, and why hadn't anyone included her?

Rebecca still had Nelson on her conscience. She told herself she had no reason to beat herself up: she and Nelson had never made each other any promises. But somehow the affair had drifted on, and it was a year now. And, which was unusual for Rebecca, until

Juan she'd not slept with anyone else. Truth be told, she hadn't had any offers, but all the same, that year of Nelson-only had somehow made her feel bad about Juan.

Nelson was lovely, and he was a great lover. But she still meant to find a man to marry. Someone with some money. Long term, Nelson would not do. Nor had she let Nelson meet Angelica. She wasn't sure why. Perhaps because she knew it wouldn't be permanent. And anyway, Angelica preferred to ignore the men in her life, indeed she'd once told her so.

'Look Mum, when you meet someone you are going to live with or marry, I'll do my best not to be the resentful daughter. But while you are just flirting for fun, or whatever it is you do . . .'

Rebecca had attempted to interrupt but Angelica had put up a weary hand.

'No no, don't protest . . . I don't mind, it's your life. But just don't tell me about it. I really don't want to know, and most of all I don't want to ever have another conversation with one of your guys about your relationship, how he adores you, how he wants to be friends with me. And all that blah blah blah . . .'

So Rebecca told herself she was keeping them apart for her daughter's sake.

Nelson often expressed an interest in Angelica and Rebecca could never resist the temptation to boast about her. These conversations would generally end with Nelson saying he'd like to meet her. Lately he'd been more insistent.

'Becca, you know we've been together over a year and I've still not met Angelica. Let's make an effort.'

'Sure, we should do that,' Rebecca said – even though she knew she would not follow through.

Nelson said in his Eminem accent, 'Wassa madder, baby? Don' you want I meet yo' girl? You 'shamed of this big buck nigger, dat it?'

He was teasing of course, but there was truth in the charge that Rebecca was ashamed. It wasn't of his colour. It was that she'd

returned to her old habits and was screwing around with other
guys.

Rebecca's infidelity had started that night with Juan. It was as if,
having tasted freedom again, she had to have it. Rather like how
having just one cigarette when you've given up, or one drink when
you're on the wagon, leads to a whole lot more. In the six weeks
since her single night with Juan she'd had a brief flirtation culminating
in a single (disappointing) night with one of Bill's fabric suppliers
and a week-long dalliance with an American friend of a friend, dull
to talk to but rich, attentive and terrific in bed. It had been wonderful,
but since he wouldn't do for a husband – even Bill was twenty
times more interesting – she'd not replied to his emails since he
returned to the States. This was partly because Angelica, who had
come home unexpectedly and met him, was so dismissive. Angelica
was the one person whose disapproval really got to her.

Right now there were a couple of guys she'd not say no to if
asked. And she'd seen very little of Nelson. Their love affair was
definitely on the slow burner, but it was still a pleasure, and
Rebecca never really liked to let lovers go completely. She needed
admirers like daisies need the sun, and she knew it.

Happily, Nelson was not the jealous or inquiring kind so it had
not been a problem. Except, occasionally, to her conscience.

One afternoon Rebecca, returning from the supermarket laden
with bottled water and loo paper and other boring stuff, had
telephoned Angelica with a request to help unload the car. As she
pulled up outside the flats, she was surprised and alarmed to see
Nelson walking down the steps with Angelica.

'Hi, Becca,' said Nelson, 'aren't you the lucky shopper? A daughter
and a friend to dance attendance?'

Rebecca's heart contracted with anxiety. Had Nelson said anything
about them? Her daughter looked her usual calm and cheerful self,
but why was Nelson here?

'Hello, Nelson,' she said, climbing out of the car, trying to sound super-casual, 'this is a surprise!'

'Ya, well, I figured you'd dreamt up this daughter of yours, so I jus' mosey down to look see for mysel'.' Dropping the street talk, he went on. 'I didn't reckon on you being out shopping, but it was cool. Angelica is one great young woman.'

In spite of her anxiety, Rebecca could not help being pleased, and she smiled at Angelica and nodded. 'She is. She puts her mother to shame.'

'No, she does her mother credit.'

'Could you both stop this?' said a blushing Angelica. 'Mum, let's get all this stuff into the kitchen.'

They unloaded the groceries and made coffee.

Angelica, smiling at Nelson, said, 'Mum, why haven't I met this guy before? I knew he was your singing teacher but I didn't know he was a good mate, and that you'd been to the Aldeburgh festival together.' She turned to Nelson. 'God, Nelson, how did you do that? Get Mum to go to a bunch of classical concerts? It's impossible to wean her off *Pop Idol*.'

'Rubbish, darling,' Rebecca said. 'You know I love classical music . . . And I thought you weren't interested in meeting my friends – you said so, remember?'

Even as she said it, Rebecca realised it was a mistake.

'No, Mum, I'd love to meet your friends if they were like Nelson. Interesting friends with brains.' She leaned over to squeeze Rebecca's shoulder. 'It's the good-looking Latino dancers and sleek fat-cats that you flap your eyelashes at that I don't want to meet. Like that idiot American. Nelson, honestly, you should have seen him. He looked like a Marlboro ad but all he could talk about was his company's chocolate-covered crisps. That and my glamorous mother. They all talk about my glamorous mother.'

Nelson said, 'Wow, I am learning stuff about your mother that I am not sure I want to know!' He said it lightly, with a smile, but Rebecca knew the information would not pass him by.

Sure enough, when Angelica had gone back to her computer, and she and Nelson were walking down to the Cow, he turned to look at her squarely.

'So who's the American then?'

'Oh, he's just a man I know. Angelica's right. He's a bit boring.'

'And the Latino dancers? And the fat-cats?'

'Darling, I don't know what she was talking about. I do go salsa dancing, as you know – I even invited you, remember, but you turned me down. Repeatedly.'

But trying to put Nelson in the wrong didn't work.

'Becca, be straight with me. We always said being together was just for fun. No strings, no commitments. But you should be honest with me.'

Entering the pub and ordering lunch curtailed the conversation and Rebecca went to the loo to give herself time to think. When she came back, she'd determined to do what she should have done months ago. And indeed what Nelson had asked of her. She would tell the truth.

When Rebecca had a Caesar salad and a glass of Soave in front of her and Nelson was tucking into beef and Guinness pie, she said, 'OK, darling. Here's the story. I'm not proud of it, but you want me to be honest, don't you? You *say* you do.'

Nelson looked up and held her gaze. 'I do.'

'OK, well here goes. I don't know what's the matter with me. But the truth is I have never been faithful to anyone after the first months of dizzying passion. It is as though I am addicted to stage one of a love affair: the not knowing, the hoping, the longing, the feeling sick, the shaking, and the wanting sex all the time.'

'So you are having an affair with the American?' His eyes were level and his voice flat.

'No, he's back in the States.'

Voice harder now, Nelson said, 'But you did have an affair with him?'

Rebecca met his stare and nodded. 'A short fling, yes.'

'And before that? Your daughter implied there was more than one bee round the honeypot.'

At any other time Rebecca would have liked the metaphor. Her fantasies frequently involved several men, all desperate for her, but right now she was having a really hard time under Nelson's interrogation. She'd told herself she'd be honest with him but she longed not to be. He was such a great guy and she didn't want to hurt him. And then, what good would the truth do? It could only make him think less of her.

They were both silent, Rebecca nervous of what her confession might unleash. She watched the emotions come and go in quick succession on Nelson's face: blank amazement, bewilderment, disbelief, hurt.

He shook his head as if to clear it. 'Does this mean you have been screwing around all the time we've—'

'No, no, it doesn't.' Rebecca reached for his hand but he withdrew it. He put his knife and fork down and sat back in his chair. 'In fact, I was faithful until a few weeks ago. Until after we started to sing the *Messiah*—'

'I don't want dates and details, please.'

'OK,' she said. Then, 'I'm sorry, Nelson.'

He pushed his pie away from him and took a large gulp of his beer. Then he wiped his mouth with the back of his hand.

'Actually I do want details. I need to know the score.'

Rebecca looked at him, her eyes full of tears. 'Oh Nelson, you are such a lovely guy. Have you not slept with anyone else in the whole year, no, more than a year?'

He looked stonily at her. 'No, I have not. So. Who else have I been sharing you with?'

Rebecca did not answer, but sat looking at the table, undecided whether to answer truthfully, lie, or get indignant about being questioned. She decided to duck the question.

'But Nelson, you are not in love with me either, are you? If you were, you'd want to marry me. Be with me all the time, all that.'

Rebecca saw Nelson's face darken in anger. He crumpled his napkin in his hand and banged his fist, not hard but with his hand clenched so that the veins stood out along the back of it, on the table.

'Bloody hell,' said Nelson, 'you don't have to be head over heels in love with your woman to be pissed off that she's sleeping around, do you?'

She closed her eyes for a second. Stay silent. Don't throw petrol on the flames. Nelson did not speak either for a minute or so. When he did, his voice was steely.

'OK, just give it to me straight. Who's been in your bed, or you in his?'

'Nelson, I will tell you if you really want to know. But do you really want chapter and verse? Won't it do to say that for the last few weeks or so I have been somehow open to offers.'

'Jesus! Open to offers! Great!'

'I don't know how to express it other than that. For ages after we started going together it just wouldn't have occurred to me to go with anyone else. I didn't want to. I thought of little else but you. But now it's somehow different, Nelson. We've slowed down and I'm back noticing other men.' Rebecca rolled her ring round and round her finger, her eyes on her hands. She looked up and into his eyes. 'Being faithful shouldn't be a sacrifice, an effort of will, should it?'

Nelson sat back in his chair, visibly deflating. 'No, if you have to try, it's not worth it. I suppose I just got in a bit deeper than I meant to. Male pride and jealousy I guess. I don't want anyone else having you, even though we agreed no strings, no commitments.'

Rebecca wiped her eyes on the paper napkin, thinking she probably had mascara down her cheeks, and went back to picking at her salad.

'So what now?' she said.

'I don't know. I'll call you. Or see you at rehearsal I guess.'

He stood up, leaving the rest of his pie and beer unfinished.

Rebecca watched him putting in his PIN and collecting his receipt. And failing to respond to the pleasantries of the barmaid.

She did not follow him. I deserve this, she thought. And I will stay friends with him, I know. I always do stay friends with them.

Chapter Twenty-Two

Lucy upended her wet umbrella in the hand basin, dumped her case on the floor and walked straight to the window. The view was spectacular but bore little relation to the sunny photographs of Pencarrick Joanna had shown them. The sky was ominous, the sea dotted with jerky white wavelets flashing on and off all over its wide expanse. In the middle distance monstrous waves swelled, and rolled shorewards to ricochet off the rocks below, swamping the jetty and boathouse. The rain and gusting wind joined forces, intent on breaching the old sash windows.

It was June. So much for a summer of sun and sea with a bit of mild teaching thrown in.

She turned and studied her room. It was large and square with two big windows facing the sea and one overlooking the terrace and garden. The wallpaper, a once pretty print of small pink roses, now faded and dull, was peeling away from the cornice. The ceiling sported a central chandelier (missing several crystal drops, she noticed) and a brown water stain. The bed was technically a single, but it was old-fashioned, wide and high with carved pillars each side of a mahogany bedhead.

Lucy approached it with gloomy irritation. It would be one of those lumpy, enveloping mattresses that would give her backache. She flopped backwards onto the faded silk spread. The bed was perfectly smooth and firm. Surprised, she sat up and flipped back the bedspread to find a feather-light modern quilt between fine linen sheets and pillows to match.

She refused to allow herself to be cheered by this, but noticed sourly that there was no bathroom, only the complicated plumbed-in washstand, with porcelain shelf and mirror above. She turned on a big square tap and an immediate gush of hot water further drenched her umbrella.

I should like this, she thought, it reminds me of the Winchester in New York: solid, comfortable, once classy. But while she approved of the room, of the quality of the linen hand-towel, of what would be a magnificent view if the weather ever cleared, she was conscious of a gentle dread lapping round her, a fear of her students-to-be, of having to eat with them as well as teach them, of being trapped with some foodie bore giving her his grandmother's recipe for pickled beef. Above all, she dreaded being incarcerated with people younger, livelier, happier than she.

She should never have come. She would be useless at the teaching, forgetting the names of her students, and worse, forgetting the names of ingredients, dishes, authors, cooks. How could she have agreed to teach a food-writing course?

She struggled to stop herself sinking. Brace up, she told her reflection, it's not so bad. You have family, friends, and a new summer job in a lovely part of England. And there may be nothing wrong with your memory anyway.

It was months since the disastrous incident on Paddington station and Lucy now had reason to hope it would prove a one-off, a mental aberration caused by grief. Her last visit to the Memory Clinic two months ago had supported this: all her scores were up.

Lucy slipped off her suit jacket and covered her shoulders with a soft cashmere pashmina – another purchase engineered by Rebecca – and went downstairs.

After a couple of glasses of wine with Joanna, feeling decidedly better and determined to deflect the conversation from Joanna's kind but determined questioning of her state of mind (Was she writing? Seeing her daughter? Getting up promptly in the morning? Eating properly?), she gestured at her friend's sandalled feet and long flared skirt.

'Jo, you do look amazing. Quite different from the efficient, pinstriped superwoman we know so well.'

Joanna's smile was broad and confident. 'I'm very happy. I love it here. Everything about it. Cornwall, this place, the people who come on courses . . .'

'Nothing to do with Stewart, then?'

Lucy was teasing, but Joanna frowned. 'I don't know. He isn't here, and has nothing to do with the business. But . . .'

Lucy finished the sentence for her. 'But love colours all.' Then she added, 'I'm happy for you. It's wonderful.'

They carried their drinks round the house while Joanna explained that the current dining room, with its views of the sea, would become the studio for painting classes, that the potter's wheel and kiln were in the former stables, that canoeing, sailing and diving would run from the old boathouse on the beach, and that singing classes would be held in the old library.

'Please tell me you've got Nelson booked,' said Lucy. 'If I miss the whole summer of rehearsals, Nelson will throw me out. You're lucky, shuttling up and down to London every week. You're still singing on Thursdays, aren't you?'

'I am, but yes, the good news is I've booked him for slots through the whole of August, when his Notting Hill classes don't run anyway. He's planning to stay down here a good bit too. It'll be fun.'

'What's he going to teach? Will he have time to rehearse us?'

'Sure, he's only doing a few hours a day – simple blues and gospel stuff for the holiday singers, but he's up for a bit of intensive *Messiah* for the three of us, and anyone else who wants to join in.'

'How fantast— Hey, whoa. Did you say *three* of us?'

Joanna smiled, delighted with herself. 'I did. Rebecca's due next month. She's coming armed with pattern books and mood boards and all the tools of her husband's trade. She'll be here for half of July and all of August.'

They moved into the kitchen. 'All these front rooms,' Joanna said, with a wide, sweeping gesture, 'will be knocked together for cookery classes and eating, and the back half will be commercial kitchens for the hotel.'

They looked at the designs pinned to one wall. In the centre would be a huge scrubbed kitchen table, where the cookery students would eat together. The windows were to be lowered so the sea could be seen while sitting down. Wide double doors would lead out from the side wall to the sheltered terrace. Magazine pictures were stapled to the plans, depicting Cornish blue pottery on a scrubbed pine table, blue and white cushions on chairs painted shabby-chic blue. Great jugs of flowers and rows of blue and white mugs adorned a painted dresser. Another picture showed a stone terrace with a long table dressed in Provençal print and a *tarte aux pommes*, filigree metal chairs with more pretty cushions, stone tubs of blue hydrangeas and a wooden wheelbarrow planted up with white busy Lizzies.

'Heavens,' exclaimed Lucy, 'this looks like a *Country Living* catalogue!'

Joanna laughed. 'I know. That's why we need Rebecca. We need it to be comfortable, and clean and fresh looking, but not quite so folksy. Forget the décor, concentrate on the plans.'

They walked deeper into the building, away from the light, through a warren of kitchens, scullery, flower rooms, butler's pantry and unidentifiable nooks and crannies. 'The house is dug into the hillside,' said Joanna, 'so while the seaward side is ground floor, this back bit is basement.' Lucy looked with dismay at the dingy rooms with their ill-fitting sideboards and ancient equipment, and tried to close her nose against the smell – mostly damp with a suspicion of leaky gas and stale food.

They looked at the designer's boards and Lucy thought, good, this looks more like it. The contrast with the prettified side of the kitchen would be startling. Where all was country comfort over there, this was to be nothing but efficient ventilation, stainless steel chillers, fridges, sinks and massive commercial ranges, with yards and yards of gleaming tabling.

'The kitchen alone is going to cost four hundred thousand pounds,' said Joanna, peering over Lucy's shoulder, 'so we'd better believe this makeover will pay off.'

'Four hundred thousand!?'

'If we're lucky. Commercial kit, steam ovens, walk-in chillers, blast freezer, automatic dishwashing, ventilation. Even the ice-cream maker costs thousands.'

'But how will you pay for it?'

'The chap who owns it is super-rich. He could easily afford to do the whole refurb himself, but he lacks business skills. His money was inherited, not made, and he just let the place chunter on, getting seedier and seedier, until it finally slipped into the red. He never came here, or took any interest in it until it started to lose money. He and Innovest will be the main funders, and I might take a few shares. If nothing else, the property value is there and will soar if we fix the place up.'

'So you can't lose?'

'I wish! The hospitality business is extraordinarily risky, and the property market is not much better. With the extra rooms we plan over the stable block, this will be a fifty-bedroom hotel – a big investment. But that's the fun of it – the challenge of trying to do better than everyone expects. And I really believe in this one.'

Lucy's arm went round her friend. 'You are astonishing, Jo. I'd hesitate for a year about buying a two-room cottage, but you don't blink at an Edwardian pile with absolutely everything wrong with it.'

Before supper, in the once-elegant drawing room, they met the assembled participants for Lucy's food-writing course, and Lucy was relieved. Mostly women, mostly in their thirties and forties, they seemed an intelligent group, interested in food but not obsessed.

That night, when she snuggled down into her high firm bed with the feather duvet, blissfully light after her grandson's Thomas the Tank Engine one, Lucy rolled on her side and drew her knees up to slip her arms round them. It was a position she'd used since childhood when happy or excited, like the night before an exam or a gymkhana. As an adult she found herself doing it before a job interview or a big journalistic assignment. Teaching a lot of amateur writers, she said to herself, could be fun.

The next morning was warm, still and sunny and they held their workshop round the terrace table, under a giant umbrella. Lucy talked to her students about the elements of a good cookbook: good writing; a distinctive authorial style; a coherent theme – and recipes that work.

'Occasionally you might see a cookbook published without one of the first three – a book with no real writing, or a recipe collection from a variety of chefs or celebrities, or an eclectic cookbook with no apparent cohesion. You might forgive any of these, but you will never forgive a recipe that doesn't work: a bad recipe means frustration, maybe even humiliation, for the cook, and sometimes expensive ingredients in the bin. So let's start with making sure you can write a faultless recipe.'

Some of the students, expecting a more literary or romantic approach, muttered. But Lucy knew what she was doing. She wrote the ingredients for a lemon meringue pie on a flip chart, deliberately listing them in random order.

'OK, I want you to use these to write the recipe in any style you like.'

When they were finished and their papers handed to her, she got them started on a recipe for gazpacho while she read through their lemon pie recipes.

'Right,' she said, when her reading was done, 'shall we stop a minute and I'll go through these and then you can go back to the gazpacho, having gathered, I hope, a few tips from this one.' She smiled at each student as she handed back their recipes, and repeated their names in an effort to learn them. Most of them smiled back at her. They were beginning to enjoy themselves.

'Don't worry,' she said, 'I'm not going to name and shame anyone. The mistakes in these recipes are ones that are really common, even in published recipes. So don't despair. The pitfalls are easy to avoid if you just do the checks.'

She flipped the chart over to a clean sheet and wrote:

Check ingredients against method

'I haven't had time to do a detailed analysis of your recipes, but there are some obvious problems with some of them. For example, some of you have correctly listed all the ingredients at the top, but in writing the method you've omitted to use an ingredient. Which would leave the cook wondering what was meant to happen to the sugar or the vanilla. You need to run down your finished recipe and check that all the ingredients get used. Can you just take a few minutes to do that now?'

The students bent their heads and almost immediately there were sighs and groans and a cry of, 'Oh God, it's me.'

Lucy smiled. 'Next, you need to check in reverse.'

She wrote *Check method against ingredients* on the flip chart. 'Since all the ingredients were on the flip chart for you, I don't think any of you fell into this trap. But you should always check through the method, making sure all the ingredients you have told the reader what to do with are actually in your list at the top. Nothing is more maddening for a cook than to be told to "Add the sugar" and to think "What sugar? There isn't any sugar!"'

They then discussed ingredients not listed in the order used so the reader becomes muddled and cross; instructions in the wrong order, for example, making the meringue before the pastry; instructions omitted, like failing to rest the pastry before cooking or not telling the reader to preheat the oven; instructions not detailed enough, like not specifying the finest gauge of the grater for the lemon rind which leaves the cook in danger of grating the bitter pith with the rind, or assuming the reader will know to let the pie cool and stiffen a bit before trying to lift it out of the tin.

They kept going for two hours, and Lucy enjoyed the class as much as the students did. At the end, the students actually clapped her.

Back in her bedroom, putting her papers away, Lucy took a deep breath and made an effort to shake off the emotion she'd felt at such appreciation. David had been dead for over a year and a half, but she still over-reacted. This time yesterday she'd been miserable and insecure, then Joanna had infected her with confidence and excitement, and today a bit of praise had her pathetically grateful. I'm a mess she thought, but I'm less of a mess than before.

The following Friday Joanna returned from her weekly trip to Wakefield and London with the news that she'd hired Orlando Black to teach a fortnight's practical cookery later in the summer.

'Good, isn't it?' she said, tidying the papers on her desk. 'The *Globe* are to give away a couple of places as a reader promotion, and he's so well known that a line about the course under his column, which we won't even have to pay for, plus a banner on his website, will sell all the places.' She looked up at Lucy. 'And if he agrees to mention your courses too, we'll be overbooked.'

Lucy could feel the hot blood in her cheeks. For a moment she stared at Joanna in disbelief then burst out, 'What? Are you mad?'

Joanna's head jerked up, a frown replacing her smile, 'Why? Of course I'm not mad. It's a brilliant coup. I've been working on it for weeks, but only just got Orlando's OK. What's wrong with it?'

'Jo, Have you forgotten Orlando Black is the guy who nicked my column on the *Globe*, the . . . the . . . half-brained ignoramus who doesn't know the first thing about food? Who ponces round the telly saying "Wow" and "Cool"?'

Joanna walked round her desk, reached for Lucy's hands and dragged her to the sofa. 'Sit down,' she said. 'We've got to talk about this.'

Lucy thought afterwards that being dressed down by Joanna was like being ticked off by her long-ago headmistress.

'Lucy, this is nonsense. These are holiday courses, not postgraduate degrees in gastronomic history. Orlando is charming, women love him, he has enthusiasm, he is famous. Besides, he worships you. So stop being so prickly. Orlando will be a huge success.'

Somehow her students' enthusiasm revived Lucy's own interest in writing. She had done little since she'd delivered *Peasant Soups* and now she started to plot out a follow up: *Peasant Hotpots*, perhaps. She loved all those slow-cooked family recipes like cassoulet, goulash, bollito, stoved pork, comforting and infallible. While her students were out sightseeing or having a siesta after lunch, she'd spend the afternoon at a table in the bay window of the dining room.

One day, at the end of her first week when she was absorbed with the universal spread of the tomato, its popularity in almost every culture, and its affinity with both garlic and chilli, she became aware of someone looming over her.

Mildly irritated, she looked up to see Joshua, the sixty-something food photographer who had come to a couple of her classes. He had an all-white thatch of hair and a round pink face. He looked expectant, obviously waiting for an answer.

She frowned. 'Did you say something?'

Joshua backed away at once, saying, 'Oh, so sorry, I'm interrupting.'

Lucy, regretting her curtness, forced a smile,

'No, it's me that should apologise, I was miles away. What did you say?'

'No, honestly. You're busy . . .'

She was anxious now to put things right.

'No really, please sit down.' She turned to face him and pushed the neighbouring chair towards him with her foot. He sat, but unwillingly. 'Actually, I've been meaning to ask you,' she went on. 'How come you turn up to odd lessons? You must live locally I guess.'

Joshua's smile revealed slightly crooked but very white, teeth.

'Yes, I do. I'm doing the same course as the others, only over six weeks. I came on a Monday to get your first lesson; Tuesday for the next, then Wednesday, etc.'

'And Joanna let you do that? Doesn't it screw up her ability to fully book each week?'

'I suppose it does, but she'd agreed before Orlando's article packed the place out, and she thought it would be a good experiment – maybe next year they will offer once-a-week courses aimed at locals – to develop the business unrestricted by the number of bedrooms.'

Lucy made an effort not to dwell on Orlando's help in establishing her courses. 'That's Joanna all right. She's good, isn't she?'

Joshua shifted his slightly overweight body to face her more comfortably, and replied, 'She is, very. I've known this place for donkey's years. Always nice and a great setting, but completely anarchic with nothing ever working. She's made a colossal difference. We get meals on time now. And they are edible. Indeed delicious.'

'That's because the cookery students cook them, or most of them. Must save on cook's wages too.'

'Sure,' he said. 'But that's good. It retains something of the old cooperative, greeny-goodie-hippie feel, don't you think?'

'I didn't know it before, but it sounds horrible! I'm much too old for horrible food and no hot water.'

'Agreed, so am I. It used to be chaotic. Once I signed up for a painting course and the tutor hadn't been booked. Most of the students were Londoners spending a week of their hard-earned holidays here, and I felt so sorry for them I ended up teaching photography instead.'

'Really? How extraordinarily good of you!'

'Not at all. We had a terrific time. I took them all over the region and the keen painters sat at their easels and I taught the rest of them the basics of photography. We got the local gallery owner in to crit their paintings and photographs at the end of the week when we had a little exhibition. Some of them even sold. Sometimes chaos works.'

What a nice guy, thought Lucy. And the thought that Grace, her uptight daughter, and Archie, her work-driven son-in-law, could join her here, absorbing something of Pencarrick's peace, flashed through her mind — and was instantly dismissed as fantasy.

Lucy was pleased that Joshua took to popping in on days he wasn't due for a class and waylaying her for a cup of coffee. Sometimes they strolled along the cliff tops together, or collected (and dutifully returned), shells on the beach. Lucy found him companionable and interesting and was grateful for the company.

A perfect walker for a widow, thought Lucy. Maybe he's lonely too.

One day Joshua rang her.

'When I interrupted your writing that day, I er . . . I failed to ask you what I'd come in for.'

Funny guy, thought Lucy. He's seen me a dozen times since then.

'So what was that?'

'Any chance of your skipping the community supper?'

'Sure,' said Lucy. 'It's not compulsory. Why?'

'I want you to see my photographs.'

'Not your etchings, then?'

He laughed. 'If I had any, then them too.'

Lucy was mildly excited on arriving at Joshua's cottage. It felt a bit like a date, something she hadn't had for forty years at least.

The house was on the quayside and had once been the harbour master's. It was solidly built with a boathouse underneath, living quarters above and, above that, a loft for sail-making. This was now Joshua's studio.

Lucy walked ahead of Joshua into the long open space, bright with summer light flooding the four big windows and the now-glassed in door that had once been used for hauling up sails.

They gazed down on the little harbour with its pleasure boats in the lee of the breakwater.

Then Lucy looked about her, taking in the furled black blinds above the windows, ready to drop down to exclude the light, and the massive roll of white paper, big as a broadloom carpet, suspended behind a low wooden platform, painted white.

'Do you do fashion photography as well as food?' she asked.

'I used to. And I still occasionally do portraits, mostly of cookery writers or chefs for book jackets or magazines.' He looked at the curtain of white paper. 'If they insist on wearing their chefs' white jackets, I have to spray the background some other colour. But I prefer food photography.'

Lucy drifted slowly round the studio. A clutter of stylist's props covered an old dresser and a pine table: baskets balanced on copper jam pans; Victorian cream skimmers and ladles stuck, like flowers, in terracotta jugs; bread boards, flower-patterned dishes and teacups stacked in haphazard piles. It looked like a good junk shop.

Next to this olde worlde display was its complete opposite: a minimalist kitchen in bright white and stainless steel, the worktop bare except for a shiny Dualit toaster, an Italian espresso machine, and the handles of Global knives and a Chinese cleaver protruding from a slit in the back of the work bench.

Lucy smiled at Joshua. 'May I?' she said, pulling open a drawer to reveal a blowtorch for browning, mini-whizzer for frothing sauces, and squeezy bottles for arty swirls of sauce on the plate. The next drawer, double width, had built-in compartments containing neatly segregated wooden spoons, fish slices, draining spoons, small tools like peelers, cherry stoners, Japanese mini-grater, lemon zester, etc.

She was impressed. Photographer's studios were usually full of dead coffee cups and debris from long-gone shoots. Joshua must be either a very good photographer who made a handsome living and could afford the best, or a rich fantasist who played at it with all the right tools.

She looked at him, speculating. He was absorbed in undoing the ties of a portfolio case and opening it on the central stainless steel workbench. Sensing her gaze, he lifted his eyes to hers, and his face came alive, a pleased smile spreading over it.

'Come and look,' he said.

They flipped slowly through the pictures. The photographs were divided into three groups. First came a set that looked like Old Master paintings, all soft light and deep shadows caressing the still-life objects: a round cheese, cut open, next to a pottery bowl with two apples in it, a half-folded napkin, a pitcher of wine. Lucy instinctively touched the surface of the print, half expecting the feel of paint.

Next came black and white action shots of young chefs in a modern restaurant kitchen. Lucy's attention was caught by the youth, seriousness and concentration of two young pastry chefs, both women. One was cracking eggs into a bowl, the other holding a dripping spoon at eye level to check the thickness of the syrup. Interspersed were pictures of young men during the service, moving so fast the images blurred and streaked. They had the immediacy and excitement of a trade that is not for wimps, but for those who can hold their own in the coordinated ballet that cooking at speed can be.

The third set of photographs consisted of straightforward shots of finished dishes. They were exquisite. Lucy paused at a picture of a perfectly round stack of crayfish and avocado, topped with an explosion of chervil and chives, and then at one of a thick piece of cod glinting through its herbal crust.

'These are wonderful,' said Lucy. 'They make your mouth water. Who is the cook? He's good.'

'Um. That's me.'

Puzzled, Lucy shook her head. 'It can't be. How can you do the cooking *and* take the photographs? And anyway, this lot looks like Raymond Blanc or Marcus Wareing.'

Joshua laughed. 'Good. That means I'm learning! But actually it's not too difficult. I work alone and take my time. Get the shot set up before I cook the dish. This lot are for a cookbook to be published in Holland by a well-known chef, but he can't leave his restaurant to come here. So he sent me some of his restaurant china and his wife emailed me the recipes and the digital snaps she took during the service, just before the dishes left the kitchen. It's not so hard.'

Lucy noticed that Joshua's natural reticence had been banished by his enthusiasm for his work. He bustled about the studio, showing her photographs and published cookbooks – she recognised several she'd reviewed in the *Globe* days. Then he lifted a second portfolio onto the table and undid the ties.

'This is what I really wanted to show you.' He opened the folder. Inside were A3 and A2 prints on thick matt paper. The top picture was of a stem of red chillies in the centre of the page, with, to one side, smaller photographs of the flower in bud and in bloom, and to the other, pictures of the leaf and the root of the plant.

'I love the detail and accuracy of botanical drawing,' he said, 'and I thought it would be interesting to do the same thing with the camera. And of course I'm now hooked.' He shuffled quickly through large prints of cabbages, celery, celeriac, beets, carrots, tomatoes, all similarly treated.

'Not so fast,' cried Lucy, putting out a hand. 'Go away. Let me look.'

'I'll make some coffee,' he said.

When he returned, Lucy was still deeply absorbed in the pictures, studying the delicacy of pale celery leaves with light shining through them, the precision of the tiny parallel ridges on the outside of the stalk, and the gradual greening towards the top. She barely noticed his presence, or the coffee he put down beside her. She was mesmerised.

'These are the most beautiful photographs I've ever seen, Joshua.'

Visibly pleased, he came round the table.

'Good. I could get addicted to your approval,' he said.

'This is as much fine art as photography. I think you should have an exhibition in Cork Street.'

'And I think we should ask your publisher if I could do the photographs for your book.'

Lucy looked at him, delighted. 'Josh, that's a great idea!' And then she shook her head. 'But it's too late. They've already hired Alexander Toby.'

'Alex Toby? Well, he's really good. Congratulations'

He sounded like Lucy felt: disappointed at the instant death of a good idea.

'Ah well. If we are still friends in a year's time, maybe we could work together on my next book?'

'Believe me, Lucy, we'll still be friends.'

When Lucy got back to Pencarrick she emailed her publisher: *Alex Toby is on for the book, isn't he? It's just that I've met this brilliant, very original, photographer and if Alex isn't signed up yet . . . ?*

Next morning she had the reply, *'Yes, Toby signed up. Will start shooting beginning of August. He's providing both cook and stylist so he should go fast. Will ask him to email you photos as he does them. Schedule is tight but we are still on for late October publication.*

But, miraculously, two weeks later, in the middle of July, she had another email: Was her pet photographer still available? Alexander Toby had had to cry off, his old mother ill in Scotland.

Josh caught an early train to London the next day to give a slide show to the design people at the publishers.

Joshua found Lucy in the bar that evening. She couldn't tell from his expression whether he'd been successful.

'Hi, Josh, how did you get on? Did you get the job?'

He didn't answer but handed her a packet. Inside was a book. A first edition of MFK Fisher's *With Bold Knife and Fork*.

'Ah, Josh! This is her *best* book! How wonderful. Where did you get it? And why?'

'I got it in *Books for Cooks*,' he said. 'It's to thank you.'

'You got the job!' Lucy put her arms round his neck and hugged him. 'Oh Josh, how wonderful.'

'Yup. They signed me up then and there, and they are leaving you and me to decide which fifty recipes we want to photograph.'

Lucy ordered two glasses of champagne. 'Here's to *Peasant Soups* then.'

'And to the start of the lifelong successful professional collaboration of the great food writer Lucy Barnes and the great photographer Joshua Emmet.'

'Steady on! We may fall out at the first picture.'

'We won't, you know.'

Chapter Twenty-Three

Joanna watched Stewart come out of Truro station and look around him, searching for her. For a second or two, she just watched him, thinking both how distinguished he looked, and how out of place among all the holiday-makers. He was dressed in a perfectly tailored lightweight business suit and carried his usual oversized briefcase in his hand. He looked cool and unrumpled in spite of the heat.

She didn't wave, delaying the moment when he would see her and his face would light with pleasure.

When he spotted her, it was exactly like that. His face opened in a wide smile, he lifted his free hand in greeting and hurried across the tarmac. And then she was in his arms, the now familiar pleasure of his embrace compounded by her pride in him. She could not help the delight that this beautiful man, this confident, achieving, wonderful chap was *hers*. How childish, she thought, but I like the fact that total strangers see him hugging me.

'Joanna, you look wonderful.'

'So do you. Though you're not exactly in holiday gear.'

'I know. I feel ridiculous in shorts. I did bring a short-sleeved shirt and a pair of loafers.'

They climbed into the car and he pulled her to him. 'I need a proper hello,' he said.

Joanna returned his kiss, desire mounting. His face against hers, he said, 'Jo, I miss you so. Every week leaving you gets harder.

Your yo-yo existence between Greenfarms, London and Cornwall is mad.'

She forced herself to push him away.

'Darling, could we discuss this later? I want you to look at a bit of Cornwall.'

She drove slowly, taking B roads down leafy tunnels with high Cornish walls covered thickly in greenery. Stewart seemed to relax, his hand on her thigh.

Of course she knew he wanted her to come and live with him in Yorkshire. He so loved the North, but she felt a long way from that sort of commitment. There were too many obstacles which Stewart was unaware of or would never understand.

One of them was his daughter. Joanna was now almost certain that Caroline was not going to make it as the boss of Greenfarms. Last month Alasdair had come to see her.

'Joanna, I hate to do this. She's my cousin after all, but I need some help here. Caroline is going to lose two of her department heads if we are not careful.'

'Why, what's up?'

'Yesterday the head buyer, you know, Bob Carsens, told me his order for vegetable packaging had been cancelled by Caroline. We are going to have to pay full whack for it. It's printed with our labels and is ready to ship.'

'For God's sake, why did she cancel it?'

'Because it is not a hundred per cent biodegradable. Which Bob knew and had agreed. The alternative, which is totally biodegradable, and which Caroline has ordered instead, is twice the price.'

'Well, to be fair, we pride ourselves on our green reputation . . .'

Alasdair interrupted,

'Sure, and the stuff Bob ordered is made of recycled and recyclable materials. But that's not the point. Even if Caroline is right, she should never countermand one of her manager's instructions without telling him, and land him with two bills which will make a hole in his budget and screw his relationship with his supplier.'

The other aggrieved executive had been the farm manager. Caroline had lost her temper when she'd found his tractor left running while he went into his house to fetch something. She'd banged on the front door and bawled him out in front of his wife and children and he was furious.

Joanna had promised Alasdair to have it out with Caroline, but she doubted it would do much good.

Her relationship with Caroline had never been great and it was getting worse. It was not just Caroline's tactless handling of senior staff that worried Joanna. She found herself having to badger Caroline over the factory reduction which was not progressing at all, and the issue was becoming a battleground. And Joanna did not want to tell Stewart any of this because she knew he'd defend his daughter, and besides she thought she should manage it herself.

The agreement with Stewart that they would give Caroline six months to prove herself was up: she should now be insisting on Caroline's departure. But — stupidly, unprofessionally but also magically — she'd fallen in love with Stewart, and had not done so.

She must return to it. But not now.

The other obstacle to a Yorkshire life was Pencarrick. It was beginning to get under her skin.

She came back to Stewart's charge. 'The thing is, I *like* my yo-yo existence, the variety of it — you and Greenfarms up north, singing and my little house in London. And this hotel.'

'But, when you've done the job — got the Pencarrick business on track — then you could just take assignments in London, couldn't you? You could be home with me almost every night.'

'Or you could join me in the choir and stay in London. And, who knows, you might just fall for Cornwall.' She sensed him about to give her reasons why not, so she flashed him a quick smile and said, 'C'mon, darling. Neither of us really knows what we want yet . . .'

'I do. I want you with me.'

'And I want you with me. But where? That's the point.'

Stewart dutifully admired the scenery as they meandered south and was fascinated by the quaint efficiency of King Harry Ferry which took them across the Fal by an old-fashioned pulley system hauling the ferry across the river.

As they drove into Pencarrick, she tried to see it with Stewart's eyes. He must be impressed: the house looked a little shabby, yes, and the rhododendrons and azaleas, now over, were at their worst, but the expanse of sweeping lawn was emerald green, the pine trees dark against the brilliant sky, and the sea looked like a child's picture book, dotted with little white yachts.

'Wow,' he said, climbing out of the car. 'Great location.'

They walked round to the side terrace where Lucy was holding her cookery-writing workshop. The students were writing diligently and Lucy came round to meet them. She wore no make-up, was barefoot and in faded cotton cut-offs and a loose man's shirt. Her spectacles were on the top of her head. She looked great.

'So this is the famous Lucy!' Stewart said. Joanna was glad to see approval in Lucy's eyes. How could she not approve? Stewart was at his friendly, confident, charismatic best.

That evening the sea was calm but with just enough wind for a gentle evening sail. Joanna, who had sailed as a child in Australia, had taken it up again at Pencarrick. She'd had the chef pack some sandwiches, and at about six o'clock she and Stewart took the single-handed catamaran and headed round the point and up the Fal. They tacked gently up the wide estuary. After a blistering day it was wonderful to be on the water, with enough breeze to be pleasantly cool but no need for waterproofs or windcheaters. Stewart had been persuaded into a pair of jeans belonging to the sailing club tutor, and was lying, bare-chested except for a life vest, on the flat expanse of deck between the two hulls.

The tide was coming in and it was easy going. When they'd been on the water for an hour, Joanna sailed to the edge of the river, where the water was almost completely calm, and let the sail flap impotently. She crawled over Stewart's outstretched legs to drop the anchor overboard, and, as she hoped he would, he put his hand up her shirt and captured her in a hug.

She wriggled out of his embrace. 'Here,' she said, 'you deal with this.' She pushed the drinks carrier to him, while she investigated the coolbox. There were hefty Cornish pasties and sandwiches of Cornish goat's cheese and tomato layered with basil leaves. Joanna opted for the sandwiches but Stewart said, 'I'm starving. All this sea air and inspecting every loo and broom cupboard at Pencarrick, justifies a pasty.'

Joanna noticed how good he looked. At Greenfarms he often seemed impatient or worried. Now he took a large bite of his pasty and reached for his beer.

'Well, my Joanna, this is certainly the life, isn't it?'

'Are you happy?'

'You know I am, daft woman. This is wonderful.' His face became serious. 'But I am not sure you're on quite the right track with the business.'

'No?' She could feel resentment trying to get in. I am the company doctor, she thought, I hope he is not going to tell me what I should be doing.

'Well, are Innovest ever going to get the huge returns they'll want? The place is charming, but it is not Champney's or Chiva Som, is it? And if you are going to pay five hundred pounds a night or whatever, you're going to want something grander than a workshop on a terrace with a barefoot writer, aren't you?'

'Darling be fair! There's a heatwave on! And writers are allowed to be eccentric. I agree, Pencarrick cannot work as it is now, no, but with an upmarket refurbishment and a really good spa, and lots more courses, why not? You said yourself that the location is terrific.'

She told him of her outline plans and how good it was going to be having Lucy down for the whole summer and Rebecca with them for six weeks. 'I've hired a lot of the tutors from the old regime who were popular with the students last year. And I've got Nelson coming to try out singing classes in August.'

'Blues?'

'Anything he likes really. I've advertised the courses as Sing Your Heart Out (which is Nelson's website name) without being specific.'

'Who is doing the cooking? I'd come if someone would teach me to make a Cornish pasty this good.'

Joanna laughed. 'Well you could be in luck, because up to now classes have been informal affairs with the chef and the students cooking supper together. Eventually we will have to have more celebrity course leaders I guess, though they will cost an arm and a leg – they're hardly going to do it for a free stay in sunny Cornwall.'

'Can I eat your pasty too?' Stewart asked as the wake of a passing motorboat rocked the catamaran.

Joanna held her glass up to prevent it spilling. 'Sure, go ahead.'

She told him that Orlando Black was doing a star turn and was surprised when he shook his head.

'I'm not sure about the celebrity thing. I think if I wanted to learn to sail, say, I wouldn't want to be taught by an Olympic yachtsman. I'd want a good teacher for beginners from a local sailing club, who knew the sea round here and who did it for a living.'

'Good point. But how do you stop the place feeling like a hippy community? We need to be able to charge zillions to justify the investment.'

He refilled her wine glass and they talked on, chewing over the merits of informality and companionship against those of luxury and pampering. Joanna was surprised by Stewart's preference for the simple life. Most of their time together had been in upmarket hotels, he had a chalet in St Moritz. She'd have thought he'd be for the upmarket option. Must be Caroline's influence.

'Anyway,' she said, 'we have the summer to investigate. And Rebecca will be spending her time thinking about interior designs. It will be fun, if nothing else.'

Stewart put his hand on her bare thigh and stroked it gently, almost absentmindedly. It made listening to him a little difficult. He said, 'Darling, don't be too disappointed if you are forced to conclude Innovest Five Star luxury won't wash. There is no sentiment in backers, as you know. I'd hate you to suffer the agonies that Greenfarms has been through.'

'Stewart,' she said, 'you're forgetting. Pencarrick isn't mine. I represent those hard-nosed backers here. If it doesn't look good, no sweat, we'll just sell it.'

But as she said it, she thought, I'm lying, it would hurt like hell.

Chapter Twenty-Four

Rebecca drew the curtains of her bedroom at Pencarrick against the August sun. She'd have preferred to be topping up her tan on the terrace but then she wouldn't be able to see her laptop screen properly.

She was entirely happy. Pencarrick, she thought, is the most beautiful old house, with charm and character and great-shaped rooms. Not a poky bedroom in the place and the huge sash windows seemed to let the light and seascape of Cornwall invade every room.

And you had to hand it to Joanna — she knew how to manage a business. The hotel ran on WD40, the food was delicious and the staff — Rebecca assumed they were from Poland or Lithuania or somewhere — worked like crazy and smiled all the time. And the participants (Joanna objected if she called them students) and teachers (oops, 'course directors') all loved it.

She was longing to start on the decor, which was boring and fusty beyond belief, but she was only allowed to plan, not do. She'd taken digital photos of all the rooms and was using the Make It Over software to change all the furnishings.

Joanna came in as she was playing round with an all-purple and black gothic theme.

'God, Rebecca, that's just awful!' Joanna's appalled face looked from computer screen to Rebecca in horror.

'I know,' grinned Rebecca. 'Don't worry, I'm just arsing about.

It's fun. Look, we could put skulls on the bookshelves and have a coffin for a coffee table . . . What do you think?' A few more clicks and there was a great baroque crucifix on the wall.

'Stop, stop,' said Joanna, pulling a face. 'How far are you with the real thing?'

'Oh, Joanna, I'm so excited. Look, here comes Pencarrick as I hope and pray it will be.'

She hit a few keys and brought up a cool summer bedroom design, cream linen curtains; cream cotton bed linen; old lace on the pillows – not too many pillows or too much lace which would put off the male guests; stone and brown jute carpets and the existing antique furniture, mostly dark mahogany. No colour apart from one big burgundy vase on the floor full of purple cornus stems and a modern-gothic chandelier with burgundy glass beads threaded through the shabby-tat painted frame.

'Oh, that's just perfect. Beautiful,' says Joanna, 'but won't it cost a fortune?'

'No,' replied Rebecca, looking a little smug. 'The furniture is here already, the fabrics all come wholesale from the Far East, and the vase and chandelier are more Ikea than Conran.'

She clicked her way through the navy and oatmeal plunge-pool room, the deep green and red dining room, the brown and oxblood study and the rich burnt-orange drawing room with the existing family portraits cleaned and relit. The chintz curtains would be replaced with peach Thai silk bordered in brown.

Joanna was delighted. The designs were far better than she had imagined they would be, and were everything she'd hoped for: classy, understated, but somehow luxurious and imaginative. She'd not known exactly what she wanted but she did not want anything looking skimped, or overstuffed, or boring – or too formal, or shabby, or kitsch. Rebecca's plans were none of these.

She hugged Rebecca and told her she was brilliant. Rebecca suppressed the desire to say she knew but it was nice to be told, and said a modest 'Thanks' instead.

Joanna would produce this year's figures at the end of September and the board would decide if the money for a refurb would be forthcoming. I've just got to do a knock-socks-off presentation, with great pictures of every room, thought Rebecca, and hope that Joanna will convince them of the business case for the investment.

Rebecca resolved that if she got the job, she'd make damn sure the interiors got covered by all the glossies. That would put her on the map, and, she thought, would give her famous decorator ex a well-deserved jolt. He didn't think she was brilliant, the mean bugger – only good enough to answer the phone and ring up the curtain makers.

She smiled at the thought that he hadn't a clue she'd helped herself to his software and his colour swatches. He knew she was advising Joanna – probably thought she was selecting a few new curtains or chair covers for a B and B. He'd no idea of the size of the hotel or of the budget. Or that she was doing a job he'd kill for.

Rebecca sighed deeply, thinking that this might even beat shopping. As she gathered up her swatches and pattern books, planning to stop work, have a glass of Chardonnay on the terrace and then go down to the beach, an email popped into her box. It was from Angelica:

Hi Mum,

Hope all's going well with the decor schemes. Had supper with Dad last night. Said he was worried you'd need help and not ask for it. But I told him you'd manage just fine.

Anyway, the reason for this email is to tell you that one of your male friends is now my mate too. Nelson. We went to a Smith's Square concert together you know, where they have the music in the church above a restaurant in the crypt underneath. He was just great. So interesting and kind. He bought me supper and two CDs – they are Haydn symphonies with Neville Marriner, the guy whose orchestra plays on old instruments, viols and harpsichords etc. And he's taking

*me to a rehearsal at the Royal Festival Hall (Mozart and Stravinsky)
and maybe I'll meet some of the orchestra.*

Nelson wanted me to join your choir for the Messiah. *He gave
me a little audition in the car! I'd love to, but I can't skip uni so
would only be able to come in September, which is stupid. Anyway,
Mum, I know he's at Pencarrick so can you tell him to get in touch
– I haven't got his email address and I don't think there can be any
reception at that place of yours because he doesn't reply to texts or
phone messages. Anyway, please tell him to email me or ring on a
landline or something. I want to explain why I can't do it. And see
if he really meant it about the Royal Festival Hall.*

Lots love, A

Rebecca read this through twice before she could sort out her
reaction. On reading the first paragraph, it had been gratifying to
find her daughter on her side in the long-running bicker of her
parents, and the first few lines about Nelson had pleased her: for
once Angelica was all approval, and also she was happy that Nelson
had been in touch. She thought for a second that perhaps he was
making an attempt at reconciliation through contact with her
daughter.

And then, as she read on, her heart contracted in dismay and
hurt. Nelson was getting at her by hitting on her daughter. It was
revenge. He was trying to make her jealous. How could he?

She sat there, wanting both to cry and scream. Nelson had
arrived at Pencarrick yesterday morning, and surely, if his motives
were innocent, he'd have mentioned the concert. Angelica was only
twenty-one: what did he think he was doing, a man of nearly fifty?

At one o'clock, calm now after her glass – well, two glasses –
of wine, Rebecca climbed down the huge rock steps to the beach,
treading awkwardly in her platforms. She was still angry with
Nelson, but determined not to show it. First of all, she had to
admit he had not done anything criminal, and secondly, now she
considered it coolly, there had been little time for him to tell her

anything. She had been out last night, dining in St Mawes with Orlando, and Nelson had been with his singing class yesterday afternoon and this morning.

Today the guests were having a barbecue lunch, with the cookery students cooking the fish and seafood they had bought at dawn on the quayside. Both Orlando and Nelson were on the beach.

Rebecca waved to Orlando who was grilling fish on the barbecue. Nelson was lying on his back, sunning his beautiful black body, eyes closed, and did not notice her. Having both Orlando and Nelson here together would normally have been a pleasant embarrassment of riches, full of opportunity and possibility. But she was upset with Nelson and glad she could ignore him.

She lay down on her towel, close enough to Orlando to call to him.

'Orlando darling, can you do my back?'

Orlando turned over the wire-mesh fish-holder thing to cook the second side, and instructed one of his students to take over. He came to kneel by Rebecca. Lying on her stomach she undid her bikini top to bare her back. Orlando smoothed the cream efficiently and evenly, slipping the tips of his fingers under the waist band of her bikini bottoms to make sure there were no gaps, and oiling her neck with delicious massaging strokes. Rebecca shut her eyes and concentrated on his touch. Then she lifted her arms so that he could do her sides, hoping he would include the exposed sides of her breasts bulging out a little under her weight. He did, and it felt wonderful. When he'd done he asked,

'How's that?'

'Pure heaven,' said Rebecca. 'You wouldn't like to do my legs too, I suppose?'

Orlando obediently complied and went on stroking her legs long after every bit of sun cream was absorbed, but of course she did not stop him. Why would she? It felt so good she wanted to purr like a cat.

When the fish smelled decidedly cooked and Orlando finally

stood up, Rebecca sat up and took her time to re-fasten her bikini top, telling herself that Cornwall was full of nudist beaches and there was nothing not to like about the look of her breasts.

Nelson, she noticed with satisfaction, got up, flicked his towel over his shoulder and left the beach without saying a word of goodbye to anyone, not even Joanna. Good, thought Rebecca, I bet he's jealous, serve him right. She watched his strong legs and muscly back as he climbed the huge rock steps without a pause or a backward glance.

Within minutes, more of the cookery students appeared with classy salads and desserts they'd spent the morning on, and hampers of wine, ice, crockery etc. Lunch turned into a really good party, and they ended up playing hopscotch like kids. Rebecca even managed to get everyone following her in an aerobics class, done to a full-volume blast of Girls Aloud from her ghetto blaster. She knew she looked pretty good in her bikini: her tummy was flat and she was religious about the bottle-tan. She noticed Lucy's slightly wobbly arms and pale dimpled legs and thought maybe the gym fees were worth it after all. She kept them all going to the beat, doing the routine with energy and precision and enjoying everyone's eyes on her. And, she thought, I'm moving too fast for anyone to notice the wrinkly bits at the top of my arms.

Finally, when only the younger guests were still with her, she hit the stop button.

Lucy had flopped down a few minutes before and was still panting.

'Rebecca, you're a miracle,' she said between gasps. 'That was great.'

'Yes,' Joanna added, 'I should hire you as an entertainment director, to lead fun and frolics for the guests.'

Rebecca felt a rush of pleasure. Those two were so often disapproving that having them united in praise was like champagne.

But she had begun to feel a touch guilty about Nelson, thinking she might have behaved a little crudely. Nelson hadn't reappeared and so presumably hadn't eaten either. So when they returned to the hotel, she went in search of him with a plate of grilled squid and salad. She found him in the music room, sorting through some sheet music.

'Hi,' she said.

'Hi,' he replied without looking up.

She sat on the piano stool and looked up at him.

'I'm sorry, Nelson.'

He took no notice, so she reached over and put the plate of squid on the desk. 'I brought you some lunch.'

'Thanks.' He glanced at the plate but not at her.

'Nelson . . . On the beach before lunch . . . I was just trying to provoke you.'

'Well, you succeeded.'

'And I guess I wanted to hit back at you.'

For the first time he looked up at her. 'Hit back at me?' he asked mildly. 'Why, for God's sake? What have I done?'

Rebecca knew she'd feel petty complaining of him taking her grown-up daughter to a concert, but it still rankled. And thinking of it revived the hurt. She said, 'Oh, Nelson, you know. Two can play that game.'

'What game, for Chrissake?' Annoyance and confusion was beginning to darken his face.

'Don't tell me you weren't trying to punish me by dating my daughter!'

Nelson's faced changed from irritated puzzlement to comprehension and resignation. 'I wasn't "dating" your daughter! I took her to a concert! She's a sweet girl. And genuinely interested in music.'

That hurt a bit. Nelson had known her long enough to have discovered that Rebecca's enthusiasm for culture was more about impressing people than genuine interest.

'So, it was her mind you were after, was it, or furthering her education!'

'Oh, for God's sake, Rebecca, it was hardly a candlelit supper

196

in a nightclub! I didn't tell you because I haven't seen you.' He shook his head almost imperceptibly and said, his voice much quieter, 'God, Rebecca, you are such an idiot.'

Suddenly that was exactly what Rebecca felt. An idiot.

'I know.'

He said, more gently, 'Becca, we haven't been together for months. You probably have half a dozen guys desperate to get in the sack with you. You don't have any claim on me, and I don't have any on you.'

Rebecca nodded without speaking.

'So you shouldn't mind if I go to a concert with Angelica,' he went on. 'You can set your mind at rest about my intentions too. I don't want to seduce her, OK? And if you want to make an exhibition of yourself on the beach, you have every right to. I don't know why I let it get to me.'

Rebecca frowned. 'But that's just it. I wanted to see if it *would* get to you.'

'Why? Isn't turning Orlando on enough? Or do you have to have an audience?'

'Not any audience. You.' She looked directly at him. Rebecca did feel genuinely contrite but at the same time she knew that she looked appealing: she was sitting on the piano stool below him, and with her head tilted back her face would be unlined. She could feel her eyes filling with tears, which would make them big and shiny. She said in a small voice, 'I suppose I want you to still desire me.'

It worked. He came over and put a hand on her shoulder. 'Well, I do. But the problem is that you want everyone to desire you.'

A big tear ran over her lid and down her cheek. Nelson rubbed it out with a thumb.

Rebecca, content now, stood up and kissed his cheek — a soft, friendly, sexless kiss. 'You are an angel,' she said, 'and I am a bitch.'

'No, I am a fool, and you are a tart.' He smiled to take the sting out of the remark. He had a great smile, his flawless teeth bright white against his handsome face.

'Shall I get us a glass of wine, and you can eat this on the terrace?'

But he had to sort the music for his class tomorrow and for the *Messiah* rehearsal, and said no.

The next Saturday, as Rebecca was standing in the drive trying to decide on what to replace the horrible crazy paving on the terrace with, six young lads arrived in a couple of Range Rovers, their roof racks thick with surfboards.

They were expected. They had just left school. 'Eton or Harrow, I think,' Joanna had said, 'and one of them, Sebastian, has turned nineteen and his daddy's birthday present is a two-week holiday for him and five of his mates. The boys are coming here for a week to learn to sail.'

Rebecca had shaken her head in disbelief. 'Five of them! Daddy must be rich as Croesus.'

Rebecca watched them as they clambered out. They were gloriously good-looking, unselfconscious and confident. Their voices were deep as only very young men's are. They hauled out rucksacks and squashy sports bags and flung them on the gravel with an animal energy overlaid with teenage indolence. God, thought Rebecca, youth is glorious. All of them, even the plainest, is edible.

She wandered over.

'Hello, one of you must be the famous Sebastian?'

A tall, skinny boy with dark, spiky hair and an olive complexion put out his hand.

'I'm Sebastian.' He had an angelic smile. 'But why famous?'

She shook hands with him and then with the others.

'Because we've heard all about your two-week birthday celebrations – the week's surfing at Polzeath and of course the sailing week here.'

'Oh,' he said. 'Well, yes, we've just done the surfing bit. It was amazing.'

'And,' she teased him, 'we know about the weekend partying on the beach at Rock.'

He looked immediately embarrassed, and one of the others said, 'Who told you about that?'

'Don't worry,' she said. 'No tales of your misdeeds have reached Pencarrick. All we knew is that you were going to Polzeath. I'm guessing the rest, since beach parties at Rock are famous, or infamous, round here. And you're only young once, right?'

As she watched them shuffle through the front door Rebecca was smiling, thinking that a bit of lively youth might leaven the dough of middle-aged respectability which tended to pervade the place.

Chapter Twenty-Five

Orlando had been at Pencarrick for a week and Lucy had to admit he'd been entirely charming to everyone, had run his classes professionally and with good humour and had even managed, by being nice to the chef, to make the hotel dinners rather more exciting and modern.

One morning, when his students had gone off to a local farmers' market with the chef, he had sidled into her class. 'Can I sit and listen, Luce?' he asked. Lucy wanted to say no, and don't call me Luce. She feared his glamorous presence would distract the students and his need for attention would not let him sit quietly. But she could hardly refuse, and she also relished the chance to show him just how good she was.

'Sure,' she said, indicating an empty chair. 'We've been looking at writing styles, reading passages from Elizabeth David and MFK Fisher.'

Briskly, to prevent any intervention or joking from Orlando, she addressed the class.

'So, as we've seen, if you want the reader to see and smell and taste the food, to make them salivate, get them out of the armchair and into the kitchen, it is no good saying something is delicious. Or wonderful. Or cool. Or amazing. "Wow" won't do either. These words are meaningless. You have to tell them how it actually smells or feels or tastes.'

This was a direct dig at Orlando. But he showed no sign of having made the connection, and watched her attentively.

She got the students to shut their eyes, and imagine they were holding a jam doughnut as they described the sandy dryness of the sugar coating, the tender but resilient texture, the shock of the warm squirt of strawberry jam . . .

For the next hour, they wrote descriptions of burnt toast, live lobsters, cinnamon Danish, boiling marmalade and much else. She was surprised to see Orlando beg some paper from his neighbour, and bend his head to the task. They brought their work to Lucy for comment as they finished it.

At noon the students and Orlando hurried out for an hour on the beach before lunch, and Lucy collected up the pieces of work she had not yet read, and took them up to her room. She'd been intrigued and unwillingly impressed by Orlando's description of boiling marmalade as it went from 'roiling bubble to slow heave, with occasional small spitting volcanoes'. So she flipped through the papers looking for his looping *Orlando* on the top of the page. There was no description of toast or lobsters. Just the words,

'Wow! Wonderful! Amazing! Cool! What a teacher!'

On Sunday, Lucy went with Rebecca and Joanna for a day of loafing about and self-indulgence (Rebecca called it pampering) in a spa. It was Rebecca's birthday, and last night there had been a dinner for her with a cake and lots of little presents. But Rebecca, never one, thought Lucy, to forgo an excuse for a junket, had insisted.

Lucy went unwillingly. She had been going to have lunch with Joshua and had been looking forward to it. She was also opposed to the waste of money, 'Three hundred and eighty pounds!' she gasped, 'Becca, you are off your head.'

'No I am not! You're a food writer. You should know gastronomy doesn't come cheap. And nor does expert hairdressing, massage and the rest.'

Lucy had another objection too, but didn't feel she could voice it. She had never spent a day, or indeed an hour, in a spa, thought only feather-brained women patronised them and was embarrassed at the prospect of joining their ranks.

'You'd be better off taking Orlando,' she said. 'He'd probably love being primped and preened.'

'But it's supposed to be a girls' day out.' Rebecca had looked at her oddly and added, 'What is it with you and Orlando, Lucy? Why so dismissive of him? You can't still be smarting over his getting the *Globe* job?'

Lucy had shaken her head and Rebecca, for once tactful, had dropped the subject.

Lucy did not want to miss lunch with Josh. And she was reluctant to admit to spending time and heaps of money on such nonsense. But she seldom lied, so she told him the truth.

'I'm really sorry Josh, I'm going to hate it I know, but Rebecca is all excitement and Joanna thinks it would be a good team-building opportunity or some rot like that. And I hate to be the party-pooper.'

Joshua had said, 'Of course you must go! It's just what you need. You are way too serious, Lucy!'

'But at our age! Rebecca has booked us in for every weird treatment with mud and hot stones and mumbo jumbo and it's all complete codswallop. I'm hardly going to walk out of there wrinkle-free and lithe as a dancer, now am I? The beauty business is in a brilliant conspiracy with the customer: she pretends it works so she can lie on a lounger and feel nice, and the business pretends it works because it makes money.'

Josh had kissed her lightly on the cheek. 'As I said, way too serious. Don't think about it. Just enjoy it. Join the conspiracy.'

As they set off in Joanna's Audi A8, Joanna questioned Rebecca. 'How did you swing a booking? Halcyon Days is full months in advance.'

'Easy,' replied Rebecca, sounding pleased as punch with herself. 'I insisted on talking to Armand Boucher himself – I'm good at getting past receptionists and PAs – and I said I was bringing Lucy

Barnes because she's writing about Cornish spas with great restaurants. And of course he's a huge fan and could not believe his luck, so he waved his wand, or wooden spoon or whatever. And found us a table. *And* we're getting free treatments. Not all of them but . . .'

Lucy, sitting in the passenger seat next to Joanna, swung round. 'You *what*? Rebecca, you didn't . . .'

'Sure I did. What's the point of being connected if you don't use your connections?'

Joanna chimed in. 'Becca, you should have at least asked Lucy if you—'

Lucy interrupted. 'For God's sake, Rebecca, how could you . . . It would . . . I cannot . . .' She was spluttering and could not explain that she would never ever use her position to get something for free – it would compromise her integrity. She started again: 'We absolutely cannot accept anything free . . .'

'Oh, Lucy darling,' said Rebecca, 'don't be so pompous. He's not giving you a brown envelope stuffed with cash. He's just thrilled to have you in his spa. Anyway, I thought all journalists lived on freebies.'

There was some truth in that, Lucy had to admit. 'Some do. I don't. Sure, I've had dinner with restaurateur friends for nothing, but never, ever if I'm writing about them. And as for pretending I'm going to do a piece when I'm not . . . Rebecca, surely you see . . .'

Rebecca shrugged and did not reply. Lucy faced front again, thinking crossly that Rebecca really was impossible. She had absolutely no sense of what was acceptable and what wasn't.

As they drove on and Lucy calmed down, she began to feel a little sorry for Rebecca. She had been so delighted with her coup. And when she leant forward and patted Lucy's arm to say, 'Look Lucy, I'm sorry, but it's not a big deal, surely? You *could* one day do a piece on Cornish spas, couldn't you? If you mind so much about a little white lie, you could make it true. Couldn't you?' Lucy found herself laughing.

'I guess I could. And it's true people blag their way into restaurants all the time, and anyway Armand would never notice, or care, if I wrote anything or not. He gets more publicity than the Royals. But no free massages, OK?'

Joanna was worried about leaving the hotel for a whole day, especially on a Sunday which was 'turnaround' day at Pencarrick, when usually one lot of guests checked out in the morning and the next checked in in the afternoon.

'But,' said Lucy, 'your staff are surely up to running the place without you? They have to when you disappear up north, don't they?'

Rebecca chimed in, 'And besides, half the new arrivals – the sailing lads – are checked in already.'

'It's them I'm worried about,' retorted Joanna. 'Who knows what they'll get up to?'

'Don't be daft,' said Lucy, 'you can't be their nanny. Just take their money and charge Daddy later if they trash the place.'

Lucy didn't think Joanna would have come at all if she had not remembered that this was tax-deductible research: how else would she know what the competition was like when she turned Pencarrick into a rich man's, or rather rich woman's, retreat?

The three women had set off early with the idea of getting maximum value out of their 'Premier Pamper Package', but also because Rebecca and Lucy agreed that if they'd left any later the guests would have started checking out and Joanna would have got involved.

Lucy found Joanna's attention to detail both admirable and maddening. She worried about the smallest details when she could have surely got someone else to do it. Like sorting out Mrs Hall, who had a strange preference for instant coffee, and Mr Armitage, an insurance salesman whose bottom had been scalded by his towel rail. The fact that soon Pencarrick would be much too smart to have heard of Nescafé, and would have gleaming wet-rooms with underfloor heating, rain-dance showers and expensive bath bubbles – all way beyond the aspirations of Mr Armitage and his mousy little wife – did not affect her dedication to getting things right. She's a considerable woman, thought Lucy, part control-freak and part obsessive. Last week she'd sent back a month's supply of loo paper, because it was buff, not white. Mad. Perhaps all successful businesspeople are like that? And maybe that's why I'd be so hopeless at it. I don't want to control anyone, and I don't worry about the detail either.

It was a glorious morning. Lucy thought that Josh, who planned to spend the day walking, with a stop in the pub (the one she was to have joined him in) for lunch, had the right idea. Bound to be a lot healthier than a day in an air-conditioned treatment room. Josh was forever extolling the loveliness of the coastal walks and he knew them all. But although she liked strolling while talking peaceably, looking at the view and smelling the sea air, Lucy disliked the kind of exercise that made you hot and sweaty.

So when Joanna's right knee stiffened up with the driving and they stopped to let Lucy take over, she was dismayed to hear Rebecca saying, 'Hey, what do you say we go for a walk up that little path? The sea must be the other side. It looks so . . .'

Lucy looked at what seemed like a near vertical path, with rocky steps climbing out of sight. 'Becca, Joanna just stopped driving because her knees are giving her grief – and you want to go mountaineering! Have a heart.'

'No, that's fine. It's sitting in one position that hurts, not walking. But why the change of heart, Becca? This morning you were champing to get there early . . .'

Rebecca nodded cheerfully. 'True,' she said. 'I'm nothing if not inconsistent. And right now I'd rather be out in this heavenly weather. And anyway, we're early.' She looked childishly excited and ran ahead. Sometimes, thought Lucy, I think Rebecca is twenty years younger than us.

They followed the path steeply uphill, and then the land flattened to a plateau and sloped gently down to a cliff edge. They could hear, but not see, the waves crashing onto the cliff below.

Lucy was out of breath, but exhilarated. She stopped at the top, hands on hips, and looked to the distance where the blue of sea met the blue of sky. The hackneyed descriptions are correct, she thought, the deep blue sea is just that, and the sky is exactly the colour she understood by sky-blue.

She did not dare go closer to the cliff edge, and Joanna's knee needed a rest, so they sat on the sheep-cropped grass, a little back from the drop. They watched Rebecca run down to peer over the edge. She turned to shout to them to join her, but they shook their heads.

'For God's sake be careful,' Lucy called. 'The edge could crumble.' But Rebecca just waved merrily and walked further along the edge, trying to see down to the beach or rocks or whatever was below.

Both women were uneasy until Rebecca rejoined them and flopped down with the ease of a thirty-year-old.

'You should take a look, you two. It's great. There's a little strip of pebbly beach. And then jagged rocks and white foamy sea, swirling about. The cliff seems to slope back under your feet. I couldn't see where the gulls go to. I guess to nests in the cliff face.'

The breeze from the sea lifted Lucy's hair and cooled her face. Content now that Rebecca was back on safe ground, Lucy leant back on her arms, raised her face to the sun and closed her eyes. The pungent scent of cut fields, the fragrance of sun-warmed pasture beneath her and the whiff of ozone made a heady cocktail, calming and narcotic. She listened to the gulls making seaside soundtracks. It was unbelievably peaceful and no one said a word for several minutes. Lucy could not remember when she'd sat in silence like this, just enjoying it.

But of course Rebecca broke the spell. She sat up.

'Lucy and Jo, what are you thinking about this very minute?'

'Mmm,' Lucy said, 'I was thinking how much David would have loved this.'

Something in her voice must have got to Rebecca, who said, 'Poor Lucy. Widowhood must suck.'

'No, it's getting better. Not all misery now. I'm not so lonely.' She was silent for a minute, her eyes turning to scan the sky, sea, fields. 'Sometimes I'm even happy. Last night I was daydreaming about living down here. It is heavenly, Joanna.'

Joanna smiled her agreement but Rebecca said, 'Not in the winter, I bet.'

I wonder, thought Lucy. It might be wonderful. No tourists, great landscapes, early springs. Camellias and palm trees. Very good seafood.

Rebecca interrupted her reverie with her penny-for-your-thoughts question to Joanna.

'I was thinking how nice it would be if Stewart appeared over that horizon.'

Rebecca sat up with a jerk. 'Oh God, we are all so feeble! Every one of us thinking about *men*. What's the matter with us? I was thinking that women are all very well, but what I really really want is a lover instead of you lot!'

And then everyone laughed, even Lucy. They stood up, telling each other that nothing beats the friendship of women. It's true, thought Lucy: young women seem to have a whole support system of friends, but our generation were generally so tied up in looking after our men and children, or trying to be superwomen of house and office, that we didn't realise what we were missing.

What Lucy felt at that moment was not just gratitude towards her two friends, it was love.

As they walked down the hill towards the car, she found herself saying, 'Do you know, I think I might have topped myself if it wasn't for you two.'

Chapter Twenty-Six

The longer Joanna spent at Pencarrick the more she liked it, but her initial instincts about the business were daily confirmed. The current strategy just would not work and they would have to take the hotel seriously up-market and aim for a far richer, international clientele. As it was, with most of the courses fully booked, it was a respectable small business, but would never make the level of returns Innovest required.

If they built a world-class spa, even more luxurious than Armand's Halcyon Days, with plenty of Eastern overtones, it would push the room rates up too, and give them a low-season trade. And they should begin to lose the less profitable courses and concentrate on really fancy ones with celebrity tutors. At the moment there was still a slightly hippy atmosphere to the place, fun but not expensive. They needed rich couples, learning to cook with a Michelin-star chef in the morning and being pampered expensively in the afternoon. What they did not need were school kids on a sailing course, or social workers, funded by the local council, learning about healthy school lunch-boxes.

Mercifully, they'd seen little of the sailing lads because they slept in the rooms over the stables and were out on the water all day, and Joanna had decreed that they should not come back for lunch. The cooks provided picnics which they ate in some cove or creek. They loved it, and it took some of the pressure off the kitchen – adolescent boys have appetites like racehorses, and besides, one dose a day of their boisterous company was quite enough for the older guests.

But Rebecca was proving a problem. Yesterday she'd stormed into Joanna's office.

'Joanna, it's ridiculous. I've got the whole day off today, OK? So I thought I'd go sailing, but do you think that prim little runt who's in charge would let me? No chance. I am not enrolled on the course, he says. And I haven't been through the safety instruction. And I've missed the first two days. And I haven't paid! For God's sake, what's the matter with him? Doesn't he know I'm your guest? You've got to—'

Joanna interrupted, 'Becca, Becca, calm down. Start at the beginning.'

And then it transpired, of course, that she wasn't interested in learning to sail. She was interested in the lads on the sailing course. She wanted to tag along and go picnicking with a bunch of adolescents on a beach.

'Becca,' said Joanna, 'I can fix for you to have a sailing lesson. Free. But you can't go with the Etonian dream team because they are all sailing Lasers which are single-handed dinghies. No room for passengers. And if you haven't done the course so far you won't be able to manage a boat of your own. And you don't want to capsize and be rescued by a nineteen-year-old, do you?'

Rebecca looked at Joanna with fury. Then suddenly burst into her hiccupping laugh.

'Why not? I look good with my hair all wet and my boobs half-way out of my bikini! Being rescued by that curly blond one with the angel face would do just fine!'

Joanna could not help smiling. It was impossible to stay cross with Rebecca. She was so good-humoured, and she never pretended to be what she was not.

On Friday evening Joanna organised another beach barbecue. London was sweating through an August heat wave, but Cornwall was as good as it gets, with sea breezes to temper the sun, blue skies and no humidity.

Pencarrick had been packed all week and almost all the guests, demob happy at finishing their courses, came down to the beach. They included the sailing boys, half a dozen painters, Orlando's cooks, Lucy's writers and Nelson's singers. And Lucy was there with her photographer admirer, so with staff and tutors they numbered sixty-odd.

It really was a perfect evening, one of those soft balmy ones which lift the toughest heart with gentle melancholy. Joanna felt a mild but persistent longing for Stewart. She missed him far more than she admitted, even to him. She wanted him with her when Pencarrick was, as now, at its absolute best, with the great orange sun racing for the horizon, speeding up as it sank into a gleaming sea.

Someone had put Jacques Brel on the CD player and the simple sad cadences contributed to the peace of the beach. Everyone sat talking quietly or gazing out to sea, stilled by the music and the evening light.

Things hotted up once the sun was set, supper was over and the bonfire blazing. Jacques Brel gave way to Latin American rhythms and the younger guests started to dance on the beach. Rebecca was in the thick of it, wiggling her bum and stamping her feet like a twenty-year-old. Joanna had to admit she was by far the best dancer there, and by far the oldest.

Joanna watched as she quit dancing and walked over to the sailing lads.

'C'mon boys,' she said, leaning down to take a beer bottle from the nearest young man's hand. 'I'll teach you the salsa. Anyone game?' And she began dancing, swirling about and pulling her skirt up to reveal her legs. Then she turned her back and jiggled her bottom at them. They laughed and jeered but they could not take their eyes off her. Tipping the bottle up to drain it, she went prancing round the beach on her own, as though this display was just for the pleasure of it because she was so good at it, and had nothing to do with having an audience.

She sashayed across to Orlando and took his hand in hers. With the other hand she tossed her empty beer bottle into the sandbank. 'Come,' she said, 'no one wants to dance with me, so you have to.'

Everyone's eyes were on her as she closed in on Orlando. He was a good dancer and they did the simple steps of the merengue and then the rumba, which, slow and sensuous, became progressively more raunchy.

Joanna could feel irritation flaring into anger. Why, she wondered, do I mind if Rebecca is a flirt?

Rebecca dragged Orlando over to the cluster of sailing lads and pulled one of them to his feet, then another.

Now she was dancing with both young men and Orlando, weaving her body close up against them one by one. The beat, switching to salsa, grew more frantic and the dancers became increasingly wild, kicking up sand and occasionally falling over, laughing. Rebecca pulled off her shirt to reveal a black bikini top.

The boys were all clapping now and some started shouting, 'Get 'em off, Becca.' She went on dancing and the calls got louder. Then, without losing a beat or pausing in her dance, she used both hands to unhook her bra behind her back. She did a few more stamps and twirls holding the bra in place, then suddenly she yanked it off and whirled it around her head. The boys clapped and cheered as she flung it at them.

They went on shouting 'Get 'em off!' and Joanna knew it would be the skirt and knickers next. She was tempted to intervene, but knew as soon as the thought occurred to her that she would only make a fool of herself. She turned away to hide her anger, and joined Nelson at the bar. He poured them both a rum punch.

'Let's get away from this,' he said, handing her the drink. 'Shall we walk along the beach?' Joanna, looking at his set face, realised he didn't like watching Rebecca on heat any more than she did.

'She's something else, isn't she?' he said, shaking his head.

'Becca? Yes, she is. I don't know why I get so cross. It's none of my business.'

'Yes it is,' he replied. 'This is your show and you've employed us all and she's breaking an unwritten rule: no fraternising with the guests. Besides, if she occupies Orlando's attention he will not do what you hired him to do, which is charm the women guests.'

Indignant, Joanna protested. 'That's not true! I hired him because he's a good cook and teacher.'

Nelson looked sideways at her, an amused and disbelieving eyebrow raised. He was right of course. Joanna hadn't even known if he was a good cook or teacher. She just knew he was famous and he'd draw in the punters.

'All right,' she said, 'I admit his celebrity was a factor.' They skirted some rocks and took a grassy path just above the beach. 'But Rebecca gets to you too, doesn't she? Are you jealous?'

'Yes and yes. Which is one of the reasons she does it, of course.'

'But you were never serious about her. Or were you, Nelson?'

'No, she's too demanding for me. She needs wall-to-wall attention, constant admiration, endless tributes at her feet. I just can't keep up with her. She's exhausting.'

Nelson's criticism of Rebecca somehow gratified Joanna, and she could afford to be kinder.

'But she's such fun and she's very generous. Sometimes I think her capacity for milking pleasure out of everything – shopping, decorating, flirting, lunching with her girlfriends – is admirable. Life-enhancing. She is such an antidote to my careful business instincts and Lucy's seriousness. Maybe we all need a Rebecca in our lives.'

'Sure, but on the fringes of one's life, not at the heart of it.'

Joanna's tolerance of Rebecca did not last. When she and Nelson returned to the party, all the sailing boys had disappeared. She peered at the thirty-odd remaining guests on the beach, but Rebecca was not among them. Joanna thought they might have gone back to the hotel but somehow doubted it. Vaguely anxious, she walked round the little bay, past the staff packing up the equipment and collecting scattered towels and empty bottles. She climbed up the rocks at the end of the beach and looked down on the second, smaller, cove.

The bright moonlight gave the scene a washed-out sheen, and the sea looked silky and slick, with tiny white ruffles at the shore. The scrap of beach and rocks were festooned with shorts and T-shirts, and both halves of Rebecca's bikini were draped over a piece of driftwood. The boys' heads were bobbing in the sea, and deep adolescent shouts and laughter accompanied Rebecca's exit from the water. She was stark naked and on the back of one of the boys, who was naked too. He zigzagged drunkenly through the soft sand, Rebecca's sopping hair hiding her face, buried in his neck.

Joanna watched in furious disbelief as the boy – it was the curly-headed blond one she'd said she fancied – put Rebecca down. She took him by the shoulders and turned him to face her, and put her hands on his bare buttocks and pulled his body into hers. Joanna turned away, seething, as Rebecca scooped up a towel and led Curly-head up the beach and offstage behind some rocks.

Joanna climbed the steep steps up to the hotel with her heart thumping as much from anger as from exertion. She went straight to her office and wrote a short note:

Rebecca, I'd like you to leave Pencarrick in the morning. Your behaviour tonight was absolutely out of order. I'm happy to pay you for the decor designs, but I cannot have you staying in the house. Joanna.

She felt better when she'd put the note (marked *Rebecca, Urgent*) on Rebecca's pillow. Good, she thought, that should get through her thick skin.

The next day Joanna had calmed down a lot, and when Rebecca appeared in her office looking distinctly the worse for wear, she was tempted to relent. She wanted to put her hands on her friend's shoulders and shake some sense into her.

'Look, Joanna, I am sorry,' Rebecca said. 'And yes, I agree I went too far with those boys. Only they *are* adults, and they loved it. Where's the harm?'

But Joanna remained distant. She was determined not to get into an argument and simply repeated her request that Rebecca leave.

Joanna asked Lucy to drive Rebecca to the station. She had not discussed last night with Lucy, and was a little uneasy that Rebecca would put a spin on events that would exonerate her and make Joanna into a prim schoolmarm, ice-cold and unfeeling. But, thought Joanna, I cannot run a hotel where one of the staff behaves like a whore. However much the punters like it.

Chapter Twenty-Seven

Rebecca sat in the corner of a first class railway carriage, sniffling into a handful of Kleenex. She was bunched up, huddled with her head down, rocking on her bottom just as she used to rock when unhappy as a child.

Her thoughts were running from angry to paranoid. What is the matter with me? Why does everyone want to change me all the time? Why do people always chuck me in the end? I never want to pick a quarrel. I'd never hurt anyone. All I want is for everyone to be happy, but in the end I always get dumped.

And I bet the fucking inspector comes and finds I haven't got a first class ticket.

She leaned back in the seat, gulping back tears and feeling drained. Every time she thought of that note of Joanna's a little wrench of misery wrung her guts.

She told herself she should be more resilient to disapproval. She should be used to it by now. Bill had spent their whole marriage trying to reform her: 'You are so extravagant', 'You drink too much' (which was rich since he drank like a fish), 'You are never serious', 'You are such a flirt'. Even Nelson found her 'too demanding', whatever that meant.

Rebecca half-expected men to find fault with her. But Joanna and Lucy! She *loved* those women and she had thought they really liked her. And she'd been so *proud* to have them for friends and so delighted to be taken seriously by them. She knew that they were big achievers and she was not, but they'd never let that show. They'd always been so great. So what had happened? What did she do? OK, she thought, it wasn't clever bonking Curly-head, but it's the twenty-first century for God's sake. And it was hardly a crime to be cast out into the cold for, was it?

Lucy had put her arm round Rebecca as they walked to the train, but Joanna! She would never have believed Jo-Jo could be so cruel. It had been just horrible, standing there in her office, trying to apologise, and Joanna looking at her with absolutely no understanding, no affection, nothing. Chin slightly up, mouth rigid, cold indifferent eyes, she just kept repeating, 'I won't discuss it, Rebecca. You're leaving, that's all.'

So here she bloody was. Sent home alone, expelled from the Garden of Eden. Yet again. Story of her life.

Rebecca stared out of the window onto a suitably miserable rainy Cornwall, while her mind drifted uncomfortably over previous rejections.

Of course the first time she'd got the heave-ho was when her mother dumped her in the orphanage at eighteen months old. She supposed a shrink would have some platitudes to utter about rejection and loss, but the truth was she did not remember that at all.

But she did remember being ejected from plenty of foster homes, so-called care homes, and schools. There was obviously something about her that invited the boot.

She knew she'd been difficult sometimes, but she was only trying to get people to like her, damn it. And the things that had caused the expulsions were always so bloody trivial. Ridiculous.

Like the time, she must have been nine or ten, when she nicked all the toffees hanging on the Christmas tree at the second (or was it the third?) foster home and ate them with the other children in the cupboard under the stairs. Those toffees had been meant for us, hadn't they? And it was only a day early, on Christmas Eve, that's all. The other children had thought she was a hero. A glimmer of a smile crossed Rebecca's blotchy face as she remembered their excited approval.

Anyway, she knew, and had known then, that the reason they'd sent her away was nothing to do with stealing sweets. It was because that pervert Clive was always putting her on his lap with his hand under her bum or on her thigh, and his wife didn't like it, that was the real reason.

To be honest, she, Rebecca, *had* liked it. It had been nice and warm tucked into his chest and he'd kiss the top of her head, and stroke her arms, up and down, up and down. It had felt really good. Letting him stroke bits of her that somehow she knew he shouldn't – though no one had ever said so – seemed fair enough.

A few homes and two schools later she had been thrown out of Appledorn Secondary Modern for selling joints. She used to get them from one of the boys in the care home, a sultry Elvis lookalike called Ian. He'd got them from the handyman. Ian had given her a fifty per cent discount, or sometimes even let her have the stuff for free, depending on how far she'd let him go in the gardener's hut beyond the soccer pitch. She was fourteen, he was a dead good-looking sixteen and they both enjoyed it, so it was hardly prostitution or anything.

But Rebecca, thinking back, had to admit she was heading down a slippery slope at that time. She was doing badly at school, and not 'fitting in' at home – stupid phrase, no one fits in in a care home, you just try to make a niche for yourself as best you can.

Her next school was OK though. There was this great dance and drama teacher, Miss Oxendale, who got her all fired up about acting and dancing. She said Rebecca was really talented, should concentrate, and blah blah blah, the usual stuff. But Rebecca believed it because she could tell that Miss Oxendale believed it herself and was not just giving her the routine praise that most of the teachers parroted all the time to everyone.

So the next year she was playing Juliet in the school production. And dancing in the modern dance group – they danced really sexy stuff to jazz and blues and rock. Maybe, thought Rebecca, that was the best time of her life.

Miss Oxendale had been small and skinny and generally dressed in neat grey or navy, always with stockings and high heels. She must have been forty or so. One day when the dance class was humping heavy wooden platforms to form a stage at one end of the hall, she'd called Rebecca to her. She was sitting, her shiny shoes neatly together, in a chair in the front row.

'Sit down, dear,' she'd said in her old-fashioned way, politely indicating the seat next to her. Rebecca sat, immediately defensive and anxious.

Miss Oxendale must have sensed it, because she'd smiled and said, 'Rebecca, you look as though you are expecting a ticking off! Are you?'

'No, Miss,' Rebecca lied. 'Well, yes, maybe. I'm always being told off.'

'Well, what I'm about to say could be construed as a telling off, or it could be construed as a friendly discussion. That will depend more on you than on me.'

Rebecca did not get this, but waited for the inevitable, racking her brains for what she'd done.

'Rebecca, I think you are a lot brighter than you think, and a lot more talented, but you disguise it very well.'

This didn't make sense. So Rebecca sat there, waiting for more.

'Because you don't think people take you seriously,' Miss O went on, 'you make sure you are never serious. For example, you are a very good dancer, and we'd still see that if you wore tights and leotards like everyone else. But you wear the shortest of hot-pants, the skimpiest of tank tops. Do you think that's because you don't think your dancing is good enough? That you'd better expose legs and belly to distract us from poor dancing?'

Rebecca didn't answer at first because she didn't believe it was a discussion, she figured it was a bollocking. But the teacher asked her again what she thought.

'I dunno, I just want to dress as I like.'

'But you know we all dress to make an impression on other people. I wear trousers and sweaters at home. But at school I wear these businesslike suits because I mean to be businesslike in my work. I wear high heels because I want to look smart, not dowdy. I want people to think I am a serious teacher but not a stodgy one. Do you understand that?'

Rebecca nodded. 'So,' continued Miss Oxendale, 'let's try and analyse the image you are trying to portray. What's the message you want to give?'

Rebecca could not answer that.

'OK,' said Miss O, 'do you want to be a good actress or a serious dancer?'

Rebecca knew the answer to that one all right. 'Yes, yes, of course, I want to be both, and I want to be the best, but . . .'

'Would you admit that ambition – to be the best – to your friends? Even to your school friends?'

'Of course not. No, no. They think I'm just a laugh. Which I am, I guess.'

'Let's try from the other end. Think of an actress you admire, who you think is serious about her profession.'

'Oh, that's easy, Vanessa Redgrave.'

'Describe the way she dresses.'

'Well, if she's out at a premiere or something, she wears movie-star clothes, you know, ball gowns and slinky dresses with low necks and jewellery and long gloves. But mostly she doesn't bother how she looks. I've seen pictures of her at rehearsal and she just wears jeans and pullovers. But she's beautiful anyway, without make-up or anything.'

'So are you, Rebecca. And you could be a successful actress too. But you have to believe it yourself. And I don't think you do. All this heavy make-up, false eyelashes, eyeliner, tarty clothes . . .'

'We aren't allowed make-up!'

'Not at school, no, but come on, Rebecca! I've seen you in the town, at the cinema. All that make-up and provocative clothes, they are just a safety net. It's easier if people think you are empty-headed and frivolous, because then you can't fail. But to succeed you need to commit to it, admit to yourself *and to other people* that you are serious, that you have more ambition than to be the local good-time girl.'

Rebecca remembered that she had started to protest, but Miss Oxendale had stood up and put her hand on Rebecca's shoulder.

'Think about it a bit.' She'd started to walk away and then turned. 'Oh, and by the way, you have lovely young skin. Putting all that slap on it makes you look forty.'

That hit home. Rebecca certainly didn't want to look like an old bag. From then on, she had thought about the impression she wanted to make. Her clothes and make-up, though never conventional, did get classier.

The memory of Miss Oxendale hurt. What had happened to her? Why hadn't she kept in touch with the woman? She'd got Rebecca into drama school. She'd even helped get her a scholarship. But, thought Rebecca, of course I let her down.

She had flunked out of RADA. Or, rather, she'd taken no notice of Miss O's advice when she was offered an ingenue part in a film. Rebecca could already see her name in lights, her picture in the movie mags, speculation about her boyfriends in the gossip columns, the first of a lifetime of big movie parts. She couldn't wait. But Miss O had advised staying at drama school, finishing the course, learning something more than how to pout prettily.

She'd been right of course. The movie bombed. Rebecca had done a few bit-parts and commercials after that, then waitressed like all the other wannabes.

And then, Rebecca thought, I just went back to doing what I do best: wiggling my bum and fluttering my eyelashes.

She had stopped crying by the time the train reached Plymouth, and she decided to go through to the dining car for some lunch.

She ordered half a bottle of Chardonnay, and instantly started to feel better. She told herself she would not be made miserable by those two. If they didn't like the way she behaved, then, tough. She could not become all moral and Victorian, and if they wouldn't speak to her, fine, she'd live.

Rebecca picked up her mobile, wondering who she could call. It would be good to go to the cinema or out to dinner or somewhere tonight – it would stop her moping at home. And, she thought, since she now had three unexpected days free, she shouldn't waste them. The problem was, her two best women friends were not speaking to her, and anyway they were in Cornwall and so were Orlando and Nelson.

But Rebecca was now determined not to be alone, and by the time she arrived at Paddington, she had booked a cinema ticket at the Curzon. There were generally some interesting people hanging around the bar there. Then she'd go to the Groucho Club, where she'd be sure to find someone she knew to chat to, even if it was only the staff. She'd have a lie-in tomorrow, then go to the gym. In the evening she'd reward herself by joining the Tango on Sundays class. Best of all, she'd have her first go at botox. Her Pilates coach had told her about a botox clinic run by two dentists (or ex-dentists since giving botox treatments had proved even more profitable than dentistry). Rebecca reckoned they would have steady hands and be good at getting the right amount of stuff into your wrinkles so you didn't come out looking like a plaster cast. The more she thought about it the more she liked the idea. A once-every-four-months treatment had got to be more effective, she thought, and maybe even cheaper, than all those astronomically expensive anti-wrinkle creams she kept buying. She'd made her appointment for Monday, after which she would ring Bill – it was good to stay close and friendly – propose a drink and see if he noticed anything.

Chapter Twenty-Eight

For Lucy, walking down to the harbour after her last workshop had become a habit. She liked to be there when the town's few remaining fishing boats came in, and two or three times a week she would buy fish off the quayside or food from the village store and cook supper while Joshua finished up in the studio.

Of course she dutifully ate at least twice a week with the course participants at Pencarrick. She enjoyed these dinners, and if he finished early Joshua might come too.

But Joshua was working to a punishing schedule on *Peasant Soups*. He had only agreed a contract for the book at the end of July, and he had to take fifty photographs before the end of August if the book was to be in the shops for November and the all-important Christmas period.

This meant talking to Lucy about the look she wanted for each soup, planning the set-ups, hiring the props, arranging the shots, buying the ingredients, cooking, styling and taking the shots. He was averaging two soups a day, including Saturdays. He had hired two assistants, one for the cooking and clearing, one for the set-up and actual shoot.

Lucy marvelled at just how much organisation and hard work this entailed. She had never done a glossy, picture-rich cookbook before and had always regarded the photographer's role as nothing compared to the writer's. But she was beginning to understand that pictures sold a book quite as much, if not more, than recipes and writing.

When Josh was done they often spent the evening at his house on the quayside. They never watched television and seldom went to a restaurant. If it was raining or cool they would sit in the kitchen and eat at the table. Afterwards, umbrella in hand, he would walk her slowly back to Pencarrick.

On balmy evenings they might sit at the wide open windows of the studio and watch the setting sun change the sea's colours and the sky momentarily brighten with streaks of orange.

Josh would put the open wine bottle beside her in a bucket of ice, and place a couple of beers at his feet – he liked some local pale ale that Lucy thought anaemic – and a tray of tapas from the local wine bar (or salami or cheese and bread with good olive oil to dip it in) on a stool between them. They'd eat and drink slowly, maybe for a couple of hours, allowing the sound of the waves on the breakwater to iron out the tensions of the day. They'd gossip about Pencarrick, and swap the day's news like old friends.

But mostly they would talk about books, art, politics. Not very often about the domestic issues of children or family. Maybe, thought Lucy, because Josh has never married and his parents live in Portugal.

But one day, after she had had a rather bruising round with Grace (Lucy wanted the children to come to Pencarrick before school started, but Grace said that Johnny had maths coaching), Lucy found herself saying, 'Do you know, Josh, I'm not sure I really love my daughter. I adore my grandchildren, but I seem to have lost Grace somewhere along the way.'

Joshua stretched his arm across the space between them to touch her elbow. 'I doubt it very much.' He turned to see her face properly. 'You wouldn't look so concerned if you didn't love her.'

'Maybe what I mean is she doesn't love me.' Lucy gave a little laugh, embarrassed to have said something so personal and possibly true.

'Children weave in and out of closeness with their parents

depending on their need. When they're homesick at school they cling like limpets; when they are happy they don't give Mum or Dad a thought. Except of course if they need pocket money, or new trainers or something.'

'True,' said Lucy, 'and when they have their own children, their attention shifts off Mama altogether.'

'Poor Lucy. That must make widowhood so hard. The so-called Third Age is tough for most people, but for women like you it must feel very bleak.'

'Women like me?'

'Yes, women who have been the lynchpin to whom everyone turns for answers. It must feel as if no one needs you any more.'

Lucy was impressed that Josh understood so well. 'And it's not just the children and husband,' she said, 'it's everyone around the family, like the kids' school teachers or the guy who mows the lawn. *No one* needs you anymore.'

They both digested this, then Joshua asked, 'Are you still very unhappy?'

'No,' she said, and as she said it she knew she was speaking the truth. 'Since I've been here I have cheered up a lot.'

Lucy hesitated. She wanted to tell Josh that he had been largely responsible for this, that without him she might well have given up and gone back to London, that he had shown her the charm, as well as the glories, of Cornwall. But a residual taboo about being too 'forward' inhibited her.

Yet some thanks were due, and she said, 'You know Josh, you've really helped me. And the best thing is that it has not felt like help at all. You've been wonderful.'

'No more wonderful than you have been for me, Lucy.'

Lucy, never easy with compliments and embarrassed by this one, ignored the remark and plunged on with her thank you speech. 'And then it's just so good to have an escape from Pencarrick — which I love of course, but there is only so much foodie talk that I can bear.'

'Good,' he said. 'I'm glad. I like having you here.' He stood up and closed the big studio windows. 'Shall we go downstairs?' he said. 'It's getting cold, and it's comfier in the sitting room.'

As they put dishes and glasses from their supper on a tray, Joshua said, 'This has been the best summer I can remember.' Then he looked up from stacking the empty tapas dishes and, his voice suddenly serious, went on, 'I've loved working with you, Lucy. I've never met anyone like you. But I confess that angling for the job of photographer was a bit of a cover story.'

'What do you mean?' Oh dear. She told herself he couldn't possibly mean what she thought he might. She felt her heart give a little lurch.

He followed her to the little studio sink. 'I wanted to see more of the wonderful Lucy, cookery doyenne and—'

'Oh, don't call me that, Josh, I hate it! Sounds so pompous and ancient!'

She had just put the tray down by the studio sink when he reached out to catch her wrist and prevent her starting to wash up.

'No, you don't,' he said. 'And *doyenne* doesn't sound pompous. It sounds wise and knowledgeable and sensible. All of which you are.' He did not let go of her but pulled her gently away from the sink, and then he leant forward to take her other wrist.

The cool of his fingers and the unfamiliar, long-forgotten feeling in her gut made it hard to concentrate.

'Lucy, you are one hell of a woman.'

She was up against his chest now, her face fractionally below his. She could smell his aftershave, clean and sharp.

'I am?' she said, but she was only just hanging on to the normality of conversation. Her face felt flushed and her throat tight. He's going to kiss me, she thought. And I really don't want that.

She tried to disengage her hands, but he tightened his grip.

Lucy's mind remained determinedly detached, even while her heart beat faster. He doesn't feel like David, she thought. He's heavier and shorter. David was bony, especially near the end. I cannot believe I'm going to let another man kiss me.

He did kiss her then, not passionately or deeply, but almost experimentally, with his eyes open. A dry, gentle kiss. Then he stood back and looked at her.

Oh, hell, thought Lucy, I think I have failed the test. And I want to go on seeing him too. If I reject him he'll be offended and will disappear.

Feeling oddly as though it was not her that was doing this, Lucy slipped her hands from his and brought her arms up around his neck.

She let her eyes close and allowed his arms to wrap around her, his body close against hers. When David had hugged her she felt his chest and his thighs as much as his stomach. With Josh, it was mostly tummy.

But it's not so bad, she thought. Not at all like David, but it's OK. It's actually rather nice. Go with the flow, that's what I'll do.

Joshua hugged her tighter and tried to kiss her again, this time with more fervour. But his glasses crashed into hers and knocked them askew.

'God, I'm sorry!' he said, dropping his arms and stepping back. With her glasses half off Lucy could not see his face clearly. She pushed them into place and burst out laughing.

For a moment he stood, dismayed, then laughed too. 'Bit out of practice, I'm afraid.'

'Snap,' she said, 'and I'm not sure I'm ready for it anyway.'

Lucy turned back to the sink and said, 'Josh, do you think I could just stick this stuff in the dishwasher while you make us some tea?'

'I don't think I have ever heard such a romantic suggestion!' he said. But he was smiling like the Cheshire cat.

Chapter Twenty-Nine

A week after banishing Rebecca from Pencarrick, Joanna had to go north to a Greenfarms meeting. She still felt unsettled and unhappy about the row with her friend, and she was tempted to ring her and make amends, but she couldn't do that without asking her to return. And she did not feel up to controlling Rebecca. The woman was a law unto herself, incapable of acting her age: you could not change her, you just had to let her be. But she missed her.

She usually visited Greenfarms every week for a catch up with Caroline and Stewart but last week Pencarrick's high season had forced her to cancel.

So she hadn't been with Stewart for a fortnight and she was both longing to see him and dreading it. The thought of Stewart as her lover still made her feel sick with anticipation, but Stewart as her chairman and the father of Caroline was another thing. She could not put off the confrontation over his daughter any longer.

Stewart met her off the ten a.m. train. As he put his arms around her and she buried her face in his collar, for a moment she couldn't speak. It was just so good to be where she belonged: inside that embrace, breathing in the familiar smell of him.

He drove to her hotel. She grabbed her overnight bag and jumped out. 'I won't be a minute. I'll just check in and they can take my bag up.'

But he followed her. 'I'm coming with you,' he said, 'It's only been two weeks but it's felt like for ever. I can't wait any longer, let's go to bed.'

'But we've a board meeting in half an hour!'

'No we haven't. I put it off until this afternoon. "Urgent business" I said. Which is true.'

The Wakefield Hotel was hideous, all swirly carpets and lumpy brown furniture, but to Joanna it was veritable heaven. Latterly, since Caroline had found out about her and Stewart and there was no longer any real need for secrecy, she had spent one or two nights in his big old house. But she didn't feel easy in Elaine's territory and, if she had to stay in Yorkshire, she preferred the hotel. After work, with both their mobile phones off and no one knowing where they were, they could exist in a private cocoon of love, sex and drifting sleep.

So the ugly hotel bedroom welcomed her with comfortable familiarity and she simply put off the evil hour of the Caroline conversation. She would live in the moment.

At one o'clock she woke up, ravenous. Stewart was snoring gently, and she had to ease herself from under his arm. She rang room service for sandwiches and a pot of tea.

Stewart stroked her spine idly with his finger-tips. 'No champagne?'

'No, darling, I need a clear head for the meeting.' And, she thought, to talk to you.

They ate the sandwiches and drank the tea, slowly waking to the outside world. At last Joanna summoned her courage. She went into the bathroom and quickly dressed. Somehow she could not have this conversation naked. When she returned, Stewart had got as far as his boxer shorts and one sock and was sitting on the bed, pulling on the other.

'Stewart, I need to talk to you.'

'Oh? What about?'

Joanna didn't think he was really listening and she fetched the dressing table stool and sat on it, facing him where he sat on the side of the bed. If she sat next to him he would surely put his arms around her and she would abandon her mission.

She felt her heart sink as she began.

'Stewart, the thing is, we have to persuade Caroline to resign. She's a liability.'

'How can you say that? The business is doing brilliantly.' She heard the hardening in his voice, but she kept hers steady and gentle.

'No, it's not. It's breaking even, yes. But I am getting pleas from the executives about Caroline.'

She watched Stewart setting his jaw, the colour rising in his cheeks. She ploughed on.

'Her management style is dreadful. She loves the business, she has real sympathy for the workers, but she seldom has a kind word for any of her managers. She countermands their instructions, rides roughshod over their plans.' She held her hand up to stop Stewart interrupting. 'Hear me out, Stewart. Caroline won't sit down and talk about anything. Frankly, darling, she's going to lose her senior staff. Two of them are looking for other jobs as we speak. And if they go, then more in the office and in distribution will follow.'

'I don't believe it.'

This got to Joanna and she could feel her famous cool melting. 'Is there any reason why I should lie to you? Or any reason why, if there wasn't a problem, the senior staff should appeal to me?'

She managed to keep her voice calm, but it sounded hard and bossy. Horrible. Not an hour ago it had been soft and dreamy with love. With difficulty Joanna re-girded her tough business persona.

'Stewart, it is not just the senior staff. Caroline is contemptuous of the board and only implements decisions if she agrees with them. She constantly backtracks on policies the directors have agreed upon, but which she argued against at the time and lost.'

Stewart shakes his head. 'That's not true, Joanna. Name one instance.'

Joanna hated doing this. She had become fond of Caroline despite everything, and she admired her. And since the awful business of explaining the redundancies to the workforce, Caroline had been, if not friendly, at least less quarrelsome and prickly.

Most of all she hated to see Stewart antagonistic and angry, but she told herself to be professional, wear her business hat and do the job she'd been hired to do.

'OK. You will remember that back at the start of the year we agreed to mothball half the factory. This would halve the energy costs, maintenance costs and staff costs.' She was looking into his face, but he would not meet her eye. She stopped speaking and waited until he reluctantly faced her.

'That was months ago. She only agreed the redundancies because you had me go in and sort it out with her and Alasdair. So at least that is done and dusted. But we now have the ridiculous situation of an enormous factory being used to produce very little. And of course it has to be heated, cleaned, maintained. It costs money we simply cannot afford. I've raised the question with her on almost every visit and she either agrees she needs to get on with it, or argues that it really isn't necessary, or gets emotional and says I'm hounding her.'

Stewart's expression went from angry to unhappy. He said nothing for a while, and then leant forward to take Joanna's shoulders and look into her face.

'Darling, are you sure you're not misjudging her? Maybe she's confident of winning new business that would fill the space?'

Joanna gently pushed his hands off her shoulders. 'Sweetheart, don't touch me. I need to be rational about this, and your hands on me make it impossible. You know there are no big orders in the pipeline, nor likely to be since we've agreed not to sell to the big supermarkets. The problem is that Caroline sees visible retrenchment as a sign of failure. She's an "onwards and upwards" person, not one prepared to take a step back in order to take two forward. If we asked her to add more factory space, she'd do it in a week.'

Stewart sat thinking, not looking at her. She pressed her point home.

'Our growth now is organic, slow but steady. Which is fine, since you and I are the principle investors and we are happy with slow but steady. But merely breaking even won't do. If we're to start making money, we need to save more costs.'

When he answered there was anguish in his voice.

'But why do we have to sack Caroline? We should just insist she carries out board decisions.'

'Stewart, I've tried. Believe me, I have tried. But Caroline cannot hear what she doesn't want to hear. She can't help it. She's a typical start-up entrepreneur, all imagination and passion but, like so many, a nightmare to work with.'

Stewart said what Joanna knew he would, and her heart sank.

'I can't do it, Joanna. It's Caroline's company. She dreamt it up, she got it going, and it's her life.'

One last try, thought Joanna, without much hope. 'Stewart, I have turned round a fistful of companies. This is the first time I have agreed to the existing CEO staying in post. And I'm ashamed to say I only agreed because I'm in love with you. I never should have. Of course I told myself it could work, and that we owed it to her to give her a chance. I would have loved it to work.'

Stewart countered. 'But it *is* working. We are doing better!'

'Not better enough, and not fast enough, and not with a happy workforce.'

They went on, Joanna detailing Caroline's failings, Stewart defending her. Joanna knew that with every word she said she was doing her duty by the company and ruining her relationship with her lover. She knew he saw the sense of her argument, but could not bear to follow it through to the consequences. After a while he stopped arguing, and just looked miserable.

There was a long silence. Joanna, her heart weak with sympathy, longed to stretch out her arms and pull his head into her breast, to kiss his thinning patch, to make it better.

She said, 'It's hard, darling, but it's simple. If you want to keep Caroline in post, then I will resign today at the board, you can buy me out, and you'll have a lifestyle business that will probably just about give her a living, but won't ever repay your investment. Or you can let me run the business, and make some money for all of us, including Caroline.'

He looked at her, his eyes defeated, his voice dead. 'Don't go on any more, Joanna.' He stood up, his shoulders slumped. 'You're right of course. I will tell Caroline to resign.'

As they drove to the office, Joanna wanted to beg him to say that this changed nothing between them, that it would not affect their love affair. Most of all she wanted him to say that he loved her. He had never said that. Perhaps now he never would.

But she feared the wrong answer, and said nothing.

There was not a word from Stewart after the board and Joanna would not let herself ring him.

Alone that night in the hotel, she wished she could telephone her father and tell him her troubles, but she'd never done that. She'd seldom complained as a child – trying too hard to be Little Miss Perfect. They talked only of her successes. He's got a completely skewed vision of me, thought Joanna. And it was now too late for confidences.

It was worse with her mother. On their long-ago visit to London she'd chided Joanna for her feebleness with Tom, saying she should *make* him marry her. Or come home and find some nice Australian man before it was too late to catch anybody. Her mother's certainty of her own rightness and lack of understanding had driven Joanna mad.

She could ring Lucy of course. Lucy was lovely – sensible and understanding and kind. But Joanna didn't want her friends to know her affair with Stewart was going wrong. Not while there is hope, she thought. But was there?

That night she slept the sleep of exhaustion. She was unhappy, yes, but so tired she could barely feel the pain.

*　　　*　　　*

The next morning she took herself to work with a heavy heart. That, she thought, is exactly what it feels like, as though I had this leaden lump of misery in my chest, weighing me down, preventing me from breathing. But she went to work because she had a meeting with Alasdair in the morning, and because, whatever happened, she had a hard afternoon's work ahead of her.

She suspected Stewart might have changed his mind about Caroline. There was no sign of him at the business. Caroline was in and out of the office, clearly oblivious to any impending sword of Damocles. If Stewart had decided Caroline was to stay, then she would have to resign and tell everyone. On the other hand, if he was sticking to his promise, then she would need to plan the damage limitation exercise. He was too experienced a businessman not to give her time to organise a plan of communication for the company. He would ring if he was going to sack her. Either he'd changed his mind or he was undecided.

At noon she had a text message from him. She opened it, praying it would be a personal, loving one, sympathetic to their joint plight.

'Will do the deed this afternoon at five p.m. Caroline will not be returning to work. Please inform the staff she has resigned.'

Do the deed! The unfairness of the implication! With its overtones of stabbing in the back and Lady Macbeth inciting her husband to murder. And then a curt chairman's command to follow through.

But Joanna tightened her jaw and put her feelings aside. She went into business-crisis mode. These things needed clear thinking if they were not to escalate appallingly. She drew a pad towards her and started jotting. She would need to draft the central points of the message and get the board and execs to put the right spin on it: Caroline resigning, looking for a new challenge, leaving the company in good hands, the usual stuff.

Her mind turned to timing. Five o'clock. Clever Stewart: too late for Caroline's possible histrionics to get to the office workers who left at five. And the trick would be to make sure the key people knew immediately, before Caroline could speak to them.

They had to be trusted to tell no one overnight. Then the info had to be cascaded down the organisation with no time between meetings for leaking.

She wrote:

5 pm:　　　　*Alasdair re acting CEO*

5.30 pm:　　　*Exec board*

9 am tomorrow: Execs to tell their teams

10 am:　　　　*Execs to tell*
　　　　　　　　factory staff
　　　　　　　　distribution
　　　　　　　　agric.workers
　　　　　　　　transport
　　　　　　　Me to tell office staff with Alasdair.

11 am:　　　　*Fax local paper with press release*

With luck she'd be on a train before midday tomorrow.

She picked up the telephone to her PA. 'Carla, book me into the Wakefield for one more night will you? And can you track Alasdair down and see if he could come to the office at five? Tell him it's important.'

At nine o'clock that evening Joanna was sitting up in bed, surrounded by papers and trying to make sense of Pencarrick's finances, when the telephone rang.

'I want to speak to Mr Stewart Muirhead.' It was a tense woman's voice, vaguely familiar, with a pronounced Yorkshire accent.

'He's not here, I'm afraid, can I help?'

'Oh, is that you, Miss Joanna?' Only one person called her Miss Joanna. Doris, Stewart's housekeeper.

'Doris, it's Joanna. Is something wrong, Stewart isn't . . .' And then she realised nothing could be wrong with Stewart, because Doris thought he was there with her.

'Oh Miss Joanna. Please come. It's Miss Caroline, she's not right. She's ill . . . I don't know what to . . .'

'What sort of ill?'

'She's taken something, Miss. And now I can't wake her . . . I've called the ambulance, but they haven't come and I . . .'

Joanna was already out of bed, reaching for her clothes.

'Doris, where are you? At Caroline's house?'

Doris's voice was going up. She was stuttering and shouting. 'Please come . . . please . . . I just found her . . .'

'Doris. You need to be calm. Is she breathing?'

'Please come, Miss . . . Breathing? Yes, she's moaning . . .'

Joanna tucked the telephone under her cheek and started pulling on her trousers and shirt. Forget underwear, she thought, just get a jacket, money, keys.

'Doris,' Joanna almost yelled, 'which house are you in? Stewart's?'

'Yes. Yes, the big house.'

'And you have rung for an ambulance? What did they say?'

'They said they were coming . . . but . . .'

'Good. Just stay with her, Doris. If the ambulance comes, just do as the paramedics say. OK?'

She slammed down the phone, yanked her jacket off its hanger in the cupboard, grabbed her keys and bag and ran down the stairs.

Joanna was good in a crisis, and within minutes she was on her way, being driven by one of the Wakefield hotel waiters in the hotel manager's car.

As they slowed to a halt in front of the house they heard the sound of a siren, and Joanna looked back to see an ambulance turn into the drive. Thank God, she thought, someone else can take charge.

The front door was ajar, the hall brightly lit, and she sprinted through to the drawing room. Caroline was lying on the sofa dressed in a crumpled summer dress. Doris was kneeling beside her, washing the carpet. There was the sour smell of alcohol and vomit with an overlay of Doris's carpet cleaner.

As Joanna came in, Doris looked up. 'Oh, thank God. Is the ambulance here? She's been sick. I got a bucket but . . .'

'You did brilliantly,' said Joanna, putting her arm briefly round the woman's shoulder, and sitting on the edge of the sofa. She took Caroline's hand in both of hers and looked into her face. She was pale, but conscious. Her face was covered in tiny beads of sweat and curls of damp hair stuck to her forehead and neck.

'Poor darling,' she said. 'What did you take, Caroline?'

Caroline looked at her and shook her head, then closed her eyes. Joanna used her bare hand to stroke Caroline's brow and face, half caress, half to wipe away the sweat. Caroline's eyes fluttered open for a moment, then closed, a look of relief, or maybe just exhaustion, on her face.

And then the paramedics were there, all kindness and calm efficiency, asking Joanna and Doris if they knew what Caroline had swallowed, asking Doris to give them the bucket in case it was needed for analysis, lifting Caroline onto a stretcher, carrying her out and into the ambulance, strapping her into the narrow bed.

One of them turned to Joanna. 'Could you have a look around the house, in a bedroom or bathroom, and see if you can find the pill bottle or package?'

Joanna darted upstairs and checked all the bedrooms and bathrooms while Doris checked the downstairs rooms. Nothing.

Doris agreed to search Caroline's house while Joanna went in the ambulance with Caroline. She was touched that Caroline held onto her hand in the ambulance, until the paramedic gently told Joanna that she must sit opposite, strapped in her seat.

In Accident and Emergency, they acted fast, wheeling Caroline away to pump out her stomach or whatever they had to do. Joanna sat on the hard plastic chair in reception and dialled Stewart. He did not answer and she had to leave him a message.

Stewart, I don't know where you are, but Caroline needs you. She's in no danger now but she's having her stomach pumped for a suspected overdose. She's in A & E in the Pinderfields General Hospital. She told Doris she'd swallowed a bottle of pills, but would not say what. I'm so sorry, darling. Ring me.

Stewart did not ring back, or turn up, and Joanna began to worry. Mark had moved to London when he left Greenfarms, and she didn't know any of Caroline's friends.

And then a young doctor appeared and told her that they had pumped out what was left of the contents of Caroline's stomach which wasn't much since she seemed to have vomited very thoroughly, so they saw no real danger. They had not analysed anything yet and Caroline refused to say what she had taken, so as yet they had no idea. Did she?

No, she didn't. She only knew that Caroline had said she'd swallowed a bottle of pills – but they'd found no suspect bottle in either house.

They would keep her in overnight, the doctor said, and if all was well she could collect her daughter in the morning.

Joanna was too tired to put him right, so just nodded and said fine, but could he get someone to note that Joanna's father was called Stewart Muirhead and that he would probably be in to see her tonight or tomorrow.

Joanna went home and again tried Stewart. '*This telephone is not in use.*' She rang the Howard Hotel in London and, relief, he was staying there, but was not in his suite. Trying to keep the frustration and worry out of her voice she left a similar message to the one she'd already left on his mobile.

She had a cup of tea and a bowl of cornflakes and, too tired to even turn on the TV, went to bed and was asleep at once. But anxiety woke her constantly and she slept badly until dawn, when exhaustion prevailed, and she overslept.

*   *   *

At eight a.m. Joanna struggled up and rang the Howard. Stewart had left. She checked her mobile. One missed call from him, but no message. Now she was angry. Why could he not at least tell her if he was coming home to take over the rescue of his daughter?

She rang the hospital. Caroline was asleep. She was doing well. The doctor would see her later.

Good, if Caroline was asleep there was no point in visiting her. And they'd not let her out till the doc had seen her – and by then surely Stewart would have been.

So Joanna went to the office as planned and she and the team carried out the various briefings to the staff about Caroline's resignation. Ironically, the news of her being in Pinderfields had somehow leaked, but seemed to confirm the general belief that she was overstretched and in need of rest, rather than that she'd been sacked and was taking revenge on her father by trying to kill herself.

At ten her mobile rang in her pocket and she excused herself to take it in the corridor. It was the hospital to say that Caroline could go home. The result of the stomach content analysis had revealed nothing but too much alcohol – no overdose of anything.

As soon as the last meeting with the staff, and her final meeting with Alasdair who would now be acting chief executive, were over, Joanna hurried to the hospital.

She found Caroline lying, neat and tidy, against her pillows, her newly washed hair like a thick halo around her pale face. She looked very young and vulnerable, but not ill.

Joanna sat down. She spoke without preamble, but kindly,

'Do you want to talk about it? Can I help? Or am I still the problem?'

Caroline's eyes lacked their usual glint of enthusiasm or fury. 'Where's Dad?' she said dully.

'I don't know. I'm worried about him.'

Caroline frowned, and Joanna had the feeling that the idea of worrying about her father had never crossed her mind. He was there to worry about her.

'Why? Why are you worried about him? He doesn't need worrying about!'

'Maybe not. But if you love someone, you worry about them. End of story.'

Caroline did not answer, but Joanna watched her expression go from puzzlement, to truculence, to concern.

'Do you want to talk about it?'

Caroline just shook her head, her eyes full of tears.

'Look, Caroline, I know that you did not take an overdose of anything. But I also know you would not have pretended you had if you did not need help. I presume what triggered this was either your dismissal or your dad's relationship with me.'

Again, a shake of the head.

Joanna sat for a minute or two, then decided she should say something of what she'd been thinking about all night.

'I don't think Stewart or I have been fair to you. You are a brilliant young woman in many ways but neither of us has treated you as a grown-up. We have pussyfooted around you, and not told you the truth, either about us, or about you. Do you want me to be honest now? Or to just go away?'

Joanna watched as Caroline tussled with the temptation to take the latter offer.

'No, say what you want to say.'

So Joanna did. She told him that she loved Stewart, and that was the only reason she had agreed to Caroline remaining as CEO when she knew it was the wrong job for her.

'That was my fault. I should never have agreed. You are a brilliant visionary, a great start-up entrepreneur, but not the sort of safe pair of hands for a business. You need to forget Greenfarms and do something else.' She held up a hand to prevent Caroline interrupting. 'OK, I know you don't believe that now, but one day you will. And you don't know how badly Stewart wanted to believe you could do the job. He fought like a tiger to convince himself. And when he gave in, you'd think I'd delivered a death sentence, not a business decision.'

Something of the old Caroline fire kindled as she snapped, 'So it's as I thought. It's all your doing. Why? Why do you hate me so much?'

Joanna suddenly felt too tired to go on explaining. 'Caroline, you know that isn't true. How about just believing what I'm telling you? I admire and like you, and your father loves you . . .'

'How can he if he sacks me? He hates me too!'

Joanna shook her head in irritation. 'Don't be childish, Caroline. He loves you more than life itself. I know it would be convenient for you to cast me as the villainess, and him as the cruel father, but it won't wash. We want what's best for you. And the business.'

Caroline closed her eyes, her face set in hostility, but tears were leaking out under her lashes. Joanna felt a wave of sympathy for her.

'Listen, Caroline, Stewart's love for you and Mark was the one thing that kept him going after Elaine's death, and your hostility to me is what prevents him really loving me—'

Caroline's eyes snapped opened and she interrupted. 'That's rubbish. He's always tucked up in the Wakefield hotel with you, or down in London, or even in Mum's bed, for God's sake. He's mad about you.'

Joanna tried to ignore the bitterness in Caroline's tone. 'I think he loves me, yes. But he's never said so, and now he probably never will. It came down to a simple choice between you and me, and he's chosen you. He has not spoken one word to me since I insisted you had to go. I love your father, Caroline, and if he ever changes his mind, I'll be there. But he will never do that if it means he loses you.'

Tears were now streaming freely down Caroline's pale face. 'Well, where is he then? If he loves me, why isn't he here?'

'I don't know.' Joanna passed Caroline a handful of tissues and took one for herself. She blew her nose.

'The funny thing is I sort of understand it. When you love

someone that much, you'll do anything not to jeopardise it. Maybe reject other people you could love.'

'But where *is* he?'

'I don't know.' Joanna said again. 'What happened when he told you about leaving the company? You must have been upset. Why didn't he stay with you?'

Caroline wiped her eyes with the tissues and between sobs said, 'It was horrible. I said a lot of stuff. That I hated him, that he was a control freak. That he'd always made Mum unhappy, that Mark couldn't stand him. That he could bugger off and live with you. Oh, God, what have I done? Where is he?'

Joanna put a tentative hand on Caroline's arm, and tried to look into her face, but Caroline would not look up.

'Stewart will know that none of that is true,' Joanna said. 'And he's probably on his way. I left a message at his London hotel last night — his mobile seems to be out of action. He'll be here, I'm sure.'

Caroline's weeping was now reduced to sniffles. Joanna found herself saying, 'I love my father too. Spent my childhood trying to get his attention, mostly without success. My mother seemed to just absorb all his interest. To sort of use him up. I'd have given anything for him to love me as Stewart loves you.'

Joanna smoothed the sheet unnecessarily. 'You two have something you both need to hang on to.'

They were silent for a moment and then Caroline said, 'Mark used to say it wasn't fair. That Dad loved me best. Maybe he did, but he tried to treat us the same. I got a bike, Mark got a bike. Stuff like that.'

'You know,' said Joanna, 'I'm not out to steal Stewart.' She could hear the twinge of bitterness in her own voice as she said, 'I'm in the familiar position of trying to get a look-in.'

Caroline did not reply but gave a fractional nod and buried her face in her bunch of sodden tissues.

Joanna went to the pantry and managed to get a tray of tea out of the catering staff. She carried it back to the ward, wondering where to take Caroline. She could not be alone, and she would not want to be looked after by Joanna. That fleeting dependency in the ambulance, when she'd reached for Joanna's hand, had vanished.

Joanna pushed the door open with her bottom and entered Caroline's room backwards, tray in hand. She turned towards the bed, and stopped dead. Stewart was there, his arms around his daughter. Joanna could see her small hands clutching her father's back.

She put the tray down on the trolley-shelf across the bed, and slipped out.

That evening, back in London, Joanna had an email from Stewart.

Thank you for rescuing Caroline. We are at my house. She's fine.
    Apologies for the radio silence. I stupidly left my mobile in a taxi.
    Going to St Moritz tomorrow and taking C. Fresh air might help.
    Please don't abandon Greenfarms. Stewart

Joanna looked up from her computer, feeling wretched – part misery, part anger. How dare he write her a cool little email as if she was the district nurse to whom he'd been a bit rude? The bastard.

But she knew she'd do as instructed. She could not abandon Greenfarms now.

Chapter Thirty

Lucy knew it was time she talked to Joanna. She had been hatching her scheme for weeks, and the excitement of it was building in her daily. It was late September and she had been back from Cornwall ten days now, but she thought of Pencarrick all the time.

Lucy's grand plan was to sell up and move to Cornwall. And she hoped to buy Pencarrick, preferably with Joanna. She'd found she could write there, and was much happier than in the Cotswolds. She liked the coming and going of the summer guests and lecturers, and she felt no resentment at seeing so little of her daughter and grandchildren. When at home in the house she and David had shared for thirty years, it was becoming harder to pretend she was happy. She still felt David's absence – she hated arriving at night to a dark empty house – and every weekend she longed for Grace and Archie to bring her grandchildren down. Of course she never asked them directly for fear they'd sense her loneliness.

They seldom came. They had good reasons of course: Clare had classes or parties to go to; Archie was working; Grace had theatre tickets.

At first Lucy had worried that it was Joshua who made the difference, rather than Pencarrick, but now she knew it was not so. True, he was an important part of her dream for the future, a comfortable, companionable part, but he wasn't *the* reason for it. After that evening when they had made a half-hearted attempt at intimacy, they had settled down to a close friendship which frequently included a night together. The sex was pleasant and affectionate but what Lucy liked was the talk. Joshua was well-read, clever and perceptive. He was interested in just about everything; current affairs, archaeology, birds, gardening, art. And food of course. He was so *peaceable*. He was content not to see her at all for days on end if she was working, yet happy to have her sit on a stool and chat while he cooked. He was, she thought, the perfect buttress against depression, and her passport into Cornish life. He knew everyone, and liked almost all of them.

She felt lighter, more fun, more gregarious with him. And he understood her. One afternoon on a breezy autumn day they were walking along the cliff path.

'You look good in the wind, Lucy.'

She'd laughed and said, 'Oh yeah? And with an ancient sweater and baggy jeans, I suppose?'

'Well, yes. To tell the truth, when you arrived you were a bit too grand for me. So smart, with your London haircut and fashionable clothes.'

'If you only knew! All that was because Rebecca took me in hand and gave me a makeover. It was good for me, shook me out of a slump after David died. But I confess to backsliding. Becca is deeply disappointed in me!'

Joshua took her arm and gave her a brief hug. 'Maybe that's because you are happier, and can afford to be yourself.'

'Maybe.' He was, thought Lucy, the true friend that everyone needs. Perhaps she'd found that someone to do things with, and more important, to do nothing with.

But to buy Pencarrick, and to run it, Lucy needed Joanna. She rang her mobile.

'Jo, are you going anywhere after singing tonight? Can we have supper?'

'Sure. I'm free as air.'

Lucy knew at once that something was wrong. Joanna's voice was too light, too controlled.

'Jo, has something happened? Where's Stewart? You don't sound right.'

'He's not here. I'll tell you later. After the class. I'll book a table at the Notting Hill Brasserie. We can hear ourselves speak there.'

Lucy had not come up from Pencarrick very often during the summer and had forgotten that the *Messiah* was to be sung by four choirs. So when she arrived at the rehearsal hall, she was dismayed to find Nelson getting thirty-odd people, at least half of them men she'd never clapped eyes on, to collect chairs and arrange them theatre-style. She liked their usual group of perhaps fifteen to twenty singers, and felt invaded by strangers.

She called to Joanna, 'Jo, do you know what's going on?'

Joanna shoved a chair into place and came over.

'We're joining up with the Maida Vale Male Voice Choir.'

'But why?'

'Because on the big night, the chorus will consist of four singing groups. Together we might do justice to the Tabernacle space – it's vast.'

'Oh God, yes,' she said, 'But where are the other two choirs? And who are they?'

'I think Nelson said they're the Marylebone Choral Society and the Kensington Singers or something like that. And apparently they are rehearsing together tonight too, but not with us.'

Nelson loped over then and kissed both women.

'Where's Rebecca?' he asked. 'She said she'd be back at the end of August, but she didn't show last week. Is she coming?'

'I don't know,' said Lucy. 'I haven't seen her since I put her on the Truro train.'

Joanna shook her head. 'She's not here. I looked.'

Nelson's face registered disapproval. 'Aren't you worried about her?' He took out his mobile. 'I'll give her a ring.' Within seconds he was talking to Rebecca, in that joky West Indian patois he affected sometimes.

'Greetins, honey-chile. Dis 'ere yo singing teacher, wants to know what going down? Bot' yo' lady friends is here, and we got nudder choir joinin' in. Going to be a blast, baby.'

Lucy studied his face as Rebecca answered. She could not hear what she said, but the deepening frown on Nelson's face told it all. He clipped his phone shut and put it in his pocket, then looked from Lucy to Joanna. Dropping the patois, he said, 'She's not coming. She says you two wouldn't want to see her. And she's not too keen to see you either.'

Lucy felt a wash of shame. Why had she not contacted Rebecca? Rebecca who had been so good to her when she was depressed. Rebecca who took her shopping and overhauled her wardrobe. Rebecca who would buy champagne at the drop of a hat.

Nelson was still speaking. 'Good Lord, women, you got to be friends with Rebecca. You not young enough to make a whole heap new friends now.' He looked earnestly at them and then suddenly grinned. 'Besides, she has a nice soprano voice and we need her.'

Lucy didn't answer, but she knew Nelson was right.

She opened her mouth to say something, but Nelson was walking to the front of the rows of chairs, clapping his hands for silence. Next to him was a small man with round specs and unruly hair, wearing a mustard waistcoat over a check shirt. Nelson introduced him.

'Ladies and gentleman, this is Bryn Jones, and he'll be our conductor on the big night. He's taking the rehearsal today. He's the leader of the Maida Vale Male Voice Choir, and these handsome fellas belong to that choir. Gentlemen, you are all very welcome.'

Then Bryn Jones took over. He started by organising the singers, separating the tenors from the basses, the sopranos from the altos. He asked everyone to stand and got them singing single notes, louder and louder: mmmaaaa, mmmaaa; then humming up and down the scales and doing breathing and relaxing exercises.

Lucy was faintly irritated. Warming up was good, but this seemed to be going on for ever. But she did as she was told, largely because

Bryn's eyes roved constantly over the group. He had undoubted authority and she did not want to cross him.

She was relieved when Bryn eventually said, 'Right, now for the *Messiah*. Please sit down. I know you have rehearsed all the choruses, and we'll rehearse them a good few more times. But now I'd like you to sing the first chorus, "And the glory of the Lord" without your scores. Please put them under your chairs. You should all know the music by now, and I hope the words too. God knows there are few enough words.'

Lucy, among the altos, made a face across the room at Joanna, in the soprano section. Apart from the fixed rehearsals for the group and the few they'd had at Pencarrick, Lucy had not done as instructed and listened to a CD, never mind done any practising.

Joanna smiled back. Lucy thought, I bet she's learnt every note and every word, she's so damned efficient. Lucy wondered if Joanna's throat would constrict and prevent her singing. Lately she'd been singing with the group with no anxiety at all. But an extra fifteen strange men could undo all that.

Lucy at first found Bryn's methods maddening. They took tiny passages and rehearsed them over and over again. And Bryn barked at them constantly: 'Sopranos, wake up, put some heat in it . . . tenors, slow down, it's not a race . . . *Piano* means softly – not dull and dreary. Don't let it lose life . . . basses, this is not a Bavarian drinking-hall song . . . altos, can you nasty it up a bit? It's *too* sweet now.'

Once or twice Bryn would let them sing more than a few bars before going back, and Lucy would begin to enjoy it. But it never lasted. Like coitus interruptus.

When there were only twenty minutes left, Bryn told them to stand. They were to sing the Hallelujah chorus and the Amen right through without interruption.

They didn't quite manage it, because the tenors were drowning the rest, and Bryn, who hopped about on the balls of his feet and frequently jumped right off the ground, suddenly stood still in the middle of a thumping hallelujah, his baton raised.

'No, no, too slow now. And sopranos, don't get sucked in by the tenors. Listen to your neighbours, not to those louts over there.' He smiled at the tenors, who grinned back. 'And tenors, cool it a bit please. You are hogging the show.'

When the last Amen was sung, Lucy felt wonderful. Looking round the room she could see that everyone felt the same, uplifted and satisfied. Joanna was flushed and beaming, whatever was up with Stewart obviously forgotten. She caught Lucy's eye and gave her a thumbs up. Lucy signalled congratulations by silently clapping her hands.

Bryn said, 'Well done everyone. Not one hundred per cent but we're getting there. With a few more rehearsals with me nagging the life out of you, you'll be singing like pros. Better maybe, amateur voices often have more vitality and joy in them than jaded musicians who have sung the *Messiah* a hundred times. And you are talented amateurs.'

Lucy felt childishly grateful for this. After an hour and a half of Bryn's hectoring and criticism, his praise was balm. But he wasn't finished yet.

'The bad news is that you are making mistakes. Old mistakes tend to come up at concerts, so please, learn the score! Then we can concentrate on pace and expression. Remember we have no rehearsal with the professionals so you need to be spot-on. If you cannot rehearse with another singer, then download a midi-file, and sing along until you know every word and every note. Until next week then, thank you. And goodnight.'

Joanna came hurrying over to her, eager to say something.

'Lucy, it's only nine. Let's get Rebecca to join us. Will you call her? She's bound to be more upset with me.'

Lucy's first instinct was to object. She wanted to discuss her Pencarrick plan with Joanna, and she wanted to hear what was up with Stewart. But then she thought, why not?

Lucy fished out her mobile phone. She scrolled down to *Rebecca* and pressed *Call*. Almost at once Rebecca answered.

'Rebecca, it's Lucy. Or rather both of us, Joanna and Lucy. We're going to the Notting Hill Brasserie. Why not join us? Have you had supper?'

'I thought you'd both decided I wasn't to darken your doors again.'

Lucy grimaced pain to Joanna, but replied lightly, 'We miss you, Becca. Please come.'

Lucy and Joanna walked the ten minutes to the restaurant, and were surprised to find Rebecca already there, just stepping from a cab.

There was an awkward few seconds while Rebecca paid the driver, and then Lucy stepped forward and put both arms round her. She felt skinny under the thin cotton coat.

Rebecca, stiff and unresponsive at first, suddenly gave in and hugged her back. As Lucy released her, she stood back, looking at Joanna.

'Am I forgiven?' she asked.

'Oh, Becca,' exclaimed Joanna, taking both her hands, 'of *course* you are, but have you forgiven me? I seriously over-reacted. I don't know why I got the whole thing so out of proportion. I'm sorry. Really sorry.'

Rebecca, whose eyes were full of tears, ran the back of her knuckles under them, and said, 'The problem is, I'd probably do it again. Though I would try harder not to. I do see it's not exactly the way to behave!' She suddenly grinned and added, 'But I'm not likely to get another chance with a squad of nineteen-year-olds, am I?'

They walked down the cobbled alley to the restaurant, and Rebecca shrugged out of her coat. She was wearing a green velvet miniskirt, with a tight sequined top, green tights and flat, buttoned, little-girl shoes. Her hair was fashionably bedraggled and her face was made up with a good deal of glitter round her eyes and cheekbones. She looks, thought Lucy, like a waif who has been at the dressing-up box. A rather elderly waif, it's true, but still very much younger than she was.

'Rebecca, you're all dressed up, you were on your way out!'

'No, it's fine, I'm going to that new ballroom club in Chelsea. But it goes on most of the night. I wasn't planning on being there until eleven or so. You caught me filling in time deciding what to wear.'

Lucy did her best to hide her disapproval. What was a fifty-something woman doing wearing teenage clothes and going dancing with strangers? Rebecca was incorrigible.

When they were seated, and had food and drink in front of them, Lucy said, 'Becca, you've lost weight. And you're so pale. Are you OK?'

Rebecca took a sip of her wine. 'I'm fine. Indeed very fine. I've a new fella, and I've discovered the joys of botox!'

'Oh, no!' This time Lucy could not keep the censure from her voice, but Rebecca just laughed.

'Lucy, Lucy, which do you disapprove of most, the fella or the botox?'

Joanna chipped in, 'We can't disapprove of the fella till we know something about him, but I'd certainly worry about the botox.'

Rebecca patted Joanna's arm. 'Don't worry. I'm very careful. The woman who does it for me is a Harley Street dentist, and very skilful. No Donald Duck lips or wooden forehead. Look!' She held her face up for examination, and Lucy had to admit her skin looked good. 'I'll introduce you. You'll lose ten years. Joanna, Stewart will find you even more irresistible, and Lucy, that Joshua will follow you around like a spaniel.'

Both Lucy and Joanna shook their heads. Lucy resolved to tackle Rebecca on the botox question another time.

'What about the new man then?' she asked.

'Oh, he's fine,' said Rebecca. 'Bit boring. Rich though, and takes me to lots of clubs and restaurants and stuff. He's at a business dinner tonight so I'm off the leash.'

'But who is he?' asked Joanna at the same time as Lucy said, 'Rebecca, if he's that unsatisfactory, what on earth are you doing with him?'

Rebecca, smiling broadly, answered them both.

'He's called Jean-Pierre. Works for a French bank. Married. Lives in Paris. Says he loves his wife, but he only goes home at weekends so I fill a gap. Suits me fine. He'll do until the real thing comes along.' She laughed. 'I could set up a shop with all the perfume he buys at the airport.'

Lucy felt a stab of sympathy mixed with admiration. Rebecca was endlessly cheerful, but it was sad. She caught Joanna's look, which echoed her reaction.

Joanna said, 'You're fantastic, Rebecca. I wish I could take things so lightly.'

Lucy looked at Joanna.

'Your turn, Jo,' she said. 'You sounded unhappy about Stewart. Do you want to talk about it?'

'Yes, I think I do, if I can do it without blubbing.'

She put down her knife and fork and frowned in concentration. She explained about ousting Caroline, and the drama over the supposed overdose, and that Stewart had taken Caroline to Switzerland and barely exchanged a word with her since then.

'Poor Caroline. She drives me nuts but I do feel for her. And poor Stewart, having to choose between his daughter and his lover.'

'Poor you, more like,' Rebecca said. 'Men are such cowards! They are just not up to rocking the boat, are they?'

'The sad thing is that if he'd stayed you could have helped each other, and both helped Caroline,' said Lucy. 'Now he probably resents you because he wasn't there and you took the load.'

'But why wasn't he there?' asked Rebecca. 'He must have known how she'd feel. Why go to London?'

'Caroline had a tantrum and told him to get out of her life,' replied Joanna, 'said she hated him and so on. I think he was either running away from melodrama or angry enough to take her at her word.'

Lucy watched Joanna tearing a piece of bread into tiny pieces, laying them neatly in a row round the edge of her plate. 'Isn't he speaking to you at all?' she asked. 'How are you running the business, and finding a replacement for Caroline?'

'He texts or emails and leaves messages. He and Caroline came back to Wakefield after a few days, but he never speaks to me. Neither does she. Once, late at night I answered the phone and he just hung up, then texted me. He obviously thought I'd be asleep and he could leave a message. Otherwise, nothing.'

Joanna was determined to be brisk and dry-eyed through this conversation – she had cried too much lately – but she was finding it hard. Her voice was unsteady as she said, 'I really thought he loved me. That he would go on loving me.'

Lucy watched Joanna struggling for control as she told her story. She longed to reach out and comfort her, but she knew if she did that Joanna might weep, something she'd hate doing, even with her and Rebecca.

Joanna looked from Rebecca to Lucy, her face rigid with the effort at control. 'The trouble is,' she said, 'I really love the . . . the bugger.'

Her mouth quivered and she bit her lip. She remained staring at Lucy for a second then dropped her head back to look at the ceiling, her jaw clenched.

Lucy said, 'Oh, Jo, I am so sorry. Men are such complete fools.'

Rebecca picked up a napkin and handed it to Jo, who buried her face briefly in it, then raised her head and sniffed. 'Sorry,' she said, her voice once more strong and steady. 'At least I've hired a good replacement for Caroline, her cousin Alasdair, and the business is back on track. I will sell out as soon as I can. Indeed, I guess Stewart will want me out as soon as my contract is up. Then I'll have more time for Pencarrick – at least that's going well.'

Lucy, grateful for the chance to talk about Pencarrick, took a gulp of wine.

'Joanna, I've been thinking a lot about Pencarrick. In fact it was Pencarrick I wanted to talk to you about.'

'Really?' Joanna looked at Lucy and then at Rebecca, frowning in surprise.

Nothing for it, thought Lucy. Better plunge in.

'Joanna, how about you and I buy Pencarrick?'

Lucy, excited but determined to remain cool, outlined her plan for selling up and living permanently at Pencarrick, with Joanna the executive partner who ran the business.

'The thing is, Joanna, I know your plan is for an expensive spa, and to take the whole thing very much upmarket, but I'd not want to do that. It would spoil the atmosphere. Of course the house needs refurbishing, I see that, but does it need a Michelin star dining-room and a spa? Couldn't it be made to pay at a more friendly level? I so love the feel of the place, of a comfortable home where you help yourself to drinks in the bar, where the library is full of good books, where you can walk around barefoot in your bathers, where you can go for a sail, or a ride, or wander into the kitchen for a midnight snack as if it was your own. Would people not pay for that?'

She was desperate for Joanna to agree, to approve, and to be excited by the concept. She held her breath, expecting to be told it would never work. Her eyes were on Joanna when Rebecca spoke.

'Wow, Lucy, you don't half move fast! Is Joshua behind this?'

Lucy shook her head, faintly irritated. It was typical of Rebecca to think a man was in the mix.

'Not at all. Joshua has nothing to do with this. In fact he doesn't know a thing about it.'

'But Lucy,' protested Rebecca, 'you can't moulder away in the country. You'd die of boredom talking about sailing and rhododendrons.'

Lucy laughed. 'London doesn't have a monopoly of interesting people! And I can write there. And I no longer hanker for a staff job on a newspaper – I can freelance from anywhere.' She paused, her hand stroking the stem of her wine glass, up and down. Then she added, 'And it's true Josh has something to do with my happiness in Cornwall. He may not know anything of this plan, but he'll love it. And he has become important to me. Not as Stewart is to you, Jo, but he's close and companionable and I like him being around.'

'Bully for you,' said Joanna, squeezing Lucy's shoulder.

'Wow, congratulations, Lucy,' said Rebecca. 'Lucky old Josh. He must feel he's struck the jackpot.'

Lucy felt a now familiar warmth for these two, so different, women. She turned to Joanna.

'Jo, I can't bear the suspense. Tell me what you think?'

'OK,' said Joanna, 'Pencarrick is worth a fair bit of money now, about twenty-five per cent more than it was when Innovest bought in. From a property point of view, the place will rise in value in the long run whether up-market or middle-market. The reason for the spa is to justify much higher room prices and to give it an out-of-season market. Innovest would want to sell it in a few years, not more than four at most, and would hope to at least double their money. But the refurb and spa will cost a fortune and it's high risk. On the other hand, if it's a success *and* there's a property boom, they'll be in clover.'

Joanna took a sip of water, and absent-mindedly swirled her glass as she went on. 'To advise you on your plan, Lucy, I'd need to redo all the forecasts assuming lower prices and fewer out-of-season sales, but much less capital spend. I just don't know without studying it, but my instinct is that owner-operators could make a fair living out of your kind of venture – after all, Pencarrick just about trundles along now. If we were just after a lifestyle business, without backers' ambitions to satisfy, I think it could work.'

Lucy noticed Joanna had said 'we', not 'you'. She said. 'But Jo, would Innovest sell?'

'Sure, if the price was right. That's what investment houses do: buy and sell. But they're pretty greedy.'

They discussed the finances. Even if Jo did not come in, Lucy thought she'd have enough money from the sale of her Cotswold house to buy out Innovest's shares (even giving them a thirty per cent profit for the few months they'd owned them). She might even be able to afford a more modest refurbishment, without the spa.

Lucy's heart was racing. Joanna had not pooh-poohed the idea.

'But Joanna, I can't run the place.'

Joanna smiled at her friend. 'And you think I can?'

Lucy leant forward, forcing Joanna to look at her. 'Of course I do. But would it interest you? Would you join me?' Joanna's business-like detachment was driving Lucy mad. She had to know where Joanna stood.

'Well, maybe. I've got to stop this company doctor stuff sometime. I love Pencarrick. And if we kept it seasonal we'd get a good bit of the winter off. I need to think about it. But if Stewart is out of the picture, why not? Though, Lucy, I couldn't be your salaried manager, I'd want a financial stake.'

'Sure. We'd need to be partners.'

'So, yes, it might just work. Let's look at it.'

Lucy felt the uprush of excitement might choke her. Joanna's gaze was steady and pleased. It might work. It really might. She held Joanna's gaze for a long moment, and then realised Rebecca was speaking.

'And what about me then?'

Lucy heard the complaint in Becca's voice, and looking up, saw the hurt in her eyes.

Joanna said, 'You'll do the refurb!' at the same moment as Lucy said, 'Design Consultant? How about a scaled down revamp?'

Chapter Thirty-One

Twenty minutes to go, and Joanna was dreading it. She checked through her board papers, trying hard to keep thoughts of meeting Stewart at bay. She had not seen him since that day, six weeks ago, when he had made such transcendent love to her at the Wakefield Hotel and then sacked his daughter the next day.

Joanna told herself she hoped he'd be professional and businesslike so that she would not get emotional, but the truth was she wanted him to put his arms round her and tell her he loved her.

Dream on, she told herself. He doesn't want you and you'd better get used to it.

She had been hurt and angry at Stewart's abandonment of her, but now she blamed him less and understood more. Dismissing your beloved daughter could not have been easy. She would see it as a stab in the back from an adored father who had unaccountably fallen from his pedestal: selling out to capitalism and betraying her mother's memory with a hard-as-nails City go-getter. Who, of course, was also the architect of her downfall.

City go-getter or not, Joanna knew she had done a good job for the company in the past few weeks. She had been lucky: the warehouse and factory staff had known for months that the firm was struggling and were relieved to get their redundancy packages in full – they'd feared bankruptcy and no wages. The remaining staff – and she and Alasdair had tried to keep the best – had worked like slaves to get the new regime working.

Joanna had had some doubts about giving Caroline's cousin Alasdair the acting CEO job, but there was frankly no one else, and she knew he understood the business. But she thought he'd refuse because he'd been so disappointed when Caroline and her father had torn up the supermarket contracts that he had sweated blood to gain. She had thought he would walk – he was a clever chap and could get a job anywhere. But in the event he'd chewed the inside of his cheek, frowned down at the desk for a long minute then looked up, smiling.

'Sure,' he'd said, 'I'd love to. I've been dying to get my hands on this company.'

'But I thought you were wedded to growing it with the supermarket contracts? The current plan is still the Caroline "family business" one, which will never make the returns we both planned a year ago.'

'I know, but things have changed. First, the market has moved. People want local stuff now, not just organic. And we are perfectly placed to do more of that. Caroline – I have to hand it to her – has always been ahead of the public. She has an instinct. And secondly' – a boyish grin suddenly split his face – 'you and my Uncle Stewart are not as greedy as Innovest, so' – he'd tapped the papers before him – 'the budgets are more achievable.'

He'd looked directly at Joanna and she had waited, knowing there was more.

'And I won't have to work with my manic cousin. I may admire her, but she is pure hell as a boss.'

They had smiled at each other, acknowledging what they could never say openly when Caroline was in charge.

'And finally,' he'd said, 'who wouldn't jump at the chance to run a company with potential? I'm only twenty-eight. I'm raring to go. Can't wait.' He'd looked confident and excited. 'I am determined to surprise you. If I make a fist of it, will you change that acting CEO to plain CEO?'

They had discussed this, and Joanna had agreed to give him two

PRUE LEITH

months. If he hadn't made his mark by then, she would start head-hunting for a replacement.

As he'd stood up he'd suddenly put out his hand to take hers. 'Thank God for you, Joanna. Stewart would never have bitten the bullet without your bullying him.'

When the door had closed Joanna put her hands briefly over her face. He was right of course. She had done the company a huge favour by getting rid of Caroline. But he was also right that she had bullied Stewart. What he did not know was just how much that had cost her.

Now, six weeks later, she was about to confirm Alasdair in the job, and resign herself. Stewart was contractually bound to buy her out at a fair return. She could put the money into Pencarrick.

Her job at Greenfarms was essentially done. Alasdair was turning out to be a really good boss: thoughtful, consultative and very clear about what he wanted – as unlike his cousin as one could imagine. He had motivated the staff, who were now working in a great atmosphere with a lot of laughter, he'd made all the savings they had planned for, and, to her surprise, had already landed two new contracts to deliver produce to schools. They were local authority catering contracts, and with any luck they would end up supplying most of the state schools in the county. Stewart, surely, had got to be pleased.

She looked at her watch. It was the gold Patek Philippe Stewart had given her in their heady days. She loved it. It was a touch ostentatious, not because it was vulgar – it was anything but – but because it was so recognisable as a classic. She liked the soft sheen of the gold bracelet against her skin and she was proud of it. It felt like a trophy of love. Maybe she should have given it back? She told herself that one day she would do that. Maybe today.

When Stewart walked into the boardroom, Joanna was already there with Alasdair and several executives. She stayed seated, but looked up, determined to be professional and friendly. Stewart came round the table and kissed her lightly on the cheek.

258

'Morning, Joanna,' he said, then nodded to the others and said to Alasdair, 'Well done, lad. Good set of figures.'

The meeting went well and the decision to confirm Alasdair as CEO was unanimous.

At the end, Stewart made a speech.

'That completes the business of the day, but before we adjourn I want to say a few words if I may.'

He looked across the table at Joanna and for the first time met her gaze directly. He smiled and she felt that familiar melting of the gut that only he could produce.

'Joanna, you have done a wonderful job for Greenfarms, and on behalf of the board, I must thank you. You have had a hard row to hoe, and there must be few jobs in your distinguished career more difficult than sorting out this company.'

Joanna smiled and shook her head, a lump forming in her throat. It was not that she would miss Greenfarms. She wouldn't. But she was severing her only remaining connection to Stewart. What hope would she have of him ever coming back to her once she was right out of his life?

Stewart was still making his speech.

'To pull any company round is hard but having to sort out a family business, where business matters get muddled up with personal issues and professional relationships are clouded by family considerations, is doubly so.'

Yes, thought Joanna, and ten times more so if you are in love with the chairman. She lifted her head and swallowed. She didn't want anyone thinking she was going to blub at leaving a company board.

Stewart continued. 'Joanna, you have navigated your way through this company and this family skilfully, sensitively and rightly. All your advice has been good. All your decisions have been successful. Some of those decisions have been very tough, and I have not always supported you strongly enough, but you battled on and today we have a company with a real future, and we have a family that is united and happy.'

Baloney, thought Joanna, Caroline cannot be happy. Stewart, detecting some unconscious sign of disbelief on her face nodded at her, smiling.

'It's true,' he said, 'and we have a surprise for you. He looked towards the door, and Alasdair got up to open it. Joanna thought, Oh Lord, they are going to give me a bunch of flowers or a Greenfarms hamper of organic veg which I will have to lug home on the train.

It was a bunch of flowers, but the surprise was that it was carried in by Caroline.

Joanna stood up, bemused. She looked from Caroline to Stewart and then to Alasdair, wondering what was going on. Were they going to reinstate Caroline five minutes after they'd accepted her, Joanna's, resignation?

Her smile felt glued to her face.

'Joanna,' Caroline began, 'I owe you an apology, and I thought I should give it to you in person. You were dead right to get rid of me, and it was the best thing that could have happened to me.'

Joanna looked at her, her eyes wide and mouth open. She was so used to Caroline's face fired with fury, or closed in resentment, or wretched with misery as she'd been that day in hospital, that she could not take it in. She stuttered something unintelligible and Caroline cut in,

'I'm really happy, Jo. I got a job almost as soon as I came home from Switzerland with Dad. It is with Sense and Sustainability, a company that helps growers and farmers go organic. I just love it. I don't have to organise people, or worry about budgets, or satisfy greedy shareholders. And I'm doing what I really care about.' She leaned over the flowers and kissed Joanna's cheek. 'So thank you!'

Joanna smiled foolishly at her and was struck by how very different she looked. She was always good looking: even when angry she was striking, but now her tumbling hair framed a face more relaxed and open.

Caroline handed her the bouquet – a glowing orange and red

arrangement of rowan berries, Michaelmas daisies, rugosa rose-hips and trendy grasses – all British autumn flora and innocent of air miles. Joanna dipped her head, pretending to smell the bunch – but really she was playing for time, determined not to cry. Then she looked up, and put her arm around Caroline.

'I'm glad,' she said. She looked at the others. 'Perhaps while we are making speeches I should say a few things too. This company, Greenfarms, and the family, are truly exceptional, and have taught me a lot about what fundamentally matters in business. So much so, in fact, that I am about to go in for a lifestyle business myself and run a small hotel in Cornwall with a friend. And with no other shareholders to worry about. The truth is, that having found myself talking Innovest out of two of their investments, I realise that I have changed – I've lost the appetite for venture capitalism. I no longer think that deals and coups are what make the world go round. I think good people do, like you lot. Thank you for that. I mean it.'

Then they all had a glass of champagne before Joanna had to race for her train. She again had that brief fantasy – perhaps champagne induced – that Stewart, who had said goodbye in a friendly but formal manner, would repeat his earlier exploit and follow her on to the train. But no. The train pulled out with almost no one in the compartment. So Joanna extricated her blow-up neck cushion, which she would never, ever, use if she were in any danger of being seen by anyone she knew, and tucked down to sleep until they reached King's Cross.

Joanna had agreed to have supper with Rebecca to talk about her designs for Pencarrick. Rebecca had been reinstated as chief interior stylist, but on a much tighter budget.

But Joanna, in spite of some sleep on the train, was just too tired. She rang Rebecca to cancel, explaining about her exhausting day, resigning from Greenfarms, seeing Stewart again, his straight-bat professional act and Caroline's conversion from enemy to friend.

'It's emotional overload,' Rebecca said, 'that's what it is. What you need is a shoulder to cry on. I'm a great shoulder.'

'You are. I know that. And I'm sure you're right about the emotion, but there's nothing that a good night's sleep can't cure, and I'm too tired to even talk about it. I think I'll take a pill and hit the sack.'

She did take a pill, or rather two. Not sleeping pills though – they made her wake up groggy. A couple of paracetamol washed down with a glass of whisky may not be recommended by the doc, but it worked wonders.

She filled the bath with a mixture of magnolia bubbles and lavender oil, and put on Sir Ernest Hall playing Chopin Nocturnes. She sank down into the warm water, whisky in hand.

It was unmistakably Stewart's voice and he was saying what she wanted to hear more than anything else, so it must have been a dream. His voice was low and steady.

'The truth is, I love you, Joanna.'

Joanna opened her eyes, reluctant to leave the dream, and realised three things at once: she was in the bath, the water was cold, and someone was in the bathroom with her.

She jerked up and looked round wildly.

Stewart was sitting on the loo seat, to the right and slightly behind her head. She swung round, momentarily angry.

'What the hell?'

'Oh Joanna, I'm so sorry. I didn't mean to scare you. I only wanted—'

'But . . . How did you get in?'

'I've still got your house key,' he said. 'And I'd like to keep it, if I may.'

She could not bear it. She looked dreadful. She had no make-up on, the bubbles had gone, leaving the water murky, her skin was goose-bumpy and she was wearing her ancient shower cap that made her look like a relic of the fifties.

She shouted at him, 'Stewart, how could you? How could you?'

'What? How could I what?' He sounded genuinely confused.

She struggled up, flinging off the shower cap and reaching for the bath towel. To her distress Stewart tried to help wrap it round her. She pushed him away.

'OK, OK. I'm sorry. But Joanna, ssshh-ssshh. Just listen to me.'

'Don't ssshh me! How could you come in unannounced when I'm feeling old and ugly? How could you be so formal and cold with me all day? How could you just walk in here as if you own the place when you buggered off for six weeks without a single word that wasn't strictly business?'

As she spoke her anger rose. She blundered past him and out of the bathroom. He followed her into the bedroom.

'Darling Joanna. Please, will you listen! Didn't you hear me? I love you. Will you marry me?'

This was ridiculous. He did not want to marry her. He just liked drama and excitement and having her on a string.

'Yes I heard you,' she shouted. 'But I am not stupid and you don't want to marry me.'

He came up close and took her by the shoulders. She held the towel tight round her body and tried to back away. But he would not let her go. And then what he said sunk into her.

Marry him! He just said he loved me.

'Did you say, I love you?'

'I did. Darling Joanna. I do. I love you. It has taken six weeks away from you to work that simple thing out.'

Joanna was still struggling with disbelief. She shook her head.

But the anger had somehow blown away. She stood still, looking into his face. His eyes earnest and unblinking were locked on hers.

Before she gave in completely, she told herself, she had to understand. 'But you just abandoned me. No explanation. No apology. Nothing.'

'Darling, darling, I know. I know. I behaved like a perfect bastard.

But I just could not bear Caroline's distress . . . her constant accusations, voiced and unvoiced, of abandonment, betrayal . . . I told myself I could learn to bear life without you, but I could not live with Caroline on the point of suicide. I knew she was unreasonable, wrong . . . but . . .'

Stewart's words *I love you, will you marry me?* were drumming in her head and were demanding attention. She could not speak beyond a few unintelligible buts and whys.

'What has changed?' she managed to say.

'Mainly, I realised that I had to be with you. And so I told Caroline and instead of shrieking and crying, she said good for you, Dad. And that she would get used to it. She's been in therapy you see, and I think it's helping. Anyway, she accepts that I love you and that I won't abandon you again.' He held her tighter. 'I won't, darling. I'll never, ever, leave you again.'

She became aware that her face was one elated smile, while tears of relief were somehow running down it.

They stood there, holding on, and Joanna wanted the moment to last for ever. Then he asked again,

'Do you love me, Joanna?'

She nodded and buried her face in his chest. He held her tightly, kissing the top of her head, and when she lifted her face, he kissed her brow and cheeks, her mouth.

'Is that a yes?'

'Yes.'

'To love and to marriage?'

She pushed him away a little, just enough to smile at him, more confident now. 'To love, absolutely,' she said.

His face registered surprise, and offence.

'But not to marriage? Why would you not want to marry someone you love?' He was still holding her, still speaking softly.

She shook her head. She did not want to think of marriage now. It was enough that he loved her.

'I don't know. I might,' she replied.

Stewart's puzzlement deepened into a frown. He was not used to contradiction or opposition. She tried to explain.

'I'm scared of marriage. My parents have been married for over sixty years and it's been a life sentence for them both. Marriage might spoil it all.'

'But ours will be wonderful!'

She looked up at him, and she could feel her lip trembling.

'Yes, it might be.'

'It will be.'

She pulled away a bit.

'Oh Stewart, first things first,' she said. 'Let's settle for love – I do really really love you.'

He kissed her then. 'You know, you looked wonderful in that bath.'

Joanna started to protest but he rode over her.

'No really. You looked so relaxed and beautiful, like a mermaid. You should not have been so cross.'

'I was beyond cross. Furious more like it. First I got a fright, and you can't just come in unannounced, it's such an invasion—'

'Whoa, whoa! Let's not go there again. Darling, I'm very, very sorry.' He kissed her shoulder and said, 'But I have seen you naked before, you know . . .'

'Not without my consent! Or without my knowing you were looking at me!'

'Agreed. And next time I'll warn you. And knock. And ask permission! I promise.'

He was teasing her but she didn't mind. She leant her head against her chest and he said, 'Like now. Can we take the towel off do you think?'

Chapter Thirty-Two

It was a month since Rebecca had been reinstated as Pencarrick's interior designer, and she had worked fast. The work was to be done over the winter when the hotel was closed, and it was already October. She was on edge, partly because Bill and Angelica were coming to Pencarrick. She wanted both of them to see the place, and she needed to show Bill her refurbishment plans and her progress so far. She hoped to persuade him to recommend her to any clients that he was too busy to take on himself. But that was not the only reason: she wanted to prove to him that she could be a hot-shot decorator, not just a part-time shop assistant.

Angelica would stay the weekend, though Bill had refused. Of course he had to get back to the faultless Jane and their darling sons. Mad to do Cornwall in a day, but still, at least he was coming, so she'd be grateful.

Rebecca dressed carefully in a black T-shirt with long sleeves against the October chill, and a low round neck that showed off her tan (assiduously kept up in the tanning shop), cream linen trousers and brown loafers. She added a heavy wooden necklace of brown, cream and white beads and saluted her reflection with a nod of approval. Botox had done wonders for her face and her hair, shiny clean, was fashionably untidy.

When they arrived, Angelica was excited and admiring. Bill gave her a formal little peck on the cheek, but then looked her slowly up and down.

'You look good, Becca, how come you get younger every time I see you?'

She certainly wasn't going to tell him about the botox. 'Must be because I'm working for me rather than for you,' she said, then realised how ungracious that sounded and added, glancing at Angelica to show it was a joke, 'or maybe the gym and the beautician.'

She went ahead, showing them through the house, explaining that so far they had only redecorated one bedroom, the new dining room and the conservatory because they needed those rooms photographed for the brochure and the website. And until four weeks ago, Pencarrick was full of regulars and Joanna didn't want to upset them.

Rebecca was surprised at her own nervousness. She still, it seemed, needed Bill's approval. Why did she mind so? She supposed it was because he had taught her all she knew, and she wanted to prove to him that she'd learned the lessons well. But of course he had never intended to teach her: she'd picked it up herself by working for him. And, she thought, he owed his own success principally to his charm: he was *the* master of bullshit. But he was still a damn good decorator, and if he mocked her efforts she knew she'd be hurt as well as miserable.

She led them into the big bedroom, which was all but finished, with only the carpet to be laid. She had kept the Victorian desk, the dressing table and the Edwardian basin in the corner. And of course the four-poster, from which she had removed the claustrophobic drapes and replaced them with a light and lacy suggestion of them, with the rest of the fabrics in peach, cream and brown.

'Mum, it's heaven! Can I have this room?'

'Don't think so, darling. We'll ask Joanna, but I think it's being kept pristine for the brochure photographs.'

Bill did not say much beyond 'very nice', and Rebecca was beginning to get anxious that he didn't like what he saw, but when she ushered him into the dining room and put the lights on, he stopped dead. Rebecca smiled to herself. She knew Bill's taste and she knew he'd love this. It was the sort of scheme that most of his rich clients didn't have the guts for. Rich green curtains the colour of malachite, wood-panelled walls, and straight-backed chairs covered in blood red and glowing green; dark wood tables with modern, deep-red candelabra. The two giant chandeliers were thin black metal with crystal and burgundy glass drops, and there were hidden ceiling spots to cast pools of light on tables, but not on middle-aged faces.

'Rebecca,' he said, 'this is just wonderful. Really original colour scheme. Stunning in fact.'

She turned to him, searching his face. 'Really? Do you mean it, Bill?' He put his hands on her shoulders and said, 'I do. Yes. This is a triumph.' Then he held her at arms' length and said, 'Maybe you were right, Becca. I should have trusted you with proper decorating. Not just the chores.'

'I'm glad you didn't though. You'd have sucked me into your business and I'd have stayed in your shadow for ever.'

Rebecca was so delighted with his approval she could not resist a little swagger, or rather a swing of her hips as she preceded him down the corridor. His praise was like champagne, lifting heart and body.

In the conservatory, with its pale blinds, Cornish slate floor, grey glass tables and white orchids in pots, Bill complimented her on the muted colour scheme.

'It's a perfect contrast with the riot of colour outside: blue sea, deep-green pines, strident autumn flowers and emerald lawn. Becca, it's very clever. The colours must be even louder when the azaleas and rhodis are out. You've really thought about it.'

The truth was, Rebecca had not thought of anything of the kind, but she nodded sagely.

'Yes,' she said, 'important not to compete with Nature.'

Lucy and Joanna were sitting at a table with a tray of coffee. Rebecca suddenly remembered that Bill had met Lucy at her disastrous dinner party and she had a moment of anxiety, fearing one of them would bring it up. But they didn't, and Bill concentrated on Joanna whom he'd not met before, and was gratifyingly enthusiastic about her interiors.

'Rebecca's hit just the right note,' he said. 'Good design without gimmicks or looking as if you've tried too hard.'

The women showed him the plans for the rest of the hotel, explaining that the works would be done over the winter, and Joanna produced the laptop and took them through her schemes for all the rooms.

Bill listened in near silence, mostly nodding approval, but once commenting, 'I see you are making good use of my suppliers, Becca!'

'Yeah, sorry about that, darling. I did nick some contacts from Inside Job. And I'm afraid I copied the Make It Over software. It's brilliant.' She kissed his cheek. 'So thank you.'

'Mum, you are impossible!' Angelica shook her head, but she looked amused rather than disapproving.

For a moment Rebecca thought Bill would cut up rough, but he just shook his head and said, 'Same old Rebecca, then.'

After a while, Joanna went back to her office and Lucy took Angelica to see the kitchen and the plans for next year to include the teaching space.

Left on her own with Bill, Rebecca said, 'Bill, I was hoping you'd recommend me for jobs you don't want – when I've done this one of course, and have proved I can come in on time and on budget, I mean.'

Bill expressed himself willing and almost at once came up with a client in Devon whose house, just inherited, had been untouched for fifty years.

'It's a nice job, because the client is more interested in the garden than the house, so you'd have a pretty free hand.'

'But if it's a huge house needing a total overhaul, why don't you want it?'

'Getting there all the time would be a bore, and anyway I'm

too busy for the next six months at least. He might agree to have you, and it's probably only an hour's drive from here.'

Julius Thurston, he summarised, was a sixty-year-old, divorced, mega-rich stockbroker who already had a big house in Chelsea but was keeping this one because it had enormous neglected grounds and he wanted to create a garden to beat all gardens. Rebecca's ears pricked up at 'sixty-year-old', 'mega-rich' and 'divorced'.

'What's he like? Do you like him? '

'Becca, restrain yourself, he's probably gay. And if he isn't, with all that money he could net a thirty-year-old.' This was unkind, and Rebecca was about to snap at him when he said, 'Anyway, what happened to your French banker?'

'Nothing, why should anything have happened to him? He's still around and, you'll be surprised to know, still adores me.'

Then Rebecca remembered that she was on a mission to schmooze Bill, and she decided to forgo the chance to be sulky. They had a drink on the terrace before he left and he was great. Maybe he realises, thought Rebecca, that long-term it's in his interest that I make some money.

The day was a great success. They didn't discuss Rebecca's allowance once, which was a relief, partly because she was, as usual, overdrawn, and also because she feared Bill would suggest he pay her less now that she was getting fees from Joanna. And she had not told him that she'd let her London flat for a heap of money while she was down here for four months. With luck, when the next month's rent came in, she would be just about solvent again, providing he kept up her allowance.

Instead, wonderfully, they talked almost exclusively about how he could help her get started as an interior designer. He was a bit miffed that she hadn't come clean about how big the Pencarrick project was, or asked for his help before, but he relented when she told him she'd wanted to surprise him. 'Besides,' she said, 'if you'd helped, how would I have known I could do it without you? Or that the results were mine and not yours?'

'Fair enough,' said Bill with, she thought, a hint of admiration in his voice.

By the time he left for London he'd not only agreed to passing on clients, but that she should go to a designer trade fair in his place to see what was new for both of them, and to find him a factory in the Far East that would rip off some Fortuny hanging lamps which cost a couple of grand each. Bill thought they could get them made (with Indian sari silks rather than Italian designer fabric) for a couple of hundred, delivered.

When Rebecca had waved him off she shrugged into a thick fleece and sat on the seat at the edge of the lawn. She looked down at the endless crashing sea, and realised that almost for the first time in her life she was not constantly thinking about a man; not the man she had, nor the one in her sights; or some fantasy bit of perfection. These days she spent more time thinking about the price of door handles or the shape of lampshades.

And the truth was, she had rather lost interest in the French banker.

Except in bed, she thought, he bores me to death. He's great in the sack. He can keep going for hours, and wants to please me rather than himself, which must be rare as hens' teeth, but still, I'd rather be shopping.

They couldn't use Rebecca's flat any more as it was let, so she sometimes spent a night with him in his hotel – he stayed in a suite at the Hilton next to Tower Bridge – and then he went off to work at dawn and she could have a nice lazy morning with breakfast in bed.

But, oddly, she preferred to stay with Joanna.

Rebecca stood up and walked along the cliff edge towards the rocky steps down to the beach. She started to climb down the steep path, feeling extraordinarily content. It was partly the way the day with Bill had gone, but it was deeper than that. She felt relaxed, sort of stretched out and happy.

Her thoughts returned to Jean-Pierre. Up until now she'd always preferred the company of men to that of women. Not now. Must be diminishing libido, she thought, but I much prefer my women friends' company to my lover's. The three of them often took the train to Paddington, arriving in good time for the *Messiah* rehearsal. Then, next day, Joanna would go to meetings in the City, Lucy would meet travel agents or publicists about Pencarrick and Rebecca would go shopping for bathtubs or flooring or whatever. And then they would all go back to Cornwall, first class, and have dinner together on the train.

Rebecca's new life as a professional decorator gave her more satisfaction than she could have possibly imagined. She simply loved it, even the costings and the admin.

And she relished being a serious buyer. When she told the Lighting Emporium that she was looking for lights for twenty bedrooms, suddenly she'd get the full treatment: the boss in attendance, a cup of coffee, nothing too much trouble. Feeling important was a buzz. But it was also a kind of validation of her power and independence. And it was good to be making her own money.

She crunched along the stony end of the beach, a chill breeze on her face, occasionally trying, unsuccessfully, to skip flat pebbles on the fleeting patches of smooth sea that came and went between the breakers. Rebecca smiled at beach, sea and sky and said to herself, aloud, 'If you pull off the Devon job for Bill's billionaire, woman, you'll be in clover. Could you be growing up at last, I wonder?'

Chapter Thirty-Three

Lucy held her mobile slightly away from her cheek. Her agent's voice was insistent and getting louder.

'Lucy, in four years I have never had an author turn down an invitation to be on *Orlando's Glorious Food.*'

'OK, so I'll be the first.'

'It would be mad to refuse. The only telly programme that sells more books is *Robert and Janine*. And Orlando even outsells *them* on cookbooks. Every cook and would-be cook in the country watches him. You *have* to accept.'

'But the programme is utter rubbish!'

'No it's not. It's very good television, which will help to sell *Peasant Soups*. Like him or loathe him, Orlando has a huge following.'

Lucy felt trapped. She sat down and covered her face with both hands, one still clutching the mobile. 'I don't loathe him. I'm over that I hope. But we don't get on. There is all this baggage between us . . . him ousting me from the *Globe* . . .'

'Baggage? He worships you!'

'What?'

'He was singing your praises at a foodie lunch the other day – something about you teaching him how to write a good recipe . . .'

When Lucy had given in and put the telephone down, she re-ran the conversation in her head. It was true Orlando's weekly pages in the *Globe* had improved. They were less strident and breathless, with fewer 'wows' and 'cools', but they still had a freshness and enthusiasm which kept you reading to the end. And she knew, and hated, that he had upped the circulation of the paper, and that the *Globe* was delighted with him. They were, if the gossip was right, paying him three times what they'd paid her.

And he was intensely embarrassing on television. So what if four million people regularly watched his show? It was still a mindless mix of trivia about food, glamour, gossip, the latest fad and cooking-made-easy. She just didn't see how she could fit into it. The only thing in its favour was that it was marginally less awful than the other show he hosted, the food quiz that she had been offered in her heyday and turned down as insulting to the viewer!

They'd hired Orlando instead – and put him on the telly route to fame and fortune. No wonder he 'worshipped her', she thought: every time she made way for him, he triumphed.

Lucy refused to cook on the show. The producer tried hard to persuade her to don a chef's jacket and join Orlando to cook soups from her book, but Lucy was adamant. She was not a chef, never had been, and would not pretend to be by wearing a chef's jacket.

They suggested an apron, but the truth was that Lucy did not want to cook with Orlando at all. And, surprisingly, her agent had agreed with her.

'I think you're right, Lucy,' she said. 'You could look staid beside all that razzle-dazzle, and there would be the danger that he would take over and hog the limelight. We need to position you as the grande dame of cooking, which you are: the authoritative, scholarly writer who produces the best cookbooks, with the best writing and the best recipes. Not a telly-celeb cook.'

Lucy had not liked the words 'staid' and 'Grande Dame' but she recognised the truth of them. Her agent went in to bat against Orlando's producer, and won: Lucy would talk and taste, but not cook.

Lucy arrived at the studio wearing her 'Rebecca suit'. It still had the effect of lifting her spirits and making her feel stylish and confident. She'd dithered about the purple pendant but decided it would be too glamorous for a conversation on a couch, and distracting for the viewer.

When the studio make-up artist had finished with her face and hair, Lucy looked as good as that time Rebecca had organised her makeover. Better in fact, since she was a lot happier now.

'I wish I could make myself up like that,' she said, 'but even if I learnt how, it would take me hours.'

'No it wouldn't. You'd be slower than me of course, but you should manage it in twenty minutes or so.'

Twenty minutes! That, thought Lucy, is the difference between me and other women. Rebecca probably spends more than that twice a day and Joanna would regard it as time well invested. But to me it is a complete waste of time. Poor Josh, I could be a better-looking mate for him if I tried harder, but he doesn't seem to mind.

The sound man, a jovial Australian, stuck a miniature radio mike to Lucy's skin, just out of sight down her cleavage, and hooked the battery pack to the back of her skirt. Between them they connected the two with a wire under her jacket. Then someone led her to the sofa at the far end of the studio, where the interviews and chat went on. The central section of the set looked like a street market with stalls of colourful fruit and veg, jams and preserves, breads and cakes, fish, game, even a coffee stall. Most of it was fake set-dressing, but the coffee stall was real, with a plumbed-in old Gaggia machine and little café tables with spindly metal legs. At these sat invited members of the public, who came to worship Orlando and to hope for a ten-second appearance on the telly.

The last third of the studio was set up as a country kitchen for cooks and chefs to show off their skills. Every programme had at least two hands-on demonstrations, plus tastings and chat.

Lucy rather liked the tense but friendly atmosphere of TV studios, with the dozen or more crew, directors, runners, and she-knew-not-what doing their jobs efficiently and calmly. It was like a good restaurant kitchen, she thought, no one yelling, everyone moving to the orders from the head chef, but all aware that at any moment, if one of them messed up, the whole thing could go pear-shaped. Under the blanket of calm, there was a thin sheet of shared anxiety.

The show opened with Orlando prancing onto the set to a burst of applause from the coffee drinkers, backed up with a good bit of recorded clapping. He skidded to a stop in front of a camera and went into his introduction. He was reading from the teleprompt but you would never have known it. He waved his arms around and spoke in the exaggerated manner of children's telly presenters. Lucy braced herself, hating it.

He ended his introductions by bouncing up and down on his feet and clapping his hands together. Then, stressing every important word as though the audience were a bit backward, he confided in an excited whisper, 'But now to our star turn.'

Still in the stage whisper, and arbitrarily emphasising words, he mouthed, 'I am thrilled, really *thrilled*, to introduce my *chief guest* for today's show. She is a *legend* in the food world. I doubt there is a top chef *in the country* that does not have her books on his shelf; the *only* writer ever to get as many *literary awards* for the *quality* of her *writing* as foodie awards for the quality of her *recipes*, and a veritable *inspiration* to us all. She is, of course, the *wonderful Lucy Barnes*.' He turned to her, leaning back and silently applauding. The floor manager orchestrated some well-rehearsed clapping from the mini-audience. The light on the camera trained on Lucy glowed red: she gritted her teeth and forced a smile.

Orlando then picked up his copy of *Peasant Soups* and held the cover squarely to the camera. He said, still in his trademark gushy voice, but mercifully less exaggerated now, 'One of the reasons we have Lucy here today is because you just have to know about her new book. It is *sensational*! Truly sensational. We will be sampling recipes from *Peasant Soups* later in the show, and also talking to Lucy about all sorts of stuff. She knows everything! Can't wait. But wait we must, because first . . .'

And off they went into the first item, with a clip of very young children making pizza.

And then the three winners of the Under-Six Nationwide Pizza Competition, two middle-class little girls and a black lad from Hackney brought their offerings over to Lucy, shepherded by Orlando. They put the pizzas down on the coffee table, and Orlando, kneeling on the carpet in order to get his face level with theirs, talked to them. Two of them, the boy and one of the girls, were completely unfazed by the cameras and entourage, and were desperate to tell him about their creations. But one of the girls, a tiny little blonde thing of about four, was struck dumb. Orlando did not press her, but instead elicited from the Hackney boy that his favourite food was pizza and he liked them best as his mum made them, with lots of chilli and garlic, and from the more talkative girl that everyone in her primary school was learning to cook and she could make corn muffins too. Then he tried again with the non-speaking child.

'This looks go-o-od,' he said, tipping the child's pizza towards the camera. 'How old are you?'

'I'm four.' A just audible whisper.

'And what is your name?'

'Lucinda,' said the little girl more confidently, glad to be asked a question she was used to answering.

'No!' said Orlando, affecting astonishment. 'But that's this lady's real name too! How strange is that? But' – he dropped his voice to a secret-imparting whisper – 'everyone calls her Lucy.'

The child, her shyness forgotten, said solemnly, 'I like Lucy best, but Mummy says I must be Lucinda.'

When asked why she liked cooking at school, she volunteered the information that she wanted to grow up and marry Jamie Oliver.

Orlando did not laugh. He bent closer and said, 'Well, he's got a rather good wife already, Lucy, so that might not be possible, but why do you like Jamie?'

'Because he would let me cook. Mummy only lets me lay the table.'

Poor Mummy, thought Lucy. Presumably she's in the wings somewhere, suffering agonies. But you had to hand it to Orlando – he was good at this.

They tasted the pizzas and dished out the prizes: trips for all three families to Naples, home of pizza, and a free meal at Pizza Express for their whole class at school.

Then there was an item about how disgraceful it was that cereal packs had so much air in them. Orlando asked Lucy's opinion and she told him she didn't mind being sold air since she could read the weight on the box, but she bought her cereal in packets from Whole Foods: that way you could see what you were getting and there was less packaging to stuff in the bin.

There was a lot more in the same vein, Orlando competently pushing everyone on without appearing to harry anyone and Lucy providing, she thought, boring, down-to earth, comments. They met a woman who bred pigeons on her roof in Huddersfield and sold them to butchers; a couple of young chefs doing gourmet dinner parties for media stars and hedge fund tycoons; the founders of a restaurant chain selling healthy food for children and making a success of it.

Lucy began to worry they'd have no time left to discuss her book. A chocolate maker was teaching Orlando to make chocolate holly leaves for Christmas. Orlando clowned about and made a mess of his, and let the chocolatier peel his real holly leaves from the painted-on chocolate, revealing perfect chocolate leaves complete with veins and scalloped edges.

Lucy was impressed. She knew Orlando could make chocolate leaves: any cook could. But he was playing the incompetent to provide glory for his guest. It was generous.

And then he was with her. He came and sat on the sofa next to her.

'I've got a surprise for you, Lucy.'

Her heart sank. Her agent had agreed exactly how the slot was to be handled. There were to be no surprise questions and no

278

cooking. He was to question her about her career, her book, Josh's photographs, her new life in Cornwall, her views on pretty well anything to do with food and cooking. And they would taste some of the soups from the book.

The show was live. She could not object to anything now.

'Don't look so horrified,' said Orlando, and produced a tattered old book, its spine exposed where the cloth cover had fallen off. Lucy recognised it at once and looked at Orlando in astonishment.

'This is a copy of *Simple Suppers* – your first ever cookbook, Lucy, published in 1978 – and it belonged to my mother. She gave it to me when I was eight years old. It was the book she used to teach me to cook.'

'I don't believe it!' Lucy reached for the book, and turned its pages. They were dotted with stains, and had pencil jottings in the margins: 'Very lemony. Wicked,' in a childish hand next to Liquid Lemon Pudding, and calculations for double quantities in a grown up one, next to the Meatballs in Tomato Sauce.

She said, 'Only a thousand copies were printed and it wasn't a huge success. I was completely unknown,'

'It's a collector's item now, did you know?' Lucy shook her head. 'I saw a copy advertised for a hundred and sixty pounds recently.'

'Quick, flog yours then!' laughed Lucy, but Orlando replied seriously,

'I'd never do that. It is still the book I use most at home, though I know the recipes off by heart now.' Lucy noticed that he had dropped his exaggerated telly voice. 'I think if my house was on fire, this is what I would save as I rushed for the door.'

The rest of the interview – and they had a full seven minutes, a lot for a magazine show – went really well. Orlando talked intelligently about *Peasant Soups*, gave her time to explain her passion for the origins of recipes rooted in the history and geography of a place and passed down and adapted by generations of women in the kitchen. She said she hoped that the book would be more than a useful tool for cooks but valuable as a historical document: food fashions spread so fast now she thought anyone might be making tomato soup with pesto, or ropa vieja (the Spanish chickpea soup called 'old clothes' because you put any scraps you liked into it) with no more idea of their origins than that they came off the internet.

Orlando teased her about using her boyfriend as her photographer, which gave Lucy the chance to protest that he was one of the best food photographers in the world. Orlando held Josh's picture of French onion soup to the camera. Lucy looked at the monitor and thought that you could feel the heat and smell the melting cheese.

When the show was over, she said to Orlando, 'That was great. Thank you, Orlando. You did my book proud.'

'Only because it's so good.'

He was unclipping his radio mike from his shirt while the soundman unhooked his battery pack, the floor manager patted him on the arm and said, 'Nice one, Orlando,' and half a dozen of the studio audience were crowding him for his autograph. He said over their heads to Lucy, 'Have you got time for a quick one?'

When they were sitting at the bar, drinks in hand, Lucy said, 'Why didn't you tell me about your mum and *Simple Suppers* when we were in Cornwall?'

'I wanted to, but you were a tad unfriendly, and I thought you were so busy I shouldn't bother you.'

'Oh God,' said Lucy, 'that's awful. I am so sorry, Orlando. I was a right cow.'

'No you weren't, not at all. You were just a bit stiff with me. I thought it was because I was flirting with your friend Rebecca.'

Lucy laughed. 'No, I might have been cross with Rebecca about that – she is incorrigible. But certainly not with her victims – there are too many to be angry with!'

They discussed Rebecca's expulsion from Paradise and Lucy told him about the new plans for Pencarrick and Rebecca being back in the fold and doing a great job on the décor.

'Would you come down again next summer?' Lucy asked him.

Orlando said he'd be glad to. He enjoyed the hands-on cooking with the students, the atmosphere, loved the place. Maybe they could do an item on cooking schools on *Orlando's Glorious Food*?

They discussed this for a while, then Orlando suddenly said, 'Actually, I *was* mildly put out that you didn't respond to my wow, amazing, what a teacher note. Did you read it?'

Lucy pulled a face. 'Yes I did. I should have thanked you. I was pleased, and surprised, but the next morning half my students were on about how wonderful you were, and I reverted to my grumpy old woman persona.'

'Is it because I got your job on the *Globe*, do you think?'

Lucy twirled her wine glass round and round by the stem, not looking at Orlando. 'I guess so,' she said at last, 'only it wasn't just that. It's worse than that, and more unfair.'

'I don't think you could be unfair,' he said, a little hesitantly.

'Yes I could. You see, I came to think of you as a kind of embodiment of everything I really hate about the food world just now.'

Orlando was still smiling, but the eyes that met hers were anxious. 'I didn't know I was that important!' he joked. 'Tell me more.'

Lucy looked into his face. 'Orlando, I simply misjudged you. Or rather judged you unfairly on no evidence. I'd hardly read anything you'd written . . .'

'I'm a rubbish writer. You were right there . . .'

'No I wasn't. I've been reading your pieces lately and they're good. A bit flowery for me but absolutely right for the new readers. You have far more of them than I ever did.'

Orlando politely demurred, but Lucy continued, 'And then, even though I'd never seen *Glorious Food* at all, I'd decided it was just the usual mindless telly-on-the-cheap. But it's not. The items are well researched and interesting. And informative. And you're really, really good at it.'

'Thank you, Ma'am.' Orlando dropped his head in a mock bow.
'Mind you,' said Lucy, 'that quiz show really is rubbish!'
'Isn't it just?'

Chapter Thirty-Four

I'll say this for Elaine, thought Joanna as she explored the nether regions of Stewart's garden, she must have been a formidable gardener. The potting shed, compost heaps, frames, stores, bays for gravel and sharp sand, and workshop were still ordered, clean and ship-shape. Presumably her influence on the gardener lingered on.

Joanna unlocked the tool room door and saw ranks of gleaming hand tools, the spades and forks oiled and shiny, hanging in rows on the wall. Larger tools were on shelves.

She was looking for a hedge trimmer, but when she found it she decided Elaine could not have trimmed the hedges herself. The machine was a monster, a huge electric thing that she could barely lift. Instead she chose a satisfyingly sharp, light pair of shears.

Joanna could no longer kneel to plant or to weed, so she had elected to trim the box hedges on the formal terrace in front of the house. It was a lovely day for gardening and she could do this without her knees objecting.

She liked clipping hedges. There was something predatory about the darting forward jab of the shears, the way they snapped to snatch a mouthful of box, the tiny shredded leaves falling like green snow onto the terrace.

She looked up to see Stewart emerge from the French windows and walk purposefully towards her. She thought he would congratulate her on her nice straight edge, or maybe offer to sweep up as she trimmed. Instead, he said, 'Do you think of us as a couple? As committed to each other?'

Joanna looked at him over the little hedge and lowered the shears.

'Of course I do. Don't you?'

'Yes. Definitely. But I want you to marry me. And move in here.'

'All the time? And give up my Chelsea house? And Pencarrick?'

'Well, yes. I love it that you are so independent, and clever, and brilliant at business. I really do, darling. I admire you so much. I'm really proud of you . . .'

'But?' Joanna liked the praise of course, but it was obviously going to end in a 'but'.

'Well, if we are together, we should *be* together.'

'What has brought this on?'

'Nothing. I was watching you out of the window and thinking how much I love you, and how tiresome you are being about doing the most obvious thing. So I thought I'd deal with it. Have another go at persuasion.'

Joanna wanted to laugh. Stewart was so controlling. And his idea of persuasion was to keep hammering away. From anyone else it would have grated, but it was so typical of him to want to get things straight, tackle the issue, 'deal with it' as if it was a business problem. She put the shears down and went round to his side of the box hedge. She held his head and looked into his eyes, feeling the familiar tug of desire.

'Darling Stewart, I would be no good in Elaine's shoes . . .'

'Who said anything about Elaine's shoes?'

She pushed him away a little so she could see him better. 'You did, in a way. But I don't want to take her place, live here, tend her garden, gingerly make modest changes to the décor.'

'I'd never object . . .'

'Of course you wouldn't, darling.' She stroked his cheek, soothing the indignation. 'I'm sure if I wanted to change every room in the place, you'd probably be delighted, see it as my acquiescence in this Yorkshire life.'

He put his arms round her neck. 'Well, it's true I long for you to acquiesce. To properly live with me.' He kissed her. 'You smell of you,' he said.

'Does that mean I smell of sweat?'

'No it does not, silly. It means you smell warm and sexy and not of perfume or talc or anything.'

'Stewart, I don't think I can just move in here.' She so wanted him to understand. She thought maybe he did understand that this question of where they lived was more complicated for her than for him, but he could not understand why. She went on.

'I don't think men get the importance of *place*. You think of this lovely house – and it is lovely – as just a house. Yes, it's where you and Elaine have been happy, where you brought up the children. But, all the same, to you it is primarily a building that provides what buildings should: shelter, safety, comfort, etc. Isn't that so?'

Stewart frowned at her, trying to understand. 'And isn't it?'

'No, to me this is Elaine's space. And yours of course. I'm more than happy to spend time here. But I don't feel about this house as I would if we had bought it and furnished it together, or as I do about my London house, or about Pencarrick.'

He was silent for a moment then said, 'I could move to London I guess.'

She was touched by this, especially since she knew he was unaware of the reluctance in his own voice. It's because, she thought, he's a true Yorkshireman. He may not care about the actual house, but he won't be happy in London, or indeed Cornwall. At least not yet.

The proximity of Stewart was getting to her. She undid the buttons of his shirt, half expecting him to back off in case someone came past. But he stood still. She slipped her hands around his body, which felt warm and familiar, kissed the bit where his collarbone gave way to the smooth hollow of his neck.

'Darling, it's all too soon,' she said her voice muffled against his throat. 'Let's go on spending odd weeks in Yorkshire or in Chelsea. And please, my love, come more often to Pencarrick. But let's not decide yet where we live.'

He addressed the top of her head, breathing into her hair. 'We've got to decide sometime. We're seriously over-housed. Four houses between us if you count my chalet in St Moritz and your interest in Pencarrick.'

'Pencarrick is more Lucy's than mine,' she said, pulling away a little, 'but I love the place. I couldn't bear to lose it.'

But Stewart wasn't listening any more. His breathing was faster and when he spoke his voice had dropped.

'Could we adjourn this discussion, my darling? I've got another, more important, agenda.'

Joanna marvelled at Stewart's sensitivity in bed. She didn't know how he managed to be so passionate and demanding, and yet somehow accommodate her painful knees. There are all sorts of contortions that do not come easily to women with damaged knees, she thought, and there are the dozens of daily actions that have become a trial to me.

Waiting for them to heal themselves had gone on quite long enough. She needed to get them fixed.

Joanna looked round the Harley Street waiting room and thought that it was exactly like the dozens of Harley Street waiting rooms she'd been in over the years. They were all the same, tastefully decorated in faded colours but dull, good furniture in less than perfect condition, slightly foxed mirror over the Adam-style fireplace, coffee table offering of out-of-date copies of *Country Life* and *The Field*.

She flicked through pages of country estates, well-groomed horses, over-furnished living rooms with improbably posed families grouped on the sofa. She pushed them aside, hoping for something with more meat in it. Surely some of the patients were from the City and would like the *Economist* or the *Spectator*?

Joanna gave up on the magazines, picked up the *Daily Telegraph* and sat on the arm of a fat Chesterfield. She did not dare sit down on the sofa for fear of having to ask for help in getting up again.

Her mind went back to her conversation with Rebecca yesterday. They had been having breakfast at Joanna's house before Rebecca set off for Cornwall, laden with more swatches and fabric samples and extremely heavy boxes containing sample door handles. Why they needed new door handles Joanna did not know since every door had a working pair, but she had promised to button her lip until Rebecca presented her final plans for the rest of the house to Lucy and her.

More to change the subject than anything, Joanna had said, 'I'm going to have my knees fixed tomorrow.'

Rebecca had looked up, a piece of croissant halfway to her mouth. 'How fixed?'

'Dr Carlisle is going to stick a needle into them, suck off all the liquid, and inject—'

'Urrghh, stop!' Rebecca waved her hands in front of her shaking head. 'Too much information!'

'Well, you did ask!'

'Yes, sorry,' she said, 'but I don't want the medical stuff. I'll faint. I want to know whether it will work, and how long for, what it costs and if your doc knows what he's doing – and did you check him out to make sure he's the best?'

'Wow, that's quite a few questions!'

Rebecca can be pretty beady, thought Joanna. She was looking at her over her coffee cup, like a judge assessing the truth of a witness. 'And?' she'd asked.

'My GP says it works in about seventy per cent of patients. I didn't ask how long for. He referred me to Dr Carlisle. I suppose he knows what he's doing. He's in Harley Street and he's supposed to be the best.'

'Who says so?'

'A chap I used to work with at Innovest. He had it done and was on the squash court the next week.'

Rebecca put the coffee cup down slowly.

'Jo-Jo, you must be careful. I dare say he's OK, but you need to ask him a few questions. How many of these has he done? And how often you'll have to come back, and how much will it cost. Ask if his fees come under the BUPA scale, and find out if there's any danger of infection. And have a good look to see if his hands shake. You want a guy with steady hands.'

Joanna had burst out laughing. 'Rebecca, I'm having my knees injected, not brain surgery. My knees are like half-blown up balloons. I don't think he can miss!'

The starchy receptionist appeared at the door. 'Dr Carlisle will see you now,' she said. Joanna pushed herself off the sofa arm with difficulty and obediently followed.

The doctor turned out to be a handsome young Indian. Joanna wondered if he had changed his name so as not to put off custom. She'd read of patients refusing to be treated by Indian doctors in hospitals. But of course she could not ask.

'Dr Carlisle?' she said. The doctor caught her hesitation and smiled.

'I know, it's odd. My great-grandfather was in the Indian Army.'

She smiled sheepishly, caught out. He waved her to the chair in front of his desk. Joanna sat carefully.

'Before we get started,' she said, 'do you think I could ask you a few questions?'

He looked up. 'Of course. Shoot.'

Then Joanna realised she couldn't ask him anything about his competence. He would think it was because she didn't trust an Indian doctor. So she asked him how long the effect of the treatment would last, assuming it worked at all.

'I'm afraid I don't know. Almost everyone experiences some improvement in mobility and pain relief. It can last for years, months, sometimes only weeks – though this is rare – and, sadly, sometimes the effect is minimal. If, as in your case, there is quite a bit of wear and tear to the bone as the cartilage gets thinner with age, then it is sometimes effective to have two or three procedures a year. But depending on the speed of deterioration in the knee joint, you could have a good few years' more hiking.'

'Tennis, actually.'

'Tennis then. A good few more years' tennis.'

He waited expectantly for the next question, but Joanna was chickening out of Rebecca's more difficult instructions. It was ridiculous really, she thought, you would take more references for a gardener or a cleaner than we dare take for someone who is going to stick needles into us and pump us full of drugs. Just because he wears a white coat. She shook her head. 'No, I'm OK.'

'You look a bit uncertain. Shall I answer my FAQs? Most frequently asked questions? Sometimes I think I should send patients a leaflet in advance since they quite rightly want to ask questions but seldom do.'

She smiled gratefully, and nodded.

'What people are most anxious about are MRSA, staphylococcus aureus or clostridium difficile. The answer is we carry out enormously strict hygiene protocols here, and we have never had a case of such infection.

'The next question that every sensible patient should want to ask is, how experienced am I? Well I do nothing but knees and I will have done well over five hundred procedures like this one, followed by a cortisone injection, this year alone. And it is a very simple procedure.'

'Good Lord,' she said, 'that many? What did people do before this was possible?'

'They put up with the immobility and the discomfort, and if it was very bad they had surgery to remove bits of cartilage.' Dr Carlisle continued with his catechism. 'The next question is, if it doesn't work, what next? Well, we could try again, or, if your knees continue to be so painful, you could have an operation. That almost always works, but it costs more money. On the question of cost, I'm afraid the procedure does not get any cheaper the more of them you have. No discount for quantity I'm afraid.'

By the time he had finished Joanna was almost embarrassed to have started him off.

He had her X-rays pinned to the wall, and had a long look at them before sitting her on his examination couch.

She didn't have to undress completely, just take off her shoes and trousers. He had her sit on the edge first while he prodded her knees with his fingers, probing gently. And then he asked her to lie on the bed with her legs flat.

He swabbed one knee with antiseptic and she felt her calves tense with anxiety. The syringe he held was huge, with a whopping great needle you might use on a horse, Joanna thought. She shut her eyes and screwed them up against the expected pain.

She was right. It hurt like hell. While he was drawing off the fluid round her knee, he told her it would not take a minute and just to try and hold still. It seemed to take for ever. He also said that he was sorry about the discomfort. Discomfort, thought Joanna, gripping the sides of the bed and screwing up her face, why do medics talk of discomfort? It's excruciating pain, not discomfort!

But she was clenching her teeth too hard to get into semantics right now.

When he had siphoned off the fluid from her right knee he gave her a cortisone injection into the joint and that hurt like hell too. But only briefly. As she yelped Dr Carlisle said, 'I've injected some anaesthetic with the cortisone. The pain will soon go.'

He was right: the pain evaporated fast. But then Joanna had to endure it all over again on the left knee.

And that was that. Dr Carlisle made Joanna flex her legs, and then sit up and swing them round to stand up. That sort of twisting movement had been painful for months, but now, suddenly, it did not hurt at all.

She walked out of the surgery as she walked two years ago, with a swing in her step, no limping, no pain. She even walked down the steps into Harley Street without clutching the rail.

When she got home she was so pleased with her new-look knees (the puffiness had gone completely) she decided to impress Stewart. She used her noxious-smelling hair remover on her legs, rubbed instant tan all over them, cut and painted her toenails and even gave her knees a squirt of Guerlain.

Stewart dutifully stroked her knees as only he could and kissed her legs from ankle to thigh. 'I thought your knees were fine before,' he said, 'and if they get swollen again, I'll still think they are the sexiest legs in town.'

It was, thought Joanna, good to be lied to sometimes.

Chapter Thirty-Five

Lucy looked up at the woman standing in front of her.

'Is the book for yourself, or shall I put someone else's name in it?'

'Oh, it's for my son. He's a chef. And he's your greatest fan. If you could just write something . . .'

'What is his name?'

'Alan.'

Lucy wrote, *For Alan, from one cook to another, Happy Cooking. Lucy Barnes.*

'Oh thank you, thank you.'

The woman was gushing embarrassingly, but Lucy was delighted.

Suddenly the voice of Fiona, her publisher's PR, lifted above the noise of the crowd.

'Any customers wanting plain signed copies of *Peasant Soups*, should go to the table towards the front of the shop, where there is a shorter queue. If you want to meet the author, Lucy Barnes, she is signing copies towards the back, but there is a much longer queue there.'

Lucy had been signing copies steadily for an hour. And it had been the same story at Harrods, at Hatchards and at the big branches of Waterstone's. She could not believe it, but *Peasant Soups* was flying off the shelves.

There had been a lot of publicity. There were cracking reviews for the writing (she had been hailed as the new Elizabeth David by the more literary critics), for the recipes and for Joshua's astonishing photographs. The book was already entered for the Glenfiddich awards, Cookery Book of the Year and for the André Simon prize.

Some of the recipes were being serialised in the *Sunday Telegraph* magazine, there had been interviews or profiles of her in the *Observer* and the *Daily Mail*, Foyles had given her a literary lunch, and she had spoken at a number of lunch clubs. But Lucy knew it was the TV footage that had produced the crowds. On the *Robert and Janine* show, Janine had given the book a fulsome plug. And, most of all, Lucy's appearance on *Orlando's Glorious Food* had turned it into the number one cookery book. Orlando had said he was giving it to all his friends and relatives, male or female, for Christmas.

The constant smiling made Lucy's face ache, and it was a relief to hear the announcement, 'The store will close in ten minutes.'

She found Joshua in the bar of the Mandarin Oriental. He rose and kissed her.

'Guess what? *Peasant Soups* overtook Jamie Oliver on Amazon today.'

'Good Lord! Really? How do you know?'

'Nora from the publishers has been trying to get hold of you.' He took her bag and coat from her, and she plonked herself down on the sofa. 'But you never have your phone on so she rang me in desperation.'

'I've been signing books, dammit. I can hardly have the wretched thing ringing, can I?'

He raised an eyebrow in tolerant disbelief, and said, 'Nora had more good news. WH Smith have made your book their Cookbook of the Year, and given it a whole window in the larger branches.'

Lucy leant into him and kissed his cheek. 'Not my book. Our book. We have outsold Jamie. It's the pictures that draw them, and you know it.'

'Drink?' he asked.

'Lord yes, I think I need a scotch.'

Drink in hand, she felt herself slowly relaxing.

'Josh,' she said, 'what shall I do about this television thing?'

'What do you want to do about it?'

Lucy frowned into her glass.

'It's not that easy. My agent and the publishers are dead keen. They keep saying, just look at who sells the most cookbooks – it's the telly chefs.'

'Except this one,' interrupted Joshua. '*Peasant Soups* never had a TV programme to go with it. And look where it is.'

'A fluke, according to my editor, though she's too polite to say so to me. And if I had a television series, we'd have sold even more.'

'So what's the downside?'

'Oh Josh, you know what it is! I hate doing it, that's all. You hang around for ever, you never get the dishes to work exactly as you want them to. There'll be some brainless presenter asking stupid questions and babbling inanities. Cooking is cheap to make. It's just wallpaper for afternoon telly. And they won't let me plug our book because it wasn't published by them, and anyway it's not what *Celebrity Top Table* will be about.' She paused for breath, and then concluded. 'Besides, they pay peanuts.'

'Mmm. OK, that seems to be pretty clear. You don't want what they are offering, but are you hostile to all television?'

'What do you mean?'

'If you could have a telly series on your own terms, in prime time, not this on-the-cheap afternoon one, what would you like it to be? What would make the hanging around and the lousy money worth while?'

'Oh, that's easy. I'd like the programme to reflect our book – to be about the history of peasant soups, meeting people in Sardinia or Poland or wherever who still make them and learning their history. Some of them go back centuries.'

'Could be interesting. But expensive to do of course.'

'That's the problem. But wouldn't it be great? Take the Spanish *potajes de lentejas* for example. That recipe comes from a tapas bar in Lanzarote, in the wine-growing area. People think Lanzarote is nothing but overtanned English tourists swilling lager on the beaches, but up in the hills the landscape is astonishing. The fields are covered with black volcanic gravel, called picon I think, and the vines are grown in hollows out of the wind, with each vine surrounded by a semicircular wall of black rock, and courgettes and tomatoes pinned to the ground with rocks to stop them being blown away. The place, with its low white houses, triangular hills and blue sky would be a gift to a good film maker.'

'Hardly gastronomic though.'

'Agreed. But that lentil soup recipe was handed down from the grandfather who made it for the comrades in the Spanish Civil War. When he came home it became the foundation of the family restaurant and later the winery. The family thinks they owe their fortunes to lentil soup. That could make a good programme, or part of one, don't you think?'

Joshua considered this. 'It could work. Why don't you do a treatment, and see if your agent can sell it to a broadcaster?'

Suddenly Lucy felt excited and awake again. She sat up and leant towards Joshua.

'Why don't we do it together? A couple of oldies doddering round the world talking to even older oldies about what their grandmothers cooked. You have such a gentle personality and I'm famously knowledgeable and greedy. They might just like the combination.'

'And it might make a change from all those testosterone-driven chefs dancing about and swearing all the time.'

They continued to discuss the idea over dinner, and by the time they were on the night sleeper to Cornwall, they had blocked out the main elements of the series. Lucy would do the research and provide the historical and social stuff, and Joshua would cook the food on camera and take the still photographs.

Joshua went off to the bar car to get them a nightcap, and Lucy undressed, pulling on an old shirt of David's – she preferred them to nightdresses – cleaned her teeth and climbed into the bottom bunk.

Joshua reappeared with a couple of miniature whiskies and two plastic glasses.

Lucy thought for the hundredth time what a thoroughly good guy Josh was. She studied his slightly rounded back as he washed his face and cleaned his teeth at the basin. She hoped he wouldn't want sex. She was so easy and relaxed with him, and felt such affection for him, that she wouldn't refuse.

Joshua leant into her bunk and kissed her. Then he handed her a plastic glass of whisky and water.

'Darling Lucy, best-selling cookery writer, part owner of Pencarrick, and, who knows, future telly star, good night, sleep tight.' Then he climbed into the top bunk and she could hear him pouring his whisky.

Lying so close to him in their own little cabin pleased Lucy. She liked the way the coat hangers were padded and covered in leather so they wouldn't rattle and keep the customers awake, and that everything was designed with thought and care.

'I love sleepers, don't you?' she said.

'Not a lot. You get no sleep and the breakfast is dire.'

'I know, but it's like playing house, with everything arranged just so. There's that net thing for a book and water bottle, and even a tray that comes out of the wall for breakfast. Once upon a time they even had a little hook with a velvet-lined hollow to hang your fob-watch in. But it's still pretty good, don't you think?'

'Won't get much sleep, though.'

'True,' said Lucy, 'but don't you like being rocked to sleep? And waking up and finding you're not there yet – more sleep and more rocking to come?'

They drifted into silence then and Lucy turned off her light. Then Joshua turned his off too, and said, 'Lucy, I feel I should be making passionate love to you in that narrow little bunk. Especially as you have such a romantic view of sleepers. If I were the demon lover you deserve, I would be, wouldn't I?'

'Darling Josh, I'm glad you are not. I was just lying here thinking that I hoped you didn't feel like sex because I really am too tired tonight. But I'd never say so, or plead a headache!'

Joshua laughed, and then Lucy joined in.

'Maybe if I was on hormone replacement therapy,' she said, 'you wouldn't be safe. But all I want is what we have. I love the warmth of you in bed, and your arms round me, and everything about you. I just don't want the humpy-pumpy very often. Do you mind?'

'Absolutely not. Quite a relief, really.'

They went on talking in the friendly dark until Lucy heard a gentle snore from above. She didn't mind it. David used to snore, and Lucy had rather missed it.

It was the second week of the children's Christmas holidays, and Lucy and her grandchildren were preparing a welcome dinner for Grace and Archie. The children had been with her, without Grace or Archie for ten days, and apart from one trip to London for her *Messiah* rehearsal, Lucy had devoted herself to them, and it had been wonderful.

At lunchtime they sat round the kitchen table, peeling freshly cooked prawns, piling them onto crusty chunks of brown bread, squeezing lemon juice on them, giving them a good grinding of black pepper, then wolfing them down. Johnny sneaked most of his to the cat under the table.

'Mum will never believe we ate prawns,' Clare said, 'especially that they were alive and we cooked them.'

'Don't talk with your mouth full, darling,' said Lucy. 'Maybe you and Magnificat like them, but I'm not sure about Johnny.'

Johnny looked up, his face a childish pantomime of guilt. 'Oh . . . I only gave him a few, I promise. And I do like them.'

Lucy laughed. 'Good. Let's see you eat the rest. Then you can get another tick in the box.' Johnny dutifully piled the remaining prawns on his buttered bread and ate them.

Clare watched him, rather hoping he would fail. 'I liked them first go,' she said. Then she slid sideways off her chair and fetched the pad and pencil from the sideboard. 'How do you spell prawns, Gran?'

Lucy spelled it for her and then asked, 'What's the score, Clare?'

Clare read: 'Thai red curry, broccoli, spinach, black olives – only we both still hate them – fish soup, fish stew, stuffed marrow, lamb stew, spicy couscous, smoked haddock, junket . . .'

'Urrgghh. That's gross. I still hate that,' Johnny piped up.

Clare took no notice.

'Beetroot – Johnny likes that but I think it's disgusting – porridge, mushrooms, corn on the cob, goats' cheese, and prawns.'

Lucy smiled at the pride on Clare's face. She wished Grace could see it, although she feared her daughter would see her efforts as criticism. She took the pad from Clare and studied it. It was a chart, with the new foods she was trying to get them to like listed down the side, and with the vertical columns labelled *Eaten by Johnny, Eaten by Clare, Enjoyed by Johnny, Enjoyed by Clare.*'

Every time something was successfully swallowed, a big green tick went into the relevant column.

But, thought Lucy, her holiday resolution to get the children off pasta, pizza and fish fingers had not been a total success: after one black olive the children had gone on strike, and Clare had greeted beetroot with vomiting noises by way of comment. The fridge was full of the things the children had agreed to taste daily in the belief (their grandmother's belief anyway) that they would get to like them before they went home. Olives and beetroot were obviously a longer-term project.

But Lucy was pleased with them, and with herself. The children had tried everything, and even in the *Enjoyed* columns there were more green ticks than blank spaces. At least they'd got minds, and mouths, slightly more open to new things. It was a start.

The children had had, thought Lucy, the best possible holiday.

She had banned Nintendo and television, and introduced them to the joys of Ludo, Scrabble and Draughts. They had spent happy hours on the cold lonely beaches without another soul in sight. They'd built sandcastles, collected shells, even paddled, though the December water was icy. They had read *Swallows and Amazons* aloud, which, to Lucy's astonishment, they'd loved. And she'd given them cooking lessons.

Tonight's dinner was to be made entirely out of food the children had resolutely disliked before coming to Pencarrick. The children were as eager as Lucy to show off their grown-up tastes to their parents.

Because the hotel was closed for the winter they had the kitchen to themselves. Lucy and the children had been 'prepping' all day, but when it came to serving the dinner, Lucy sat down with Grace and Archie, while the children 'did the service' under Joshua's eye, and brought it to the table. Then they sat down with their parents to eat it.

They started with a prawn cocktail made from more of the prawns they had cooked and peeled for lunch, with home-made mayonnaise doctored with a little tomato ketchup, and shredded cos lettuce.

Then came a green chicken curry with Thai spices they'd ground themselves, steamed rice and broccoli. The last course was a local goats' cheese served with home-made focaccia bread, and candied orange slices, which had been drying over the Aga for days.

Dinner was a cracking success. Lucy felt a great wash of pride at the children's concentration and commitment, and Grace was suitably congratulatory about the children eating everything. If she felt any shafts of jealousy that her mother could get her children to eat things she couldn't, she didn't show it.

Both Johnny and Clare were very excited, competing to tell their parents about the sailing, the shells they'd found, how to develop photographs (the day Lucy went to her rehearsal had been spent with Josh), how to make mayonnaise, how to cook the orange slices in sugar syrup and then dry them.

With the hubbub of the family supper at its height Lucy sat back, detached and content, as she watched Joshua helping Clare to arrange the cheese, candied orange and focaccia on a chopping board. His photographer's eye would not allow them to be piled up any old how. And yet the finished cheese board looked wonderfully unarranged, as if it had just happened, with no designer input. He photographed it with professional attention, as he had every course.

Lucy's eyes drifted to Johnny, earnestly showing Archie how to grind spices in a pestle and mortar.

This is real happiness, she thought. She considered the possibility that she had somehow negotiated the pitfalls of widowhood, and found a way of being close to her family without making demands on them. And her old fears of memory loss had receded. I'll chuck going to the memory clinic, she thought. What's the point? If I go mad, I go mad. I refuse to worry about it any more.

She looked at Grace, bent over Josh's photo of Clare and her baling out the rowing boat with a Tupperware box and a beach bucket. They were both laughing. Grace looked up and caught her gaze.

'Mum, you've given them such a wonderful time. How do you do it? Ten days of them should have reduced you to a wreck, but you look marvellous.'

'I've loved it. And I'm really happy here,' she said. It was true. Pencarrick would give her a home, a business and space to write. And would draw her grandchildren and Grace in a way the Cotswold house could not.

Somehow, in the past year, she had developed a happy independence. Grace could not control her, and indeed no longer seemed to want to. And she might, or might not, do a telly series.

But I know, she thought, what has really made the difference – it's friendship. In a family, it's the family that counts, but single people need friends. Rebecca and Joanna, and latterly Josh, had been the saving of her.

She looked up and caught Joshua's eye. He blew her an almost invisible kiss.

Late the following afternoon, when the family had left and Joshua had gone back to his studio, Lucy took the rowing-boat out in the bay. It was clear and cold and the sea was calm. Streaky clouds caught the last of the light just above the horizon. High above, stars were beginning to speckle the darkening sky.

She was warmly dressed with a good few layers under her anorak. She pulled the cowl neck of her sweater up over her ears and jammed her ancient fur hat on her head. She pulled the anorak zip up to her neck, and slipped her hands into David's old fishing mittens with cut off fingers. She couldn't bear gloves that prevented her feeling what she was doing.

She rowed slowly out into the middle of the bay, enjoying the rhythm of the oars and the way the water flashed and glinted in the moonlight. There was very little current and no wind and she could ship her oars and drift slowly towards the shore with the tide.

I expect Grace would have a fit, she thought. She'd say taking a rowing-boat out in the dark, alone, in a Cornish sea in December without a life jacket, is irresponsible madness. But I will be home long before the tide turns.

She had the urn between her knees. For the past two years, it had lived on a shelf in her study. She didn't like the urn. It was ornate and marble, and very heavy. It's too funereal, she thought. And then smiled. Of course it's funereal. It contains David's ashes.

She had the kitchen bowl from the sink with her too, and now she tipped the ashes, which were surprisingly white and gritty, into the basin and then opened the shoebox on the seat beside her, and scattered its contents on top of the ashes. These were wild flower heads (not many, flowers being rare in December, even in Cornwall), seed pods, small fir cones and leaves the children had collected in their fortnight with her. They had pressed the flowers and the leaves between blotting paper and dried the seed pods over the Aga with the orange slices. There was also the children's collection of shells that Lucy had told them they could not take to London and that she'd return to the beach. Well, not quite, she thought, but they will end up on the beach eventually.

Feeling rather odd, as if it was not her but someone else performing these rites, she gently mixed the flowers, leaves and shells into the ashes, and then scooped them up, handful after handful and tossed them into the sea. They made a pattering sound as they hit the water. She liked the way the ashes and shells sank at once, leaving the flowers and leaves floating on the surface. Goodbye my darling, she said, and realised she'd spoken aloud.

When she'd turned the plastic bowl over the side to sprinkle the last of its contents into the sea, she tucked it under the seat and reached again for the marble urn. It was too heavy and awkward to hold with one hand and she held it with both as she leant over the side. The boat, tipping with her weight, allowed her to reach the water. She lowered the urn slowly until it filled with water and then she let it go. She watched its white form sink rapidly out of sight. I'm not polluting the sea, she told herself, a few winters of Cornish storms and the urn will be part of the beach, a few hundred years and the beach sand will have an infinitesimal percentage of Italian marble in it. She shifted back to the middle of the boat, feeling it obediently right itself and settle to ride the gentle swell.

It was so still and peaceful in the bay that Lucy was tempted to stay. She took her flask of Macallan out of her jacket pocket and took a gulp. The whisky ran a fast warm path down her body. It felt good and Lucy smiled. Then she tucked the flask back in her jacket and rowed slowly back to shore.

Chapter Thirty-Six

The Tabernacle's tiered seats encircled the central stage on three sides, and the audience was sandwiched between the tenors and sopranos on one wing and the altos and basses on the other, with the orchestra occupying the stage in the middle.

Lucy fiddled with the purple pendant at her neck. She was wearing her 'Rebecca suit' in honour of the occasion. It wasn't strictly blue – the choirs had been told they must wear blue – but it was blue-ish, and she felt good in it. She'd not worn it since her appearance on Orlando's TV programme last month and before that it had hung unmolested in its dry cleaner's plastic for months. Pencarrick did not require smart clothes, and besides, she'd regressed into her former unfashionable ways since she'd met Josh.

But she still loved the suit. It represented the turning point when she stopped feeling useless and wretched and started to feel human again. Until then, grief had leached all the joy from even the things that used to give her such reliable pleasure: opening the curtains to a sunny day, her cat trampling her thighs, stripping redcurrants from the stalk with a fork, even the act of singing. This summer has restored all that to me, she thought.

The lights were still up and the audience was shuffling and bumping into their seats. She was pleased to see Rebecca's daughter, Angelica, arrive and Nelson beckon her to come and sit next to him. Angelica was coming to stay at Pencarrick after Christmas with a friend. And Lucy was going to fulfil her promise to teach her to cook.

Josh was on Nelson's other side and Grace and Archie just in front with the children. She caught Clare's eye and the child's excited wave was quickly brought to heel by Grace's restraining hand.

Josh noticed the exchange and smiled across at her. Nothing changes, the smile said.

Lucy ran her eyes over the two blue blocks of choir. We must be a hundred strong, or near it, she thought: the audience hardly outnumbers us.

The musicians were tuning up, shifting their plastic chairs a fraction to right or left, adjusting the music on their stands, and producing a medley of discordant noises. Lucy had always liked this cacophony before a performance: it stirred a familiar anticipation of pleasure to come. You only got that thrill, she thought, with live concerts: no recorded CD, however good, no televised Prom, could produce the buzz. She was just old enough to remember when theatres dropped a solid fire-curtain before the start of a play or panto. It was the sure signal that soon a magic world would envelop her. The frisson had not lessened.

There was a small stir on the far side of the auditorium and Lucy looked up to see their now familiar conductor from the Maida Vale Male Voice Choir, Bryn Jones, walk, or rather bounce, on his thick-soled shoes from the side of the stage to his podium.

The conductor bowed to the audience, turned to the orchestra and raised his baton. And then they were into the sinfonia.

When they stood to sing the first chorus, Lucy thought, this is going to be wonderful. You sing better when you are happy. But then she reminded herself, don't let the beauty of the music get to you. You cannot sing when all choked up.

His back to the audience, Bryn Jones coaxed and commanded his players and singers. He jumped on his small feet, swivelled and swayed, his eyes sometimes closed with concentration, sometimes wide and demanding, his tiny baton a never-ceasing encouragement and goad.

*　　*　　*

Joanna looked across at Lucy, and envied the ease with which she could just open her mouth and sing. But Joanna was determined that she would not end this evening in tears of frustration. This was her chance to prove she could sing before an audience like she sang without one. She sang carefully and quietly at the start, gingerly testing herself. Her contribution to 'And the glory of the Lord' was at best tentative, and she was still more nervous than happy in 'And he shall purify', but by the time they were into the third chorus she knew she was going to be all right. Her throat was fine: relaxed and without a hint of strain or pain. The words were as wonderful as the music. 'O thou that tellest good tidings' was just thrilling. She relaxed and sang.

When they sat for the instrumental interlude Joanna listened to the orchestra with a feeling of pleasure and relief. They had got this far, and so far so good. She so badly wanted the performance to go well. Not just for her, or even for the choir: if she shut up altogether they'd probably do better without her. But Stewart was in the audience somewhere and she wanted to end the evening happy and elated. If he thought they were rubbish, she would mind. She didn't know where he was sitting and she made up her mind not to know. Just think about the music, she told herself.

She hoped that if Stewart was impressed with them, then maybe he would agree to sing with them. Nelson's little group was not, of course, as impressive as this amalgam of four choirs, and probably not as good as Stewart's old Wakefield choir, but, she thought, they were not half bad. And it would be so good to have something regular to do together, which would bring him down from Yorkshire every week.

As they sat down after the first part, Joanna looked across at the sopranos and smiled. In the middle of the second row stood Rebecca. All the female members of the choir wore blue, but that did not stop Rebecca standing out in a crowd. Her idea of blue was a brilliant turquoise dress, beaded and sequined with a pattern of silvered discs like fish scales. It clung like a bathing suit and was skilfully cut and boned to hold and lift her ever-tanned breasts from underneath, displaying their swell without wrinkling the skin above them.

The dress was sensational, a showstopper all right, but there was nothing vulgar about it. Rebecca looked, Joanna thought, like the top half of a mermaid. Her hair, currently highlighted with blond and russet, was pinned back from one side of her face but fell straight to her shoulder on the other. And even across the Tabernacle's central stage, Joanna could see that her make-up was perfect, dramatic slanting eyes emphasised with shimmering shadow. She was unquestionably overdressed: most of the choir were wearing simple blue tops or blouses, and even the evening gowns of the soloists were modest in comparison. But Becca didn't care. She liked to be the centre of attention, and her obvious enjoyment of it somehow stopped anyone minding.

Joanna returned to the score in her lap, still smiling. She and Lucy would probably grow old more or less gracefully, but Rebecca would turn growing old *dis*gracefully into an art form. And good luck to her.

No one could bear to break the silence after the last 'Amen' with anything as crude as clapping. But then Nelson gave a sharp couple of claps and unleashed a torrent of applause from the audience. In seconds they were on their feet, and the singers were grinning at the audience and each other. Even the professional musicians smiled at each other briefly as they lowered their instruments and closed their music. As Bryn left the stage, one of them touched his back in congratulation. It had been a good *Messiah*.

Grace and Archie had to take the children home as they couldn't get a babysitter. Stewart had to catch the train back to Wakefield for a meeting first thing, and Josh was driving down to Cornwall, so what had originally been planned as a party, turned out to be the three women, Rebecca's daughter Angelica, and Nelson at Carluccio's in Westbourne Grove.

Rebecca clicked her glass of Tinto against Nelson's and then lifted it towards the others. 'Nelson,' she said 'don't you think leading the applause for your own choir was a bit rich?'

Nelson barked a short pleased laugh. 'That audience was catatonic. They were going to stay silent and mesmerised all night. Besides, it wasn't my choir. It was Bryn's, and it was good, baby. Really good.'

'It was, Mum. It really was,' said Angelica. 'I was just so jealous. I spent the whole time mentally singing along and wishing I was allowed to open my mouth.'

Rebecca basked in her daughter's praise as if she had achieved the *Messiah* single-handed.

After the penne al pesto and the osso bucco, Nelson turned to Rebecca.

'You're not going to have a hissy fit if I take your daughter off to meet some young fellas half my age? I promised Bryn I'd meet him in his local pub, which will be full of Welshmen. They all sing, or play rugby. Some do both. How about it, Angelica?'

'Cool. Love to.'

Rebecca met Nelson's eyes and smiled broadly. 'Of course I don't mind. Just keep an eye out for a suitable middle-aged one for me, OK?'

Nelson stood and leaned over to kiss Rebecca's cheek.

'It's a deal.'

As soon as Nelson and Angelica had gone the women's conversation turned to the men in their lives. 'Is Stewart for keeps then, Jo?' Lucy asked.

'He could be, I think. He says he wants to marry me.'

Rebecca exclaimed, 'Oh Jo-Jo, how wonderful. When's it to be?'

'But how about you, Jo?' Lucy cut in, her face serious. 'Do *you* want to marry him?

Afterwards, Joanna realised that it had been at that very moment, when, confronted by the question from Lucy that she had been asking herself hourly for weeks, she suddenly knew the answer.

'No. I don't. I did before he vanished. When he'd never even said he loved me. I thought I'd lost him, and I realised how badly I wanted him back. I had this schoolgirl idea of ever-after love-and-marriage, maybe because I've never been married. But then, when he came back, I was so conscious of the spectre of my parents' marriage – sixty years of incompatibility – and I was sure I could not sustain a relationship . . .' She trailed off, shaking her head.

Then she jabbed into her panna cotta, her eyes on the spoon. She felt the others watching her, knowing she hadn't finished her speech. She looked up.

'Anyhow, I'm now sure that what makes him so exciting, what keeps us in love and desperate to see each other are the gaps when we are *not* together. Apart from absence making lust grow fonder, we have more to say to each other if we aren't in each other's pockets all the time.'

'But do you want to spend the rest of your lives together? That's the test question, isn't it?' asked Lucy.

'Yes, I think I do. If he were ill, for instance, I could not bear anyone else to nurse him. I feel he's mine, and I'm his, but I don't want him every hour of every day, or even every week of every month.' She sat back, content that she was telling the truth, to herself as well as to her friends.

'Oh, I so understand that!' said Rebecca. 'Wouldn't it be great if you could lease men by the week, or for a jolly weekend, and hand them back when they fell asleep in front of the football.'

Lucy laughed and said, 'Becca, that's exactly what you do already! You've just dumped that poor Frenchman, haven't you? But Joanna really cares about Stewart, don't you, Jo?'

'I do, but I'm not ready for a routine retirement. And nor is he, though he thinks he is. He has his family in Yorkshire, he's still chairman of Greenfarms, and he has directorships all over the place.' Joanna frowned down at her empty pudding plate. 'The thing is,' she said, 'I've had a lifetime of making my own decisions, and I'm not used to considering anyone else much: wondering if they would like fish for supper; asking whether it's time to change my car.'

'Makes sense,' said Lucy. 'You're both such Alpha characters. Retirement for captains of industry is difficult enough with well broken-in wives. But even they object to having the chap who's said "very nice dear" for forty years suddenly taking a controlling interest in her garden.'

'Exactly,' said Joanna. 'Anyhow, I just want to see what happens. See how he likes Cornwall – next week he's coming down again – see how I get on with the new-model Caroline. See if we can stay in his house without the ghost of his dead wife haunting me!' She sat up straight and shook her head. 'And besides, we all need to concentrate on Pencarrick and make it work. So I think we'll just stay as we are.'

'But,' said Rebecca, 'I'm sorry to be crude, but if you love him, hadn't you better grab him now, rather than wait for him to fall out of love with you and go for a younger model?'

Both Lucy and Joanna laughed. It was so typical of Rebecca to get right to the meat of the matter. Joanna nodded.

'There's that risk. Sure there is. Men in their sixties want women in their thirties or forties, I'm very aware of that. And if they are as rich and charming and unattached as Stewart they can get them too. He wants me now because he missed me so much while he was trying to forget me, and he's so impressed that I could do what he couldn't – turn round his business. But of course he could leave me. Well, OK – better before we get our assets tangled up. That's all.'

Lucy leant over and kissed Joanna's cheek. 'Oh Joanna, you are so logical and businesslike. But it's right. It's good sense.' She sat back, smiling. 'Bully for you, Jo.'

Joanna suddenly felt extraordinarily content, on a wave of optimism and satisfaction combined. She shook her head as though to dispel a dream, then, aware that the conversation had been all about her, said,

'So c'mon, you two, let's have it. Have you really ditched your banker, Rebecca? And Lucy, Josh looks as adoring as ever. Is that good?'

Lucy told them about her relationship with Josh being the reverse of Joanna's with Stewart. Maximum time together, occasional cosy sex, a close, for ever relationship.

'I'm sure we're together for good or ill,' said Lucy, scraping her pudding plate for the last traces of cream. 'We're working on another book, probably going to do a TV series together. The only reason he doesn't stay with me every night is because he likes to start working early when the light is right, and so he sometimes stays in his studio. But more often than not he's with me, and it's good.'

'But are you in love with him?' asked Rebecca, frowning.

'God knows. But whatever it is we have, it's good enough for me.' Frowning slightly, she added, 'You know, when David died the hardest thing was not the lack of a mate to do things with – I can always do things with you two, or with the family – it was having no one to *do nothing with* that was so devastating. And Josh is wonderful for that.'

When they turned to her, Rebecca confirmed that indeed the banker was history. 'And,' she said, 'my big news is that I'm going to take a break from the man-hunt to get into shape to do it better.'

Lucy frowned. 'What do you mean?' she asked.

Rebecca looked at each of them in turn, trying not to laugh at their solemn faces.

'I'm off for a dose of cosmetic surgery. In Russia!'

A moment of shocked silence followed this and then Lucy and Joanna both tried to speak at once.

'Rebecca, you are off your head! Why for God's sake? Is it some new chap half your age you are doing this for?' Joanna sounded almost angry.

In milder tones, Lucy said, 'Darling, you look really good, younger than I've ever known you. Isn't it a mad risk? How do you know they won't screw up? Or give you some horrible hospital bug?'

'Because I've checked out the clinic, and they have a great record, and because I just know it will work.' She placed her fingers each side of her neck. 'Look,' she said, 'I'm going to start with just a mild neck-lift. Nothing that could go disastrously wrong.'

She eased the skin gently backwards. She'd tried it out in front of the mirror dozens of times and knew that her neck, soft and a little crêpy when relaxed, instantly became youthful and wrinkle free. 'And if that works, I'll go back for the bags under my eyes, and maybe a tummy tuck too.' She turned to Joanna. 'And then maybe I'll ensnare a thirty-year-old. But to answer your question, Jo, no, I'm doing this for me, not for some man.'

Joanna at once looked contrite. 'Sorry, Becca,' she said, 'but I hate the idea of you risking . . .'

Rebecca put one hand on Joanna's arm and one on Lucy's. 'Don't look so worried, darlings. I'm fine, and I know what I'm doing.' She looked round the table, leant back in her chair. She wasn't finished yet. 'There's more! I've bought a Mercedes SL 500 with my first decent earnings. Second-hand. Can't quite afford eighty grand. But it's in mint condition and it's fantastic. Goes like a bullet and the top comes down at the touch of a button, and it makes me feel a million dollars. That's why I need the face-job. I don't want people thinking, "What's that geriatric old bird doing with a car like that".'

Rebecca was pleased with the sensation both her announcements had made. She sensed that Joanna, at least, was impressed by the sports car – not just the car, but the fact that she'd blown her savings on it.

And once they had got over their initial prejudice, their questioning about the cosmetic surgery showed an interest beyond their avowed concern for her: all women, without exception, she thought, are tempted.

'OK,' Rebecca said, 'I can see however intrigued you two might be, neither of you will have any nips or tucks. But that is a kind of vanity too, isn't it? Being too proud, or too ashamed to want some help in the looks department? At least I know what's important to me.'

'But,' countered Lucy, '*should* it be important to you? You're a good looking woman. You're in your mid-fifties and look ten years younger. Isn't that enough?'

Joanna sat silent, thinking maybe Rebecca had a point. She could tell the world truthfully that she'd had her knees fixed out of medical necessity. But half her pleasure in the result was that her knees had lost their swollen look. Was there such a difference between her and Becca?

Rebecca was answering Lucy's question. 'No, of course it's not enough to look younger than I am. Not if I can improve things further. My body is an ongoing project. If I look younger, I feel younger. If in thirty years time I'm the only old crone in the rest-home still shaving her legs and dyeing her hair, then good. I'll be proud of me.'

Lucy and Joanna laughed, and Rebecca felt a glow of happiness. She knew that her new spirit, her reborn confidence were due mostly to her new career, but also, a little bit, to Bill's now admiring attitude and Jean-Pierre's astonishment at being dumped. She was flying high and high-flyers deserved a treat or two, like a new face and a new car.

It was well after eleven when the three of them emerged, none of them quite sober. It was raining gently, and there were no cabs. In the end, Joanna managed to flag one down by sprinting across the road. As she did it, she thought, medical necessity, that's what it was. I'd never have managed this six weeks ago. She called across to the others.

'C'mon, we'll share. Lucy, we'll drop you first.'

As Lucy climbed into the cab, Joanna asked, 'Pembridge Square? You're staying with Grace, I suppose?'

'No, I was going to, but I've changed my mind. Can you take

me to Paddington Station? I think I'll take the sleeper and follow
Josh down to Cornwall. He has a new exhibition in Falmouth
tomorrow. I'll surprise him.'

Joanna looked at Rebecca, lifting her shoulders in mock despair.
'Definitely love,' she said.

Rebecca nodded. 'No question.'

Lucy smiled. 'Of a sort, yes.'

'But you've no night bag,' said Rebecca.

'No matter. I'll sleep in the buff. And they give you a little pack,
toothbrush and stuff. I'll be fine. Josh won't even notice that I'm
still in this suit.'

Joanna and Rebecca watched Lucy hurrying into the station, her
curvy hips swinging under the flared jacket.

'You know what, Becca?' Joanna said. 'We're all pretty good at
this growing old business. You just keep dancing, Lucy has settled
for affection, and I'm keeping my options open. All good stratagems
for holding the inevitable at bay.'

'Yeah, and none of us is droning on about our growing list of
ailments . . .'

'. . . or the price of everything, or how the world is going to
hell in a handcart.'

'At least not yet.'

'It'll come,' said Joanna.

'But not yet,' said Rebecca.